Good Intentions

Good Intentions

A Novel

MARISA WALZ

ST. MARTIN'S PRESS
NEW YORK

First published in the United States by St. Martin's Press,
an imprint of St. Martin's Publishing Group

EU Representative: Macmillan Publishers Ireland Ltd, 1st Floor, The Liffey Trust Centre, 117–126 Sheriff Street Upper, Dublin 1, D01 YC43

www.stmartins.com

The Library of Congress Cataloging-in-Publication Data is available upon request.

ISBN 978-1-250-39740-9 (hardcover)
ISBN 978-1-250-39741-6 (ebook)

Our books may be purchased in bulk for specialty retail/wholesale, literacy, corporate/ premium, educational, and subscription box use. Please contact MacmillanSpecialMarkets@macmillan.com.

First Edition: 2026

10 9 8 7 6 5 4 3 2 1

For Dan Jr. and Isla

1

The sun is leaving for the day, and I probably should, too. I shouldn't be here at all. This has to stop, everyone says so. *It's not healthy, Cady. It's not right. Not normal, not* legal.

But I'm only watching. Watching never hurt anyone.

There's not much to see anyway—just another house sucked dry, the only sign of life the pulse of a television's blue light. It flickers from the back of the house, where I've always imagined her living room to be. I can't know for sure, though. I've never been invited in, despite those months when we were what I would consider friends.

The house, a small brick bungalow, has the look of something kept nice out of duty, not love. The driveway and sidewalk are neatly shoveled, but that's all that suggests someone cares. There's no months-old Christmas wreath she's too busy to take down, no welcome mat for visitors to wipe their snow-packed boots on, no sled lying forgotten in the yard, no smoke curling from the chimney. Not even the bronze lantern hanging over the door has been left on.

Away from the house, closer to me, azalea skeletons guard her concrete walkway. Their fleshy leaves and magenta flowers fell off a long time ago, blowing away and decomposing beneath the weight of the snow, leaving behind a network of woody rib cages. Above: a gray sky. Below: a dirty white carpet—snow, slashed by the brown dirt of boot treads and the spray of muddy tires.

It didn't have to be this way. It did not have to be *like this*. Her, in there with the TV's sad blue light casting ugly shadows on her pretty face. Me, out here in my car, lights off, engine cold, winter biting into my bones until my muscles cramp protectively around them.

I tried to help her, the woman inside, the one watching TV alone and dutifully keeping her driveway shoveled. But it's hard to help someone hanging on by a thread, Dana. Impossible, if you're hanging on to the same one. At some point, despite your good intentions, the instinct to survive kicks in, and you claw for that last piece of the fraying thread for yourself.

This, though—the watching—it has to stop.

And it will, soon. I've promised the therapist it will. We had a session tonight, right before I came here, and I told him I've given myself one last visit. (This was when he suggested I start talking to you. He thought it might be easier for me to tell you all the things I can't—won't—tell him.)

Anyway, he wasn't impressed. *And then what?* he wanted to know. *Then what will you do, Cady?*

Wrong question. He always asks the wrong questions. It's not what I'm going to do that we should be talking about. It's what's already been done.

But I can't tell you that, Dana—I can't tell you anything—without telling you *everything* you've missed.

2

The beginning. Where exactly should I begin? June 14, thirty-three years ago? The day I came barreling (Mom's words) out of the birth canal?

I beat you by four minutes, Dana. Mom and Dad loved to joke that the moment I was born, I was already late for my next appointment—that it was you who was supposed to go first, but I pushed you out of the way at the last second . . .

But you already know all that. So let's start over, and I'll tell you only what you've missed, starting with last February.

February. You know how much I hate winter, Dana, and as far as I'm concerned, February is the Wednesday of the Midwest winter—three months of cold and gray under the belt, another three looming ahead. I mean, what is there to love about five o'clock sunsets and snow that's no longer clean or pretty?

The first thirty-two Februarys of my life weren't so bad, though. Back then, nothing was too bad. In fact, things were pretty fucking great. Even in February.

The sky was still the color of razor blades, the cold still bit my fingers, the frozen sludge still barnacled itself on to our windows and car doors and boots and Champ's haunches, but I survived it all by breathing life into the glamorous parties I planned for my clients. With family get-togethers at Mom and Dad's and girls' nights out in the city. With date nights in by the fire, just me and Matt and a bottle of wine, maybe a Netflix series rolling on the screen or Phoebe Bridgers drifting out of the speakers. And if that didn't cut it, if I got fed up with it all like I tended to do by the time March hit, Matt and I would just leave, jet off to someplace warm, somewhere I could replace the slush under my Moncler boots with sand under my bare feet . . .

Anyway. February 14, a year ago, midafternoon. I was downtown, preparing to walk my biggest client, Nora Donnelly, and her daughter Quinn through the space where Quinn's sweet sixteen party was set to commence in just hours and Oh. My. God. Quinn Donnelly. That girl's sixteenth birthday was going to make my beautiful backyard wedding look like a potluck picnic at a tractor pull, Dana. But whatever. I could've bought a new car with the money Nora shelled out for that five-hour blink in her daughter's eye.

The location: an old factory that had been converted into a luxurious bathhouse. The vibe: Restoration Hardware meets ancient Rome. Ten thousand square feet of towering ceilings and wood beam rafters and ubiquitous brick. Pool after turquoise pool of water—warm, hot, cold, saltwater . . . even a private soaking tub of Spanish red wine. There were marble benches and glass steam rooms, an honest-to-God waterfall and giant stacks of pink Himalayan salt. The sun streaming through the clerestory windows offered just enough light; in a couple hours, when the sun set, the job would be left to the city lights twinkling outside the massive windows and the hundreds of candles clustered on the stone floors. It was a stunning location, the perfect spot to fulfill Quinn's aesthetic.

Sexy, she'd declared months earlier, when I'd asked this fifteen-year-old for her vision. *But edgy. Lots of gold. Glamour. Opulence. And, like, I want Insta photo ops everywhere.*

Now the time had come to show what I'd managed to do with that vision—and Nora's high five-figure budget. So there I was, in a black wool jumpsuit, Valentino heels clicking over Spanish stone floors as I led my clients toward a dramatic brick archway. On the other side, a masterpiece of a sweet sixteen party awaited. Nora, in cream cashmere, and Quinn, in a tiny gold dress, teetered at my side in their own designer heels.

This, the reveal, was one of the best parts of my job, second only to the event itself. I led my clients through the space, pointing out every detail: Straight ahead, a wall of peach- and pearl-colored roses whose singular purpose was to linger prettily in the background. Overhead, five hundred clear balloons filled with twinkling white lights floating high above the water like escaped champagne bubbles. Over there, a gold monogram, bigger than the birthday girl, glittering over a waterfall. Tables draped in cream linen and gold sequins. Giant, gold-dusted lily pads floating in pools. Above the largest pool, a glass dance floor.

As Quinn leaned over to peer at the gold-leafed roses climbing the ivory walls of her birthday cake, my phone vibrated rudely from the bottom of my Birkin. Nora raised her eyebrows but didn't tell me to go ahead and take it. Not that I would. It was probably just Matt, making sure I didn't forget about our Valentine's plans that evening.

Quinn looked up from the cake and clapped daintily, then pressed her palms against her gold-beaded chest. "It's perfect," she declared.

Her mother nodded in agreement, and I hid my exhale. No matter how good my work was, there was always the chance it wouldn't be up to snuff for clients of a certain caliber—and Nora Donnelly was definitely a client of a certain caliber.

Now there was just the small matter of collecting the last payment, which Nora transferred to me on her phone while my own phone buzzed three, four more times with calls, the subsequent vibrations telling me my voicemail was filling up fast.

That was my life back then. Just a year ago. So full. A full inbox and another full payment. Days packed with client meetings and staff meetings and vendor calls, weekends loaded with double-booked parties and girls' nights and date nights and fundraising galas. A closet jammed with more clothes than I could wear, a contacts list too long to keep up with. I had you, and Mom and Dad. And Matt, the husband I'd wanted since I was seventeen. A business so hot, I was turning down jobs I once would have died to take, and a bank account balance that would have made college me choke on her Ice House.

I'd worked hard, very hard—you know that—so nothing came easy, per se, but it did come: the year-over-year revenue growth that paid for the Birkin and the Range Rover and the big white Colonial at the end of a tree-lined street in the most desirable section of the most desirable suburb in northwestern Chicago, and God, Dana, looking back now it makes me sick. Not that I had it all, but that I lost it and can't ever get it back. Not the actual *stuff*—the house and the business and all that—but the innocence, the naïvety. The thinking that it was all mine to keep forever, no matter what.

3

On my way out, Quinn casually mentioned that she'd literally die if anything went wrong at her party that night.

Nora rolled her eyes. "Nothing will go wrong," she muttered. "I've paid an arm and a leg to ensure it doesn't." She shook her head and gave me a little smile that said, *Teenagers!* but behind it there was a warning.

I had three offices back then: my home office, my office office, and my car office. I sat in the latter in the venue parking lot as I drew a neat black line through *3:00 Donnelly Walk-through* in my day planner. Just one appointment left (a new client consultation in Lakeview), trailed by a long list of to-dos: *Make hair appt. for Friday . . . RSVP to Lindsey's Mardi Gras party . . . Hostess gift for Adlers' dinner party . . .*

The math was impossible. An hour, at least, for this next appointment, forty-five minutes to get home, twenty (if I rushed) to change for dinner . . .

I snapped a photo of the list and texted it to Jamie with a request: Can you pls take care of the first 3 items?

I tried not to use my assistant for personal stuff, Dana—you know how I felt about being *that* kind of boss—but I was paying Jamie, and it was that or be late to dinner. Not that V-Day was terribly important to me, but it was to Matt, and as usual, he'd made an effort—reservations at Il Poggiolo. Who knew what else he had up his sleeve, but knowing Matt, there was something.

I gave myself a glance in the rearview mirror to make sure I was ready for this next appointment. The image-is-everything cliché was especially true with the type of clients Eventually, LLC brought in. I was a reflection of my company; I had to look as polished and expensive as the events I was selling. And I did. Every strand of long, shiny, honey-highlighted brown hair perfectly styled and in place. Every last centimeter of my face smoothed into submission with foundation and setting powder, every angle elegantly accentuated with an expert cocktail of highlighter and contour. And somehow my lips were still "Firebrand" red, two grande lattes later. That Tom Ford stick I'd picked up at Neiman's was worth every one of the sixty-two dollars I'd paid.

My phone buzzed back with a call. Jamie. I picked it up, launching into an embarrassed apology, but she cut me off.

"Cady, no worries—I'll take care of everything. Actually, I was calling because we've hit a snag with Quinn's sweet sixteen tonight."

I smothered a groan. "What's the deal?"

"It's the limos."

I rolled my eyes. Quinn had insisted on having a fleet of white limos waiting outside the venue to drive her and her guests home, as if it were gauche to subject her friends to riding home in their parents' Benzes and Beemers and Bentleys.

"One of the cars allocated for Quinn's party is having mechanical issues," Jamie said, "and it's Valentine's Day, so demand is hot, and well, long story short, we're down one white limo. They can send a black one, but . . . look, if it were me, I wouldn't care about one black limo sticking out from the rest, but I know Quinn specifically asked the photographer for shots of her fleet, and I'm just guessing here, but I don't think she'll be happy about—"

"Call them back," I interrupted, glancing at the clock on my dash. I had to get to that client in Lakeview. "See if you can get something else in white. Something bigger or more special than the other cars—a Lincoln or something vintage? Or one of those Ferrari limos, like we got for the Singh wedding. Have them position it at the front. Quinn and her inner circle can take that home, and the other limos can take the rest of the guests. It'll stick out, but it will look intentional."

"That's brilliant, Cady!"

I smiled. Jamie was great, but she was new. Soon she'd learn that there was always some sort of snag the day of an event, and it always got resolved, one way or another. Admittedly, I'd had to get really creative at times, but this—the limo thing—was nothing.

I hung up and thumbed over to my missed calls, wondering if Jamie'd been the one blowing up my phone for the last hour. Though it wasn't like her to panic. More likely Matt confirming our dinner plans. Or Ramona Crawford triple-checking there'd be white orchids at her anniversary party, or maybe a slew of new clients from that feature in *Chicago Life*.

Or . . . not. I squinted at the name responsible for all five missed calls: *Sean.*

Huh. I mean, we'd exchanged the occasional text, but I was pretty sure I'd never received an actual phone call from your husband before, Dana. Definitely not five in a row. He never called. Not me, anyway, and definitely not me lately. Not since . . .

Oh God. Was that what this was about? Was he calling to put me in my place? To defend your honor? If so, I would have to laugh—how "only child" of him.

But that wasn't it. Something inside me, something instinctive and ancient and primal, knew.

4

Accident. What a lazy fucking word. It could mean anything. A wet diaper. A glass of spilled merlot. Two tons of steel and glass and bones and flesh colliding.

You were not dead, thank God. Not yet. Sean didn't think so, anyway. He'd gotten the call from the EMTs when you were en route to the hospital. He was on his way there now, would be there in five minutes. Could I come?

Could I come—was he kidding me, Dana?

I turned to my GPS and fumbled with the buttons, pressing things out of habit without thinking, until I realized the stupid thing had routed me home. I jabbed my finger at the screen, accidentally exiting out of the navigation. I didn't have time for this. *I did not have time for this.* I had to—

Stop.

Just stop.

Deep breath.

Dana. Get to Dana. Get to the hospital. Type it in, press the buttons: Nav. Address. Illinois. Oak Park. Rush Hospital.

Go.

The correct directions finally loaded. I shifted into gear and pressed the sole of my pump down on the pedal, only peripherally concerned with what the Donnellys might think if they happened to step outside just then and catch my Range Rover peeling obnoxiously out of the lot.

The GPS took me down side roads to avoid rush hour traffic—Ogden, then Washington and Madison, through the West Loop, into Garfield Park—but it was still going to take forty-five minutes to drive those nine miles.

"Siri," I ordered, "call Matt."

"Calling Matt."

The ringing filled the cabin, obscenely loud. Not to be outdone, the GPS woman's voice interrupted to demand a right turn.

Matt's voice countered: "You've reached Matthew McKenna. I can't . . ."

I turned right as I hung up and instructed Siri to try again.

"Calling Matt."

The ringing started again, Dana, so loud and unanswered it hurt my ears.

"You've reached Matthew McKenna . . ."

"Matt," I begged his voicemail. "Call me back, please. It's . . . just call me, okay?"

I turned left at a four-way stop like the GPS was instructing, cutting off a red Camry. I hadn't meant to, but the driver didn't know that. He laid on his horn as he rode my ass the whole next block before he turned onto another street.

The horn's blare resonated in my ears. My fingers cramped from their stranglehold on the steering wheel. The darkest, ugliest corners of my mind conjured up images I didn't want to see: A head-on crash that threw your body against your seat, shattered windshield glass spraying your face. A sideswipe that sent you skittering into the fray of a half dozen other cars. A semi plowing into your driver's side door, instantly snuffing you out of your life, out of my life.

I squeezed my eyes closed.

Don't think about all that; think about Dana, the real memories, the good ones.

But I couldn't, Dana. Every time I tried, our last conversation reared up in my consciousness. I tried to push it back down, but my brain insisted on looking at it, shoving our last words into my ears, pressing your heartbroken brown eyes right up against mine.

Think of a different time.

A happier, better time when everything was right. You, full of life and light. You, giving our Barbies pixie cuts and Sharpie tattoos. You, the way your nose scrunched up when you laughed really hard. You, two years earlier, tipsy from champagne, dancing in big circles in a sparkly green dress at a New Year's Eve party in Manhattan—

Party. Fuck. The client in Lakeview.

"Siri, call Jamie."

"Calling Jamie."

She picked up right as I crossed Cicero. Just a couple more miles now. Ten more minutes, maybe less, and I'd be there, Dana.

"Jamie. Sorry. Me again. I need you to cancel the Lakeview appointment. Just tell them I had a family emergency, would you please?"

"Of course, I'm on it. I hope everything's okay?"

"I'll let you know."

She didn't ask for more. Jamie was great, a lifesaver. Now if only Matt would pick up—why wasn't he answering? He always had his phone on him. Maybe if I blew it up enough, he'd realize this was a real emergency.

I tried him again. Nothing. Dictated another text. Thirty seconds later, another. Nothing, nothing.

Another stop sign approached, and the car rocked back from the sharp tap I gave the brakes. I picked up my phone. Maybe the GPS or the bad memories had drowned out the ringing of Matt's return call.

But no, there were no notifications waiting. Unbelievable. I'd texted him a stupid Valentine's Day meme that morning, and he'd responded instantly with a perfect rejoinder. But now, *now*, he was unreachable.

The GPS was in my ear again: *Make a left-hand turn in three hundred feet.*

It was so loud; everything was so loud.

The GPS.

Your disappointment.

My angry words.

Two hundred feet.

A voice in my head: *Let her be okay. Don't let Dana die. Don't let the baby die.*

Matt's voicemail: "You've reached Matthew McKenna . . ."

"Matt, call me. As soon as you get this. It's bad . . ."

5

Did you know there are secret waiting rooms in hospitals, Dana? There's the big one where you wait for news, any news, where you pray as hard as you can, even if you don't believe in that sort of thing. Then, once the worst materializes, when it's too late for prayers, they put you in another room. A smaller, special, secret room to keep you from upsetting the others, the ones still holding out hope.

Sean and I sat in one of those rooms, waiting for Mom and Dad to arrive. We could have called to let them know not to hurry, that it was too late, but they were already on their way. It would be better—kinder—to tell them when they arrived, when we could put our arms around them and share whatever air was still hanging in that special, secret, suffocating room.

We didn't talk right away. When the door closed and we were finally alone, Sean reached for me, and I fell against him, because here was a piece of you, Dana, something that was yours.

Had he held you earlier that day in this same shirt? I latched on tight, inhaling deeply, trying to find a hint of your smell through his soap and aftershave. Was there something left of you there? Your makeup? A hair? An eyelash?

Was Sean doing the same? Did it kill him or comfort him to see me and feel me and know that maybe you—by a very long, very desperate stretch of the imagination—lived on in your literal other half?

Except we hadn't only lost you, had we, Dana?

"My baby." Those were the words Sean whispered when we sat down. I didn't know if he meant you or the ten-week-old life in your belly.

Ten weeks, Dana. A sickening coincidence, if you believed in coincidences, which I did not.

The air grew thin; I felt as though I were caught inside one of those

Chinese finger traps we used to get as birthday party favors. On the one side, something powerful pulling me back to the hospital parking lot, to my car, to the road. On the other, the overwhelming urge to run so fast and far the other way that I'd never have to face this. Both sides pulled with such well-matched force that I was left stuck, suffocating there in the middle— sitting inertly, helplessly, stupidly in that horrible room. I stood up.

"I can't be in here."

The words burst forth like they'd been stuck inside and finally escaped. Sean pulled his face out of his hands.

"Sorry," I said. "I just . . . I have to go to the bathroom."

There, that was better. Sean nodded and returned his head to his hands. I hesitated, then leaned down and wrapped my arms around his shoulders and squeezed him like it was going to be all right. Easier to lie that way than with words, Dana.

***

In the bathroom, coming out of the stall, I saw you in the mirror above the sinks. Your long brown hair and round brown eyes, both speckled with amber. Your high cheekbones and heart-shaped lips. The dimple on the left that was twice as deep as the one on the right when you smiled.

I tried to smile at you—I wanted to see the dimples—but you didn't smile back, so I looked down and concentrated on washing my hands under the automated taps. The water was barely lukewarm, evoking a mundane memory of us washing our hands in the bathroom at Penumbra.

It blows my mind, you'd said. *The water's not hot enough to kill anything. What's the point?*

And in a restaurant, I'd said.

We always agreed on stuff like that, Dana, the little inanities and petty injustices of the world.

Now, at the hospital, I took my time drying my hands, working the paper towel into the spaces between my fingers. Then I threw the battered towel into the waste bin.

Now what? A shitty coffee from the waiting room? A stale pastry from the cafeteria? Maybe I could wander the halls until I got lost or find an empty bed to lie down in. If a nurse came by and asked what I was doing, I'd stare up at the ceiling and be quiet, and maybe they'd let me stay. Maybe they'd put an IV in my arm and warm blankets on my legs. Anything would be better than being back in that room, where the only thing to do was face . . .

Oh God, Dana.

Gone.

Gone.

Such a small word for such a big, forever, horrible thing.

When Sean had pulled away from me earlier, we'd sat down across from each other, less than a foot separating our knees, and he'd cried these awful, wracking sobs. It took him ages to stop. Once he did, his face was still twisted, tears still falling, silently now.

We stared at each other for a long time. I wasn't sure what we were looking for. Words? An alliance? A fix? Whatever it was, Sean kept searching long after I'd had my fill.

Finally, he looked away, wiping his eyes on the sleeve of the shirt that did not smell like you. "It hasn't sunk in for you yet, has it?"

Ah, so that was it. Tears. He'd been looking for tears, and I hadn't yet cried.

I didn't know what to say. *It* had definitely sunk in. I mean, the knowledge was there, Dana. I could feel it in every part of me, and I got it, trust me, *I fucking got it.* You were dead and you were not ever, ever coming back. *I got that.*

But Sean was right. I hadn't fully plunged into my grief, not yet. Something held me back. Something far worse was holding my grief hostage.

6

The big waiting room in the trauma ward was more tolerable than the little room in which I'd left Sean. There were other people there. People who didn't know you were gone, who didn't know you at all. People who woke up not knowing that this was what the day held in store for them and therefore had not prepared childcare or snacks or outfits. Most wore sweats or hoodies, jackets thrown hastily over their loungewear, the first shoes they'd come upon shoved on their feet. To my right, a woman pulled a pen and a crumpled receipt from her purse and offered it to two bored children—a boy and a girl. Twins.

There were others. A young couple holding hands, his eyes closed, hers absorbed with the phone in her free hand. Across from them, a middle-aged man shifting restlessly in his chair. Beside him, a teenage boy with earbuds attached to a phone with a broken screen. A woman tearing apart her cuticles. A man directly across from me, maybe early forties, zipped up in a green Patagonia, disheveled hair and eyes that . . . I think . . . yes . . .

Yes, they were, they were definitely watching me, Dana. But not just watching—searching. *Delving.* Trying to pry into me the way Sean's had back in that room. I hadn't minded much when it was Sean, but this . . .

I looked away and pretended to check the time on the clock hanging on the wall.

Ten, fifteen seconds ticked by. I glanced back.

Still watching.

Okay, Cady. He was only watching. Watching never hurt anyone. I'd watched while the twins played with their new pen and paper, hadn't I?

It was just . . . there was something in those eyes, something I rec- ognized, something that made the blood swim faster in my head. He looked like—this sounds ridiculous, Dana—but he looked like he *knew,* like he knew what—

"Please!"

I jumped. We all did. A newcomer—a woman—had arrived. She was reaching an arm out to a passing nurse.

"Please," she begged. "Can you tell me where my son is? He's twelve years old. Christopher Keller. A neighbor—they said he fell off his bike, and his head . . . I . . . can I see him? Is he okay? *Where is he?* Please . . ."

Around me, people looked away, respectfully pretending not to listen. But I kept watching, Dana. I couldn't pull my eyes away. Twelve years old.

The nurse touched the woman's arm and said something I couldn't hear. They talked more, then the nurse walked off. The woman was left standing at the edge of the waiting room. With the hopefuls. And me.

Her brown eyes flitted around, her head making tiny adjustments as she went, like a bird at a busy park. She had a small, oval face with pretty features. Business-casual black pants. A dowdy winter jacket. Not much makeup, maybe some mascara and brow filler. Her dark blonde hair was pulled back in a low ponytail. Mid-forties, maybe? Not sure; you know how terrible I am with ages.

The woman's eyes landed on mine, and I was struck by the urge to help, to do or say something—no idea what—but it was too late anyway, she was already moving on to—

"Morgan!"

The woman turned. Another new arrival. A man, out of breath, jacket in hand, his head thrown back the way Matt's had been that time we'd finally found Champ after an hour spent searching the neighborhood. He walked over and put his hand on her shoulder.

"Morgan." He choked on her name, like it was a question, and their bodies snapped together like two big magnets. Then, just as quickly, almost awkwardly, they pulled apart. He asked something in a low voice, and she shook her head. Her lips moved, but I couldn't make out the words.

The man nodded and ran a hand through his hair, curling his fingers around the strands, giving a small, sharp yank. I knew the move. I did the same when I got one of my migraines; the best way to get over one pain is to inflict a new one.

The others in the waiting room returned to their phones and magazines and naps. I couldn't. I feigned interest in a beat-up copy of *Us Weekly* as I tracked the couple's movements from the corner of my eye. The man gestured toward something near me, and then they were moving, and then suddenly they were there, right next to me. For one horrifying second, I thought they were going to confront me.

What the hell was my problem? Did I think they wouldn't notice me staring? Did I think their situation was entertaining? I should mind my own goddamn business.

But before I could see the absurdity of this, the woman sat down wordlessly in the chair beside me, the man in the seat beside her.

I lasered my eyes onto the magazine, trying to look interested in the latest Travis and Taylor sighting.

I barely heard the man's whisper to her: "Tell me again how it happened?" There was some sort of an accusation in his tone, and the woman bristled.

"I told you everything I know, Reid."

"But why was he by himself?" he pressed.

I felt the woman's head snap his way.

They didn't say anything after that.

Seconds ticked into minutes.

I texted Matt: Why aren't you picking up?

Then: Something's happened. I'm OK but I need you. Come to Rush as soon as you get this.

It was chance that I looked up, or maybe instinct. Whatever it was, I caught him. The man in the zipped-up green jacket and knowing eyes was watching me again. Maybe he'd never stopped.

A strangled sound escaped my mouth. Almost instantly, I felt something cold touch my hand. I looked down.

Another hand. The woman—the mother—was squeezing my hand.

I looked up to meet her eyes, but she only gave me the briefest sideglance and a . . . well, I guess you could call it a smile, Dana. Except it wasn't, even though one side of her mouth contorted itself into something resembling one. I understood what it meant, though: *I know. Me too.*

The whole thing lasted a second, then she took her cold hand back.

I wished I'd done something. Whispered thanks, maybe. But the moment had passed. I rubbed at the goose bumps still prickling my arms and avoided any more contact with that man's eyes.

What was his deal, anyway? Just curious? Bored, perhaps? Maybe he'd seen me and Sean in the hallway earlier, being escorted to that little room, and now he was wondering why I was back out here with the hopefuls instead of with Sean. Or maybe I just looked famil—

Movement.

Movement again, Dana, at the end of the hall. The nurse from earlier was returning, another woman—a doctor?—by her side.

Morgan—could I call her that now?—stood and broke into a run, then slowed. Self-conscious, maybe. Or maybe that's when it hit her, that she might be rushing into the arms of something she did not want.

The man followed. When they reached the doctor, he cupped his big hand over her—Morgan's—shoulder. Reassurance, or maybe he was bracing himself. I wasn't sure, and it didn't matter; his hand wasn't there long. It fell away when the woman crumpled to the floor. Her scream, one word—*No*—was so cutting, Dana, so animal and raw. I would never completely get it out of my ears.

7

I couldn't stop seeing her. She was like those spots that imprint on your retinas after you look at the sun. Morgan. The mother of the twelve-year-old boy. The mother who . . . well, what do you call a woman who loses her child? We've got widow and orphan, but nothing for losing your child. Or your twin, for that matter.

Everything happened quickly after that scream, like it was the cue for us to get on with it. With these new lives. With everything that would come next. The parents of the boy were ushered away, probably to their own secret room, like the one I'd left Sean sitting in.

He was startled when I opened the door. He pulled his face out of his hands and stared at me. "Where . . ."

But his question died. He shook his head, like he'd decided against it.

"Your parents will be here soon," he said instead.

I nodded. But I was not prepared for our parents, Dana. I hadn't decided on the right words yet, the ones they would replay in their heads for the rest of their lives.

I sat down in the empty chair across from Sean.

He clasped his hands together and pressed them to his lips. "They didn't know about . . ."

He couldn't get it out. *The baby.* You hadn't told Mom and Dad yet. Why, Dana? Because of me?

Sean dropped his hands and leaned back in the chair. "I don't even know how to tell them, Cady. How do you tell someone their child is gone?"

I saw the face of that mother again. Saw her fall to the ground, heard her scream ringing in my skull.

Sean stood up and began pacing the tiny room, making it feel even smaller.

"And how," he asked, his voice cracking, "how do you tell them, *Wait, there's more*?"

I felt my throat close up at the idea of saying it out loud. I stood and put my hand on Sean's arm so he'd stop moving.

"We don't," I managed to get out. "Not yet. We'll tell them later."

Sean shook his head. "I thought about that. But they'll want to talk to the doctors when they get here, right? And if not now, when? How does more time help? It seems cruel to drag it out, doesn't it?"

It seemed cruel either way, Dana.

"It's your call, Sean."

He blinked in surprise. I doubt I'd ever conceded anything to him before. We weren't exactly on the best terms, were we? I knew you'd told him about that argument, because you'd made sure to text me his verdict later that night, after you'd ignored all my calls and texts. Sean pointed something out to me tonight. Of all the things you've said and done over the years, this is the worst, Cady.

"It was your baby," I said gently.

He flinched at the last word. Or maybe it was the past tense.

"I shouldn't have . . ." The words stuck in my mouth. My eyes watered, but I refused to let the tears fall. Not now. My first tears could not be for myself. God.

"I'm sorry," I whispered lamely. "I'm really, really sorry."

Sean's eyes filled with something—I don't know what. I suspected forgiveness, but that couldn't be, could it? He opened his mouth, but whatever he wanted to say died as a thought. Something behind me had caught his attention, saving us both. I turned.

"Mom. Dad."

I let them pull me into their arms, Dad's glasses pressing into my brow, Mom's nose bent against my cheek. Their touches felt desperate. Needy. Like they had to reassure themselves I was real. Alive. Maybe words wouldn't be necessary. Maybe they would just know, the way I'd known when I'd gotten there and seen Sean's face.

They spoke at the same time. Mom: "Where's Dana?" Dad: "How is she?"

I tried to put the answer in my eyes, Dana, but they didn't see it, or maybe they didn't want to. Mom shared a panicked look with Dad: *Why is no one saying anything?*

Sean reached his arms out to Mom. He wrapped her up and sobbed into her hair, and he was the one who said it, kind of: "Lisa, I'm sorry. I'm so sorry."

The words don't exist for what it felt like to watch it hit them, Dana, but this is what it looked like: Mom, pressing a fist into her chest like it might stop the bleeding, something light and beautiful escaping her eyes, something that would never come back. Dad, taking off his glasses to hide his crumpled face with one of his big bear-paw hands.

There was more, of course. I looked to Sean. He couldn't say it. I could see him trying to put the words together, his eyes dancing back and forth between Mom and Dad, but it was too hard.

I reached for their hands. Mom's nails looked newly manicured, which somehow made this even sadder, and Dad's hand felt limp, giving away the façade of his rigidly composed face.

"Dana was pregnant."

I felt sick. It shouldn't have been me. It should have been you telling them, with matching GRANDMA and GRANDPA coffee mugs or a special cake or ultrasound pics slipped inside the Sunday paper. It wasn't right that they had to learn about their first grandchild in the same breath it was taken away from them, there in that awful little room.

That's when Matt finally arrived. Nobody had to explain anything. It was written all over us. He closed his eyes like it hurt to have them open, then he pulled me against him, wrapping himself around me. I hugged him back, squeezing handfuls of the back of his shirt in my clenched fists. It was the first time I cried.

"Where were you?" I whispered into his shirt. "*Why didn't you fucking answer?*"

8

Dogs are supposed to sense our emotions, and goldens are supposed to be especially astute, but Champ greeted us at the door like that night was any other: mouth hanging open in a big dog smile, panting from the exertion of greeting us, his tail—the only part of him that still worked like it had when he was a puppy—wagging like a windshield wiper in a Chicago blizzard.

Matt squatted down to scratch behind his ears. "Hey, old man. Sorry we're so late."

It was disorienting, Dana. All of it. The normalcy. Champ's big dopey eyes and happy tail. The landscape lighting outside, showing off our elms, welcoming us home. The slow crawl up the driveway. The mudroom door opening, the sound of the weather strip unsticking from the threshold. The unnamable smell that was our home's. The long blue kilim in the hallway, the satin shine of the recently refinished oak floors underneath. It was all familiar but not. Everything looked the same but felt different, as if someone had snuck in and replaced our things with impressive replicas.

The clock in the hall claimed it was nine o'clock. What would we do now? Watch TV? Read the paper? Work? All the normal things seemed absurd. Pointless. How would I ever be able to do any of them again?

What would I do with my life from now on?

I told Matt I was going to bed. He didn't say anything, just wrapped his arms around me. Again. His blue dress shirt had dark smudges from where my mascara had bled on it at the hospital.

I'd almost reached the second-floor landing when I heard him pounding up the stairs behind me, calling out for me to wait, his voice breathless and urgent. I prepared myself for an argument, for his second thoughts about leaving me alone *at a time like this*. I couldn't take any more of his empathy, though, I just couldn't, Dana. I continued my climb as I voiced my plea to be left—

". . . alone," I finished dumbly.

Red petals. Roses, strewn across the landing, forging a path to our bedroom.

Valentine's Day. Right.

Matt mumbled an apology as he brushed past. "Just stay right here," he murmured.

A small commotion ensued, the sound of things being shoved off dressers and countertops into some box or bag or laundry bin. Finally, Matt let me know it was safe to come in.

Everything inside our bedroom felt familiarly different, too. But I knew it wasn't the things that had changed; it was me. I was not the same person who had smoothed the creases from our spotless white comforter that morning, and I never would be again.

In the master bathroom, I pulled my earrings off and tossed them onto the counter, sending one skittering into the side of a bottle of prenatal vitamins. Funny—after everything that had happened that day, *this* was the thing that finally took me down.

Matt came running at the sound of my animal scream. He looked around frantically for the cause as he reached for me, but the only thing out of place was the bottle of vitamins, rolling to a stop by our feet after ricocheting off the mirror I'd hurled it at.

He held me tightly against his body, stroking my hair with his hands, making the sort of ocean-wave shushing sounds mothers make to soothe their babies. I let him lead me back to the bedroom, toward our bed. I reached behind me for the zipper of my jumpsuit. Matt's hands got there first, tugging it down for me before my fingers could find it.

"What else do you need?" he asked.

It was a simple question, Dana, but that night the answer seemed very complicated. Much more complicated than crawling into our bed, under the covers that smelled like us. *Us* before *this*.

I pulled back the comforter and climbed in. Matt went around to his side and joined me under the downy folds, pulling me to him. We lay tangled together, silent.

Long, wordless minutes passed as I waited for the quiet to be broken. Matt took his time. I think my silence scared him. I couldn't fault him for that—remember how Grandpa Flynn always used to say, *Cady could talk the hind legs off a donkey*? Well, the day you left forever, I had no words, Dana, let alone enough to endanger anyone's hind legs.

The whole time Mom and Dad and Sean and Matt had talked to the hospital staff, making arrangements for you—what funeral home you would go to, what to do with your organs, the ones that had survived you—I was quiet. Quieter still when the cops came to talk about the accident, the witnesses, the liability. How they were still investigating what had happened, but initial analysis indicated you might be at fault. Dammit, Dana. You were always such a bad driver. It was a family joke. *It was a joke.*

Anyway, my words that day were few. *Amen,* when we prayed with the chaplain. *I love you guys,* when we hugged Mom and Dad goodbye. To Sean: *Call if you need anything.* To Matt: *Let's take your car; I'll come back for mine tomorrow.*

On the ride home, I'd only smiled—sadly—when Matt told me, for maybe the forty-fifth time, some variation of *God, babe, I'm so sorry.* I patted the hand he placed on top of my leg, nodding when he said we should call Sean and Mom and Dad that night, to make sure they got home all right, to see if there was anything else we could do. As if *they* were the ones who'd lost the most.

And now: "You've been so quiet."

I pulled back a little, so I could see his face. "You didn't pick up your phone."

I couldn't blame Matt for the look he gave me. If things were the other way around, I'd have thought the same thing: *That's* what you're worried about right now?

"I'm sorry," he managed. "I was in a meeting. I called you back as soon as I could, and then I came straight to the hospital."

We left it at that.

9

Remember that Cinco de Mayo party at the SigEp house freshman year? How hungover we were? Well, cheap tequila doesn't have anything on ten hours of crying, Dana.

I barely slept that first night. Every time I tried to close my eyes and drift away, I heard loud bangs and the crumple of steel and the unanswered ringing of Matt's phone and Sean's *I'm so sorry* and that mother's horrific *No*.

Matt was already awake when I came downstairs the next morning, but Champ got to me first. He pressed his big head into my leg. I scratched his ears until he got his fill and returned to his big pillow in front of the living room windows.

Matt was right behind him, pulling me into a wordless hug. I appreciated that he didn't say *Good morning*; we both knew it wasn't.

"I made coffee," he said.

"Smells delicious. Thank you."

I made my way to the French press, grateful Matt didn't jump to get it for me, as if I were too fragile to pour myself a cup.

I usually popped two pieces of rye or sourdough in the toaster before I sat down with my coffee, but Matt didn't comment on this break in routine, nor did he point out that we didn't eat last night. He just pointed at his laptop and said he'd let his staff know he'd be out of pocket for a while. I almost laughed. *Urban Land* magazine's "Commercial Real Estate Developer to Watch" and *Crain's* youngest ever "40 under 40" recipient could never be *out of pocket*.

We drank our coffee in silence as I looked around our newly remodeled kitchen. Up until right then, it had given me such pleasure, the way all those details and deliberations had paid off, creating my favorite space in the house. The dark green cabinets I'd had to talk Matt into, the brass pulls that popped against them. One of those big, fat French ranges with gold knobs. The copper vent hood and polished black walnut counters. But that morning, day one, all that those things made me feel was empty. I couldn't believe I'd ever cared so much about fixtures and finials, Dana.

But also, I wished I could get back to the world where I had.

Matt was talking again, something about going somewhere. I shook my head. "Sorry, what? You're going where?"

"The hospital, to get your car."

I blinked. "What are you going to do with your car if you're driving mine home?"

"I won't take it. I'll take an Uber."

"That's stupid." The words snapped out of me like a rubber band. "Why would you do that? Just wait until I'm done with my coffee, and we can go together."

Matt blinked. I never spoke to him like that.

"I'm sorry," he said. "I didn't think . . . of course I won't leave you alone."

***

It started in my stomach as I crawled into Matt's car. Then we were backing down the drive and there it was again, but in my throat now, my head. Some internal storm. My body and brain working together to stop me from doing this, from going back. I ignored them. I told myself I should have tried to eat something. But it wasn't hunger, Dana.

We were passing the emergency room doors when I said, "Right here's fine."

Matt glanced around. "You sure? I don't see your car."

"It's over there." I waved an impatient hand toward the back of the lot.

"Where?" Matt let up on the accelerator and turned his head to follow the direction of my wave.

"Seriously, Matt. Just let me out," I begged. "I lost my sister, not my mind. I can walk twenty feet to the goddamn car."

"All right, all right. I just . . ." His voice trailed off, defeated.

"I'm sorry. I just . . . I don't want to be here."

"I know," he said. "That's why I was—"

"*I know.* But it's fine. I'm fine. I just need to get out of this parking lot."

Matt didn't believe me, I could tell, but he didn't argue.

I tried to soften my tone. "Do me a favor? Please don't wait for me or trail behind me the whole way home. I've got this, okay?"

"I know you do." Matt leaned over. I gave him the kiss he was looking for and told him I'd see him back at the house.

A few yards from my car, I looked back. Matt was disappearing from sight, his head turned to get one last look at me before he was gone.

I was wrong. I so did not *have this.* A snowflake fell on my nose, and I brushed it away with much more force than was necessary.

Inside the car, I jabbed at the GPS buttons to navigate home. I may have been the better driver, Dana, but as Dad always loved to say, I couldn't find my way out of a paper bag. He still talks about the time I got lost in the Woodfield Mall parking lot.

"Proceed to Osler Drive," the GPS woman instructed.

You again, I thought. But this time, I wasn't in a hurry. I was not desperately trying to reach you, Dana. Or Matt. I no longer feared the worst happening—arriving minutes too late to say goodbye, to say sorry—and so the GPS and I got along fine this time.

The drive home felt shorter than the one out. The snow crunched loudly under the wheels as I turned into our driveway. The sound was so ugly, so distracting, that I nearly scraped the side of the car against our big brick mailbox. The contractor had built it way too close to the driveway, and I hated it. It was one of the first things Matt had insisted on replacing when we moved in. I'd been focused on the big stuff—repainting and landscaping and furniture—but Matt was hell-bent on having a respectable mailbox.

"Who plops a stock Home Depot mailbox outside a home like this?" he'd said under his breath as we'd left the open house.

The car was halfway up the driveway, garage door shuddering open, when the idea—the impulse—came.

My hand went to the shifter, the shifter went into reverse, and the car backed slowly down the driveway. I'd barely come to a halt before we were back in first, my foot pressing down on the accelerator—and this time, I didn't miss.

10

When I woke up Friday morning, you'd been gone thirty-eight hours. That's how I started thinking of time. Not as Thursday or Friday, or the fifteenth of February or the sixteenth, but as *how long has Dana been gone?*

Someone, I don't know who, decided the funeral planning should be done within forty-eight hours. Before we left for the funeral home, Matt and I had our morning coffee, and this time I had my toast, even though I didn't feel like it. It seemed to please Matt.

It wasn't until after breakfast, when I was pulling on my jacket and Matt was heading out to the garage to warm up his car, that I remembered.

I finished pulling my arms through my coat as I ran to the garage. Matt's keys were dangling at his side, his eyes assessing my car, taking in the gouges and depressions running along the back half of the passenger side.

He looked over at me, confused. "What happened?"

"I hit the mailbox yesterday."

"Our mailbox?" He turned his head to look down the drive. "Is it okay?"

"The mailbox is fine, Matt. And so am I."

He shook his head. "Right, sorry. I just . . . how did you hit it?"

"I've almost hit it a thousand times before, I've told you that. The guy built it too close to the edge of the driveway. I have to maneuver around it every time I pull in. I knew one day I was going to—"

"Okay, okay." Matt walked over to me, put a leather-gloved hand on my shoulder. He opened his mouth to say something, then stopped and stared, thinking.

I hoped he wasn't remembering. I hoped he wasn't thinking of senior year of high school. *That was fifteen years ago.*

I gave him a pathetic smile.

His hand fell away from my shoulder, and he relaxed. "It's okay. Accidents happen."

I nodded. "I really am sorry."

"It's not a big deal, Cady."

We got in his Audi A-whatever and pulled on our seat belts. The heat was blasting, and the fact of it warmed me more than the heat itself. Matt preferred the car and the house ten degrees cooler than I did, so this little generosity spoke loudly to me.

He slowed at the end of the driveway as we passed the mailbox. There was a thick black scrape of paint all across the brick.

"I'm sure we can fix it," I said. "Some paint thinner will probably take it right off."

"I'm not worried about it."

"Maybe a wire brush or something." I felt really bad now.

Matt sighed. "Don't worry about it, Cady. It doesn't matter."

We had to drive back to Oak Park, a few miles from the hospital, to make the *arrangements*. Cramer-Bernstein Funeral Home. That's where you were staying for the next couple days, Dana. Then it would be off to the local cemetery.

I hadn't thought about your body until we pulled up outside the funeral home. Now I did. You were inside. And wherever you were, you were cold, even if you didn't know it. You weren't even a *you* anymore, Dana. You were just a body now. Not to me, of course, or to Sean or Mom or Dad or Matt. But to the rest of the world, and definitely to the stout prick who introduced himself as *Howard Bernstein, Funeral Director.* He sometimes referred to you as *your sister* or *your daughter,* but he never used your name, and sometimes you were just *the body. The body arrived yesterday. Did you want to cremate the body, or will you be doing a burial? The body can be made fit for an open-casket wake, if that's of interest.*

There were a lot of decisions to be made, a lot of guessing as to "what Dana would have wanted." Sean said you definitely would have wanted a burial, not cremation. I didn't think you would have cared one way or the other, quite frankly, but I held my peace. This was for them, for us. For Sean and Mom and Dad and me. You were gone, and it made us feel better to make decisions we told ourselves were for you—the stain and wood grain of your casket, the songs we'd play at the funeral, the passages we'd read at the wake, the font on your headstone—but really, it was for us.

There was a lot of discussion around flowers that day. We weren't big flower girls, were we, Dana? Either of us. We both agreed they were awfully expensive for something that lazed prettily in water for a week before up and dying. But Mom and Sean wanted to nail this for you.

"What do you think?" Mom asked me, pointing to the options they'd narrowed down for your casket cover.

I blinked at the choices as my phone buzzed from inside my purse. Someone had been trying to get ahold of me for the last hour. I'd texted Jamie the day after you . . . your accident, to let her know what had happened, but I hadn't left anyone in charge, hadn't said when I'd be back. No doubt there was a problem to be solved. A last-minute snafu with an event, probably. Maybe a bottle of wine worth more than my car had been dropped, or maybe we couldn't get the permit for Asher Belman's helicopter entrance to his bar mitzvah. Like I said, Dana, there's almost always a hitch right before an event, and we almost always get it resolved—if this time we didn't, so be it.

I feigned interest in the options Mom was pointing to. White roses. Yellow roses. Lavender cremones. Pink lilies. What did it matter one way or the other?

I'm sorry, Dana. When I say things like that, it sounds like I didn't care. I cared a whole lot that you were gone. I just didn't care about the damn flowers, because I knew you wouldn't have given a flying fuck which ones we threw in that hole with you.

"Let Sean pick," I said. "He'd know better."

He chose white roses for you.

"And yellow ones for the baby," he said. "Ten stems, one for each week."

11

Breakfast. Sixty-two hours since you'd been gone. Matt said, "Your parents called. The police want to meet with them today."

I put my toast back on my plate. "About what?"

Matt shrugged and wiped his mouth with a napkin. "Standard stuff, I imagine. There's probably some sort of investigation to determine liability, for insurance purposes."

I wrapped my hands around my coffee mug. "That's all they want? To talk about which driver was at fault?"

"Pretty sure. Unless they found out about that Blow Pop I stole from Walgreens twenty years ago—or you've been up to something nefarious I don't know about."

I caught my breath before I spoke. "Hilarious, Matt."

His face turned serious. "Your parents asked if we wanted to come along. I told them I'd ask . . ."

"No. I don't want to."

Matt nodded. He carried his dishes to the sink, then headed to his home office to take care of some emails. I headed to mine.

On a typical Saturday morning, I would have been in full ringmaster mode, pulling together last-minute details for that evening's events and putting out the inevitable eleventh-hour fires and smoothing over any wrinkles from the previous night's events, but on this particular Saturday, I couldn't face the chaos.

I did try—I opened my email and studied my long and many to-do lists and even pulled up Jamie's number to check in and make sure everything was covered, to see if I was needed. But the emails remained unread, the to-do lists unchecked, the offer of help undelivered. Instead, I found my fingers on my keyboard, typing *dana stoll* into Google.

The only thing that came up related to your death was your obituary, which I'd helped write. It didn't say anything about the accident, just that you'd unexpectedly passed away.

Why had we chosen "passed away," Dana? It sounded so . . . passive. And peaceful—like you'd floated out of reach in a hot-air balloon or been carried away by a strong tide. I guess we'd just followed protocol, sparing everyone else the words we couldn't get out of our own ears: *impact, crushed, organ failure, blood loss.*

I added *illinois* and *accident* to the search bar, but still nothing came up. I tried several variations of *fatal accident oak park pregnant valentine's day tragedy.* Still nothing, like it hadn't even happened. That's what you get for dying in the greater Chicagoland area, Dana. If you'd been a small-town girl, or maybe even from a couple suburbs farther west, you'd be front-page news. But out here, so close to the city, the reporting of your death would be relegated to three formulaic sentences in next week's Oak Park police blotter:

> *Police and emergency technicians responded to a fatal accident on Oak Park's west side Wednesday afternoon. The victim, a 32-year-old female from Downers Grove, was pronounced dead on the scene. Another driver, a blah-blah-blah from blah-blah town, was treated for minor injuries and released.*

No mention of the fact that you were coming home from the school where you worked as a guidance counselor. No acknowledgment of how you poured everything into those kids, helping them see that their bad grade could be turned around, that their parents' divorce was not their fault, that the comments in that TikTok post wouldn't mean shit in ten years.

No talk of the girl who'd cried when Bambi's mother died, or the woman who'd cried when, even though it was probably our thirtieth time watching *The Notebook*, Noah told Allie *It wasn't over, it* still *isn't over.* No reference to the hiccups you got on your first sip of beer or how good your Kardashian impressions were, especially after a second margarita. Your random, occasional good morning, gorgeous! and night, sis! texts, just because. Your Sunday-morning doughnut deliveries to Mom and Dad, the softness in your eyes as you said your wedding vows, how tenderly you'd touched your belly when you told me you were pregnant.

Not a twin. Not a daughter. Not a wife or a friend or a soon-to-be mother.

Just a 32-year-old female from Downers Grove.

Downstairs, a kitchen counter stool scraped against the new travertine floor. My eyes flew to my closed door, then back to my computer screen. What would Matt say if he saw my search history?

I'm worried, Cady. This isn't healthy. What's the point—why are you doing this to yourself? I hope this doesn't turn into another one of your—

Another screech from below. The stool being pulled back in. I backspaced over each letter of each word, one by one . . . *tragedy day valentine's pregnant park oak accident fatal.* Hypothetical Matt was right. This was pointless and unhealthy. I doubted Mom or Dad or Sean were punishing themselves like this.

Or the parents of the boy I'd seen in that waiting room.

God, Dana. That mother. Her scream echoed in my ears like the ringing after a good show at the Metro. I'd survived three nights since February 14, and for three nights that sound had played on a loop inside my head. It was so loud, so *real,* that I'd glanced over and over at Matt, worried it would somehow wake him.

And her hand. She'd placed her cold, soft hand on my trembling one. She didn't have to do that. She had her own fears, her own pain. She did not have to give me anything.

I turned back to the search bar and my keyboard.

morgan keller illinois

There were a fair number of Morgan Kellers, including several in Illinois and at least one in the Chicago area who, with her high-waisted jeans and prolific #makeuphaul posts, was definitely not the woman in the waiting room with the sensible black pants and minimal makeup.

I added *christopher* to my keywords and tried again. Maybe it would yield a birth announcement, or something on a school PTA page. Something about the family before they'd become a tragedy, when they were just a normal mom and dad and son worried about normal things like messy rooms and bad grades and who wasn't pulling their weight around the house. Or maybe some well-meaning friend or cousin had posted something on Facebook—a request for prayers or a GoFundMe, I don't know. People do shit like that all the time, Dana. Like God gives *Facebook likes* any heed as he decides who gets to stay and who has to go.

I found nothing, though, even after a review of all eighteen pages Google had to offer. If Morgan or her son had social media accounts, they were private ones I couldn't see. Not unless I dared send a follow request, and I wasn't going to do that, Dana. What would I say?

Hey there, remember me? From the hospital? You held my hand, and I can't stop thinking about it. About you. And I thought since my sister and your son died on the same day, we could be friends or something?

Actually, I will admit I considered a (less flippant) version of this. If anyone could understand what it was like to lose a twin—an actual piece of yourself—it would be a mother, right? People bonded over much less every day: sushi and country music and *Ted Lasso*. So why not this?

12

Birthday. Anniversary. Sympathy. Get Well. Nothing for *Thanks for trying to save my sister.* I settled for a nondenominational vase of white lilies and a card with watercolor flowers on the front and nothing inside.

"Can I borrow a pen?" I asked the woman in the hospital gift shop. She had precisely coiffed white hair and rheumy blue eyes. Her entire getup looked swiped from the shelves of the shop, from the rhinestone chandeliers dripping off her earlobes down to the embroidered slippers on her feet.

"My goodness, of course."

I smiled my thanks and let the pen she gave me hover over the finely textured paper. I started and stopped a dozen different sentiments that sounded either slightly sardonic or excessively maudlin, and settled on signing the card *From the family of Dana Stoll.*

Vase in hand, I walked through the now familiar maze of corridors, beneath the unforgiving lights. In the trauma ward, I was greeted at the nurses' station by a woman in green scrubs whose name tag said *Miriam.* I held out the vase and awkwardly explained what the flowers were for. Miriam's head tilted as she exclaimed over how thoughtful the gesture was, as if I'd invented this custom. I smiled weakly.

"It's the least I could do." Literally.

"I'll be sure the right people get these," Miriam assured me. "And the card too, of course."

"Thank you."

"You're most welcome. And I'm so sorry, Ms. McKenna, about your sister."

"Thank you."

A lot of people had told me that. That they were sorry about my sister. Like you were some regular old sister I shared half my DNA with, Dana, not every last nucleotide.

I stood unmoving, flowers and missive successfully dispatched, my mission completed. It was time to turn around and get back in the car. To go home and tell Matt how nice it felt to get out of the house, how well received the flowers had been. But there was one other thing, an after-thought, really—not my purpose in coming—but since I was there . . .

"There was a woman here that day," I told Miriam. "Morgan some-thing. I recognized her from high school. I . . . I overheard that her son had an accident and that he . . ."

Miriam's whole face fell. "Oh yes, I heard about that. So sad. The boy was only twelve."

"I know." I pressed my hand to my chest. "I keep thinking about her. I wish I'd said something, but what with my sister and everything . . . it didn't seem like . . ."

"Oh, no, of course not," Miriam said, shaking her head.

I didn't intend to use you like that, Dana. I only wanted to offer an explanation for why I hadn't talked to my supposed old friend that day. But since Miriam seemed sympathetic . . .

"I don't suppose," I said slowly, lowering my voice, "that you could help me out with something?"

"Oh. Well, yes, of course, if I can."

"I'd like to reach out to Morgan, with my condolences. I tried to find her online, but I struck out. I was hoping maybe you could give me her address? Or at least a street name?"

Miriam pinned one side of her lower lip between her teeth, like she was thinking, and I let myself hope. But in the end, she screwed up her face in a display of regret.

"I'm sorry," she said. "I can't give out any information on patients, unfortunately—HIPAA, you know. I'm really sorry . . ."

I shook my head. "I understand. I shouldn't have asked."

I should have let it drop, Dana. I should have gotten back in my car and minded my own tragedy. But a bit of the old Cady, the determined twenty-seven-year-old who'd quit a safe, decent-paying job to start an event planning business with zero guarantees and unfavorable odds, must have been on standby somewhere in there.

"Maybe you could just confirm the last name she's using?" I asked.

"I thought it was Keller, but she must have changed it. If I had the right name . . ."

Miriam chewed her lip again. Her eyes darted around the room, looking for would-be witnesses to this potential crime.

"I suppose," she said, lowering her voice, "that wouldn't hurt."

13

On the fifth day, we buried you, Dana. But first we had the wake, which seemed like a cruel word to describe the event from which you would never rise.

There are many things people don't get about being an identical twin. I don't have to tell you that. You knew all about the push and pull of wanting to preserve our special bond, but needing to be seen as your own person, too. The perks and pitfalls and all the stupid questions. *Do you have telepathy? Can your parents tell you apart? Have you ever made out?*

But there are a lot of things you never got to learn about being a twin because you didn't have to lose yours. For example: what it feels like to see yourself lying in a casket.

There I was, staring down at you, Dana, your face frozen and caked in the thick paste they were trying to pass off as makeup, and I couldn't help but think, *This is what it would look like if I'd been in that car instead.* I could hear you teasing me about it: *Nice, Cady. Way to turn my wake into your existential crisis.*

But anyway, your big send-off. It's impossible to convey what that day felt like. All the adjectives I know are insufficient. I will say, though, I was glad we got the stupid flowers. It would have been that much harder to watch your casket being lowered into the frozen ground without anything beautiful or alive to keep you company.

Matt spoke at the burial. I didn't. I'm sorry, I know I should have, but I just didn't think I could, so Matt volunteered, and I helped him prepare. He talked about your unapologetic love for reality TV dating shows. How badly you used to beat him in Monopoly. How funny that was because, you know, his career. How we'd tried and failed to pull one of our infamous switches on him.

It was hard to look at the other faces as he spoke. I wasn't a big crier—neither were you—but we were both hopeless if we saw someone else doing it, and let me tell you, Dana, seeing *Dad* cry like that . . . well, I just couldn't.

I studied the cemetery instead. It was empty. You were the only service that Monday. *An unusual choice,* according to that awful man at the funeral home. But you loved Mondays because you said they were a fresh start, and we were doing this for you, remember?

My eyes went back to Matt. He was talking about Sean now. About the first time you'd brought him over for dinner, how Sean had turned to me as I loaded my burger up and said, "I thought you hated onions, babe." We'd all laughed, good-naturedly, at his mistake. At his pink cheeks. Most everyone at the cemetery already knew the story, but we still smiled at the punch line.

Matt moved through the stories we'd selected, expertly telling each one. I tried to focus on his words, on the remembering, on the feelings I was supposed to be having, but I . . . I . . .

Dana.

He was there.

He was there.

The man from the waiting room, with those knowing green eyes. He was back, at another grave site maybe fifty yards away. Not part of our huddled, grieving mass, but not far. He was *there,* still in that same coat, a small bouquet of yellow drugstore flowers in his gloved hands. I couldn't see the color of his eyes from where I was, but I knew they were green.

I knew it was *him.*

Beside me, Matt grabbed my arm and I jumped. He was done speaking, was returning his notes to his coat's breast pocket. I'd missed the end of his eulogy.

"Doing okay?" he whispered.

I shook my head, my eyes fastened on the man.

Tchaikovsky's 1812 Overture started to play as you were lowered into the ground with your big white roses and your baby's little yellow ones. I watched carefully, trying to be in the moment, because maybe I needed to see this—you in the casket, the casket in the ground—to really grasp it and one day, hundreds of years from now, accept it and carry on.

But I couldn't, because all I could think was—

"Do you see that man?" I whispered to Matt.

"Which one?"

"At your ten o'clock, way over there by himself."

"Oh. Yeah. What about him?"

"He was at the hospital."

"When?"

"The day . . . Valentine's Day. I saw him in the waiting room."

"Are you sure?"

"Positive."

"Huh." Matt stuffed his hands down deeper in his coat pockets. "Small world."

"It's not a coincidence. He was watching me in that waiting room—like *really* watching me, Matt. It creeped me out. And now he's here."

"Cady . . ." The music had stopped. "I think you're supposed to throw your flower in," Matt whispered.

I glanced around. Sure enough, all eyes were on me, waiting.

I stepped forward, gripping the stem of a single white rose in my gloved hand. You were down there, Dana, in that glossy wooden box. This would be my last chance to say something to you. I looked for the right last words, but nothing was good enough. *I love you and I'm sorry*—that's what I thought, really hard, as I tossed my flower down.

I returned to Matt's side and let my arm slip into the little crook he made for me with his.

Mom and Dad dropped their flowers next, then Sean.

I checked the spot where the man had been. Gone.

"He's not there anymore."

Matt didn't respond, except for the almost imperceptible flare of his nostrils.

"Did you see where he went?" I whispered.

Matt shook his head. His eyes were fixed on the pastor, who was inviting everyone to join the family for refreshments back at the church.

People began to disperse. Cousins we hadn't seen in years had come. Old neighbors I'd forgotten about. Friends I hadn't texted back since the news had spread and the condolences started piling up. They shook hands, embraced, murmured their excuses or intentions to join us for refreshments.

Matt released my arm so I could receive their hugs and handclasps. Over their shoulders, in the gaps between their frames, I looked for the man with the green jacket and yellow flowers. He'd vanished.

"Shit," I said. "Gone."

Matt moved his hand to my back, steering me toward the car. "He left flowers, Cady—he was visiting someone. It was a coincidence. Maybe it wasn't even the same guy, just someone who looked like him." He said this in the voice parents use in the grocery checkout to explain to hysterical toddlers why they can't have a candy bar.

"It was the same guy. *I know it.*"

Matt's hand pressed more firmly into my back. Like a warning. "Don't do this," he whispered. "Don't start another . . ."

I fixed him with a look, daring him, but he gave up. Or chickened out. I shook my head and took off, leaving his hand hanging empty in the air.

"Where are you going?" he called.

I didn't answer. Matt called after me again as I neared the spot where the man in the green jacket had stood. He was on my heels by the time I reached the grave with the freshly laid stems. I used my foot to clear away the snow covering the small headstone.

Maybe Matt was right. Maybe it was a coincidence. Maybe it wasn't the same guy. There were probably hundreds, even thousands of men in the area with green Patagonia jackets and dark hair and stares that could cut you open from a distance the length of the Aragon Ballroom.

But tell me, Dana, who visits someone who died in 1889?

14

At just over a week since we'd lost you, many of my friends had already stopped checking in. I didn't mind. They weren't really friends, not like you'd been. Most of my circle was casual—up for a happy hour or a juicy group text, but not on call for the heavy stuff. That had only ever been you, for me.

So it was fine, I got it. I'd been in their shoes once, with my sincere but arm's-length sympathy, dispatching expensive condolence bouquets and laboring over just the right sentiment to include in my letterpress sympathy cards. I too had put on somber black dresses and made appearances at wakes, all the while still caught up in the minutiae of my life, still caring about the overgrown roots in my hair and the new wallpaper in the dining room.

It was okay. I didn't want to talk to anyone anyway.

Just you.

My fingers often itched to open our last text exchange, to tell you that I needed you to come back, to see what you would say.

Then I would remember.

Not that you were gone—I would never forget that—but that our long-running chain of daily, sometimes hourly, text messages had died two weeks before you did.

I didn't want to open it up. I already knew what your last words to me were. I didn't have to look.

Of all the things you've said and done over the years, this is the worst, Cady.

The worst.

Oh, Dana.

I wish that were true.

Anyway. It was a Friday. Matt was officially back "in pocket," but still working out of his home office. The hum of serious conversation and productivity buzzed through the house like a trapped fly I wanted to snap down with a dish towel.

I'd never realized before how stressful my husband's days were. Lots of tense conversations, the occasional raised voice that just as suddenly became hushed.

He'd taken a short break earlier that afternoon to grab some lunch from the kitchen. I was still there from breakfast, sitting at the table with a cold mug of coffee, watching Champ sleep by the window.

"Have you checked in at work lately?" he asked as he pulled a container of leftovers from the fridge. It came out a little snappish, and I shot him a *Don't even* look.

I could see how it might be irritating, to spend the morning busting your ass and fighting on your phone, only to find your wife sitting in the same chair you'd left her in three hours earlier. But it had been nine days, Dana. *Nine days.*

After that, I'd escaped to my own office, the implication being that I was *checking in*—answering emails or planning events. But I was not working. Not on Eventually stuff, anyway. I was looking for Morgan again, this time with her real name, which, according to the sympathetic nurse from the hospital, was not Morgan Keller but Morgan Hess. She must have divorced or never married the boy's father, or not taken his name, I didn't know.

All that mattered was that now, when I put Morgan's name in the search bar, I was able to find her. On LinkedIn, on the Meet Our Team page of a small accounting firm's poorly designed website, in a Western Illinois alumni directory, in online real estate records.

The latter offered up her current address, which I pasted into Google. I was about to click on a result from Zillow when my phone buzzed.

Work.

Jamie.

I remembered her seventeen missed calls over the last few days and picked up.

"Cady! Thank God. I'm so sorry for all the calls, but we've run into a problem with Ramona Crawford's anniversary party. But um, first . . . I just want to say how sorry I am about your sister."

"Thank you, Jamie."

I had to get used to that. People being *sorry* about you.

"What's up?" I asked.

"Well . . . you know how important it was to Ramona that there be white orchids tonight?"

"Not important," I corrected. "Imperative."

"Right, well, they were delivered to the venue this morning and they're gorgeous—and gigantic, just like she wanted—and I knew how important they were to her, so I sent her a quick pic to put her mind at ease, but . . . well, she says they're supposed to be *double* orchids, Cady."

"She never said anything about double orchids."

"She said double orchids have some sort of special significance and she'd rather have no orchids at all than these."

I rubbed at the sides of my head, where a migraine was blossoming. "Okay, call the Hausermann greenhouse in Villa Park—"

"I did. They're wiped out from Valentine's Day. I called around to some other distributors, too, but no luck. I can get a few that size, but they aren't white. The white ones I can get are too small or still budding. I have the team calling florists now, but it's not looking good. If I can't—"

"If you can't, then Ramona will just have to wipe her tears on the *single* white orchids she originally asked for. Or on the sleeve of one of those Balmain blazers she lives in. Or better yet, in hubby number five's doughy-ass, never-lifted-a-finger, man-baby arms."

There was nothing from Jamie for a long beat. I never talked like that about my clients, no matter how difficult or spoiled or needy they could be.

But what did I care anymore if Ramona Crawford had a little smudge on her big fat entitled life?

"One more thing," Jamie said slowly, proceeding with caution. "This is probably a stupid question, but I'm just confirming . . . you're not going to be there tonight, right? At the event?"

I sighed more heavily than I'd meant to. "It's not a stupid question, Jamie. I've dropped the ball on this, I'm sorry. I was supposed to be there, but do me a favor. Gabriella's more than capable of managing everything—ask her to take over, will you? And if you're not doing anything tonight, why don't you go and back her up, get some actual event experience? I'll pay you overtime, of course."

Yes—*yes,* of course Jamie would go. She'd *love* to. She thanked me for the opportunity. *The opportunity.* I tried not to feel bad about that, but I had presented it that way, hadn't I?

I put my phone down and turned back to my computer, to all the open tabs on my screen offering up small pieces of Morgan, to that Zillow link I'd been about to open. I clicked it, and the page loaded, offering up a Google Street View and all the usual facts.

My hand shook on the mouse. This was where she lived. In a two-bed, two-bath, 1,400-square-foot single-family home, purchased six years ago for $289,000.

There were no interior shots from the last listing—it had been too long—but the seller's description remained, letting me know that this *exquisite vintage property* had a stainless-steel fridge, a brand-new water heater, a freshly stained redwood deck. Walking score of eighty-seven. A seven-rated elementary school, a five-rated middle school.

I played with the map. Google Street View showed me a squat, redbrick bungalow with a tidy yard on a quiet-looking street. I clicked around, circling the block, lingering on the homes of her neighbors, pacing up and down her street with my mouse until I felt like I'd driven it in my car. Like I would recognize it, if I ever passed by.

Back in my search results, I sifted through the pieces I'd collected. Morgan was an accounting analyst and had once—twenty-five years earlier—been a business major at Western Illinois University. She'd run a 10K with some coworkers to raise money for Lurie Children's. She'd been quoted in her local newspaper as being in favor of a new school district referendum. She may or may not have been the Morgan Hess behind a half-hearted attempt at a baking blog, and she had a Goodreads account—she'd given five stars to all three books on her "Read" shelf: two Colleen Hoover titles and one Elin Hilderbrand. She had a Facebook account and Instagram, but those were private. I wouldn't be able to see them without requesting to friend or follow her, and I'd already decided

I wasn't going to do that. That would be absurd. She wouldn't accept a stranger's friend requests—and even if she did, it's not like we'd become *real* friends. Right?

Or could we? Morgan had lost her child on Valentine's Day, and I'd lost you. A coincidence, if you believed in coincidences, which, as you know, Dana—

"Refill?"

I jumped. Matt. He was at the door, French press in hand. My mug from breakfast sat empty on my desk, but I shook my head. I'd cut back considerably now that my days required less fuel.

Matt set the press on the edge of my desk and placed a gentle hand on my shoulder. "How do you feel about me taking your car to the shop?"

He must have felt the way my body tensed because he pulled his hand back. Apparently, I was now one of those people you had to feel out on every minor matter. Two weeks earlier, Matt would have just said, "Hey, if you don't need the car today, I'll take it in."

"That would be helpful," I said. "Thank you."

I had to remember that Matt was just trying to find ways to make it all better, to help me get through it, even though he had no idea what *it* really was. If I resisted, he'd protest or give me one of his defeated sighs. He was sighing a lot lately, so I didn't argue, because that was another new thing we were doing a lot of, Dana. Arguing.

We'd never been one of those couples that pecked at each other or were unsufferable to be around. We were *fun*. The couple that partied for every little reason or no reason at all. The first ones jumping into the pool, the last ones dancing at the wedding. We'd *tutted* over the couples who bickered about savings account balances and speed limits and whether the forks should be placed in the dishwasher tines up or tines down.

Now look at us. Matt, tiptoeing around his offer to get my car fixed. Me, driven to the outskirts of sanity by the sound of his Teams chat alerts.

Maybe that's why, when Matt asked what my plans were for the day, I said, almost without thinking, "I'm going into the office."

"The office office?"

"Yeah. Think I could take your car?"

Matt tried to downplay his enthusiasm. "Yeah, of course. But . . . are you sure you're ready?"

"No. But if I have a bad day, who's gonna fire me?"

It took a while to get out the door. In a little over a week, I'd forgotten how to get ready. I was so used to being in a hurry—putting on earrings while slipping into heels while talking into my speakerphone—that getting ready for nothing pressing, with no set appointment time or competing priorities, was problematic.

I stood staring at the clothes in my closet, the possibilities overwhelming. Finally I settled on black pants and a dark green blouse. I brushed my hair, then my teeth. I didn't feel like touching my makeup—I hadn't even worn any to your funeral—but I wanted this to be convincing, so I curled my eyelashes and put on some mascara and lipstick.

Matt's eyebrows jumped when he saw me. I flinched, fearing he'd do some stupid whistle or something, but he just smiled and told me I could do this.

We kissed goodbye at the door. Matt still looked like he couldn't believe this was really happening, and honestly, Dana? I couldn't believe what I was about to do either.

15

I adjusted the seat and mirrors and steering wheel in Matt's car—probably the only time I wouldn't get in trouble for messing up his settings—then plugged the address into Google Maps on my phone so it wouldn't appear in his car's navigation history. A voice that sounded like Grandma Ruby's *tsked* in my head: *Anything worth hiding is worth not doing.* But then came a louder one, offering up one of Grandpa Flynn's nuggets: *If you can't be good, Cady girl, be careful.*

I knew when I was getting close, thanks to those satellite and street views on my computer. There was the pink Queen Anne on the corner and the American foursquare with peeling white paint and just ahead, a tree with a burl the size of Champ.

The neighborhood was empty and quiet, the homes modest but tidy, the trees old, their branches heavy with snow. A strong wind blew that day, and each gust shaved a layer of snow off the branches' reserves, the iridescent flecks drifting down to dust my windshield.

The house—her house—was a classic brick bungalow. Small, but well cared for. A Christmas wreath still hung on the door, lights strung in the naked azalea branches, glow-in-the-dark stickers clinging to a front window. Footprints zigzagged across the yard and a headless snowman stood right in the middle of it.

I imagined the house two months earlier, in December. The wreath thumping against the door as the family went in and out on their way to holiday parties, coming home from school, going out to build the snowman. I saw Morgan stringing the lights in the bushes, then calling the boy over to watch as they turned them on all at once.

I traveled over every inch of that house, reading into each quirk and crack as if they told a story, imagining the hands that stuck the stickers on the window and the feet that slid into the boots that ran up and down the yard, making those prints.

What had caused that snowman's head to lie smashed on its side like that? Had it lost a sword fight with the boy? Fallen victim to a snowball? Was it the work of teenage passersby and, if so, had the boy cried when he'd discovered it?

Probably not. He was twelve. Maybe it hadn't even happened while he was alive. Maybe Morgan—or the father—was responsible. Perhaps the beheading was not done in fun.

The paint on the garage door was starting to crack and peel; I wondered if there were plans to fix it, if Morgan cared about that sort of thing. If we were friends, if she ever asked my advice, I would tell her to paint her brick a creamy white, those shutters a light black. The house would look cleaner but not stark. Bright and homey.

She should tear out the azaleas, too, Dana, and replace them with evergreens, to cheer up the curb appeal during winter. And in that big front window, swap out those blinds for sheer curtain panels. Something more welcoming that let a little light in . . .

I hadn't had any appetite in a week, but at some point, my stomach began to growl. I ignored it. My phone, too—now and then it buzzed to remind me I had other things I should be doing. A missed call from Jamie. Two more from Gabriella, who'd covered Quinn's party and Ramona's anniversary dinner. A text—How's it going?—from Matt. Another, an hour later, asking, Everything good?

I watched for hours. I didn't mean to, Dana, not for so long, but . . .

Do you remember going fishing with Dad in fifth grade, when he and Mom rented that cabin in Wisconsin? Remember how long it took to get him to leave the lake? At first, before it became annoying, we thought it was funny how hell-bent he was on catching something. He was so sure a big bite was just around the corner, that if we pulled our poles at that point, we'd miss our chances by a hair.

This was like that. I'd waited so long for a glimpse of her. If I waited just a few more minutes . . .

And then it happened. It took almost the entire day, but finally, the front door opened—maybe an hour before sundown—and she emerged, her arms wrapped tightly around her torso as she walked down the driveway to the mailbox. She was in yoga pants and a purple Western Illinois sweatshirt, no coat. Her snow boots were unlaced, and the stack of mail she retrieved was thick, like it had been several days since she'd last checked. She showed no interest in the contents before trudging back up the slight slope of the drive.

From where I sat, her eyes were little more than two dark dots on her face. I couldn't tell if she'd been crying. I could not gauge her exhaustion, or her grief, or her anger. For that, I would have to get closer . . .

Oh, I know.

I know.

But seriously, Dana, do not worry about me. I know how all this must sound, but it was really truly harmless.

I was just watching.

16

Ten days, Dana. Ten days.

"Babe," Matt said at dinner.

Already I knew I was not going to like whatever came next. I put down my fork.

"I was thinking . . ."

Yep, here we go.

"I was thinking maybe it would be good for you to talk to someone."

"Like a shrink?"

"Yeah, or a support group or something."

"I don't think they have support groups for losing your twin."

"Actually, they do." Matt pushed a piece of paper forward. On it were a couple websites, spelled out in his block lettering. I hadn't even seen him reach into his pocket. "I did some googling and they're—"

"Probably not local," I said, pushing the paper back. "How many identical twins are dying every day in the northwest burbs? It's probably some online forum of old folks who got forty or fifty more years with their twin than I got with Dana."

"There might be a subgroup or something . . ."

"No thank you."

"Cady—"

"*No, Matt.*"

Dead silence. He was going to drop it. I picked my fork back up. Matt waited until I had a roasted brussels sprout in my mouth to try again.

"I get it," he said. "You don't want to talk to me about Dana. I don't blame you—I have no idea what you're going through—but you should talk to *someone*. Someone trained to help with this sort of thing, or someone who's going through something similar, maybe—"

"Just stop, Matt!" My chair squealed as I pushed away from the table.

"*No one* is going through what I'm going through. Okay? Talking isn't going to fix this. It won't undo . . . it just . . . it's too late."

"It's *not* too late, Cady!" Matt was shouting now, too. He never did that. Ever. "You're not going to be able to get through this on your own. You're not . . . you've never been able to . . ."

I lifted my eyebrows, daring him to finish the thought.

"You've always had a hard time letting go," he said carefully. "You know that, Cady. And I mean, shit, I know it's hard for everyone, but you . . ." He trailed off, his eyes pleading with me to be reasonable, to at least consider it.

I put my napkin back in my lap and picked up my fork. "I'm not talking to a fucking therapist."

Matt turned back to his plate. His jaw looked like it might snap as he chewed. But this was more than anger. This was fear. And maybe hurt. He'd just wanted to help—he always wanted to help, Dana.

That's how we met, remember, Matt helping me up off that football field? The powder-puff game junior year? He was the first to reach me after Mackenzie Arlington *accidentally* tripped me as I was going for a senior's flag. He was wearing a short, pleated skirt and false eyelashes, one of which was only half on, clinging for dear life.

"You okay?" he asked.

Well, I was a lot better now that Matt McKenna, senior varsity soccer player, was standing over me with his rusty brown hair and eyes so dark blue they were almost black. I saw something in them, something feverish and turbulent, that I couldn't name but instantly recognized.

I accepted his outstretched hand and let him yank me up.

"I'm Matt," he said.

Yeah, I knew.

"Cady," I said, "with a *C* and a *D*, not a *K* or a *T*."

"Good to know." Matt was reaching into his shirt, into his stuffed bra, for something. His phone. He pulled it out and started plugging something in. "C-A-D-Y . . . right?" He looked up and his eyes literally *twinkled*, Dana. "Better give me your number," he said seriously, "so I can check up on you later."

That next weekend, we had our first date. *Nick and Norah's Infinite*

Playlist at Classic Cinemas. He kissed me halfway through. My first kiss. More followed—more kisses and more movies, chill nights on the couch in our den or his parents' basement, school dances and football games.

The *Things I Love About Matt* list grew quickly: His dry sense of humor. That he seemed not to notice or care that he was a big deal at school. That he wasn't embarrassed by his National Honor Society status or his parents cheering loudly at his soccer games. I loved how seriously he took soccer and his grades, how he'd rekick a single missed shot for hours and study, over and over and over, facts and formulas and theories he already knew. I loved how he cranked the stereo in his car so loud the bass felt like it was in my throat. I loved how pensive he got when he listened to music, how he'd replay a song he didn't feel he'd appreciated hard enough the first time.

We became inseparable—I know, I know, total cliché. The *inseparable* teenage lovers, a tale as old as time. But you know, Dana. You were a twin—*my twin*—so you knew the weight of that word. You knew me. You knew that if I loved you, *I. fucking. loved. you.* That I would build myself around you with bricks that wouldn't be easily knocked down. That was just me. My way. Why bother with anything if it doesn't feel like *everything*?

I knew, even then, at seventeen, that most guys didn't want a girlfriend like that, that they made jokes at the expense of girls like me. But Matt wasn't most guys. He loved it. He loved being loved the way I loved, even if it scared him a little—maybe *because* it scared him a little. Because he was like me, Dana. Intense. A force.

That's the thing I loved most about Matt, the way his energy matched mine. I was too much for some people.

Things changed when he went off to Northwestern the following year. None of you got what that was like for me. Matt, out there, on his own, in a new place with new people, a legit adult doing whatever he wanted in his shiny new world. A world, I saw right away, that had the power to take him from me. New friends and frat parties and professors and majors and dorms and *those girls*. When I came to visit, I noticed them acutely, all the girls with the tiny outfits at the big parties that they didn't call parties, Dana, they were *mixers*. Those girls, with their Greek letters stretched proud and tight across their chests, who didn't choke on the smoke from a joint, who sucked beer out of bongs like it was water, who didn't have to be home by twelve. Who didn't have to come home at all.

I had built *my* world so small, around you and Mom and Dad and Matt. But now Matt was there, in that other, bigger world that felt a lot further than thirty-two miles away.

You saw my fake smiles in the hallway at school and the tears that came out of nowhere at dinner; you were there when I ran to your room in the middle of the night because it felt like I might literally die, because I physically couldn't breathe. You knew I slept with one of his sweatshirts balled up like a teddy bear. I saw that look in your eyes when my AP Bio exam came back with a C-, then again at State, when you set that volleyball so perfectly, but it fell right in front of me like a big, blurry raindrop. I heard Mom and Dad's whispers behind closed doors: . . . *always been a little . . . I just don't think . . . not healthy . . . I hate to say it . . . should probably see someone . . .*

Look, Dana, I wished I was the sort of girl who didn't give a fuck. The sort of girl who took whatever the world handed her with blind faith and a smile, who didn't bat an eye when another pretty girl walked in the room, who didn't put all her stock in one teenage boy, who didn't feel that boy's leaving like he'd been cut away from her with a knife, who didn't stay home from parties to refresh his Facebook page, whose fears didn't spread like the dandelions Dad fought in the backyard, who might cry but would be okay if things didn't work out.

I wished I was that sort of girl. But I wasn't.

Our senior year of high school, I spent more time studying Matt's social media accounts than trig or world lit or biology. I zoomed in on every smile in every photo, running each one through the database of memories in my head, analyzing whether *this* smile was bigger, brighter, better than the ones he gave me when he came back home every other weekend.

I researched every girl behind every like and comment and photo. If she was anywhere on Matt's socials, I was on her. On her stories and comments, her likes and photos, on her *friends'* comments and likes and photos.

I even looked into his new guy friends—you never know, and *I had to know, Dana*, what kind of people Matt was hanging out with. If this pledge brother Lucas who kept popping up in all Matt's photos said he was *In a Relationship* with a cute brunette named Emma, then why was he posting pics with *these* girls? These peroxided, halter-top-wearing girls? Was that the kind of person Matt wanted to hang out with? Was that the kind of person Matt was? Or was becoming?

I created a fake Facebook account I filled with provocative selfies yanked from some wannabe model's page and DMed Matt, to see what he would do. I disabled the typing indicator on my phone so he couldn't see me starting all the texts I never sent. When I came to visit, I smelled his dirty clothes while he was in the shower. I counted the condoms in his top dresser drawer and ran my hands under his bed to check for forgotten earrings or tubes of lip gloss.

And yes, Dana. That car accident, my one and only accident, where I hit that telephone pole and got that little scar on my forehead that made me, for the first time ever, not look exactly like you? It wasn't a coincidence that it happened the day before Matt was set to board a plane to Cancun to celebrate spring break with his new college friends. There are no coincidences. I know you wondered—I saw the question in your eyes when you came to the hospital—and *you were right.*

And I got it. I got it, okay? For whatever reason, my brain wasn't put together according to the same instructions as yours, and that was scary for you. For Mom and Dad. But was it really so bad, Dana, to feel life so hard? To be so all in?

Then it came time for you and me to decide where to go to college. I knew you'd fallen in love with U of I's campus, and I knew you wouldn't follow Matt to Northwestern with me. I couldn't go to Northwestern if it meant leaving you—we'd promised each other—and besides, as much as I loved Matt, as much as I'd fought to make it through senior year so we could finally be together again, I couldn't just chuck you aside for him.

Matt was my world, but so were you, Dana. Since day one. *You* were *me.* Literally.

We would make it, I promised Matt. We'd already gotten through one year apart. What could 149 miles do that 32 couldn't?

We lasted—what was it? Three weeks? Four? Not long. It turned out an extra two hours between us was fatal. Matt had a job that year and "frat responsibilities," and you and I didn't have a car, and I could not—*could not*—survive another year like the one before, let alone four, so the first weekend Matt finally made it down to Champaign, I ended it.

He cried. I almost took the words back, but I knew I'd eventually wind up in the same spot again, with the same impossible decision hanging before me: Go to Northwestern and be with Matt, or stay there in Champaign. With you.

So that's what I chose, Dana.

You.

I would choose you every time. Over anybody or anything, under any circumstances.

You don't even know.

17

It was a Tuesday, the thirteenth day you'd been gone, and for the last two, I'd been watching Morgan's house—sorry, does that sound bad? Should I say *visiting* instead? It's not like I was leaving dead animals on her doorstep or sifting through her trash bins or anything, though I did mosey into her yard one time when I was pretty sure she was out, pretending to look for my lost dog, sneaking a peek inside her front window and gently touching the snowman's head, returning his carrot nose to its rightful place. But other than that, I was only watching. What was the harm in that, Dana?

Okay, look at it this way. Remember when you and Jared Mason broke up junior year and we drove by his house to see if the lights were on in his room? Remember how we sat there in the car, wondering whether he was crying buckets over you or playing *Grand Theft Auto*? Well, this was kind of like that. Besides, I never stayed long—and that Tuesday, I was only there a few minutes, maybe half an hour. A quick stop before heading into the office.

It was my first time back. Matt thought it was my third. I did not blame Jamie or Gabriella or Pam from payroll or Edgar from graphic design for the panicked missives their eyes dispatched to one another as I walked through the door. I should have texted Jamie a heads-up, so she could have spread the word and let them bounce their awkward condolences off one another before delivering them to me.

I thanked them for their sympathy and asked Jamie to stop by my office in fifteen minutes.

I closed my office door. Set my Birkin on my spotless desk. Sat down in the Eames Chair that advertised how important and successful and tasteful I was. I noted the colorful abstract paintings on the walls, how they felt as familiar and foreign as everything in the house had felt that first night.

From my purse, I pulled out my phone and my monthly planner. I hadn't touched that planner in two weeks, but now I opened it to February. My eyes traveled over the neatly recorded appointments and reminders, odd remnants of an old life that no longer made sense.

I stared at the back of my closed office door, unsure, for the first time since I'd started Eventually, what to do. It was really hard to give a shit about parties anymore, Dana. If I'd been a nurse or a teacher or something—or a school counselor, like you—maybe it would have been easier.

I'd once upon a time convinced myself that my work was important, that I was making dreams come true, creating memories my clients would cherish forever. I don't know, maybe that was true once. But not anymore, not with the sort of clientele I'd graduated to. If I didn't plan a sweet sixteen party that rivaled most weddings, someone else would be happy to step in and figure out how to put a dance floor on top of a pool or finagle a white limo out of thin air.

Jamie knocked softly on the door before entering. I'm sure she'd waited precisely fifteen minutes, but it felt like two.

"What can I do to help you settle in?" Her voice sounded different, unnatural. She didn't know how to proceed—she didn't know how *I* wanted to proceed—so she was trying to cover all bases. *Let's get down to business, shall we—unless you want to talk about* it?

I glanced around my office for an answer to her question, then looked back at Jamie, at her eager, waiting face.

"I guess what would be most helpful," I said, "is if you could catch me up. I can't remember where I left off . . . I've never been away this long."

Jamie looked down at the notebook in her hands. It was opened to a page crawling with blue ink. "Well," she said, "I could really use your help circling back to clients on some of our bigger events. I've let them all know about your . . . your sister, and they were all very sympathetic and understanding—well, most of them were"—she made a face—"but there are some urgent things I could use your guidance on. For starters, Mei Liu is completely rethinking the menu for her husband's surprise fiftieth. Oh, and the Farrells pooh-poohed the design I put together for their daughter's engagement party—and of course Nora is champing at the bit to see what you have planned for her annual black-and-white ball."

I smiled. "Of course." I had nothing in mind for Nora's event. I could see in the planner lying open in front of me that I'd blocked off half of last week to work on it. "Why don't you put together a list for me?"

Jamie grinned and slid a paper from her notebook. I took the printed list, shaking my head in wonder. I was about to thank her for her foresight—for everything—when her phone rang in her pocket. She pulled it out and made an *Eek* face.

"Ramona Crawford," she explained. "Again. We ended up repotting those orchids to make them doubles, but that meant we only had enough centerpieces for every other table, so Gabby whipped up these cool candelabra things. They were absolutely gorgeous, but it wasn't what Ramona had in mind and—I'm sorry, Cady, I've been trying to handle it on my own, but when I said earlier that *most* of our clients were understanding, I was specifically *not* talking about Ramona. I just don't think she's going to be able to move past this until she gets to give you a firsthand earful—"

"Here." I motioned for Jamie to hand over the phone. Part of me hoped I'd be too late pressing that green button, but another part . . .

"Hello, Ramona. This is Cady."

There was a long pause. I thought maybe I'd lucked out, that I was too late picking up the call. But then: "Hello, Cady. I take it your assistant has filled you in on what transpired with the orchids?"

"Jamie has filled me in, yes."

"Well," came Ramona's huffy response, "may I ask what you intend to do about it?" There was another small pause as I debated how to proceed, then she added, "And I just wanted to say Jane told me about your sister, and I'm very sorry for your loss."

Jane. Of course she couldn't be bothered to remember Jamie's name, even though I'd just said it.

"Oh, thank you, that's very kind, Ramona." I let that sit. For a long time.

"Cady?"

"Yes?"

"Did you . . . did you hear the question? About the orchids?"

"Oh yes, I'm sorry. You were asking about a refund, right?"

A little gasp came through the phone. I took a scrap of pleasure in knowing that vulgar word—*refund*—would settle unpleasantly on Ramona's diamond-studded ears. Nora Donnelly had taught me that lesson many years earlier.

"I said nothing about *money*." The word left her mouth like spit.

"Oh? What was it you were looking for then, Ramona? I'm afraid I don't know what other restitution can be offered, other than my deepest apologies for the pain and stress it caused you on your special day."

"It wasn't my—" Ramona started, then stopped. "Forget I asked," she said shortly. "I'll consider the matter closed, but I'm afraid this entire ordeal has left a sour note in my mouth. I don't see how I could be persuaded to hire Eventually again in the future. I'm terribly sorry, Cady, I just don't see it happening."

"I understand."

I thought I heard a little sniff, then, "And please remove me from any mailing lists."

I rolled my eyes at Jamie. I could tell from her ever-widening eyes that she'd heard every word.

"Sure thing, Ramona." I pulled the phone from my ear and hung up, not bothering to see if there was anything further on her end.

Jamie swallowed and took her phone back. She glanced down at the blue scrawls in her notebook. I could almost make out the next item on her list—something to do with future bookings. Before she could get to it, I gathered my phone and my planner and placed them back inside my bag. Adrenaline thrummed through my veins, making me lightheaded. I'd never lost my composure or behaved remotely unprofessionally with a client. Or a vendor or a contractor or my staff—or anyone.

"I think I'll finish the day at home," I told Jamie. I smiled and waved the list she'd typed up before stuffing it into my bag. "Might be easier to tackle these there."

Jamie looked disappointed but relieved. She followed me to the front door, where she and the other staff issued spirited goodbyes, all of us pretending not to find it noteworthy that I'd barely lasted thirty minutes on my first day back.

I walked to my car, climbed inside, and started the ignition. Whatever had overcome me in the office clung to me as I backed carefully out of my spot and exited the parking lot.

I didn't know where my car was taking me until I was there, Dana.

The cemetery.

I pulled up to where we'd buried you not even two weeks earlier. The slam of my car door echoed through the empty graveyard. I walked to you. I knelt down. I pulled my coat sleeve over my hand and used it to wipe the thin layer of snow off your headstone.

I wanted to talk to you so badly. I wanted to tell you. Everything. And maybe I would have, right then and there, and maybe things would have turned out differently if I had.

But I didn't, because something stopped me.

A bouquet of frozen, wilted yellow flowers. The cheap kind you grab from a bucket in the Walgreens checkout line. The exact kind that man, the one in the green Patagonia jacket, had laid on that old gravestone the day of your funeral.

I stood and started to walk toward the site where the flowers had been placed two weeks earlier, though it wasn't necessary. I could see from where I was that the flowers were gone from that grave. They'd been moved to yours.

18

Bursting. That's what you were when you told me you were pregnant, that first day in February. Brimming with hormones and pride and the anticipation of my enthusiastic reaction. Sean was the only other person who knew (you'd just hit the eight-week mark) and, you admitted, you'd almost told me first, before him.

I took my time taking a sip from one of the coffees I'd just poured us. It was hot and burned my throat on the way down, but I didn't care.

"I didn't know you were trying," I finally said.

You were so happy, so pleased with yourself, that you didn't yet realize I wasn't.

"We weren't," you said, smirking conspiratorially. "Not really. I mean, yeah, I stopped taking my birth control a couple months ago, because we wanted to *start* trying, but we weren't, like, timing anything or keeping track. We just thought we'd pull the goalie and see what happened. I wasn't even on prenatals! I never even got my period—I just stopped taking the pill and—*bam!*—pregnant."

Bam. The word hit me like a slap. I'm surprised I didn't flinch.

Then again, maybe I did. Either way, you didn't notice.

"Sean was so shocked," you went on. "Like, *shocked*. He didn't think it would happen so quickly. Neither did I. I took three tests just to make sure. My first reaction—" you laughed, throwing your hands over mine. "It was so funny, Cady. I—get this—I broke into a sweat and thought, *Shit, Dad is gonna* flip. I mean, you spend the first part of your sexually active years trying *not* to get pregnant and sweating bullets every time you're a day late, then the next thing you know . . ."

"Bam?"

"Yes!" you said, laughing again, nodding, all the giddy things. Your hands tightened over mine on the new walnut table I'd bought for the breakfast nook. "You're going to be an aunt—Aunt Cady. Aunt Cady and Uncle Matt. Wild, huh?" You sighed, dreamily. "I guess what's meant to be is meant to be."

What's meant to be.

How nice for you, Dana. That all those motivational posters hanging in your office and the cutesy plaques littering Mom's kitchen walls turned out to be true.

For you.

"I mean, seriously," you continued, giggling. "Can you believe it?"

You finally stopped talking, took a sip of your coffee. When you were done, you put your hot mug down on my new table. I pushed a leather coaster toward you.

"Believe what?" I asked. "That you're going to have a baby? Or that you broke your promise?"

My words were a sharp pin landing on the tautest part of the bubble straining inside you. The happiness whooshed right out. I could hardly tell it had been there seconds earlier, threatening to rupture you.

"What promise?"

"The promise we made and kept for twenty years? That we'd raise our kids together?" It came out like the *Uh, duh?* retorts we'd tortured Mom with as teenagers. "We can't exactly raise them together if we don't have them at the same time."

You laughed, kind of. "You're joking, right?"

I wasn't.

"Cady . . ." You didn't know what to say. I was supposed to be jumping out of my seat. I was supposed to be ruining my mascara and smiling so big my face hurt. "I can't believe you're turning this into a *you* thing."

"I'm not thinking of myself, Dana. I'm thinking about our kids. Sean's an only child, Matt's just got the one brother, and God knows when or if he'll ever get married, let alone have kids. You and I only have each other. I thought we'd agreed . . . I mean, don't you want your kids to have cousins to grow up with? A big, close family? My kids and your kids, best friends?"

"Of course I want that," you said. "But I can't wait around forever for you and Matt to be ready. Besides, who's to say it won't still happen? Sean and I want more, at least two or three. Maybe next time . . . And if it's really that important to you, why don't you start trying? You and Matt are way more—"

"It's not a good time," I said.

"Well," you said, sadly, "it is for me."

You looked like an entirely different person than the one who'd been waiting for me to pour those coffees, biting your lip to hold in your exciting news until I sat down.

I was wrong, I knew that. And stupid; I was being so stupid. It just hurt, really fucking bad. But that wasn't your fault, Dana. I came within a breath of apologizing—I almost explained everything—but then you said, "This is about Sean, isn't it?"

I'm sure I blinked. "Sean?"

"Yes. You hate him. You always have. You've never liked anyone I've dated. You've never liked any of my friends, for that matter. Not if they weren't your friends, too."

"I don't hate Sean."

You gave me your *Come on, Cady* look. "Well, you definitely don't *like* him."

"I do too! I have nothing against Sean." I didn't, not really. He was fine. He just . . . wasn't who I'd pictured you ending up with.

Your laugh scared me. "Cady, you tried to break us up!"

"I never tried to break you up. I tried setting you up with someone else."

You did your scary laugh again. "Yeah, Matt's friend. *Six months* into my relationship with Sean. You pushed it every day for weeks and weeks. You said something about it in front of Sean once!"

I shook my head. How could you not see? "I just wanted you to be happy."

"I was happy." You slumped back against your chair and closed your eyes.

"I wanted you to be *more* happy. I wanted you to be with the right person." I sighed. "Why are we even rehashing this? None of this has anything to do with your . . . news. This is about your promise to me, Dana. You promised—"

"This is bullshit, Cady." Your eyes flew open and you slapped the table with your palms. The coffee in my mug rippled like someone had tossed a pebble into it. "This is . . . this is like if I'd made you feel bad about marrying Matt. Because didn't we have a pact about that, too? Something about marrying twins or best friends or something?"

The reminder made me laugh, bitterly. "I'd sacrificed enough for you by that point, Dana."

"What are you talking about?" Your eyes were as dark as the coffee in your mug.

"I kept our college pact—I didn't go to Northwestern, I chose U of I, I chose *you*—and I almost lost Matt because of it."

You didn't say anything for one whole breath, like you were waiting for the punch line. Then: "Give me a fucking break, Cady. Are you for real? I never asked you to choose between us. You did that on your own. You almost lost Matt because *you* chose to move three hours away from him because you couldn't stand the thought of me doing my own thing, without you, for once in our goddamned lives. This is some first-rate revisionist history bullshit."

"Oh, well, I'm sorry I wanted to go to college with my sister, with my best friend, *like we'd planned to do our whole lives*. If keeping that promise stopped you from living your best life or doing your own goddamn thing, then I'm sorry."

"I'm not just talking about college, Cady." You were crying now. Still angry, but crying. "Every time I wanted to do something without you, you'd get a *bad feeling*, and I wouldn't do it; I wouldn't go through with it. I was too scared because you'd been right that one time, about me going to Mackenzie's house, and you knew that—you knew I'd be scared—so you used it to keep me close, to keep out everyone and everything else that might take me away from you. But this, Cady? You can't control this. You can't stop me from having this baby."

The longest seconds of my life passed while you gathered up your purse and coat and I tried to find my voice.

Before you walked away, you pulled a small white box out of your purse and slammed it down on the table.

I waited until I was sure you were gone, then I opened it. I pulled out the little onesie, newborn size, and ran the tips of my fingers over the words.

PARTY ANIMAL, JUST LIKE MY AUNTIE.

I still have it. It's in a drawer in my nightstand. It'll probably stay there forever. One day I will die, too, and someone will clean out my things and find it.

Maybe one day soon.

19

Four weeks to the day. That's when everything really changed, though it was hard to see it then.

Matt was back to his normal routine, his days spent visiting properties and running the office. Before he went back, he'd taken my car into the shop and had it all fixed up. He handed over the keys as we stood admiring the repairs together.

Like nothing ever happened, he'd said. Like I hadn't spent the worst hour of my life inside that thing and then, the next day, dragged it along his beloved mailbox and set off the alarm bells in his head that had him sighing and tiptoeing all around the house.

I didn't go back to the office, but sometimes I made an effort from home, chipping away at design concepts and email replies—solitary endeavors that didn't require interacting with staff or clients. I left the event facilitation and client interfacing to Jamie and Gabriella, though that wasn't sustainable. When clients spent the kind of money mine did, they wanted the face of the brand, not an assistant or understudy. It was me they were hiring, not Eventually. My face. My stamp. My fire. I just didn't think I could hock up any convincing empathy should someone bitch about the thread count in a table runner or lament the hopelessness of securing white truffles this time of year.

It would get easier. That's what I had to keep reminding myself. This world had once been my natural habitat. If I could just get myself there, to the office or an event, if I could just show up, it would all come back.

But just showing up proved more difficult than I'd expected. Every morning I left the house with a thermos of coffee and good intentions, but I never made it.

Instead, I found myself at Morgan's house. I didn't stay long. Just a few minutes, sometimes an hour, maybe two. There was rarely anything to see. Most days, I didn't see her at all. Maybe a shadow crossing the window, or the blinds tilting up.

Afterward, I'd go home, put on the TV, take Champ for a walk. The hours would slip away too quickly, and Matt would be walking in the door. The next morning, it would happen like that all over again. And the next.

Then, one morning, I came earlier than usual and caught Morgan's garage door lifting as I pulled up. Inching forward, I was able to glimpse her before she disappeared into her car. She had on sensible flats and black pants; one of those key card badges dangled from her waist—she was back to work. She was doing better than I was.

I changed my routine and started visiting her house in the evening, which got me home later. Sometimes Matt would beat me, or we'd pull into the driveway at the same time, and he'd beam, so proud of me for putting in another full day at the office.

I could usually count on Morgan's little red Honda turning into her driveway at around a quarter after five. Sometimes I would park on the street a couple houses down. Sometimes I would circle the block and catch her going in. On less frigid evenings, I would get there early. I'd park a block or two away and flip up my big, fluffy hood and happen to be strolling by her house as she pulled in.

On those nights, I could make out the sound of her mudroom door squeaking open before the garage door shivered closed. A light, presumably the kitchen one, would come on. It would stay on for twenty minutes or so while she prepared and ate her dinner. Then it would go off, and the house would stay dark the rest of the night, except for the blue glow of the television.

On this particular day, a Wednesday, exactly four weeks after your accident, Dana, I arrived at my usual time. I parked as many houses down as I could without losing sight of Morgan's driveway. I tried to switch up my spot each time. I didn't need the neighbors spotting a pattern, or my Range Rover becoming a known fixture in the neighborhood.

It was warmer—high forties—so I let my window down an inch. I noted the sort of little things I'd failed to register for a long time. The crisp air, the warmth of a rare sunny March day, the pink glow of the sun beginning its descent. I welcomed them in through the cracked window. It had been a hard day, Dana. For some reason, anniversaries of your death—one whole month this time—hit hard, though I knew the numbers were arbitrary.

Morgan's red Honda appeared on the horizon at the usual hour. The orange-pink sun lit up the windows from behind, like one of those sun-catchers we used to paint as kids.

Her car drew nearer and turned into the drive, then the garage, the door shimmying down behind her. I turned on my car and pressed down on the gas pedal slowly, inching closer before stopping between the two houses closest to hers.

Twenty, thirty seconds, and then yes, there it was, the kitchen light. Seventeen minutes later, it went off. Dinner was over. Any minute now, the TV's light would broadcast from the back of the house. I waited for it. My signal to leave. My sign that everything was under control, just as it should be.

The minutes ticked by—one, then an unprecedented two, then three—but still no blue light. I crept closer, narrowing my eyes at the big front window. The glow-in-the-dark stickers were gone. I watched and watched, but the TV's light did not appear.

Then the garage door was coming back up. Something was going on. Trash night? A neighborhood stroll? The mail?

None of that, I realized, as the taillights on her Civic lit up. Something more exciting, then. Maybe dinner with friends.

Her car rolled slowly down the drive, then pivoted its back end my way before taking off.

I started the engine and followed, staying far behind, waiting to see where our paths would diverge. It happened at the second stop sign. Morgan put on her signal to make a left on Harlem. I signaled right to go home.

And then, on second thought, I pushed the lever back up.

Okay, Dana, here's where you gasp and grab my arm and get all, *No, Cady, please don't tell me you—*

Yes, Dana. I did. I followed her, okay? South down Harlem, a left and then another, all the way to Morton West High. I tailed her right into the parking lot.

I wondered, at first, if this was where the boy had gone, if Morgan had come here to torture herself with memories of school drop-offs and first-day pictures outside the glass doors. But no, that couldn't be. We were in—I checked the GPS—Berwyn, a full town away. And this was a high school and the boy had only been twelve—his mother had said so, and the nurse I'd given the flowers to, Miriam, had confirmed it. There was even a big blue magnet on the back of Morgan's car that boasted PROUD PARENT OF AN HONOR ROLL STUDENT AT BROOKS MIDDLE SCHOOL.

Now, before I tell you what happened next, Dana, please know that I did have a debate with myself—give me some credit. Up until then, I'd only been watching Morgan, and only from a distance. Following her into that school and seeing what this was all about? That was something else. A line that perhaps I shouldn't have crossed.

But then again, I'd come this far.

20

"Where have you *been*?"

We weren't the sort of couple that gave each other a hard time about coming home late or doing our own thing, so this accusation, disguised as a question, took me aback. No, literally, Dana. I stumbled back when Matt hurled the words at me. I'd only just stepped into the kitchen, my shoes still on, my purse still slung over my shoulder.

I considered telling him the truth: *I followed a woman I don't know to a parent bereavement group.*

But I went with an apologetic smile and a lie. "Work," I said. "We're *so* busy right now, and I'm still playing catch-up. In fact, I may—"

"Stop," Matt interrupted. "Just stop, Cady. I can't listen to this."

He knew I was lying. My insides ran hot, then cold, like two taps twisted open inside me. My brain scrambled to stitch together a story, like it had back in ninth grade when Mom walked up to us on the couch, laundry basket under one arm, lips perfectly horizontal, a half-smoked joint sticking up from her free hand like a middle finger.

"You weren't at work today. You haven't been to the office in weeks."

Had it really been that long? I stared emptily at him across the big island, gripping the thick countertop to steady myself.

"I talked to Jamie," Matt said. "She hasn't been able to get ahold of you all week. She was worried something was wrong—and she said you've put her in charge? Of everything?"

"Not *everything*. Gabriella is helping her, and Jamie is perfectly capable of handling things on her—"

"Jamie's perfectly capable of being a great *assistant*, Cady. You can't just throw her into the fire like this. It's one thing to give her more responsibility, but she isn't prepared to be *you*. She's drowning."

"She's fine."

Matt threw his hands in the air. "How do you know? You haven't talked to her in a week!"

I closed my eyes, breathed in through my nose. "You literally need to mind your own business, Matt."

There was no quick comeback this time. I opened my eyes. Something dark and unfamiliar had crossed my husband's face.

"I am minding my business, thank you," he said. His voice was deadly calm, something dangerous humming beneath it. "Mine *and* yours. It's not like your actions—or lack of them—don't affect anyone else, Cady. You have staff. And we've got bills to pay, ends to meet."

I laughed. "Ends to meet? Give me a break, Matt. Eventually had a great year last year, and you make more than enough to float us if I have one bad quarter—or is that it? You don't think I'm pulling my weight?"

Matt glared. "That's not it."

"You must be forgetting how I supported us when you started up MLG."

Matt balked. The shot had landed too close to home.

"Of course I haven't forgotten. And I haven't forgotten how I returned the favor when you started Eventually." His guilt washed away. Back to that smug outrage. "That's not the point, dammit. We're not talking about years ago; we're talking about right now, Cady. If you don't run Eventually *right now,* or delegate to someone capable of overseeing a multimillion-dollar company . . ."

"Please, Matt." I held up my hands, as if that could curb his frustration. "Don't tell me how to run my business. I don't tell you how to run yours."

Matt gave me a dubious look. "If I were running mine into the ground, I sure as shit hope you'd say something."

"Eventually is a well-oiled machine," I snapped. "It can do without me for a bit."

"It's a great fucking company, Cady, but it doesn't run without you. And it hasn't been a bit, it's been a month—"

"Are you fucking her?"

Matt's jaw dropped so low, I thought he was doing it on purpose, *trying* to look like a cartoon character. "Who?"

Wrong answer.

"*My assistant,*" I hissed. "Are. You. Fu—"

"Oh my God, Cady. No." He looked at me with disgust, like *I* was the one screwing *his* assistant. "Why would you even ask me that?"

"Well," I said smartly, "you've been working an awful lot of hours lately, haven't you? And now I find out you *talk* to Jamie?"

Matt's hands went to the sides of his head, his fists curling in his hair. It reminded me of the boy's father at the hospital. The way he'd yanked the strands.

"How did we even get down this hole?" he asked. "Forget Eventually—where have you been if you haven't been going to work?"

Oh, so *now* we could stop talking about Eventually?

"In my car," I said.

Matt looked behind me, like he was checking for a hidden camera or something, like I'd made a joke and everyone was going to pop out and yell *gotcha*. "What do you mean? Like driving? Like cruising around town?"

"No. I stop at . . . places. I go for walks or just sit and watch . . . people."

Truth—kind of. Sort of.

Matt wasn't buying it, I could tell. He reached down to reassure Champ. The dog had been craning his neck back and forth between us, his ears pulled down in concern. We never argued. Not like that, with raised voices.

"Next time you go to the park for that long, at least bring Champ. How long was he sitting in his crate today?"

I laughed, a bit nastily. "Bring Champ? He can barely walk to his food bowl anymore, Matt."

He gave the dog another rub on the top of his head. A reassuring *Mommy didn't mean that* kind of pat that pissed me off. "I'll take a few days off again—"

"Matt—"

"I'll take a few days off," he said firmly, holding up his hands to deflect my protests, "and try to help you figure things out. From what Jamie said, at the very least, we need to ensure you're ready for all the spring garden parties—and then graduation season, of course. But I have my own business to run, Cady. This isn't sustainable. We're going to have to—"

"*Matt.* You don't have to do this."

"We don't have a choice, Cady."

"This isn't a *we* thing," I argued. "This is *my* company—"

"And I'm not going to let you lose it," he said, pounding his fist on the walnut counter. "One day, you'll be back to your old self, and you're going to want your old life back. When that time comes, you'll be crushed if you don't have Eventually. I'm not going to let that happen. You would do the same for me."

We stood there in silence. Matt was waiting for something. A fight, or my surrender. But I had neither of those things in me. I let my purse slide down my arm and fall onto the counter, hesitating, so he would know I'd at least given it some thought—we knew each other so well, we could pick up on those things—and then I turned and left.

He was right, Dana. As hard as it was to drum up any of my old enthusiasm, as dirty and hollow as the very idea of a party made me feel, it would hurt—badly—to lose Eventually.

And I *would* do the same for him, and I *had* loved my job.

But we were never, *ever* going back.

21

Matt tried to stay home the next day. I'd confirmed his niggling suspicions that I wasn't okay, that I wasn't *coping*. The Cady he knew wouldn't abandon Eventually. She wasn't lazy, or a quitter, or a liar.

I insisted he go. I did not need a caretaker. To prove it, I got dressed in real clothes—a pair of jeans and a black sweater—and brushed my hair and almost curled my eyelashes. I went to the grocery store and bought staples—bread, coffee, fruit, TP. I took Champ on a walk. One spin around the block. He had to lie down halfway through; I went through an entire bag of treats getting him the last leg home.

It was not a comeback, not even close. But it was the most productive day I'd had in a month. I had an idea, Dana. A plan.

Ten minutes before Matt got home that night, I put some dirty dishes in the dishwasher. Five minutes before, the Thai food I'd ordered had been delivered. I'd thought about making something, but that would have aroused Matt's suspicions.

He walked through the door a little after six and entered the kitchen, making a show of sniffing the air, smelling the amalgam of curry and basil and coconut.

"You made dinner."

"I made a phone call," I corrected.

"You made my *night*," Matt said, slipping out of his jacket. "I'm starving."

I pulled out plates and cloth napkins. Matt opened the white cartons, exclaiming over each one as if they were carefully chosen Christmas presents. As usual, I'd ordered way too much for just the two of us.

"How was your day?"

"Good." Matt plucked a stick of chicken satay out of a box and placed it on top of a pile of noodles. "How was yours?"

"Productive."

"Good."

"I took Champ on a walk."

Matt lifted an eyebrow. "Did he make it?"

"Almost halfway."

"Good boy."

Across the room, Champ lifted his head from his pillow.

We brought our plates to the big round table in the kitchen nook. Matt said something about switching Champ's food; he'd read about some expensive-sounding brand that might help with the arthritis. I nodded, waiting for him to hold up his chopsticks and say *Cheers* the way he normally did, but he just broke them apart and hovered over his plate, debating where to start.

My own chopsticks didn't break apart cleanly, so I picked the splinters off while Matt dove into a pile of glass noodles.

"So." I took a deep breath. "I was thinking about what you said a few weeks back, and you were right."

"About the car?"

"No."

"About Trump?"

"*No*," I said. "About me needing some sort of outlet."

Matt's chopsticks froze. "So you've made an appointment with someone? A therapist?"

"Not a therapist," I said. "A bereavement group."

22

Wednesday. 5:58 P.M. Morgan's little Honda pulled into a spot near the front of the lot. If she hurried, she would be right on time. I'd have to hustle behind her to avoid being late myself, and I had been warned by the group leader, Moira, not to be late.

That was on Monday, when I'd called ahead to inquire about the registration process. "You're just in time," Moira had told me. "That group started last week, and we don't allow newcomers past the second session—a closed-group model builds trust."

I'd never given much thought to what a bereavement group leader might be like, but nonetheless, Moira was unexpected. I guess I'd anticipated someone gentle. Someone with a balmy voice who wore nondescript, pilling sweaters and a dainty gold cross.

Moira was . . . well, the first word that came to mind was sturdy. She stood like a tree, her shoes planted on the linoleum; I could imagine roots growing under them. Whatever had turned her hair a brassy orange had grown out four inches ago, and her body was a downright rectangle, though maybe that was due to her clothing: an oversized ZZ Top tee, boxy blue jeans, and a pair of white Reeboks—*Reeboks,* Dana.

At exactly 6:00, she squatted on her metal chair in the center of what appeared to be, judging from the posters and books, a history or social studies classroom, and slapped her hands against her thighs—our cue to quiet down, I guess, because we promptly did.

She started by welcoming me and welcoming back the others. Her voice was not exactly loud, but it was forthright. She didn't speak her words; she threw them, like tightly spiraled footballs.

"Since our first session," she said, "you might be experiencing a certain degree of anxiety. What will happen here? What will you be asked to do? Will it always be so hard? You might be scared of what you'll feel or worried that hearing someone else's pain might make yours worse. Maybe you don't like talking in front of the group—we're still strangers at this point, and who likes public speaking anyway, right? But let me tell you right now, folks: These fears are normal. *You* are normal. Everything you're going through is *normal*. It sucks, but it's normal."

Across the circle, Morgan smiled faintly and nodded. One of those active-listener types.

I'd wanted to sit next to her, but I'd been the last one in. The only seat left was on the other side of the circle, which I was thankful for now—it was easier to watch her this way, to take in the details. The pink rims of her brown eyes. The white cracks of her chapped lips. The fake Rothy's on her feet, the scuffed black Aldo tote beside them. Her polyester black pants, maybe the very same ones she'd been wearing in the hospital. And her straight, straight hair, hanging like reeds down the sides of her face, her left ear poking through the strands.

You know how I hated that, Dana—one of those little things that ir-ritated the shit out of me for no explicable reason—but with Morgan, there was not even a twinge of annoyance. I just wanted to walk over and carefully rearrange those dark blonde strands. I imagined her soft smile of thanks, for fixing it. For helping her.

"Now," Moira continued, "I'm not saying what you're going through isn't *personal*." She pointed to a man in green flannel. "Your loss," she told him, "is not the same as my loss. And neither is yours or yours or yours." Her index finger moved to each of us like a little pistol. "We're all special snowflakes, okay? Your story is yours, and mine is mine, and so your progress will not look like mine—and that's okay. There's no wrong or right way to do this, just like . . . damn, what's that candy commer-cial I'm thinking of?" She snapped her fingers to make it come to her. "Oh yeah, Reese's—there's no wrong way to eat a Reese's, right? Someone might tell you you're doing this wrong, but screw them. Your grief is a Reese's Peanut Butter Cup—there's no wrong way to eat it."

Moira paused. "Have I lost anyone yet? Go on, put your hand up," she said, raising her own. "I usually lose at least one of you with the peanut butter cups."

No hands, just some accommodating smiles, and an especially warm one from Morgan. It must have hurt her chapped lips; she pulled out a tube of cherry ChapStick. Someone, not me, should tell her that just makes it worse.

"Now for the good news," Moira went on. "This is going to become your safe space. A no-judgment zone to process all the shit you're dealing with."

She got a few polite laughs with the bad word.

"What?" she asked, holding up her hands in defense. "It's shit, isn't it? Everything you're going through? Not just the grief, but the people who think they know what you should be thinking and feeling? The asshole who tells you what stage of grief he thinks you're stuck in? It's all *shit*. Tell me I'm wrong."

Our ten heads bobbed in agreement. From the corner of my eye, I watched Morgan rub her lips together.

Moira proceeded to lay out the ground rules: Number one, no new members after tonight. Two, what we do at home is our business, but no one better walk into group under the influence of drugs or alcohol. Three, confidentiality—what happens in group stays in group. Four, respect—no side conversations, no phones or other devices, no showing up late. And finally, absolutely no judgments allowed, not of ourselves and certainly not of our fellow members.

She clapped her hands together. "Okay, who's ready to grieve?"

No, Dana, definitely not what I'd expected.

Now that we had the housekeeping out of the way, Moira suggested we do intros again, since I was new. She went first: Moira. She'd lost her only child, a boy of nineteen, twenty-two years ago to drugs. "Heroin, but it was probably the four milligrams of fentanyl it was laced with that really did it."

Morgan paid close attention, bobbing and angling and shaking her head as the others introduced themselves and retold their stories.

There was a mother whose sixteen-year-old daughter had succumbed to cystic fibrosis, a couple whose six-year-old had lost a two-year battle with leukemia, a father who'd found his adult son overdosed on benzodiazepines in the basement on Christmas Eve. A mother whose daughter had been killed in a drunk driving accident on the way back from her freshman homecoming dance. A couple who'd lost their son to a heroin overdose, like Moira had.

The tragedies—eight so far—piled up in the center of the circle we'd made with our metal folding chairs. I was going to leave feeling infinitely heavier than when I'd walked in, but I tried to pay attention, like Morgan, and to attach names to faces, on the very off chance that I came back the following week.

Then it was Morgan's turn. I already knew her voice, or thought I did. Her frantic pleas to the nurse and that excruciating *No* ricocheted between my ears when I tried to sleep at night.

This voice, though, was softer than the one from the waiting room. The urgency was gone. It rang out, desolate, like an echo in a long tunnel, but there was something solid about it, too. Some grit. I liked the sound of it.

"My name is Morgan. I lost my son Christopher thirty-five days ago. He . . . he crashed his bike on his way home from school. He wasn't wearing a helmet. I'd tried to get him to be better about that, but I . . . he just never remembered. It was Valentine's Day."

The hand of the mother whose daughter was killed on homecoming fluttered to her chest.

That was all Morgan said. Someone else started to speak, but I'd stopped listening. I could only hear Morgan's voice. Forty-eight new words for my collection. They resounded in my head. I played them over and over.

The woman sitting on my right gently pressed my arm. I must have missed my cue.

"My name is Cady," I began. "I'm not . . . my situation is a little different, I'm sorry . . . I—"

"Ah, ah, ah," Moira tsked. "No apologies, Cady."

Right.

"My name is Cady," I started over. I tried to put some of that grit I'd heard in Morgan's voice into my own. "I lost my daughter in a car accident last month. She was just a baby, just ten weeks old. Her name . . . her name was Dana."

23

I was not going to come back. Being there, hearing everyone else's sad stories, did not make me feel less alone. It was depressing as shit, and I was lonelier than ever. I was not like the rest of them, Dana. They were innocent survivors. Victims. I was . . . I was something else.

Definitely not a parent.

They thought I was. My fellow group members—those grieving parents of real children—thought I'd lost a precious baby girl. But when Moira asked me to talk about her, I couldn't. I felt sick enough, dirty enough, for having made up the baby in the first place. I couldn't take it any further, Dana; just the thought made me ill.

But I had to talk about something; that was the whole point. So I'd told them about you, too. A couple of the faces in the circle had gasped when I'd revealed my double tragedy.

"And what was your sister's name, Cady?" Moira gently asked.

"Dana," I answered, without thinking.

"Oh," Moira said, momentarily confused before coming up with an answer, sparing me. "You named your daughter after your sister?"

This possibility demanded a staggering amount of tragedy and irony and suspended belief in order to be true. My daughter and my sister, both named Dana, both lost to me within weeks of each other? But Moira appeared ready to accept this, so I nodded.

People always look for the answer they can stomach, not necessarily the one that makes the most sense.

Now that the group thought I'd suffered this surreal dual tragedy, I had to qualify, in every story I told, whether I was talking about baby Dana or you. Total fucking mess.

So no, I decided as I walked out that first night, there was no way in hell I could go back.

But when Wednesday rolled around again, I thought of that circle of faces, how they got it, what it was like to lose a literal piece of yourself. And I especially thought of that one face, of her soft voice and those gentle new words she'd given me to play over the sound of the old one—that horrific *No*—and I went a second time.

Then Matt said he thought it was helping, so I went again.

My interactions with Morgan consisted only of eye contact and the encouraging nods we all gave each other in the circle. The one time I'd stuck around for the postsession mingling, and she came within three feet of me, I pretended my phone was vibrating in my purse and scurried away, rummaging through my bag like I had an urgent situation unfolding at home. I must have, at some point, drawn a line for myself, and talking to Morgan was apparently it.

Anyway. Fourth session. You'd been gone fifty-six days. Moira announced we would be diving deeper into our *loss stories*.

"Tonight," she said, "I want you to share something about your relationship with your deceased loved one. Share as little or as much as you're comfortable with—but remember, if it doesn't hurt, you aren't stretching, and if you don't stretch, you don't get stronger."

Ten heads nodded. Yes, we remembered.

"And one more thing. I challenge each of you tonight to talk about your loved one's death in frank terms. Don't be afraid to use the *D* words. *Dead. Died. Death.* These are not bad words. My son is dead. He died of a drug overdose. These are facts. When I avoid these facts, when I say he is *lost,* I am avoiding the truth, and there is no healing in avoidance, friends."

Morgan was usually one of the better sharers. Sometimes she even volunteered to go first when the room was crickets. But tonight, she didn't look very keen when Moira suggested she kick off our go-round.

"Christopher," she began uncertainly, "was my son. Still is, of course. He'll always be my son, even though . . . even though he's dead."

Ten nods—*Yes, yes, good, use those* D *words.*

"His father and I divorced when he was seven. I had primary custody, his dad had him every other weekend. My ex would've taken him more often, but we'd agreed it was in our son's best interests to have a routine and that breaking up that routine to fulfill our own needs would be self-ish. So I kept Reid—that's my ex—up to speed on baseball games and back-to-school nights and that sort of thing.

"Actually," Morgan said, as if just now realizing this, "it worked pretty well. We were much better co-parents than spouses. Sometimes we even took a family photo or got pizza together after a game. But I . . . I didn't have a lot of free time for Christopher. I'm an accounting analyst in a medical billing office—exciting, I know—and my schedule is consistent, but still, I didn't have a lot of time. What little I did have—half an hour in the mornings, a couple hours at night, every other weekend—I tried to make really count, you know? I tried . . ."

Her words started to come out unsteadily, then not at all. My fingers twitched in my lap. They longed to reach across the circle for hers.

She tried again. "On the morning Christopher . . ." She shook her head. "It's so stupid that this is so hard . . ."

"Just do it," I whispered gently. "Count down from three and do it."

This was one of Moira's techniques for getting us to break through a stubborn wall. If you gave yourself a short countdown, she insisted, you could trick your brain into acting, into thinking that time was up.

Morgan shot me a small, grateful smile and drew in a breath. "I have so many regrets," she said. She stared intently at her hands in her lap, like she was talking to them, not us. "I wish I'd gotten on Christopher harder about wearing his damn helmet. I wish he hadn't needed to get himself to and from school. I wish I worked different hours or that I could have afforded after-school care or that I'd arranged for him to come home with a neighbor or something. But the thing I keep coming back to, for some reason, isn't his death."

We nodded, waiting, letting her put the words together.

"I had an important meeting at nine that morning, and I wasn't pre-pared," Morgan said. "And I had a coffee stain on my shirt, which meant I had to change into one I didn't like because of course I was behind on the laundry—and all these things wouldn't mean anything to me now, if I had that morning to do all over again, but they all seemed to mat-ter immensely at 8 A.M. on that February 14. And here comes Christo-pher, complaining that he can't find his Nintendo Switch, asking if I've done something with it. I hadn't seen the damn thing. *Wasn't my day to watch it,* I think I said. Besides, it was time to head to school—*past time,* actually—and why hadn't he combed his hair and wasn't that the T-shirt he wore yesterday? *Go change your shirt right now,* I yelled. I knew I'd feel bad when I got in the car and even worse once I got to the office—that's how it always went—but I told myself I'd do better the next day. That's what I always thought. That I'd get my shit together so I could be a better mother *tomorrow.*"

I wanted so badly to grab her hand. So badly.

"I thought about apologizing," she said. "But there wasn't time. *I had to go.* Christopher came back in a new shirt, and he was dragging his backpack down the hall the way he always did; it got under my skin every time. I told him I was leaving, that he needed to focus on getting out the door, and to remember to lock up, and that starting tomorrow he needed to start showing more responsibility. Waking up earlier, planning ahead, focusing on getting done what needed to get done and not worrying about finding stupid shit he didn't need for school anyway."

Morgan finally looked up at us, disgust in her eyes. She let loose a bitter laugh.

"Can you believe it?" she asked. "I didn't realize the irony until way later. Me, telling Christopher, my twelve-year-old son, to be more responsible. Christopher, who—for almost three years—had been getting himself to and from school every day. Me, telling that child to be more responsible when the whole reason I'd lost my shit in the first place was because I'd been running behind, because *I* hadn't prepared enough for that meeting, because *I* hadn't focused on what I was doing and *I'd* spilled coffee on my shirt . . ."

I swallowed hard. I wanted to tell her I understood all too well. The wrong words, the wrong decisions, the naïve certainty that anything could be taken back or fixed . . .

"Anyway, those were my last words to Christopher: *You need to be more responsible.* That, and *Don't forget to lock the door.* I didn't even look at him, just threw the words over my shoulder."

A tear slipped down her cheek. She flicked it away angrily, but more were piling up.

"I hate myself for that," she cried. "There were so many mornings I made sure to tell him I loved him. Why couldn't it have been one of those mornings?"

Morgan blurred before me. I felt her pain like it was mine, like it was radiating off her, burning me with its proximity.

"Listen to me," Moira said sternly from the other side of the circle. She was leaning forward in her seat, elbows digging into her denim-clad legs. "You loved Christopher, Morgan. *You loved your son.* And if I can see that—if we can all see that," she said, gesturing around the circle, "then your boy surely knew it, too."

We all nodded—*Yes, he knew, Morgan, he knew you loved him.*

Morgan didn't seem to hear Moira, though.

"The thing is," Morgan said—and just barely; I had to lean closer to hear—"that morning should never have happened. If I . . . if I hadn't . . ."

Her words stopped. I looked to Moira; she was never intimidated by silence. She let the uncomfortable spaces hang there until she got another sentence or two out of us, another little tear of the muscle that would make us rebuild and grow stronger.

But not tonight.

"Thank you, Morgan," Moira said.

"Thank you, Morgan," the rest of us murmured.

But I didn't want Morgan to be done. I wanted her to keep talking. I wanted her to tell us everything.

I went last. I hadn't given much thought to what I would say. I'd been too busy dissecting Morgan's words, letting her pain wash over me, trying to absorb some of it for her, wanting to help, to see that little smile she'd given me one more time. I wondered what unspoken things reverberated among the ellipses in her story. She was holding back; Moira should have pushed harder.

Now I had to say something, and it had better hurt, or Moira would surely pull it out of me. She wasn't going to let two of us walk easy in one night.

But my mind was blank. I couldn't think of a single story to tell about my daughter. Of course I couldn't. She didn't exist.

I should have been able to drum up something, though. The story of her birth, her first smile, something. But I couldn't. I couldn't bear to shit all over the very real story Morgan had just shared about her very real son. It was too much, too far, too—

"I can see this is hard for you," Moira said.

My head snapped up to meet her eyes. They were full of something I didn't deserve.

"It's too hard," I said, my words barely making their way out. I cleared my throat. "I can't talk about her. Not tonight."

Moira nodded. Maybe she was going to let me off the hook.

But no.

"Maybe," she suggested, "it would be easier if you told us a story about your sister instead?"

Yeah, it probably would, Moira, but it would still really fucking hurt.

"You said you shared a unique bond with her," she pressed. "Maybe tell us about that. About a time you felt how special that bond was."

I looked down at my hands like it was seventh-grade geography and the answer might be written on them.

"Okay," I agreed.

You know what story came to mind, don't you, Dana? Of course you do—or you would, if you were still here. Excuse me, still alive. Excuse me, *not dead.*

"My family calls this the Mackenzie Arlington story." I could picture you rolling your eyes over this old yarn getting more airtime. "My sister and I were very close," I told the group. "We did everything together. Had all the same friends, liked all the same things. If she went to a birthday party, I went. If I wanted to do soccer or take piano lessons, Dana was right there with me. But one day, when we were in sixth grade—so eleven years old, I think—Dana gets invited over to this girl's house. *Mackenzie Arlington.*"

I said her name in that bitchy voice I always say it in, and everyone laughed.

"Anyway, Dana gets invited over there, but not me, which creates a legit crisis at home, because this is simply unheard of. We're twins—everyone knows what that means. If Dana gets a present, I get a present. If I do ballet, Dana does ballet. If Dana gets invited to someone's house, *I* get to go, too." I shrugged. "That's just how it was. And this was the first time anyone had challenged that."

Fucking Mackenzie Arlington.

"So anyway, there's a lot of tears and screaming while Dana's getting ready. I'm sobbing, begging my mother to let me go with, insisting I cannot be left behind. Dana's crying and yelling back, begging my mom to please not let me ruin her plans with stupid, pretty, popular Mackenzie Arlington, that I'm being such a baby, and she'd never do this to me if I was the one who'd gotten invited over to Mackenzie's house. So my mom's in the middle of all this, trying to calm us both down and get Dana out the door. Then there's my dad, seconds away from putting a kibosh on the whole thing and not letting anybody go anywhere. And I know how all this must sound, but I truly feared Dana leaving that day. It felt *wrong*."

I paused for a breath, just long enough to wonder at the ease with which all these words were falling out of me.

"So Dana goes to Mackenzie's house, and after several minutes pass and the earth is still spinning, I settle down, but there's something churning inside me that makes it hard to relax, so I turn on the TV and watch *Lizzie McGuire*, and eventually my mom comes back from dropping Dana off.

"Then, about ten minutes later maybe, I get this intense pressure inside my chest and this . . . this inexplicable pain. And somehow, I know it has to do with Dana, that she's in trouble, that something is wrong. So I run to the kitchen, where my mom is, and I'm at the doorway when the pressure starts, like, *exploding*, shooting pain through me, from my chest straight down into my legs, and it hurts so bad I can't breathe.

"I try to explain to my mom, but she gets this look on her face—like *Not this again*—so now I'm screaming because she doesn't believe me, and if she doesn't believe me, then we can't get to Dana and help her. Meanwhile, my dad hears the commotion and comes running, and he's terrified at first, thinking I'm like dying or something, the way I'm carrying on. Then he finds out it's about Dana again and he makes the same face my mom made, and now they're both trying to calm me down—

gentle at first, but then they start to lose it because, I mean, holy shit, right?

"And then the phone rings. My dad goes to answer it and he says, *Lisa, Lisa*—that's my mom's name—he says, *Lisa, Lisa,* and he holds up the phone." I paused, for impact. "He tells us that Dana's been hurt, that Mackenzie's parents have called an ambulance."

I nodded at the ten faces staring back at me.

"She'd landed badly jumping off Mackenzie's swing. That's something we liked to do, jump and do fancy landings and rate each other on grace and technique like it was some sort of Olympic sport. And somehow, I knew. I knew Dana was hurt."

***

I was definitely not lingering afterward. My body was vibrating like a plucked guitar string, and I was *sweating*, Dana. I could feel the dampness behind my knees leaching through my pants onto my metal folding chair, my fingers sticking to the handouts being passed around—more homework I wouldn't do.

Bodies rose. The murmur of private conversation hummed to life. I pulled myself up and reached for my phone as I walked toward the exit. Staring importantly at my phone was my new go-to avoidance mechanism. *Please don't bother me,* it said. *I'm handling important things.*

"Cady?"

Morgan. She knew my name. We all knew each other's names by then, but still. Morgan knew my name, and that terrified me a little.

She was smiling. "I just wanted to say, good job tonight. I could tell it was hard for you to talk about your sister. You should be proud of yourself."

I was not proud of myself, Dana, not at all.

"And thank you," she said. "For the encouragement. Talking about Christopher . . . it was hard for me tonight, too."

Yes. I knew. I'd seen. *I know you, Morgan, more than you realize. I've been watching you so carefully. I've been waiting for this . . .*

Oh God, of course I didn't say any of that aloud, Dana.

"It feels good to get it out, doesn't it?" I asked.

Morgan nodded—*Yeah, sure.*

She was right. We were lying to ourselves. We'd both held back. I'd seen the way she stopped herself from finishing her story, swallowing down the words.

"Actually, you know what?" I shook my head. "No. It didn't feel good. That really sucked."

Morgan laughed. It was short-lived and quiet, but she laughed. And now she was smiling. At me. Not the fake half smiles we all gave each other in the circle. The real kind.

"Morgan, would you . . ."

She looked up, her eyebrows raised like maybe she was hoping for something. Or hoping *against* something. Second thoughts hit me hard. Were we allowed to talk outside of group? It probably violated some sort of boundary or ground rule or something.

But then again, what the hell.

"Would you like to get some coffee? Sunday?"

She hesitated.

"Or any day," I said. "Doesn't have to be Sunday."

I waited for her to concoct whatever excuse would most easily extricate her from my invitation, but then—

"Yeah," she said, "I'd like that. Sunday is . . . Sunday is great."

24

It wasn't your fault. You were making a left-hand turn, and the light was red, but you had already been in the intersection when it turned yellow. The other driver had the green light, but he failed to yield to you.

I'm sorry, Dana. I just assumed it was your fault. You were a terrible driver. You once rear-ended two cars in the same week.

Sean called a family meeting. As your spouse, he could bring forth a wrongful death suit, but he wanted this to be a family decision. I appreciated that. I didn't appreciate that there was any question as to what our decision would be.

We gathered around Mom and Dad's dining table after dinner. Mom made decaf and served cheesecake—*cheesecake,* Dana. As if this would be fun. As if we were deciding where to vacation or who would host Thanksgiving.

Your husband took charge. He laid out the facts: Your left turn. The yellow light that turned red. The other car—a black Mazda. The other driver—his excessive speed, his distraction. His slightly-more-than-half share of the culpability.

"So he was distracted," I said.

Sean nodded. "According to the DA, yes. He said the guy feels terrible."

"He should feel terrible. My sister is dead because he was changing the song on his playlist? Or unwrapping his cheeseburger? Or what?"

"It was his phone." Sean twisted his wedding ring around his finger. "He got a call or a text or something and looked down."

The little hairs on my arms rose up. It hurt. I could feel every goose pimple. "Well, I hope it was important."

Sean sighed.

"Remind me again why we're debating this?" I asked. "I mean, what is there to discuss?"

"The facts, Cady." Sean's words came out fatigued, as if I'd already asked the question a thousand times. "We need to discuss the facts, so we can make a decision."

"We already know the only fact that matters: Dana is dead, and he killed her."

There was a long silence. I could feel their eyes on me. I shifted mine away, to one of Mom's little signs, the one above the sink. THIS IS OUR HAPPY PLACE.

Dad was the first to speak. He wanted to confirm he'd heard Sean right, that there were no drugs or alcohol involved. I wanted to roll my eyes, Dana—what did *that* matter?—but it was Dad, so I didn't.

Sean shook his head. "None. They did a Breathalyzer at the scene and drew blood at the hospital. The guy was clean as a whistle."

I flopped back in my seat. "Oh, then all's forgiven. As long as he didn't kill Dana while he was *high,* we should just let it go."

"That's not what anyone is saying, Cady," Sean said through his teeth. "This isn't so straightforward. Dana had some liability, too. The law—"

"I don't understand you!" I cried. "The facts. The liability. The law. The fifty-one percent responsible bullshit. We're talking about *Dana,* not some case study."

Matt squeezed the top of my leg under the table. I didn't know if it meant *there, there* or *knock it off.*

Sean cleared his throat and moved on to his next fact, the 911 call. Several witnesses had called in, but the other driver, William—his name's William, Dana—was the first. He was already talking to the operator by the time he got to your side. He stayed with you until the EMTs arrived.

Mom tore at a crumpled tissue in her hands. "That means a lot to me," she said, "that he stayed with her. That he held her while she . . . I'm just thankful Dana wasn't alone."

Right. You were in the arms of your killer, Dana. I bet that was very nice for you.

"It makes me sick."

All four of their merciful, rational heads swiveled my way.

"I hate that she died in his arms," I said. "It's wrong. She didn't know him. I'd rather Dana died alone than . . . than like that."

I thought of Ramona Crawford, insisting that if she couldn't have double orchids, she wanted no orchids at all. But this was different, so different.

"Can we please not discount the fact that Dana wouldn't have died in *anyone's* arms if it weren't for this guy? Shouldn't he have to pay for that? I can't believe you're considering letting him wash his hands of this."

Dad shook his head. "No one's absolving him of anything, Cady. We just—"

"Absolution is exactly what we're talking about! Not doing anything *is* absolving."

"There are a lot of factors to consider," Sean said quietly. "Yes, this guy—William—was at fault. Do I want to show up on his doorstep and take justice into my own hands some days? Yes. But there's more to this than that. And look, we're not talking about some asshole who fled the scene or sat shaking in his car or shirked his accountability. The guy did everything he could to save her. And shit, another day, another time, that guy could have been any one of us."

"But it wasn't."

Someone sighed.

"The question I keep coming back to," Mom said, her eyes watering, forcing me to look away so I wouldn't catch her tears, "is what good does it do us—or Dana, or the baby—to punish this man anymore? The district attorney is bringing criminal charges, and it sounds like this man is very sorry. I'm sure his own guilt is already the worst sentence imaginable. What good will a civil suit do? Will it heal us? Will it bring Dana and the baby back?"

Sean shook his head. "That's where I'm at too, Lisa. It won't bring them back or give us peace." His eyes shot to mine. "Not me, anyway."

God, your husband could be insufferable, Dana. I bet he'd been that kid who pointed out his good behavior to the adults when the other kids misbehaved—I'm *being good, right, Mom?*

"And honestly," he said, "I don't think Dana would have wanted us to avenge her."

Oh, here we went with that again. Trying to guess what you would have wanted. You would have wanted to not be dead, to have your baby safe and alive in your belly, that's what *you* would have wanted.

"Not to mention the toll of a trial on all of you," Matt added.

I gave him A Look.

Sean gave him a *Good point* nod.

"I guess I'm outvoted." I snatched my hand off the table before Matt's could reach it.

We all looked to Mom for the last word. Everything on her—her down-turned mouth and limp hair, her sagging shoulders and droopy clothes—looked like it was being pulled down by a heavy, invisible weight.

"I'd hoped we'd all be on the same page with this," she said.

So that was that, apparently. Majority ruled.

"There's one more thing," Sean said. "He, er, William . . . he wants to meet with us, if we want to."

"Meet with us? For what?"

"To apologize, I'm assuming. I don't know, Cady."

I leaned back in my chair. "I'm interested to see what you all have to say about this one."

"Personally," Sean said, "I don't think I'm ready for that." He grimaced when he said it, like it pained him to be so ungenerous to the person who'd taken you and the baby from him. "But if you and Lisa are open to it," he said, looking to Dad, "I can help arrange it. You too, Cady."

I snorted.

Dad looked at Mom. "I don't know . . . it might be good, to get some closure."

"Dad. Come on. *Closure?* For who? You, or him?" I tried to say it gently, to get him to see reason.

"I don't know, Cady." He sighed. "I don't know."

As the air left him, everything on his face seemed to fall another quarter inch. Despite his efforts to put up a good front, he always looked tired now. Mom too. If you'd miraculously come back to life and walked into the kitchen right then, you'd have taken one look at them and figured you must've slept through a whole decade.

"Mom?"

Mom pushed her cheesecake crumbs into a little pile on her plate. "I don't know. I worry it'll be difficult, or that it's somehow . . ."

Disrespectful to Dana? I didn't say it, though.

"I suppose I'd go," Mom said, "if your dad goes."

Well then.

Sean started wrapping up the meeting, talking about *next steps*. I went to the living room, knowing full well I would become the new topic of conversation, and sat on the couch while they talked in hushed voices in the kitchen.

After a while, Dad joined me. He didn't say anything; he just squeezed my shoulder on the way to his La-Z-Boy and turned on the Blackhawks game. I don't think I've ever appreciated the quietness, the unobtrusiveness of his affection more than I did in that moment.

We watched the game together in silence, Dad actually watching, me just looking in that general direction. After some time, Sean came in and shook Dad's hand and hugged me goodbye.

"Take care, Cady," he said.

I tried not to, but I couldn't help picking up on something in the tone of your husband's words. *Take care, Cady,* as in, *Get it together, Cady.* I could feel his disapproval as plainly as I'd felt his hot breath on my face.

Sean was always disapproving of me, wasn't he, Dana? Like when I'd confronted him, that first year you were married, about your holiday plans. He'd made you spend Christmas with his side of the family, even though he *knew* you and I had never spent the holiday apart. When I hadn't cried in that awful stuffy waiting room, the day you died, or two weeks earlier, when you'd told him about our little tiff in my kitchen— and that's all that was, right? A tiff? If you'd lived a day or two longer, we'd have resolved it, and it would have become a nonissue, something we'd have to pause to remember if anyone ever brought it up again down the road.

If you'd been there in the living room that night, Dana, you'd have rolled your eyes and said I was being paranoid, that Sean doesn't have a passive-aggressive bone in his body. I would have smiled and kept my mouth shut—or tried to, anyway.

But you weren't.

I followed your husband to the front door. If he heard or sensed me on his tail, he didn't show it.

"Are you really okay with all this, Sean?"

He stopped but didn't flinch. He'd known I was there all along.

"With all this," he repeated, turning around. "Are you asking about the decision we just made or about"—he gestured around the foyer as if to indicate the whole world—"all this?"

"Not pressing charges," I said impatiently. "That's really what you want?"

Sean grabbed his forehead. "Want? I don't want any of this, Cady. What I want is to have Dana and our child back." He glanced down the hallway and lowered his voice. "This isn't as simple as you make it seem."

"Maybe it's not as complicated as *you* make it seem."

"Look," he said softly, dropping his hands down at his sides like they'd grown too heavy to hold up. "I get where you're coming from, okay? But this isn't a decision for *us*. This is what Dana would want."

"Yeah, well, Dana didn't always know what was best for her."

Oh God, Dana. Sean's face . . . I regretted the words as soon as they left me.

Sean wouldn't have been my pick for you, you know that. He knew that. He was too staid and pliable; you'd have been at your max with someone who challenged and pushed you the way I always had. I'm sorry, but it's true.

I'd known it from our first meeting, when Matt and I invited you both to dinner at our little apartment in Logan Square. Your big brown eyes never left Sean's small, rather close-together gray ones as you told the story of your school's career day—how you'd volunteered to help organize it and ended up falling for the guest speaker. You beamed at Sean, like you were introducing me to a pediatric heart surgeon or a Pulitzer nominee, not the assistant regional manager of a midsized chain of self-storage facilities. Not the guy with a fresh Supercuts crew cut who'd primly asked if he should take his shoes off before bothering with a *Nice to meet you* or *Thanks for having me* or even a simple *Hello*. The guy who would eventually make comments about how often and at what time of day I texted, whose jaw would twitch if I showed up unannounced to suggest brunch or shopping or a walk through the arboretum. The boy-friend who would turn into the husband who would tell me to *Take care* in a way that suggested that maybe I fucking couldn't.

Still, I shouldn't have said it. I was about to tell him that; I was opening my mouth to apologize, but he beat me to the draw.

"Dana was perfectly capable of making her own decisions, Cady. But you couldn't let that happen, could you?" Sean's eyes flashed with a fury I'd never seen him wear before. He was always so in control. The most I'd ever managed to do was make him sigh or shake his head.

I'd finally gotten a rise out of your husband, Dana, and I hadn't even meant to.

". . . didn't like who she married," he was saying, "and you didn't like when she wouldn't come work at Eventually with you . . ."

That again? Did he still think I'd tried to *force* you to come work with me? Is that what you told him?

No. You wouldn't have. He'd misunderstood, like always.

I'd just wanted you to want more out of life, Dana. Something bigger and more exciting than settling for whatever crossed your path. Your first job offer out of college. The self-storage manager from career day. I wanted you to feel what it was like to burn for something. The thrill of not knowing if you'd get it.

In the end, it didn't matter. I'd seen right away that you wouldn't be swayed. "I'm happy doing what I do, Cady," you'd said. Then you'd smiled. Sweetly. A little sadly. Like maybe *you* felt bad for *me.*

". . . and Christ, Cady"—Sean was still at it—"you even tried to control when we started our family!"

I shook my head. "I did not."

But Sean wasn't listening. Years of pent-up complaints and swallowed accusations were bubbling up like lava. "But you know what?" he hissed. *Hissed,* Dana. Your husband. "Dana was finally starting to see it."

I blinked. "See what?"

"You, Cady. *You.*" He pointed—stabbed—his finger at me. "Dana finally saw you for what you are. And she'd had enough. She was starting to stand up to you. She was escaping you. And then . . ."

Escaping me? *Escaping* me, Dana?

Oh God, he didn't get it. He really didn't get it, did he? Us.

I shook my head. "You don't have a clue, Sean. No one does. No one gets what being a twin is—"

"Stop, Cady. Just stop, okay? Stop using the twin thing as an excuse."

"An excuse for what? No, never mind," I said, waving off his attempt to respond. "It's not your fault you don't understand, Sean, but Dana and I . . . our relationship was special."

Sean's eyes narrowed. "It wasn't special, Cady. It was unhealthy. Toxic."

I shook my head, tears falling down my cheeks now. How dare he say that. How dare he use those words to describe us. "No. I loved Dana."

"You suffocated Dana."

I gasped. It was a disgusting choice of words, considering. It almost felt like an accusation, like I was somehow—

"This is stupid." Sean rubbed his temples. "I don't want to fight. The past doesn't matter anymore."

Then he was gone, the door closing quietly behind him.

I didn't know what time it was, but it felt late. I walked past Dad in the living room to collect Matt from the kitchen. As I got close, I heard two voices mingling, Mom's and Matt's, like a familiar song. They weren't exactly whispering, but they were quiet. I let my footsteps fall more lightly.

". . . how she can get," Matt's voice was saying.

Mom sighed. "I do. Cady was always my . . . intense one."

"Intense. Yes, that's a good way of putting it, Lisa."

"Sometimes it's her superpower, you know?"

Matt made a sound of agreement. "It's the thing that drew me to her, the thing that I sometimes love most about her. Other times . . ."

There was a pretty big pause here.

"A blessing and a curse." I could hear the sad smile in Mom's voice. "Well," she said, "keep me posted, will you?"

"You know I will, Lisa."

I cleared my throat and moved into the doorway. We all smiled stupidly at each other and pretended no one had been talking about me. I told Matt we should be getting home.

Dad joined us at the front door, where we took turns hugging goodbye, Matt and I promising to drive safe and text when we got home. As I pulled away from Dad's hug, I caught the brief clasp of Mom's hand over Matt's—a reassuring, good luck squeeze.

Because we all knew *how I could get.*

25

In the car on the way home, Matt was quiet. I pressed my nose against the cold window and looked out at the stars and let my mind go, the way I used to when we'd drive home late from Grandma and Grandpa's on Christmas Eve or after losing a volleyball tournament.

The intense one.

That was me.

Apparently.

You . . . you were the careful one. The good one. Have you ever thought about that, Dana? How we came to be that way? I think about it a lot.

We were alike in so many ways. Of course we were—sameness is what you get with twins. But people have an inherent problem with sameness. With twinness. They don't get it. They're raised to believe they are utterly unique; they can't fathom existing any other way.

So they look for something, some way to tell us apart. A scar, or a higher math grade, or a louder laugh, whatever. That's how a twin gets branded the smart one or the quiet one or the funny one or the wild one. That's my theory, anyway—that maybe you weren't really the good one and I wasn't really the intense one, but maybe someone saw or imagined something in one of us at a young age and labeled it and fed it, allowing it to take root and grow.

Or who knows, maybe we really were programmed that way. I just don't know.

I said earlier—didn't I?—that we shared 100 percent of our DNA. Every last nucleotide, remember?

That's not exactly true. I read somewhere that identical twins are born with *nearly* 100 percent identical DNA. It's like 99.9999999 percent similar or something. Close enough for me. But over time, this article said, external factors—our environment—come into play, tweaking our DNA.

Slowly, over years and years, the little differences proliferate, and we become more and more different, further and further away from being a 99.9999999 percent match.

For so long, there'd been so little to separate us, Dana. Everything you did, I did. Everywhere you went, there I was. If you liked something, I liked it, too. We finished each other's sentences with disturbing frequency. We shared a bedroom until we were fourteen. We did the whole matching outfit thing for far too long.

And then there were our pacts, Dana. Oh my God, our pacts. We promised, pinkies hooked, that neither of us would play varsity volleyball unless both of us made the team. We swore that no matter who we went to prom with, we'd ride there together, and we'd go to the same college and join the same sorority, though ultimately we agreed neither of us would go Greek at all.

And we were going to marry twins. Twins, or at least best friends. I know you remember that one because you pulled it out, like a gun, that day you told me about the baby. The day you broke our other pact, that we'd have all our children at the same time (because that's something you can just, you know, plan for and make happen).

The one thing we never promised each other—because it didn't seem like something that needed to be said—was that no one and nothing would ever come between us.

Do you remember when Matt asked me to be his girlfriend? At our front door, a couple weeks after we'd met at that powder-puff game? I suppose that doesn't really matter for the point I'm trying to make, since my relationship with Matt didn't truly alter our bond until another six years, two proms, one breakup, and one makeup later, when he proposed in the backyard at our college graduation party.

I said yes, and with that, my promise to you was broken.

As Mom and Dad passed out plastic flutes of Moët to our guests, I remembered our pact and the champagne soured in my stomach. You laughed when I pulled you aside and apologized. It took me a long time to figure out why I didn't laugh along with you that night, what it was about breaking that stupid, childish pact that scared me so much.

But now I know, Dana. Somehow, I sensed that I'd unwittingly pulled the first thread from the bond that was holding us together, that it would fray and unwind from there, until whatever magic had sent your broken leg's pain shooting down my own would become so faded that when you died, I wouldn't feel so much as a tingle.

26

Mid-April, a little over two months without you. It was the Sunday after I'd asked Morgan to coffee. I was waiting for her to arrive at the café she'd suggested. Cuppa's. Awful lighting, surprisingly decent coffee.

I'd gotten there early and scored the best table—a cozy booth near a window, away from the door. By around two minutes before our appointed meeting time, I'd convinced myself she wouldn't show. I let my doubts unfurl like the ivy climbing Grandma Ruby's front porch, imagining how awkward group would be next Wednesday, how maybe Morgan would make it worse and apologize—or worse yet, maybe she'd be so embarrassed she'd stop coming to group altogether. Maybe I should stop going so Morgan wouldn't have to—she'd been there first, after all.

All the hypotheticals were for naught. Morgan ended up walking into the café about ten seconds after the clock on my phone ticked from 9:59 to 10:00. I had the strangest sensation when I saw her, Dana, like I was back in elementary school running into one of our teachers at the grocery store, finding out she was a real person and not just some avatar that waited in the classroom for us to return every morning.

Of course, I'd seen Morgan plenty of times outside of group, but never like this. All those other times—her shadow passing by the window, the rare sighting in her driveway—were like watching a movie. This was real.

"You made it," I said.

"I made it." Morgan glanced at her watch. "I'm sorry, am I late? It's totally possible this thing is off."

"Not at all. I got here a little early—I had an errand to run nearby."

Morgan settled into the booth across from me, keeping her big Aldo tote close by like a chaperone. She tucked a lock of that stick-straight hair behind her ear and curled her fingers around the sides of a small white box she'd placed on the table between us.

I pointed to it. "What's in there?"

Morgan looked down at the box and sucked in her breath. "Cupcakes."

"Oh." I wasn't sure why—

"Today is Christopher's birthday."

My breath caught in the back of my throat. "I'm sorry," I said, not sure that was the right thing to say, not sure anything I said would be right. I remembered her hesitation at group, when I'd suggested this day for our coffee date. "Do you want to talk about it?"

Morgan shook her head, but then our server came by to get our coffee orders, and when he left, she proceeded to do just that.

"I thought," she said, "I was doing pretty good, you know? I was back at work, and I was going to group every week and sharing my pain and saying *dead* and *death* and doing everything I was supposed to do. I mean, I'm still alive, right?"

She paused, like she was actually asking me, like she needed me to confirm it.

I nodded.

"I'm still kicking—and I feel bad about that, Cady. Sick. Like, what kind of mother am I? I always thought I would die if anything ever happened to Christopher—you know?"

"Yes." Kind of. Yes, I did know.

"Before Christopher died," Morgan said, "I would imagine—I would fear what it *would* be like. Every parent does. When you see a school shooting or a pool drowning or some other tragedy on the news, or hear about the friend of a friend whose kid got hit crossing the street on the way home from school . . ." Her voice broke on that last word.

"I used to plug my ears," she said, closing her eyes, "like *Nah-nah-nah, not thinking about that*. But every once in a while—" She opened her eyes back up, the pupils huge and black for an instant before they retracted. "Every once in a while, the horrible possibility of Christopher's death would sneak its way into my consciousness, and I'd let myself look at it, like a bad wreck on the highway, and I'd panic. Like I'd somehow jinxed my kid by allowing the thought in, like it was a premonition or something. But I always knew one thing for sure—that if Christopher died,

I would die. Hands down." Morgan swallowed thickly. "But here I am. Still kicking. Sometimes just barely, but . . ."

She looked up at me, then back down at the box. Two glassy tears skimmed her cheeks. "Today is Christopher's thirteenth birthday. It's . . . hard. Obviously. But not because he's gone, or at least not just because of that . . ." Her tears fell onto the white box; I stared at the spots as they bloomed. "It's the guilt, Cady—not just that I failed to protect Christopher, or that I'm still here and he isn't, but that I haven't done anything to rectify that—that I haven't killed myself yet. I'm sorry, I know that's, like, *wow*." Morgan widened her eyes and made an explosion gesture with her hands.

I wanted so badly to grab her face and say, in that voice Mom used with me when you went to Mackenzie's house, *Don't you fucking dare. Don't do that to me, Morgan. I have plans for you. For us. Don't even* think *like that.*

"No apologies," I said softly instead, "remember?"

Morgan nodded—*Yeah, yeah.* She rubbed her hands over the flat surface of the box, across the gold sticker in the center.

"We went to his grave this morning," she said. "Me and my ex, right before I came here. We brought balloons and Pokémon cards and these graphic novels he liked. And the cupcakes . . ." She shook her head. "I know it sounds stupid, but I just couldn't imagine not getting them today. It's tradition."

"It's not stupid, Morgan. It's . . . I get it."

She half smiled. "You know, no one's called today? Not my parents, or my brother . . . it's like now that Christopher isn't here anymore, he was *never* here. I know it's tricky—delicate—finding the right thing to say on a day like today. But . . . they could have at least sent a text. *Thinking of Christopher today,* or something. Right?"

I nodded.

"Well," Morgan said, pulling the box toward her. "I decided to get the damn cupcakes instead of pretending like this day doesn't mean anything anymore." She pushed the box forward. "Do you want one? I have more than enough."

"I . . ."

Did I want one, Dana? God no, I did not want this dead child's birthday cupcakes. But there was no polite or graceful or sensitive way to decline, so I watched as Morgan slid her nail through the clear tape securing the lid in place, and I accepted the cupcake she handed me, and I held it in my palm and studied it until I couldn't delay any longer. Morgan was already chewing her first bite and watching me, expectantly, with a peculiar lightness in her eyes.

I took a bite, my teeth severing the buttery yellow cake in two. The cream cheese frosting smudged the top of my lip, then my nose. I covered my face as I chewed, in part to hide the frosting, in part to hide my horror.

Morgan was completely oblivious to the absurdity of this. Completely unaware of the wrongness. She was smiling, Dana. A real smile that went all the way to her eyes, and I realized that this was making her happy, or something like it, and I found it spreading from her to me, that joy.

It was the oddest thing. I was suddenly the happiest I'd been since you'd died. It wasn't a pure happiness—it was tinged with something dirty, like the snow that's left at the end of winter—but it was better than nothing.

I swallowed my last bite and smiled back. "So, do we talk about death now? Or do we pretend we have other things on our minds?"

"I think we pretend," Morgan said matter-of-factly. She'd finished her cupcake, too, and was wiping the frosting off her fingers with a napkin. "I mean, we've beaten a dead horse with all the dead and death business on Wednesdays, haven't we?"

"The horse is long dead," I agreed.

"Okay, so tell me about the other stuff. Do you work? What do you do for fun, or what did you used to do for fun? Favorite color?"

I blinked. "I do work." I was surprised Morgan didn't know this about me, that I hadn't mentioned it when we'd gone around introducing ourselves at group. Rewind the tape a couple months, and you couldn't get me to shut up about Eventually. "I have a party planning business, but—"

"Party planning?" Morgan asked, frowning.

"Yes, well, event planning, but I primarily do parties. Pretty big ones, actually."

"Huh," Morgan said. She still had that frown.

"What?" I asked, laughing. "Don't you like parties?"

Morgan gave her head a little shake and the frown disappeared. "Sorry, I just . . . never mind. It sounds like a really fun job."

"It is. But, to be honest, I've been pretty hands-off lately, letting my staff run things until I feel up to the task again, you know?"

Morgan nodded. "It's hard. At least you have a cool job. Try toiling over spreadsheets and answering emails that should be meetings and sitting in meetings that should be emails. Planning parties has to be better than that."

"Yeah, except I haven't exactly felt . . . festive lately."

Morgan smiled. "Fair."

"Let's see. What else did you ask me about?"

"Fun."

"Oh, right," I said. "Fun. Well, I used to go to parties, in addition to planning them. My husband Matt and I always had something going on—parties, dinners, trips. I had friends back then, kind of." I shrugged. "Anyway: I used to be an event planner, I used to be fun, and my favorite color is green. At least, it used to be. I'm not sure I have one anymore."

Weird but true, Dana. I'd had to reach way back in time to recall my favorite color.

The server came back with our coffees, and I burned my tongue on the first sip.

"What about you?" I asked. "You do spreadsheets, you said."

Morgan nodded. "Yep. I do numbers stuff in a beige, windowless office." She squinted like she was thinking hard. "I don't remember what I used to do for fun. Play with Christopher, I guess, when he was younger and time allowed. Honestly, it's been so long since I've had time to do anything. I used to be so resentful of that—isn't that horrible? I mean, I loved Christopher, but I'd get so frustrated, because I barely had time to be his mother, forget about being a woman." She laughed bitterly. "Now I could give a shit about being a woman. I just want to be his mother again."

"You are."

"Yes," she said, "I am. And I'd give anything to have my biggest problem be not having time to do anything for myself because I'm too busy driving Christopher to baseball practice and helping him with his home-work and keeping up with dentist appointments and sports physicals and school emails. You know?"

I did. And I didn't.

"Oh, and my favorite color is orange."

"Orange," I said. "Interesting."

Morgan smiled. "It used to be blue, but Christopher's favorite color was orange, so now it's mine, too. I look for it everywhere I go. It's fun—there's more orange out there than you think, if you pay attention. Like how you don't realize how many pregnant women are out there until *you're* pregnant, you know?"

I must have flinched because Morgan gasped and reached for my hand. "I'm so sorry. I wasn't thinking. Your baby . . . and, oh God"—her eyes widened—"your sister, too. I'm such a jerk."

"No . . ." I shook my head. "It's not that."

"Oh?" Morgan's hand tightened over mine, and something made me tell her, Dana. I never even told you. I know, I know—impossible. We told each other everything—*everything*—even after we had Matt and Sean to confide in.

But this . . . this I never told you.

27

Two years earlier. You and Sean were engaged, counting down the days to your wedding. Matt and I had just bought the house. Eventually was doing well—really well. Well enough that I'd started to feel comfortable, and I didn't like being comfortable. It made me restless. Itchy. I wanted the next thing—the next goal, the next accomplishment, the next adventure. I decided it would be kids. A family, with Matt.

But it wasn't as simple as that.

It started with the new house. It felt so empty. Of course it did. We were coming from a little apartment in the city to a stately five-bedroom in the burbs. I threw up curtains and laid down rugs, ordered bigger couches, stocked shelves with picture frames and books and travel souvenirs.

It still felt empty, though, so Matt and I spent our weekends scouring art galleries and estate sales until the walls were filled with color and character. I hit up HomeGoods, loading up a cart with marble bookends, embroidered pillows, decorative towels and soy candles, little sandstone Buddhas and tiny marble busts, sure each new tchotchke would be *the* thing that finally made our place feel like home.

And still something about the space rang hollow. I started to think maybe it wasn't the house that was empty, but that all the things I'd put in it—the candles we never lit and the coffee-table books we never looked at—were as empty and unsatisfying as the calories in a doughnut.

Then, at our housewarming party, Matt's mom looked around with approval, clasped her hands to her chest, and said, "It just needs the pitter-patter of little feet, and it'll be a home."

As much as I wanted to object, to say that our house *was* a home and that Matt and I *were* a family, she was right.

I always knew we'd have children. Matt and I were on the same page about that. We wanted at least three, maybe four. Enough of us gathered around the dinner table each night to make it feel like a party, that was our thinking.

So it wasn't that I hadn't thought about children. I'd just been too busy to stop and *really* consider it. Matt and I had businesses to run, a full calendar to juggle, a new house to make ours . . . it hadn't occurred to me to add something else to the mix.

Once it did, though, I was all in.

I brought it up to Matt one night in an Uber coming home from the Ballengers' annual white party. We were both a little tipsy—okay, Dana, we were plastered—and I went for it: "When should we have kids?"

"Immediately," Matt said, "let's start trying tonight." He lunged clumsily for my neck with his lips—that poor Uber driver—and when we got home, despite the five whiskey sours Matt had gulleted at the party, we had sex. It was the first night I didn't take my birth control since going on it more than a decade earlier.

It was absurd, Dana, but when I got my period a few weeks later, I was stunned. What had happened? What went wrong?

No matter. I responded in classic Cady fashion: I swallowed the disappointment and doubled down.

Now, I should probably stop here and tell you that Matt and I had talked since the Uber ride and agreed we wouldn't force anything. We would stop *preventing* a pregnancy and let whatever happened, happen. It would be fun and exciting, we agreed, to be caught off guard a month or two down the road, like buying a lottery ticket and being shocked when your numbers were actually called. That would be us. That would be the enchanting story of how we started our family.

But you know better, Dana. *You knew me.* I wasn't a sit-back-and-see-what-happens kind of girl. Each month that passed without two pink lines appearing on those at-home tests, I became increasingly anxious—and strategic.

I started tracking my cycle and initiating sex with Matt on my fertile days. My old lists—*Renovation Ideas, New Restaurants to Try*—gave way to new ones: *How to Get Pregnant, Natural Fertility Boosters.*

When I still kept getting periods, I bought an ovulation kit.

When more months passed without a positive result, I added temperature charting.

Then I started assessing my cervical mucus. I steered Matt clear of hot tubs and trashed anything in the house with fragrances or artificial sweeteners or BHT or MSG or high fructose corn syrup. I bought organic fruits and vegetables. I tried acupuncture. Meditation. Prayer.

I tried it all, Dana. But I didn't tell Matt. I let him think this was all some cute new health kick. I wanted that beautiful, artless story—and if I couldn't have it, maybe Matt still could. I could fix this. I could do this.

But I couldn't. After about a year, it dawned on Matt that quite some time had passed since we'd made our drunken resolution in the back of that Uber. He casually mentioned, during a movie where the main character finds herself pregnant, "I'm surprised we haven't gotten pregnant yet. You're still off your birth control, right?"

I burst into tears and confessed everything.

The very next day, Matt and I teamed up against Mother Nature and Lady Luck together. *We* would fix this. It wouldn't be the carefree well-would-you-look-at-that! fairy tale we'd envisioned, but we would still have our family.

Enter the vitamins and the new sex positions and the consultation with a fertility specialist. The wasted dollars spent on round after fruitless round of artificial inseminations. The books and massages and online forums. The hormone tests and the genetic tests and the egg counts and the semen analyses.

Still no second pink line.

Frustrated with our lack of results, we switched specialists five months before you died. We were not giving up. We were not quitters, Dana; this is why we were together.

Our new doctor read our history, heard our desperation, and recommended IVF. Whatever it takes, we said. We'd tried everything else.

So I stabbed needles into my belly and ass, stuck hormones up my vagina, slapped patches on my abdomen, swallowed more vitamins, sat for more blood draws, lay down for more ultrasounds.

I was in the clinic three, sometimes four days a week, getting stabbed and probed until finally they said it was time. Time for more shots, new shots, bigger shots, the trigger shot—all for *the shot* of finally, finally having our baby.

The doctor extracted twelve eggs (a full carton!) from my swollen uterus using a catheter and a tiny needle. I watched it happen live on ultrasound—the gentle suctioning of each egg from the follicles that festooned my ovaries like clusters of tiny champagne grapes.

Then it was time for the eggs to be whisked away to a lab, to dance with the sperm Matt had released into a plastic cup.

Over the next several hours, six of Matt's guys found six of my girls, and three days later, five of the embryos were still going strong. On day five, we implanted one of the best—a high-grade 3ab—into my uterus and giggled and hoped and celebrated with takeout and sparkling water.

We passed the time by discussing names and nurseries and whether or not we'd find out the sex. We calculated that the baby would be born sometime in August. August! We would have a son or daughter by fall. We would take family walks around the neighborhood, stopping to pick leaves out of the stroller and fuss over blankets.

Our little one would be here for Halloween—what would we dress him or her up as? They would be just months old, of course, but this was *our* child, and *our* child would have a costume because *our* child would be fun, like us!

Four weeks later, we got the call. I put it on speaker, so Matt could find out with me: *You're pregnant.*

Pregnant! We'd done it. It hadn't been easy, but like Matt and I always said, there's nothing you can't have if you're willing to do anything to get it. The proof was there, in us and Eventually and McKenna Land Group, and now, our little 3ab.

It was hard to keep it to ourselves, but we'd waited years to get to this point, so we could wait a couple more months, until the second trimester, when it was safe to tell you and Mom and Dad and the world. Sometimes, when Matt and I were placing bets on whose side of the family the baby would most resemble, or when I fantasized about the moment we'd tell you and Mom and Dad the big news, I'd remember our old promise, Dana, how you and I were supposed to have our babies at the same time. But then I'd remember that you'd laughed when I'd brought up our pacts at our graduation-turned-my-engagement party, and I would feel better about the secret growing inside me.

I turned down alcohol and salmon crostini at parties, secretly hoping someone would guess why, and I'd have to confess or smile slyly and change the subject.

I bought maternity clothes even though I'd only gained two pounds.

I kept a *Nursery Inspiration* Pinterest board that grew longer each day.

I started jotting down first birthday party themes—I couldn't help it, Dana, and besides, it was never too early to start planning a party.

Two weeks away from my second trimester, when our little miracle was ten weeks old, I felt a pinch deep in my pelvis. It was electric, like lightning.

I googled the possibilities: *round ligament pain, non-pregnancy-related cramps, bladder infection*. I reassured myself it was the round ligament pain, though I was still a couple weeks away from my second trimester, when that symptom was more common.

The pain grew steadily worse. By the time Matt came home from work, it was unbearable. We called the clinic, who paged the doctor, who sent us to the ER, where it was confirmed: a miscarriage.

The next morning, I began to bleed, just a spot at first, then much more. For such a tiny little thing, our 3ab made quite a mess as it left my body.

Matt held me as we lay on the couch and pretended to watch movies. He didn't leave my side until the worst of the cramping had passed. When it finally relented, I wanted it back, to numb the new pain that was harder to bear.

What had gone wrong? I must have done something wrong, Dana. Our embryo had been healthy, strong, a 3ab, such a good grade, a 50 percent chance of resulting in a live birth—odds that grew steadily each week of my pregnancy. By the tenth week, when I miscarried, the stats were on our side. Less than a 10 percent chance of something going wrong. Something must have happened. *I* must have done something. Life doesn't just stop for no good reason.

I pulled myself off that couch somehow. Valentine's Day was coming up. I had parties to plan. I had to think of a gift for Matt. I had to stay busy. If I stayed busy, I would be okay. Thank God I hadn't told Mom and Dad and you—I could spare all of you this.

But, of course, I couldn't spare you, could I? I would *have to* tell you, Dana. I had to warn you. I had to advise you to start trying now, *right now*—either that or freeze your eggs. We were identical twins. Ninety-nine-point-nine-nine-nine-nine-nine percent the same. Same eyes and mouth and hair and dimples—that was us. If I did volleyball, you did volleyball. If you took piano lessons, I took piano lessons.

If I couldn't have a baby, *you* couldn't have a baby.

28

Morgan and I left that first coffee date agreeing it would have to become a standing thing, and soon we were jumping into our new friendship with the shameless urgency of a pair of schoolgirls.

Every Sunday morning, we met at Cuppa's and made a point of talking about you and baby Dana and Morgan's son without talking about your deaths. Death was for Wednesdays.

Instead, we talked about what her son was going to be when he grew up. What you were like *before* you grew up. She told me about Friday movie nights with her son, how they took turns picking what to watch, how they themed their snacks to the film. I told her about our first-Sunday-of-the-month brunch ritual, how I always picked the restaurant because you could never decide, how we'd been on a forty-six-month streak up until February.

I tried to discuss baby Dana as little as possible, fearful of being buried under the weight of my lies, terrified that the next one would be *the one* that collapsed the whole stack.

We talked marriage. Divorce. Pregnancy. Miscarriage. Sometimes we talked through our tears. Sometimes we laughed so hard we contracted hiccups.

There was never enough time to fit it all in, so we'd pick up our parting thoughts in text conversations that would run all day long and into the next.

At some point, Morgan accepted my friend requests on social media, though neither of us ever posted anything.

We became a recognized entity at group. Everyone knew that the empty seat next to hers was mine.

My world became more orange. I started noticing the color everywhere.

A basketball lying forgotten in a neighbor's yard. The reduced-price stickers on the dented cans at the grocery store. A small school of Goldfish crackers, clutched in a tiny fist. When I spotted an especially good one—a Garfield sticker on an orange VW Bug or a man in a tangerine top hat and matching three-piece suit—I'd send a photo to Morgan.

You're smiling, aren't you, Dana? You're happy for me. It sounds like things were looking up. I had a friend, and we had a connection that wasn't based on proximity or a shared hobby or a Netflix series. And because of this, the standard rules of friendship did not apply. We did not worry about propriety or appearances. We did not have to smile and be happy. We did not have to impress each other; we did not *want* to impress each other. We did not hold back. I could text her thirty or even one hundred times in a single day if I wanted to.

I wanted to.

Morgan quickly became the closest thing to you I'd ever had, besides Matt. We had our texts and our Sunday mornings. And group.

But every time I sat in my empty car after a Wednesday night session, or waved goodbye to Morgan outside the coffee shop, or sat waiting—sometimes hours—for her to respond to my latest text, I felt as though a warm blanket had been snatched from my lap.

29

Come the end of April, Matt was working longer and longer hours, converting his frustrations with me into new condominiums and strip malls.

Supposedly. An awful lot of closed doors and hushed, heated conversations for the world of commercial real estate, if you asked me.

I spent those hours getting closer to Morgan, unearthing the steady rhythms of her days. Learning where she got her groceries and filled up on gas. What day her trash was collected, what time her mail carrier came, how often an Amazon package arrived. What face she made when she dropped her keys or forgot something in the car. Discovering what the grass in her yard and that magnet on the back of her Honda felt like under my fingertips. Living for Wednesday nights in that little classroom, where we wouldn't be separated by the brick walls of her house and the steel frame of my car. Where Morgan tilted and nodded her head as I talked about you and your baby and my supposed baby and faced your deaths and said *death* and listened to everyone else talk about *death death death*.

Then I would come home to Matt—or to our empty house, since he was so often late now. I was always relieved when he walked in the door, but it was not like before. It was no longer the best part of my day. We'd begun to feel like roommates, Dana. Worse, like roommates who'd found each other on Craigslist. The silence in the car ride home from Mom and Dad's weeks earlier had followed us into the house that night and hung on for dear life.

On the weekends, we made unspoken compromises—silent, respectful stakeouts of our territory. If I was watching *Love Island* in the living room, he'd open *The Wall Street Journal* in the den. If he was watching *Yellowstone*, I'd open the Celeste Ng novel I'd been pretending to read for the last five months. It was ridiculous, Dana. It was absurd to dance around each other like that. Matt was my husband. It shouldn't be so hard to simply *be*.

But *easy* is the luxury of a healthy relationship, and ours seemed to be dying of a mysterious illness.

Matt finally pointed it out one night, on one of the rare occasions we found ourselves in front of the same TV. He told me I seemed distant.

Distant. I let the word wedge itself between us on the couch. Matt stopped flipping through the latest Hulu releases. "I'm right here," I said. Literally sitting on the same piece of furniture, maybe three feet separating us.

Matt's eyebrows twitched. "That's not what I meant, and you know it."

I did know it, Dana. But I didn't appreciate the tone.

"If you're mad or something, just tell me, Matt. Don't give me this oblique shit about distance."

"I'm not *mad*." He tossed the remote on the coffee table and turned to face me. "I'm worried. If anything, I'd say you're the one who's angry."

"I'm not angry."

He crossed his arms. "Then what's with the silent treatment?"

"What silent treatment? We're talking."

"We're fighting. Whenever I try to talk, you shut me down. Especially if I bring up Dana."

"Well, you have to admit, Matt, that's a little confusing."

Matt's eyebrows did that thing again.

"You never used to want to talk about Dana before," I said. "Why do we have to talk about her now that she's gone?"

Dead, Moira's voice whispered in my ear. *Now that she's* dead, *Cady.*

"I never used to . . . what are you talking about?"

"You were jealous of her, Matt."

He looked at me in disbelief. Maybe he'd truly never been aware of his resentment. "I was never jealous of Dana."

"You didn't like when I talked about her."

"Sometimes I didn't like how *much* you talked about her," he said. "It was . . . your relationship with Dana was . . ."

"Was what?" If he used any of the words Sean had used—unhealthy, toxic, suffocating—I was going to . . . well, I don't know what I would have done, Dana.

Matt shook his head. "I don't want to talk about this. It feels wrong, now that . . ."

Dead. Dead dead dead. Say it, Matt. Say it.

"I thought Dana was exactly what you wanted to talk about." I made a little smirky face, to match my tone.

"I want you to talk about *what happened*," he corrected me. "I want you to tell me what's going on inside there." He nodded at my head, like it was a bad place we shouldn't name out loud.

The screen saver came on the TV. *Samsung* floated around, changing colors as it hit the edges of the screen.

Matt sighed. "You blame me, don't you? For your family's decision not to sue that . . . the guy who . . ."

I narrowed my eyes. "The guy who killed Dana?"

"Well, is it? Do you blame me for that, for not taking your side that day? Is that why you won't—"

"That's not it."

"Then what is it?"

"*I don't know.* But it's got nothing to do with you, okay?" I sighed and fell back against the couch. "It's me."

Matt shook his head. "No. This isn't you, Cady. You don't wallow. Ever. You act, you do. You have a plan; you always have a plan. But not anymore. Now you've given up or something, I don't know, but if you never face that day, you—"

"Never face that day, Matt? *Never face that day?*" I sat up, ramrod straight. "I face that day every Wednesday night. I go to group, and I open up and I share and I hurt and I let it all out. Okay? Every fucking Wednesday. And I'm doing *great* there. I even made a friend."

And the plan I always have, *but not anymore,* according to Matt? Well, I did have one, Dana. But I sure as hell wasn't letting Matt in on it.

He looked skeptical, but he gave a conceding sort of sigh. "I'm glad you found a friend, Cady. Really, I am. I just . . . I've never felt so far away from you, not even—"

"Oh my God, this again? You want to talk about *distance,* Matt? About not being there? Then let's talk about why you couldn't pick up your god-damn phone on the worst fucking day of my life."

That knocked the wind out of him. When he finally recovered, he almost laughed. "Is *that* what this is about?"

Oh, I nearly told him right then, Dana. I wanted so badly to wipe that look off his face. He looked *relieved*—what a relief for him, to discover that this whole time, *this* was what I'd been so pissed about. A couple missed phone calls.

I left, Matt's words chasing behind me as I climbed the stairs.

"I told you."

"I was in a meeting."

"My phone was on silent."

"I called you back."

"You didn't answer . . ."

"What more could I have done?"

"What could I have done differently?"

"What could I have done differently, Cady?"

30

With Morgan safely tucked into my little world, I felt some of my old motivation flickering back to life. I even started spending time at the office. For real now. Just a day or two, here and there, but at least Jamie and I were having regular touchpoints again. She always came armed with lists of concerns. Each week, her bullet points grew increasingly bleak.

May 7's *List of Bad Things to Tell Cady*, in the order they were presented to me:

1. People were quitting, and nothing could convince them to stay.
2. They could not be replaced. No one wanted to come work for Eventually. Word had spread that we were going down the shitter and swirling fast.
3. We hadn't booked a new client, or even a new event, in almost two months.
4. The clients we did have were growing impatient. They'd been sympathetic at first, but their compassion had an expiration date, and it was rapidly approaching.
5. Four more one-star Yelp reviews had been posted since Jamie's last update, and two of them said, *If I could give zero stars, I would.*
6. Jamie appreciated the pay raise I'd offered, but her paychecks still didn't reflect her new duties.
   a. Gabby's either.
   b. Oh, and Pam Fitz (who handled payroll) quit last Friday, so until we replaced her, no one would be getting paid anything. But refer back to item number two for why that wouldn't happen anytime soon.

I laughed. Not in a funny way, but in a losing-it way. Jamie looked alarmed. And mystified.

"It's hilarious," I told her. "Everything is deteriorating or declining or disappearing. More *D* words to add to my list."

She was thoroughly confused now. "*D* words?"

I didn't answer her.

She chewed the cap of her pen, an anxious tic I'd never noticed before. Jamie was usually so composed and carefree. I wondered if there was a seventh item on the list she hadn't shared. Maybe Nora Donnelly had pulled her black-and-white ball off our docket. Or maybe Jamie had accepted another job offer—maybe Matt was right; maybe she was drowning. Maybe I'd given her too much responsibility. Become the kind of boss I'd started my own company to avoid.

Or maybe it was just that she was secretly talking to my husband.

Or worse.

"Did I ever tell you Eventually's origin story?" I asked.

Jamie blinked. "No," she said. She uncrossed her legs and closed her notebook.

"Really?" I said. "I never told you how Matt and I built our little empires?"

Jamie shook her head and moved to the edge of her seat. "You've never told me anything about how you got started. I'd love to hear it, though."

"All right." I smiled, making sure to look a little sheepish. "It's actually a pretty romantic story."

I watched her carefully, searching for a flinch or a flush, but she was either too good or too innocent.

"So before I blew up on the luxury event planning scene," I began, "I was a business operations analyst for a wholesale food distributor."

Remember that, Dana? Mom was so impressed, because the title was a mouthful.

"I was so excited when I got the job," I told Jamie. "I mean, I was going to *analyze operations*. I pictured late hours in some posh think tank, coming up with novel solutions to whatever sort of problems a wholesale food distribution company might face. Presenting my findings in a smart blazer and pointy heels."

Jamie smiled.

"In reality," I admitted, "all I did was update Excel spreadsheets, then figure out why the formulas never added up right. But I was good at it, and I worked hard, so I moved up quickly, which made it harder to see how unhappy I was."

A few years earlier, I explained to Jamie, Matt had been in a similar boat. He'd been an analyst, too, at a commercial real estate development firm. McNally Something or Other.

"This company's a joke," he told me one night in our tiny eat-in kitchen. "Zero communication from the top. No organization. The partners contradict each other every time they open their mouths." Heavy sigh. "I'm on a sinking ship, babe."

"So jump ship," I told him.

Matt snorted.

"I hate seeing you unhappy," I said quietly.

"I'm not unhappy, I'm just . . . dissatisfied. And frustrated."

"Sounds unhappy." I twirled my fork, creating a little linguine tornado.

Matt stabbed his noodles.

"Why don't you stay on a little longer, learn the ropes better, then go into business for yourself?"

"I already know the ropes. Enough, anyway."

I raised my eyebrows, challenging him. "Then do it now."

Matt balked. "With what money?"

"Investor money. Isn't that how McNally does it?"

"Yeah, but who's going to hand over that kind of money to a kid fresh off the farm?"

"Smart people who value passion and work ethic and good business sense over the number of bullet points on a résumé." I lifted an eyebrow. "Maybe even some of McNally's current investors."

Matt scoffed. "That's a big maybe."

"Don't make this so difficult."

He laughed. "Sorry if I make launching my own commercial real estate firm from nothing sound difficult."

"You're not starting from zero," I argued. "You said you know the business—well enough, anyway—and you have contacts. It's not illegal to lure investors away. I mean, you didn't sign an NDA or noncompete, did you?"

Matt shook his head.

"There you go," I said. "Recreate McNally, but do it better. Fix all the things that are broken, the things that piss you off and keep you up at night. Those are your competitive differentiators. Use them to woo away some of McNally's investors and snatch up new ones. Then make mistakes, get back up, learn from them, get better. Repeat in perpetuity. Voilà."

I locked eyes with Jamie over my desk, smiling at the memory, at my old naïvety and moxie.

"Matt was profitable within two years," I told her, "and dominating within five."

It was my turn next. We were eating dinner again—lasagna this time—and I was telling Matt all about my latest side project, a farewell party for a friend's mother's uterus. Those were the sort of events I was doing back then, mostly as favors. A friend's wedding. *Her* friend's nonprofit launch. Now another friend wanted to throw her mother's uterus a farewell after the mother had a hysterectomy to beat Stage 3 uterine cancer, and how could I say no to something like that?

"Cady," Matt said. He'd been watching me talk with a kind of wonder. "Do you seriously not realize what's going on here?"

I looked around the kitchen, confused.

"You're so alive right now," he said. "This is your calling—parties, they're your thing. You have to turn this into a real business."

I laughed. "I don't know the first thing about event planning. I'm just winging it, Matt."

He arched one of those dark eyebrows, an impish something flickering in his blue-black eyes. "You know as much about putting on a great party as I did three years ago about commercial real estate."

"And what, throw away a perfectly good career?" I shook my head. "I'm a senior analyst. I could be in management in the next couple years."

"Ooh, management." Matt gave me jazz hands, and I scowled at him. "I'm just saying," he went on, "you don't talk about frozen vegetable inventory the way you talk about these parties."

He wasn't wrong. Right then and there, at that little table in our little kitchen, I began to envision a different future. One where I spent my days creating and executing and making my own decisions. Working with people, not pivot tables. Touring venues and meeting with clients instead of sitting under fluorescent lights within the concrete-colored fabric walls of a cubicle.

I could even feel the liberation of handing in my two weeks' notice to my needed-help-PDFing-a-Word-doc-but-managed-to-find-a-typo-in-every-email boss.

"And, oh God, Jamie," I said, "the ecstasy of knowing I would never again have to chart the five-year outlook on tomato freight costs . . ."

Jamie giggled. "That sounds *horrifying.*"

"It was torture," I agreed. "And Matt was right. I *could* make it work. I could put in the time at night and on weekends, and if it really started taking off, maybe one day I could quit the spreadsheets forever and do parties full-time . . ."

The memory—the excitement, the terror—was so clear, bringing me right back to that kitchen, remembering how Matt . . .

"So you'll do it?" he'd asked.

"Yeah." I nodded, a plan taking shape in my head. "Eventually, yeah. I'll start small—"

"Eventually?" Matt said, frowning. "Fuck eventually. Start next week. Start tomorrow."

"And I did," I told Jamie. "I handed in my resignation the next day."

Jamie's eyes were shining with admiration. "You're so brave," she said.

I shook my head. "I was terrified."

"Yeah, but isn't that what being brave is? Being terrified but doing the thing anyway?" She gasped, and her hand flew to her mouth. "Oh my God, I just realized . . . is that where you got the name? Because you said . . . and Matt said . . ."

I laughed. "Yep."

Jamie's jaw fell like three inches. "*I love that,*" she cried. "That is amazing. Why haven't you told this story before? There's like a million articles about you and the company, and this story is nowhere to be found. We need to change that." She opened her notebook and started scrawling, her chewed-up pen cap dipping and bobbing in frantic little loops. "I've been trying to think of marketing angles to get new clients in the . . . Cady?"

She'd finished scribbling and looked up, stopping when she saw my face. I was lost in my own head, far away.

"Sorry," I said. I smiled apologetically, but not too big, so the tears wouldn't fall. "I was just thinking."

Jamie smiled uncertainly. "About what?"

A traitorous tear slid down my cheek. "How hard it is to single-handedly build something—and how easy it is to single-handedly tear it all down."

"Oh."

"Sorry," I said. "That's not very inspiring." Another tear. "I'm a terrible boss."

"No, you're not."

"I am." I swiped at my wet face. "Don't bother with reassurances. Despite the melodrama, I'm not looking for sympathy."

Jamie reached out an arm anyway, laying it across the desk that separated us. "You lost your sister, Cady. But you're here, you're trying. No one expects more than that."

"Some people do."

"Fuck them."

My eyebrows must have jumped an inch. Despite my earlier tears and self-pity, I burst out laughing. I'd never heard Jamie utter so much as a firm *Dammit,* not even when she'd knocked her elbow into the side of the Singhs' eleven-thousand-dollar wedding cake.

She was laughing now, too. "Sorry," she said, looking a little horrified and very red.

"For what? That's the hardest I've laughed in a long time."

Jamie turned serious. "You could do it again, you know."

"What's that?"

"Build Eventually back up."

I looked at the list she'd printed off for me. All the things I'd messed up. Could I really fix it? That seemed a lot more daunting than quitting my safe office job and starting Eventually from scratch.

I was suddenly very tired. I made an excuse to Jamie about having to leave early and pretended to reread her list on my way out. I kept it up all the way into the parking lot.

That's probably how I got so close, just a few car lengths away, before I saw him. A man in a gray T-shirt walking toward the front door of the office. He was speeding toward me—on a mission—when suddenly he stopped.

For a half second, my heart leapt—a new client?—but then I saw, *I recognized*, those eyes.

Even without the green jacket, I knew those eyes.

We both hesitated, like two wild animals coming upon each other in a clearing. He'd looked so determined a moment ago, Dana, so convinced of something. But now he looked scared. Terrified.

Of me.

Before I could move, he turned. He began walking away, fast, then faster. He made it probably twenty yards before I found my voice and shouted for him to wait.

He turned, just for a second or two, long enough for me to see him weighing his options, and then he turned his back again and disappeared into a black Jeep.

I ran toward the car. I was not going to let him leave. Not this time. I should have been quicker at your funeral, Dana. I should have confronted him, found out what he wanted. But I'd been too afraid he knew the truth, too afraid he'd speak it in front of everyone, all our friends and family.

Now? Now we were alone in this little parking lot. I closed in on his Jeep as it began to reverse out of its spot. The car rocked to a hard stop as I reached the back end.

At least I knew he didn't want to hurt me.

I ran around to the driver's side door and banged on his window.

"Roll down the window!" I started to demand, but I only got out "Roll" before his Jeep was doing just that. He was free to go now, now that I was no longer blocking his way, and so he did. Quickly. Stupid move, not blocking his path out. In a blink, he was halfway out of the lot, then all the way.

I stood staring at the empty spot. It had all happened so quickly—*did it really happen?* Why would he appear—again—and then leave? Did I imagine him? Or had there been a man, a different man, and I'd mistaken him for the one from the cemetery and the waiting room?

Was I just seeing what I wanted to see? Was scared to see?

The parking lot blurred before me. I reached for the nearest car to steady myself.

No, no. I would never forget those eyes. It was him; I was sure of it.

That, and one other thing: He would be back. And next time, he wouldn't get away.

31

May 16. It was supposed to be a special day, but Matt forgot. I don't know how. It'd been a couple months since we'd put it on our calendars, but I'd made such a big deal about that date.

Not that it would have made much difference if he'd remembered. That morning, I watched 9:59 roll into 10:00 from the comfort of our couch. At 10:18, I let the call from the doctor's office go to voicemail.

After the miscarriage, I'd had a follow-up appointment to make sure my body was healing as expected. Matt came with and we talked next steps with the doctor. We still had four embryos and a lot of determination left. We told our doctor we wanted to try again, at the earliest safe date, so the doctor told her nurse to book us a baseline blood work appointment for three to four months out.

The nurse consulted her computer. "How's 10 A.M. on May 16?"

I looked to Matt; he nodded.

"Perfect." I flipped to May in my planner and wrote *IVF Round 2* in the square marked *16*. "Such a pretty date," I murmured.

The nurse paused her typing. "It is, isn't it?"

Matt looked up. He'd been plugging the appointment into his Google Calendar. "It is?"

"Yeah," I said. "It just sounds nice. Like a day you might want to have your wedding on, or your birthday."

"If you say so."

I rolled my eyes. The nurse caught me and hid a smirk.

"Okay," I said. "Try this. Would you rather live at 1802 West Windsor Avenue or 391 South Braintree Road?"

Matt squinted at me. "Which one has a bigger garage?"

"I can't tell you that. You have to pick one based off just the address."

"Okay, say them again?"

"1802 West Windsor Avenue," I said slowly, "or 391 South Braintree Road."

"The first one, Windsor."

"Exactly! That's what anyone would pick. It just sounds . . . nice, right? Like May 16."

"Wah-huh," Matt said. "*Oui, oui.* It has a certain *je ne sais quoi, non?*"

He said this in the most ridiculous French accent, Dana. Then he grabbed my face and kissed me. Urgently. Enthusiastically. Frenchly. Like the poor nurse wasn't right there. She closed her laptop and slipped out of the room.

"West Windsor Avenue," Matt muttered, returning to his phone. "I hope our kids don't get your weirdness, babe."

I laughed and slid my planner back into my bag.

"No, really," he said, his face serious but not his eyes—he could never mask that telltale twinkle. "They better not be weird, or I'm out."

I laughed harder. Matt would never be *out*. We'd both been *all in since 2010* (our private joke to make light of the fact that I'd nearly destroyed us that year).

God, it felt good to laugh. It was the first time I'd felt light—hopeful—since the forty-two painful, messy hours it had taken me to miscarry our baby.

The loss, Dana, had been hard. Real hard, especially those first couple weeks. *Especially* when your good fortune was shining a hot spotlight down on my pain.

But now I could see I still had so much to keep me going—Eventually and Matt and four more viable embryos . . . and now May 16.

You and I, we needed to talk soon, so I could apologize and explain everything.

That was February 13. The last day I still had all the time in the world.

32

On June 14, Matt didn't say happy birthday. Instead: "Thirty-three. Do you realize we've spent half our lives together?" Then he kissed my forehead and asked if he could cook me dinner that night.

He always used to surprise me with something for my birthday—dinner reservations, concert tickets, a party. On my twenty-ninth, he'd just said, *Pack a bag.* I'd laughed and asked, *Shorts or pants? Whatever,* he said, *destination TBD.* He never harbored any fear or doubt that I wouldn't be up for whatever plan he hatched. Now he was asking permission to cook me dinner.

My phone saw more action that day than it had in four months.

Jamie texted Happy Birthday trailed by thirty-three pink hearts.

Mom: Dad and I would like to take you out to lunch today. Would that be all right?

My dentist: Dr. Eagan and team wish you the best birthday yet! Enjoy 20% off any whitening treatment this month, on us. Just mention code BDAY20!

Some of our mutual friends sent some version of: Thinking of you and Dana today. Alexis Channing, bless her heart, texted, Have the happiest birthday ever, girl! accompanied by a GIF of a tuxedoed monkey chugging from a champagne bottle. I suspected she sent the same thing to you. I hearted it anyway. Someone would tell her one day.

I took Mom and Dad up on lunch. Matt came with. We met at La Za' Za', and I did my best to look put together.

For mid-June, it was a pretty mild day. We waited for a table on the patio since, as Mom pointed out, you had loved to eat outside.

Literally everybody enjoys dining alfresco, Dana, but I understood what Mom was doing. She was keeping you alive. We needed to remember and say out loud all the things you'd loved and stood for, so they wouldn't fade away like the edges of the new sod covering your grave already had.

We talked about Champ's cataracts. How Sean was. What a nice day it had turned out to be. I asked Dad how the Cubs were doing, and Mom asked after my work, and Matt's. We toasted the occasion. You slipped in here and there—what you would have ordered, what you'd have said about the new boutique going in across the street. It would have been wrong to not bring you into the conversation, but we sprinkled you in judiciously: not so much that it became a sad affair, not so little that we excluded you from your fair share of the celebration.

At only one point did we drop this delicate balance. Dad was talking about dessert—"Who wants to split the chocolate *tartufo*?" "Does anyone else want coffee?" Mom wasn't paying attention. She was looking off in the distance, the tears in her eyes rising to precarious heights. It was impressive they stayed put until she blinked when my hand covered hers.

"Sometimes I still can't believe it," she said. She was smiling. She wasn't happy, just . . . wistful. A story was coming, Dana, and it would hurt. They all did now.

"Do you remember your seventeenth birthday?" she asked.

I nodded. I remembered them all.

"We went downtown," she said. "To see that play. The one set in World War II, with the long-lost twins who get reunited. It was so funny . . ." She snapped her fingers, trying to shake the name loose.

"*The Comedy of Errors*," I supplied.

"Yes! *The Comedy of Errors*. Dana was so excited to go to the theater and you were just happy to be in the city. *Downtown*."

I smiled, remembering how hot shit we thought we were, strutting down Michigan Avenue in the outfits we'd spent all week planning. My ill-fitting Express blazer and your crinkly satin Bebe dress with the pleather belt.

Mom's eyes drifted away. "We'd gotten our snacks and were headed to our seats," she said, "when Dana noticed that little boy, remember? He'd gotten separated from his mother. He was so upset. Dana and I tried to comfort him while your dad found someone to help. Dana was so good with him, told him the story of that time you two wandered off in Target, how you were scared at first, until you stumbled into the candy aisle. By the time you'd opened a pack of peanut butter cups, I'd found you and all was well."

She smiled sadly, her eyes coming back to earth. "She got him to stop crying, remember, Cady? Even got a smile out of him, didn't she?"

I nodded. I didn't remember one way or the other.

Next to her, Dad's eyes were misty. But he was still Dad—no clue what to do in the way of words or gestures during a moment like this. I realized my hand was still on Mom's and squeezed it tight. She swiped at her eyes with her other hand and drew in a deep breath.

"I always knew Dana would end up doing something with kids, or maybe nursing. Somewhere she could *help*. That was her calling."

Was it, Dana? Your calling? I'd always suspected you chose that path because you knew it was one I wouldn't follow you down. You would be free from me there.

Mom attempted a smile, but her face had already surrendered to the weight of that story. Everything on it had fallen, like it had the day we'd decided not to go after the other driver.

I remembered Dad's claim that meeting him might bring us some closure. I pulled my hand away.

"I've been meaning to ask. Did you ever end up meeting with that . . . with the . . ."

Mom looked at Dad before she answered.

"William," she said gently. "Yes, we did."

I reached for my wineglass. My fingers tightened around the stem. I imagined it snapping between them. I imagined a severed finger bleeding onto the white tablecloth.

"How did it go?"

Mom dabbed at her eyes with a cloth napkin. "It was healing, actually."

Healing.

"How so?"

"Well." She glanced at Dad again. He'd nodded at her choice of words. "Your father and I agreed that it was a relief, to let go of our anger."

You ever notice, Dana, how Mom says *your father* when she's upset? We never called Dad *father,* but that's who he became when one of us was in trouble. *Your father and I were talking. Your father and I have decided. Wait till your father hears.*

"You let go of your anger."

Mom looked at her hands. "Yes."

"So you *forgave* him."

Somebody sighed.

"Yes, I suppose we did."

"Did you *tell him* you forgave him?"

They didn't answer with words, just another exchanged look.

Matt placed his hand on my leg under the table.

I looked down at the fly that was pillaging the carcass of my half-eaten salmon finocchio. I reached for my wine again. It was flat, but it suddenly tasted really good. I felt Matt's eyes on me as I took a big long swallow.

"It was a good talk," Mom said. "Good to get closure. Did you . . . did you know that William pulled Dana from the car? He jumped out of his car and ran through the intersection to get to her—he nearly got hit himself."

So now he was a hero.

"Do you *really* forgive him, though?"

"Of course," Dad said, but I thought I heard a question mark in there. "Why? *How?*"

Mom sighed. Dad leaned back in his chair and watched the people walking by on the sidewalk. Matt's hand slid off my leg.

"I'm not being an asshole," I said. "I'm genuinely curious. I'd love to forgive and forget. I'd love to be okay with all this."

"I haven't forgotten anything," Mom snapped. "And I am not *okay* with losing Dana. But I don't want to hold on—"

"Dana dying," I corrected. "It's okay to say it, Mom. You're not okay with Dana *dying.*"

"Okay, Cady," Dad said, standing up. "That's enough."

That's enough. Like I was a teenager again.

Mom gestured for Dad to sit down, and he did. Matt stayed quiet, eyeing my wineglass like it might be to blame for all this.

"It's not about William," Mom said. "I could give a rat's ass about him, if I'm being honest. I didn't forgive him for *his sake*. I forgave him for myself. And no, I'm not sure I meant the words, Cady. But telling William I forgave him was . . . it was like letting myself out of a cage."

I didn't like that we were using his name, like he was part of our circle. He wasn't. He was the asshole that drove his black Mazda into our circle and broke it.

***

That night, I sat in our living room as Matt made my birthday dinner. He left me with a glass of pinot noir, Fleet Foxes rolling out of the speakers to keep me company.

I turned the volume down. I preferred the sounds coming from the kitchen. The efficient *shwish shwish* of something being sliced on the mandolin. The *click click voom* of a gas burner coming to life. The *plop* and *sizzle* of something cold hitting a hot pan. I took another sip of pinot, savoring the way it was uncoiling the tightly wound nothing inside me.

My phone vibrated on the marble coffee table, startling me out of my trance. I leaned over to look at the screen. A text. From Morgan. I'd been waiting all afternoon for it.

Despite Mom and Dad's revelation at lunch, we'd ended up having an okay time. Dad ordered that *tartufo*. We all had coffee. Mom and Matt steered the conversation back to safer topics. A Yorkie in an orange sweater-vest trotted by, and I took a picture. I sent it to Morgan and she hearted it right away.

But I couldn't let it go, Dana.

The forgiveness. Of that man.

I'd texted Morgan about it on the way home. I'd asked her, as a parent, if she thought she'd be capable of the same. She'd taken until now to respond. I opened her message. Grief is a Reese's PB cup, Cady. Ain't no wrong way to eat it.

I actually smiled at that, though it wasn't the answer I'd been looking for.

Another message came through. And happy birthday, BTW. If I'd known, I'd have taken you out for a drink or something!

A drink. We'd never gotten a drink before, Dana. Just coffee. Friends who got a drink together were different from the sort of friends who met for coffee. A level up.

Matt appeared in the doorway with a dish towel in his hands. "Your birthday dinner awaits." He gave a slight bow.

I glanced down at Morgan's last message. I'd have taken you out for a drink or something!

I grabbed my wineglass off the coffee table and followed Matt to the kitchen. There, on the table in the breakfast nook, was a spread of my favorites: chicken coconut soup, pork satay skewers, Penang curry . . .

My eyes filled. "You made me takeout."

"I call it *take-in*," Matt said proudly.

He pulled my seat out. A tear escaped as I sat down. I tried to smile so Matt wouldn't mistake it for something else, but he did anyway.

"What's wrong?"

I shook my head. "Nothing—they're happy tears." One fell onto my plate. "This is so thoughtful."

He'd managed to surprise me again, this year of all years, even as I'd privately lambasted him for not doing so.

Matt flicked his napkin open and placed it in his lap. I copied him, then served myself a generous helping of everything. He'd put all the food in the plastic takeout containers I kept a small supply of.

"For authenticity," he said.

I laughed as I picked up my chopsticks. "I dig. It's a whole vibe."

I put the first bite in my mouth and almost moaned. If I hadn't heard and smelled all the preparation, I'd have thought he cheated and ordered in.

After dinner, Matt revealed a cake that had been hiding in plain sight in a box on the counter. A tiny chocolate number he'd picked up at the bakery in our little downtown. No candles and, mercifully, no singing.

Just one slice for me, one for him, and our fork tines clinking together in a toast.

Matt watched me carefully as I took my first bite. "You seem better lately."

I lifted a brow. "Better?"

"More yourself. I can see some of the old bits sometimes."

"That sounds bad."

He laughed.

"But, for the record, I think I'm starting to feel them again."

"The old bits?"

"Yeah."

Matt raised his eyebrows. "Yeah?"

I shrugged. "I don't know. It's different. It's hard to imagine I'll ever feel completely *restored*, but maybe . . ."

"Renovated?"

I snorted. "I'm not one of your big, empty buildings."

"I know." Matt's lips twitched. "You're a castle. A beautiful princess castle, with turrets and little pink flags."

I rolled my eyes and made a face.

"You're doing it!" Matt dropped his fork and pointed. "Your old crooked smile."

"I don't have a crooked smile."

"Yes, you do." Matt grinned at our old joke. Then his face turned serious. "So what's driving this renovation? I have to know, so I can help keep it up."

"Actually, I think it's . . . I think it's Morgan."

Matt blinked.

"My friend," I reminded him. "From group."

He made a little face. "I know. You talk about her a lot."

"I do?"

He shrugged, and the look slipped away. "Yeah, sort of."

"Oh. Sorry."

"Nothing to be sorry for. I shouldn't have said anything."

What did *that* mean? Was Matt feeling slighted? Jealous? Had he somehow figured out, or sensed, that the real—

"Another glass?" He was holding up a second bottle of pinot, moving his hand to uncork it.

I looked down at the glass in my hand. "Actually," I said, "I should probably pace myself. I forgot until just now, but I . . . I promised Morgan she could take me out for a drink tonight."

33

Morgan suggested some fancy cocktail lounge in Riverside, halfway between us, but I countered with a dive bar in Forest Park, conscious of her wallet, knowing she'd insist on buying the first round, given that it was my birthday.

We squeezed in at the crowded bar, the sides of our legs and arms brushing against each other every time we reached for our drinks or our purses or swiveled around in our stools to check out the cause of some ruckus coming from the pool tables.

We had to lean in close to hear each other. Her breath warmed my cheek when she talked. My lips brushed against the strands of her hair when I talked. We discussed my text earlier that day, about Mom and Dad *forgiving* that man, and we laughed about the *F* word, how it was harder to get that one out than all the *D* ones Moira was always on our case about.

My birthday drink soon became birthday drinks, plural. We ordered a second round of High Lifes, then a third. Morgan told the bartender it was my birthday, which earned us free lemon drop shots, which made me feel like I was in college again, which made me want another beer.

"Happy birthday to you, friend," Morgan said when we had our fourth bottles. She'd toasted me for every drink so far.

I lifted my beer and clanked it against hers.

"And," she added, "to Dana."

My eyes filled with tears—of course they did, Dana—but this time it wasn't because you were gone. It was because Morgan had said it. Your name. Because she knew what it was like, the rest of the world pretending your birthday didn't exist anymore.

I raised my bottle to hers again and smiled as the wet drops ran down my face. "Happy birthday, Dana."

I took a swig but noticed Morgan didn't. I pulled my bottle off my lips and pointed it at hers. "It's bad luck not to drink after a toast," I told her. Or so Dad always says.

Morgan did the half smile thing we were always doing. She picked up her beer and took a giant swallow before putting it back down on the bar. "I wasn't going to say this, because it sounds bad . . ."

I rolled my eyes. Since when did we care about things like that? "Say it."

"It's just . . . I almost toasted to a better year ahead. But then I didn't, because that didn't seem right." Morgan laughed. "I mean, how dare we hope for something like that? How dare we think it's possible?"

Exactly.

"But screw that," she said, getting animated, pounding her beer-free fist into her thigh. "This next year might not be good, but it can't be any worse than the one behind you."

I raised my eyebrows. "True."

"I mean," she said, her chestnut eyes widening, "you lost your daughter, your sister, your unborn niece or nephew, *and* your own unborn child. In one year! In just a *couple months*."

"Thanks, Mor." I laughed. Sort of. I don't know why. Because she was right? Mostly? Because it was so absurd? I don't know why I called her *Mor*, either. I'd never tried to give her a nickname before.

Morgan frowned. "I don't get the timing, though."

My laugh had faded into a smile by then, and now that smile slipped off my face altogether. "What timing?"

"Well, the miscarriage. The math doesn't math. If your daughter was ten weeks old when she died, and if you'd lost a ten-week pregnancy just a couple weeks before, then wouldn't . . ."—Morgan rolled her eyes up and off to the side, like she was calculating the numbers on an invisible chalkboard—"wouldn't that mean you got pregnant with your second baby while you were eight and a half months pregnant with the first one?"

My head began to swirl like the ice in the frozen margarita dispenser at the end of the bar. I hadn't thought of the timing. Why hadn't I thought of the timing? Why hadn't I said the miscarriage happened years ago, instead of months? Why had I even told Morgan about the miscarriage in the first place? It was a stupid, careless mistake. The kind of lie that could be *the lie* that I'd feared this whole time, the one that would bring everything crashing down.

Though, to be honest, even faced with Morgan's suspicion as I now was, I wouldn't have gone back and changed my story. I didn't regret it. It was the first—only—completely honest story I'd told her—anyone—since you'd died. And it had felt good to have someone other than Matt know about our baby. A woman, a mother, who got it.

I looked in Morgan's eyes, debating. I could have made something up. Could have said she was misremembering, or that I must have misspoken, that baby Dana was ten *months* old, not ten weeks. I could have said my first child was adopted. I don't know why I didn't.

I just remember Morgan's ear, how I could see the pale, tiny hairs at its opening and the three little pinholes where her lobes had been pierced. How naked and vulnerable that ear seemed. How welcoming, like it was waiting for something, a confession or a promise, to be deposited inside.

"I lied to you," I whispered. "I lied to everybody."

Morgan went so still. "About what?" she whispered back.

Everything.

"Something really bad."

She leaned forward, shaking her head like this was all just some alcohol-induced nonsense. "Cady—"

"I didn't have a baby girl," I said slowly. "There is no baby Dana. There never was."

Morgan blinked. She looked confused. Annoyed. "There's no baby Dana."

I shook my head.

She squinted at me, like it might help her understand. "But I don't get it. Why . . . why are you in group then? And what about your sister?" She put her hands on the sides of her head, like the logic—or lack of it—was giving her a headache. "Oh my God," she whispered. "Did you even have a sister?"

I nodded. The movement made the room start to blur and swirl before me. Or maybe that was the tears. "Dana—my sister, Dana—was real. She died. And I wasn't lying about the miscarriage, either. I was pregnant and lost the baby, just like I told you."

Morgan shook her head. "But . . . why? Why did you . . . ?"

I could have kept going, could have told her the truth about everything right then. But I'd already confessed so much. I started to feel like I was losing control of the whole delicate narrative I'd strung together.

"I wanted to join the group," I told her. "I'd lost my sister, yes, but it was the baby—the pregnancy I lost—that I really needed the group for."

Morgan's eyes shone with sympathy. No, not sympathy. Pity. And confusion. "But don't they have support groups," she said, "for women who . . ."

"I didn't want to join a fucking miscarriage support group!" I snapped.

Morgan flinched away from me, and I instantly regretted my reaction. My hand shot out to touch her arm. "I'm sorry," I said gently. Pleadingly. "Morgan, I'm so sorry. I shouldn't have gotten upset with you. But I didn't want to talk to other childless women about *pregnancy loss*. I didn't lose a fetus. I lost a person—a whole real person. A literal piece of me, Morgan."

Just like you'd been, Dana.

Morgan was listening carefully, like maybe she got it. Or was at least trying to.

"Don't you remember being pregnant with your son?" I asked her. "Imagining what his smile would look like? What his laugh would sound like? How it would feel to hold him? He was so real, wasn't he? You pictured him, at three, making all sorts of messes. In kindergarten, drawing you pictures. All the trouble he'd get into later, and how proud you'd be when he graduated high school, how you'd cry when you dropped him off at college. You thought about what his friends might be like and whose side of the family he'd take after. He was real, right? Even though he wasn't *here* yet, even though he isn't here now, he was real. Right?"

Morgan choked on something, nothing. She was nodding—she had been since I'd mentioned her son's smile—tears streaming down her face.

I caught the bartender eyeing us. Regretting those free lemon drops, I bet.

Morgan finally spoke. "That explains why you never talk about baby Dana," she said slowly; it was all still coming together in her head. "I thought that was . . . interesting, how you'd just lost a child, but all you ever talked about was your sister." She smiled a sheepish smile. "To be honest . . . I always kind of sensed something was off with your story." She reached her hands out and placed them over mine. "Now I know why."

I forced myself to smile back. "Yes. Now you know."

Morgan frowned and let her hands slip away. She took a long swig from her bottle.

"You think I'm a terrible person." I hated how pathetic I sounded.

Morgan shook her head, swallowed the beer in her mouth. "No," she said. "I don't. I . . ."

"It's okay," I insisted. "I am."

"You're not," Morgan insisted back. She set her beer back on the bar. "You're not. I mean, yeah, you shouldn't have lied—and what a thing to lie about . . . But I get why you did it."

"You do?"

"Yeah. I mean, the way I see it, it wasn't really a lie, was it? Like you said, that baby growing inside you was as real as if you'd gotten to hold her."

My eyes grew thick with tears.

Morgan's glimmered back at me. "Knock it off," she said, swiping at them. "No crying. This was supposed to be fun, dammit."

I laughed. Laugh-cried. "I'm sorry. It's just, it means a lot. Your understanding. I don't even think Matt got it, not really."

Morgan smiled. "He wasn't physically connected with the baby yet. That doesn't come as naturally for a lot of dads, not until they have the real physical proof of their progeny in their literal hands. I swear, sometimes Reid seemed to forget I was pregnant. But once Christopher was here, he was a great dad. Matt will be, too."

I picked at the gold edges of my beer's label, eyes wide to keep the tears at bay. Morgan was right. We were supposed to be celebrating or whatever.

I smiled. "I never thought . . . when Dana died, I didn't think I'd ever . . ."

Morgan lifted her eyebrows.

I wasn't comparing her to you, Dana. I would never, ever, ever. She and

I could not replace you and me. No, I had something different in mind for Morgan.

I reached out my hand for hers. "You don't know what it means to me," I told her. "Your friendship. You're a good friend, Morgan. I'm going to pay you back somehow."

She rolled her eyes. "Stop."

"No, really, I am."

"Okay, next round's on you, and we'll call it even."

"*No*," I said, the word long and heavy on my tongue. I hadn't drunk like this in months. I should have been putting myself in an Uber or calling Matt for a ride, not trying to convince Morgan that this wasn't just the beer and lemon drops talking, that I was serious. Dead serious. "That's not enough. I'm going to get you back," I insisted.

Morgan gave me a funny look. "That sounds more like a threat than a promise."

"*Morgan.*" I tried hard to look sober, which never works. "I'm *serious*. You're my friend, and when you're my friend . . . when I care about someone . . ."

"You what? Reward them?" Morgan giggled. "Seriously, Cady, you don't owe me anything. All I did was listen and give you the benefit of the doubt. That's what friends do. You'd do the same for me, and that's all I'd ask in return."

I shook my head. "It's not enough."

Morgan sighed. "You're impossible," she said, but she was smiling. She downed the last of her beer. I finished mine and signaled the bartender for another round. He gave me a skeptical once-over. Morgan realized what I was attempting to do and started to protest, but I shushed her, mouthed *Last one* to the bartender, and implored him with my biggest puppy dog eyes. He shook his head, but he reached under the bar, and when his hand emerged, he held two more bottles.

Morgan laughed. "Like I said, impossible."

We thanked the bartender for our beers and toasted to me—and you—again.

A mischievous smirk was creeping up at the corners of Morgan's mouth. "So you were saying something about buying me a new purse?"

she said. "One to match yours? Bestie Birkins?" She giggled at her little joke.

"I'd buy you a Birkin."

Morgan's giggles escalated into a full-out laugh. She thought it was funny—hysterical—that I would do such a thing. She didn't get it. I would show her though. She would see, one day.

"I'm serious, Morgan. I'd do anything for you. Give you anything. A Birkin. A kidney. A lung. I'd give you one of my goddamn embryos, if you wanted . . ."

I caught myself, stopped.

Morgan's laughter stopped, too. Her eyes suddenly looked very dark. "If I wanted what?"

If you wanted another child.

But I couldn't say that. I wasn't *that* drunk.

"Nothing," I said. "Nothing. I was just being drunk and stupid. I would obviously never . . ."

But I would. I really thought I would, Dana.

I shook my head and tried to laugh it off—stupid drunk-birthday-girl talk. "Okay, forget that last part. No . . . no organs or body parts or anything like that. But there must be something . . . What do you want, Morgan? What do you need? Money? I have money. Or a job—I could get you a job! You *hate* your job."

"I don't hate—"

"Yeah, you do," I slurred, pointing a blurry finger at her, "you hate that fucking job. I'm going to give you a new job. At Eventually."

Morgan snorted. "What would I do at Eventually? Plan a debutante ball? Or some heiress's sweet sixteen? I haven't even *been* to a party in years, Cady. Not unless it had an ice cream cake or Minecraft balloons."

"I need a numbers person."

"That's ridiculous."

"It's not ridiculous, it's perfect. I need you, Morgan."

And I need you to need me.

Morgan shook her head. "I can't just quit my job. I've been there fourteen years."

I sighed and reached into my purse, fumbling around for a pen.

Morgan kept making her excuses. "I mean, the pay's not *great*," she said, "but I have stability and a little 401(k). Sixty hours saved up in my PTO bank. And my company picks up part of my insurance premiums, and most years I get a two percent—"

Morgan stopped. I'd just slid a cocktail napkin in front of her. She picked it up and looked at the number I'd written on it. Then she looked back at me.

"Get out."

"I'm serious."

Morgan considered the napkin for several more seconds, then laughed and tossed it back on the bar. "No, you're drunk." She pulled out her phone. "I'm ordering us Ubers, birthday girl."

I didn't want the night to end yet, but I had just enough wherewithal left to realize that five more minutes with Morgan, one more drink, would be trouble.

We waited for our Ubers outside the bar. The air was thick with middle-of-summer humidity. My skin was tacky, like glue, and I could feel my hair frizzing and curling around my face, but I didn't protest when Morgan put her sticky arm around my shoulders and leaned her head against mine. I rested against her, two opposing forces holding each other up; if either of us pulled away too quickly, the other would fall.

"Happy birthday, Cady."

I closed my eyes. "Thank you. Really, thank you, Morgan. This ended up being an okay birthday, all things considered."

Morgan's grip on my shoulder tightened. "You know," she whispered, our heads still pressed against each other, "you still have a whole lot to live for, Cady."

The slightest breeze skirted over us and made the skin on my arms and neck tingle with goose bumps. I opened my eyes and turned to face Morgan, slipping out from under her arm.

I never told you this, Dana, because you always said I worried too much about the most ambiguous shit, but I'd always, even as a kid, worried I had it too easy in life. A loving family. Good health. A roof over my head. Nothing fancy, just the sort of boring childhood every kid with real problems dreams of.

But the longer I went unscathed by some great misfortune, the more I feared what waited around the corner. Surely the ease with which I'd glided through my first thirty-some years would have to be repaid someday, somehow.

I just never anticipated the interest on that debt, Dana. Or that it would be demanded from me almost all at once. The baby, then you, then . . .

"Do you believe we can be punished for things we haven't done yet?"

Morgan blinked. "What, like in *Minority Report*? Like a psychic police force or something?"

"No. Like . . . I don't know. Never mind."

But Morgan's eyes were round with curiosity. "No, tell me. I'm intrigued. You don't mean like—"

"Never mind."

"Cady—"

"Morgan, please. Forget it. Just forget I ever said it."

34

June 17 didn't start out too bad.

It had been a good weekend. I'd been on a high after my birthday. Matt had been put out—maybe even hurt—when I left after dinner, but he didn't make a big deal about it. Just greeted me at the door when I got home and looked my face over like he was checking for something, then smiled when he realized I was drunk. He kissed my forehead.

All weekend, Morgan and I texted back and forth about our hangovers, the free shots, the cute bartender, the couple fighting next to us, my silly drunken proclamations—had I seriously offered up my embryos? No! And that business about preordained punishments at the end of the night? Wow, I must have been *really* drunk. I remembered none of it! Too funny!

But seriously, it meant a lot that she understood about the baby. I remembered that part.

Morgan laughed it all off. The alcohol had been my downfall and my savior that night, forcing careless confessions to slip off my lips, but also giving me the most timeless of all excuses—*Oh that? I was just drunk.*

Anyway. It felt good to have one less secret, Dana, even if the others were still inside me, metastasizing.

Something lifted ever so slightly in the days that followed—a weight, a burden, my heart, my guilt, *whatever*. Its name was unimportant.

So come Monday, I was feeling good. Or maybe just better, which was good, too. I washed my hair and put on clean yoga pants. I made a to-do list, things I had never let slip in the past but were now long overdue. *Performance check-ins with staff. Q4 marketing plan. Hair appointment.*

I doubted I'd get around to crossing anything off, but I used to subsist on my lists, and I hadn't made one in four months, so this had to be some sort of win, even if all it wound up being was an inventory of little failures.

I rarely experienced true hunger anymore, so I was surprised when my stomach growled in protest of its empty state late that afternoon. I decided to make something on the stove, still feeling productive and ambitious from all my list-making. I pulled out a loaf of sourdough, a block of sharp cheddar, another of Havarti. A thick pat of butter melted in a frying pan while I slathered more on two slices of bread and added my grilled cheese secret ingredient. (It's Jane's Krazy Mixed-Up Salt; I can tell you now, Dana. Now that you can't tell anyone else.)

The butter hissed as I placed the sandwich in the pan and gave it a good press. Of course, Champ chose that critical moment to beseech me with his most urgent *let-me-outside* whine.

I hurried to let him out and rushed back to the stove, sure I'd find a grease fire tearing through the kitchen or a brick of charred bread smoking in the pan. But there was only the smell of butter-fried sourdough and cheddar and Havarti drippings. When I flipped the sandwich over, it was a golden wonder with perfect, crisp edges.

I got to enjoy one crunchy, gooey bite before my phone pinged with a message.

Mom, just checking in. And also, she wanted to apologize about the whole William conversation on Friday. She should have saved it for another time, not my birthday.

I put down my sandwich and texted her back. Nothing to be sorry for. I was the one in the wrong. (I was feeling generous after the high of the last couple days.)

And, I added, I'm glad it helped you and Dad. Really. Maybe I'll consider talking to him, too. One day.

Too generous? Whatever. I hit Send.

Mom texted back, Really? And then a long three-part message about what a great idea that was, how it would bring me so much peace and heal me, yadda yadda yadda.

I was hearting her messages when another *ping* sounded on my phone. Mom had shared a contact with me.

Oh God. First of all, didn't know Mom knew how to do that. Second of all, she wasn't *really* sending me his info, was she? I'd said *one day*, not *as soon as I finish this sandwich.*

I tapped the bubble to open it.

Sure enough, it was him. William. *William Fahey,* apparently. I'd never asked his last name. Didn't want to know. I'd rather think of him as the thing that took you away, not an actual person with a last name and a cell phone number.

William Fahey.

I held my finger over his name and pressed Copy. Then I pasted it into Safari, added *Illinois,* and hit Go.

There were a lot of William Faheys in Illinois, some very close. One from Hoffman Estates, one from Downers Grove, another in Wheaton, two—a senior and a junior—living in Addison . . .

I returned to the contact info Mom had shared, but all I had was his first and last name and cell number.

I swiped back to Safari and clicked Images. Rows of faces—Irishmen, mostly—filled my screen. But then one of the faces . . . his green eyes . . .

The dots scrambled to connect in my head, making me dizzy. I felt as though I needed to sit down, but I already was.

I pressed down on his image with my thumb, then drilled down into every link attached to that face.

William Fahey. Forty-three years old. Systems engineer at Northrop Grumman. Northwestern grad. Wheaton resident—very nice-looking house.

Aside from the headshot on his company's website, the internet offered few photos of William, just a slew posted several years back by his wife, Melissa Fahey—professional family photos, the kind where everyone is color-coordinated and at least one person looks to be on the brink of tears.

He had a wife, Dana, three kids, a black lab . . . all the makings of a nice, normal, quiet life. The sort of life you should have gotten to have.

The sort of life he took from you.

35

I found his address online in under a minute and was there—my door to his curb—in thirty-eight.

What can I say, Dana? I'm a professional now. It's frighteningly easy these days. No matter how careful you are with your social media and your passwords, it's virtually impossible to hide from the internet. I couldn't find a single instance of William putting himself out there, but in the end it didn't matter, because his wife, his company, his local newspaper, his alma mater, and his city, county, and state all did.

His house was nice. Very nice. Not as big as mine, but much bigger and statelier than Morgan's. A new build. The style—modern farmhouse?—was in the fashion of all the new builds lately. Tall and multi-gabled with a black asphalt roof. White vinyl clapboard. Stone base. I bet anything there was a big open floor plan and a white kitchen tucked inside.

Why? Why had he shown up at my work? At the funeral? Why the interest in the waiting room that day?

Only one person knew, Dana, and that's why I'd come here.

But could I really do it? Go up to his door, ring the bell, and ask him? Could I face the man responsible for the fact that *this* was the only way I'd ever be able to talk to you again?

I didn't even know if he was home.

I checked the time on the dash. 4:18. Probably not. Systems engineer at Northrop Grumman sounded like a nine-to-five if I ever heard one. Maybe no one was home.

But screw it. Only one way to find out.

Three, two, one, and suddenly my seat belt was unbuckled and zipping away from me. I opened the car door, got out, and slammed it shut. I even crossed the street, to the side his house was on. I was doing this, Dana. I was really fucking doing this.

Or at least my legs were. The rest of me . . .

I mean, what was I going to do? What exactly would I say? What if his wife answered? Or one of the kids? And why were my legs shaking like this? *I* shouldn't be the one terrified.

As I stood there at the end of his driveway, alternately working up the courage to ring the bell and the good sense to go home, the garage door lifted and one of the children, the oldest one—ten? eleven?—emerged in Under Armour shorts and an I PAUSED MY GAME TO BE HERE shirt, a basketball tucked under one arm.

The kid looked bored. Or maybe annoyed. He dribbled the ball as he moped down the slope of the driveway, his curly red-brown hair swinging over his eyes. He was only a few strides down it when he noticed me. He stopped his dribbling and caught the ball, pinning it under his arm again.

We stood there squinting at each other from opposite ends of the driveway.

I supposed I had to say something.

"Hi," I called out. I tried to sound cheerful and casual, but I may have overdone it.

"Hi?" He started dribbling the ball again but didn't move closer. "Are you here to see my mom?" he asked. He glanced back at the house like he might run and go get her.

"No," I said quickly. "No, I, uh, lost my dog."

"Oh," he said, a little of the mopiness slipping away. "What kind?"

"A golden retriever."

He came a little closer, the basketball thump-thumping against the asphalt. "My friend Marty has a golden retriever," he said. "They just got it." *Thump.* "It's a puppy." *Thump.* "It pees in the house." *Thump, thump.* "One time, it peed in Marty's dad's shoes."

I laughed. "Well, *my* dog is definitely not a puppy. He's very old, actually, and he can't see well, which is why I'm worried about him."

He stopped walking and scrunched up his nose. Only a couple feet separated us now. He had a tiny smattering of freckles on his nose and under his green eyes. His father's green eyes.

"Did you try the park?" he asked. "Marty's dog *really* likes kids; every time he sees one, he goes chasing after them. Maybe that's what happened to your dog."

"You know," I said, tapping my finger on my chin, "that's a really good idea. He does love kids. I'll have to check the park next. Thanks for the help."

He nodded and turned around, thumping the ball back up the drive. He stopped a few feet shy of the hoop and took a shot. Miss. It bounced off the rim and came bounding down my way. I ran to intercept it before it reached the street.

When I turned back around, he was holding his hands up, expecting the pass. I held on to the ball. A seedling of an idea was taking root inside my head, Dana. I didn't have a clue what it would grow into, only that I needed more time to let it unfold, to see what might become of it.

"Do you want to help me look for him?" I asked. "I could really use an extra set of eyes."

He scrunched up his face, thinking.

"And," I added for good measure, "I don't know where this park is."

He was thinking about it. I could read the deliberation in his eyes. It would probably be more interesting than shooting hoops by himself in the driveway, but he didn't know me. I was a stranger.

Then again, I was just some old lady. Old ladies like me never hurt anyone. And there was the poor old dog to consider . . .

"It would be a real big help," I said. "And it shouldn't take too long."

I finally tossed the ball his way. He caught it and spun it around in his hands like it might have the answer written on it, like one of those Magic 8 Balls we had when we were kids.

"All right," he said. "I'll help."

He ran back into the garage and tossed the ball into a tall bin. Then he cracked open the door into the house and yelled, "Going to the park, Mom! Be right back!"

He waited half a second for any objections, then slammed the door shut and ran back down the driveway.

"Thanks for helping me," I said.

He shrugged. *No big deal.*

We set off down the sidewalk. He dragged the bottoms of his shoes when he walked, the way you used to do, the way that drove Dad up the wall. I tried to think of something to say, but I didn't have the slightest inkling what to talk about with a boy his age—and anyway, a bigger, louder part of my brain was trying to figure out where I was going with this, what the plan was. Was I going to question him? Cross-examine him for information about his dad? Send him home with a message pinned to his shirt? Kidnap him?

Kidnap him?

No, God no. Of course not. I laughed at myself in my head for taking it that far.

Or no. Must not have just been in my head, because he stopped and gave me a funny, uncertain look.

"Sorry," I said. "I just thought of something funny."

"Oh," he said. He started walking again. Kids are so easy, the way they take your word for things just because you're an adult. "What about?"

I shook my head. "A grown-up thing. You wouldn't get it."

He made a face. I couldn't blame him. I used to hate that line as a kid.

"So what's your name?" I asked.

"Billy."

Billy. "Short for William?"

"Uh-huh."

"Interesting," I said. "Where'd your parents come up with that name?"

Billy raised his eyebrows at me, like, *Really, lady? William?*

But he muttered an answer anyway. "I'm named after my dad."

Billy didn't ask me my name. Typical kid. I didn't mind, though. I didn't have an answer ready.

I wanted to ask something about his dad—what he was like—but it seemed too strange a question, even after he'd just mentioned his father.

Billy continued to lead the way, shuffling across the street at the end of the block.

"You seem a little down," I said.

He shot me another of his funny looks.

"I mean, you seem disappointed or unhappy or something."

Billy rolled his eyes. "I know what *down* means. I'm going to be a fifth grader."

"Oh, sorry," I said. "My bad."

He laughed.

Yes. That's it. Get him to keep talking. Get him to keep walking with you. The farther away you get . . .

"So what's got you in a bad mood?" I asked.

"My mom."

I rolled my eyes. Kids. "Okay . . . what about her?"

"She made me go play outside, but I was in the middle of a Fortnite battle."

I made a sound of commiseration. I had only the faintest idea what Fortnite was.

"There were only fourteen people left," he said, as if that meant anything to me. "I could have gotten a victory royale. But she said it's too nice out to play inside."

I bit my tongue from saying that didn't sound so bad to me. It wasn't what he wanted to hear, Dana. It wouldn't get him to see me as different from the other adults.

I wanted to be the kind that got it. The kind he could trust.

Yes, I would get him to trust me. If he trusted me . . .

"Well, that sucks," I said.

"I know."

"Next time, you should try negotiating," I told him. "Like, *Hey, Mom, if you just let me finish this game, I'll go right outside when I'm done.* Or offer to do some chore or something in exchange for more time."

Billy snorted. "Yeah, right. That sort of thing doesn't work anymore. My parents are so lame now."

Good. That was real good. He was upset with his parents. I could use that. I could get him to come with me.

And what?

Take him?

No, no, that wouldn't be good . . .

I turned my attention back to Billy. I tried to remember the last thing he'd said. Oh, right.

"What do you mean *now*?" I asked. "They weren't always so . . . lame?"

Billy sighed, like he couldn't believe he had to explain this. "They used to be less lame, but then my dad crashed his car, and they had to buy a new one. He's been really sad about it. He really loved that car."

He steered us to the right at the end of the street; up ahead, the park came into view.

What if I got him to go somewhere else after the park? To keep looking for the dog. Somewhere farther. Just until *he* got home from work, just long enough to make them worry, to make *him* feel . . .

Stop. I had to stop this thinking.

Billy was still talking. Something about his mom being mad that his dad wouldn't get over it.

"Get over what?" I asked.

He shrugged. He did that a lot. "The car, I guess. It got totaled. That means it got so messed up they couldn't fix it."

I made sure to really exaggerate the eye roll I gave him. "I know what totaled means," I said. "I turned thirty-three a few days ago."

He tried to suppress a smile but couldn't; I'd gotten a full-on grin out of him.

That was good, very good.

"She says he needs to move on," Billy said. "For our family. She says it was horrible what happened, but he can't keep—"

"Billy!"

We both spun around to face the big black Suburban rolling to a stop. The driver was a woman, middle-aged, with a plain white T-shirt and a messy updo, not the stylish kind, but the I-fucking-give-up kind.

"William Junior, what on earth are you doing?"

"Going to the park," he muttered.

"What?"

"Going to the park!"

"Don't yell at me," his mother said, pointing a finger at him. She had yet to register my presence.

Billy rolled his eyes for maybe the tenth time in the fifteen minutes I'd known him. "Well, you didn't hear me the first time."

She gave a tired sigh. "Just get in the car, please. We need to pick Olivia up from swimming, and I'm running late enough without having to track you down. You were supposed to be playing in the driveway, not running off to the park."

"I asked you if I could go!"

"Stop arguing, please, and *get in the car.*"

Billy sighed and hung his head, but he trudged toward the back door and jerked the handle out, pulling the door open. Before he hopped in, he turned around to mutter a short "Bye," and finally the woman noticed me.

I held my breath, waiting for her to recognize me somehow, but she just turned her gaze slowly back to the road in front of her as Billy's door slammed shut. Her eyes flitted to the rearview mirror as she drove off. I could just barely make out her voice as she asked Billy who that woman was.

It must have been eighty-something degrees that day, but as I made my way back to the car, my whole body shook like it was the middle of January. I don't know why. It wasn't like I would have done anything, Dana. You know that. You know me. I would never—*could never*—hurt a child.

It was just an idea. Not even. Just a bit of hypothetical make-believe, like getting mad at your parents when you're a kid and thinking about what it would be like to run away, to show them. This was like that. A fantasy, to test out what it *would* be like. To hurt him. William, not his child. For God's sake, not the child. I just wanted . . .

But it doesn't matter; I would have never gone through with any of it. I would never hurt anyone.

You know that, right?

36

My body hummed with the aftershocks of my encounter with William's son. I would have never hurt that child. I'd never even come close. Not really. Which is why my body's reaction made no sense. My weak legs stumbling to the car, my hands fumbling with the door handle, and now my death grip on the steering wheel, the nausea, the road blurring in front of me.

I must have temporarily lost my senses, luring the boy away from his home. And those thoughts. They were just thoughts, Dana. They didn't mean anything.

And why wouldn't some sleepy, primitive part of my brain think that way? Why wouldn't it occur to me to even the score with the man who'd taken you away from us? After everything I'd been through? The miscarriage, then the accident, you dying, the man with the green eyes and green jacket showing up everywhere . . .

And then to find out he was the man who took you away from us, Dana?

He killed you.

Then he showed up at your funeral. And my work.

Who does that? Why? *Why?*

The garage door lifted as I inched up the driveway, revealing Matt's car. Relief swept through me like a drug, easing the pinch in my neck, stilling the tremors in my muscles. I would be better once I had the reassurance of Matt's arms around me, the liberation of telling him who the man in the green jacket was.

"Hey," he said when I came into the kitchen. "Where've you been?"

The emphasis was on *you* this time, not *been*. He was pleased I'd been out. Curious, not concerned, about what I'd been up to.

Then he kissed me. Just a peck, a casual afterthought as he moved past me to get a glass of water. The kind you don't think about but just do, the very best kind. Easy. Natural. Normal. Not old normal. New normal. But that was okay. More than okay.

I would save the revelation about William for another time, Dana. I didn't want to rock this boat.

I smiled. "Just coffee," I said. "With Morgan."

Matt looked behind me, like he expected to find her there. But, of course, I was alone. This seemed to puzzle him. I worried I'd gone and done something stupid or wrong again, this time without even realizing it.

Or maybe it was the mention of Morgan. I remembered Matt's comment from the other night, on my birthday, about how often I brought her up.

"Did you bring Champ with you?" he asked.

I gave him a funny look and moved around him to clean up the mess I'd just noticed I'd left earlier. "No, why would I—"

Oh God. Champ. The grilled cheese. He'd whined, so I'd let him out, but . . .

"He didn't come when I called him, so I—*shit,*" Matt said, grabbing his forehead. He looked at me, eyes round with horror. I knew what he was thinking. "Do you think he . . . ? They say they go hide somewhere . . ." He strode from the room, still holding his head.

"Matt," I called, chasing after him.

"It's okay. You stay here. I'll find him. You don't have to see—"

"He's not in the house, Matt." I shook my head. "I let him out before I left, and I'm pretty sure . . . actually, I know I didn't let him back in. I forgot."

I couldn't read Matt's face when he turned around.

"I'm sorry." The tears came down my face quickly as I bent over to put my shoes back on. I fumbled with the laces, choking on another apology, but Matt was already out the door. I ran to catch up to him.

"We should split up." He said it without turning around, and for a second, I thought he was talking about forever. But no, he was talking about the search.

"I'm going to drive around in my car," he said. "You go on foot, check people's yards, ring doorbells."

I nodded, though Matt didn't see. He was already climbing into his car.

I turned and walked quickly in the opposite direction, trying to cover as much ground as I could, desperate to find Champ and set everything back to the way it had been ten minutes earlier, when Matt had greeted me with a smile.

All right, breathe. Think. Think, think, think. Champ couldn't have gone far. He could barely get to the end of the block.

And this wasn't the first time he'd wandered off, Dana. His eyesight had gone south over the last year. Several times now, we'd discovered him tangled up in a bush or a soccer net. Today would be no different. Within the hour, we'd find him ambling obliviously through a neighbor's yard.

Or maybe someone had taken him in. Champ didn't wear a collar anymore—it irritated his skin—but he was well-known in the neighborhood and had a microchip, so if—when—someone found him, we would be reunited.

I peered over fences and pushed apart hedges. I whistled. I yelled. A Nissan drove by too fast, and I screamed for it to slow down. I called the police (*Not yet, but we'll keep a lookout*). I called the 1-800 number for the microchip place (*No, ma'am, sorry*). I texted every neighbor in my phone book and went door-to-door knocking. I hardly cared how frazzled I must have appeared—over a dog—or if my neighbors were thinking, *Oh no, first her sister, now this.* All I wanted was to find Champ and bring him home and make everything better.

When I got back to the house, Matt was still gone. I looked at the clock. Champ had been outside for five hours. We'd been searching for more than two of them.

I spun my wedding ring around my finger as I watched out the front window for Matt's headlights. He wouldn't come home until he found Champ—and Champ *would* turn up; he had to. He was so old, Dana. He could barely see, just like I'd told—

Oh God.

Just like I'd told Billy.

I'd lied to the boy about my dog being lost and now, less than an hour later, Champ was gone.

The *whir* of the garage door sounded, and my hopes lifted with it. I rushed to greet Matt and Champ, praying they would be so relieved at having found each other that all would be forgiven.

But Matt entered the house alone. He hugged me, but it felt forced, or obligatory, like something he'd planned to do on the drive home to prove he wasn't mad. To show he understood that it was an accident and that you can't hang a mistake like this over someone's head.

"Do you want me to order something for dinner?" he asked.

I shook my head.

Matt ate pretzels from the bag in front of a nature documentary while I pretended to read a book in the den. David Attenborough's voice drifted in from the other room, narrating some feral drama unfolding on the screen—foxes and goats squaring off in the Alps.

. . . the young ibex instinctively run back to steeper ground . . . the fox has them trapped, or so it seems . . . will have to find its meal elsewhere . . . her seven-foot wingspan . . .

I might have fallen asleep in my chair, dreaming of hungry foxes and snowcapped mountains, if it weren't for Matt abruptly changing the channel to some drama. A thriller, maybe. A man's voice, low and stern and secretive, whispered urgently, but I couldn't make out the words. Matt had turned the volume down too low.

Wait, no . . . it wasn't a show, Dana. The voice was Matt's. I hadn't recognized it at first, it was so hushed, but that voice definitely belonged to my husband.

I sat up, instinctively turning my ear to better capture the words. Maybe a neighbor or the police or the microchip place had called to say they'd found Champ?

I walked quietly to the living room. When I got there, Matt was no longer talking. He was holding his phone, staring at it, debating something.

"Who was that?"

Matt's head snapped up. He looked . . . guilty.

162 | MARISA WALZ

"Nobody. Work."

"Oh."

He shoved his phone into his pocket. "I need to get out of the house for a while. Grab a quick drink or something."

He was lying. It was wrong, all wrong.

"Don't go," I begged.

He moved past without looking at me. "It's just one drink, Cady."

No, no it wasn't. I could feel him slipping away. Just like before. The old panic rose up.

"*Please*, Matt, don't—"

"Stop!" he yelled, spinning back around to face me. "Goddammit, Cady, just stop. Don't start your . . . don't do this shit right now. Please. I can't . . ." He held up his hands, his fingers straining so hard the tendons were popping. I'd never seen him so tightly wound, so barely in control of himself. "I'm leaving," he said firmly.

And then he did.

37

I didn't protest when Matt left. I waited. I stared out our bedroom window, watching for his headlights to come stabbing back through the darkness as he returned home to me.

He would come back.

He always came back.

He'd come home from Northwestern, and he'd come back to me after that breakup, and he would come back tonight. I knew this. Still, that fourteen-year-old wound had been reopened.

If I'd thought having Matt 149 or even just 32 miles away was unbearable, it turned out to be nothing next to not having him at all.

I'd ended things so I wouldn't have to do three more years like the one before. So I wouldn't waste the remainder of what were supposed to be the best years of my life. So he could be happy, and I could be healthy, and you wouldn't have such a miserable roommate, Dana.

But despite my official relinquishment of Matt's heart, I found I could not let him go, or stop the old habits.

I should have been listening to lectures and contemplating a minor. I should have been dancing at toga mixers. Pregaming with our floormates. Dressing up for homecoming parties. Getting sick off jungle juice and Jägermeister. Sneaking into bars, sweating my bad fake ID. Making memories that would last forever and mistakes that wouldn't.

But I wasn't doing any of that. I spent my first semester at college thumbing through Matt's social media. Just as I'd done the year before, I scrolled and scrolled, living for and dreading each new picture that popped up. Matt and his roommate giving hard faces in front of a row of empty liquor bottles. Matt and two frat brothers with their arms around each other, grinning like fools, a throng of girls in the background wearing tight pink shirts with sparkly sigmas.

Matt, doing a shot of tequila with some bitch in a coconut bra.

Matt, playing flip cup, sandwiched between a crop top and a minidress.

Matt, in his dorm, wearing a Northwestern sweatshirt I'd never seen before, laughing about something, I didn't know what, with someone, I didn't know who. Laughing harder, I was sure, than I'd ever seen him laugh before.

Did that mean he was happy?

Already?

Or worse, happier than he'd been with me?

Was he better off without me?

Mom said it would be okay and maybe it would still work out, you never know. Dad said Matt was an idiot if he didn't come crawling back (never mind that I was the one who'd done the breaking up). Our friends said, *Did you really want to marry the only guy you've ever done it with?*

You, Dana . . . you held me and let me cry.

If you're going to be heartbroken, a college campus is the place to do it. On the rare occasions I was able to pick myself up off our dorm room floor, I found it easier to cope if I dulled the pain with other things. I partied a little harder, drank a little faster, and then—ugh, okay, cringe—then I gave that D-Chi pledge Ian Doyle a blow job at a toga mixer, remember that? I came home and told you about it, and we were so ecstatic, so sure it was a sign I was cured.

But the next morning, without the haze of pot and Coors clouding my head, I was less enthusiastic about my recovery. I pointed out that I'd hooked up with a Delta Chi—Matt's fraternity—so rather than getting over Matt, maybe it had been some sort of subconscious *fuck-you,* or worse, a subconscious substitute.

You said it was just a good old-fashioned blow job and also that next time I shouldn't be so generous.

A couple weeks later, I was sitting up in bed doing homework on my laptop. You were on your bed doing something on your phone. I reread the question I was supposed to be answering. It was the fifth time I'd read it; it still didn't make sense. I snapped my laptop closed.

"What are you doing?" I asked.

You jumped.

It was an innocent question. I was tired and bored. I was going to see if you wanted to turn on a movie or something.

But you jumped. You looked guilty as fuck.

"Nothing," you said. You purposely didn't look down at your phone when you locked it.

We watched a movie. It was funny; you forgot all about your phone, and afterward, you took a shower. When I unlocked your phone—*061491,* our birthday—I saw what you were hiding. Matt. You'd been texting each other all night. He was depressed. He missed me. How was I doing? Should he call me? If this was what I really wanted, if this was what was best for me, he should respect that. Right?

You'd told him I missed him, too. But I was doing better, and a call from him might undo all that. Some more time might do both of us good. It would give us clarity. And this might be a good thing for me—I needed to learn how to be by myself. That's what was best. And you would know.

I wasn't angry with you, Dana. I knew you meant well. I knew you believed every word you said. You always trusted the universe to work things out—what's meant to be, will be, right? You were just trying to help. Everyone was always trying to *help.*

You ended up misplacing your phone that night. It disappeared for a whole week.

That didn't stop your conversations with Matt, though. You told Matt, on second thought, maybe he should give Cady a call. Cady was a total wreck without him. She wasn't getting better at all. Sometimes you were worried I might . . . oh God, you didn't even want to say it. Maybe he and I really were meant for each other. Yes, you were certain, Dana.

Oh and BTW, all the guys in our circle wanted me; it was only a matter of time before I moved on if he didn't do something. Yes, you were positive now, Dana. Matt and I belonged together. No one else in the world could love him the way I did. Sure, I could be a handful, but I was worth it. It was all worth it, to be loved by someone the way I loved. And you would know.

Matt was so thankful for your support, for the advice. You told him no problem, but asked that he never bring it up again. You shouldn't have told him all that; you felt bad. If Cady ever found out . . .

166 | MARISA WALZ

Matt promised it was your little secret, just you two.

The next day, I found your phone when I was rummaging through your laundry bin, looking for a top I'd misplaced. You swore you'd checked there. Twice.

I shrugged, laughed, said, *Third time's the charm.*

You didn't laugh back, or even smile. You just looked at me, thinking whatever you were thinking. You looked at me that way for a week.

***

A couple weeks later, Dad came down to Champaign to drive us home for winter break. When we pulled up to the house, Matt's rusted Wrangler was parked alongside the curb. He was standing on the front stoop in a ski cap, hands jammed into the pockets of his jeans.

"What's he doing here?" Dad muttered.

"*Dad,*" you and I jinxed.

My heart was going wild inside my chest by the time I reached Matt. We stood so close, our breath clouds kissed like a little Venn diagram. You nudged Dad inside, leaving me and Matt alone.

"Hi," he said.

"Hi."

"So life kind of sucks without you."

I tried not to smile. "That's what you came here to say?"

"That, and I dropped out of Northwestern. I talked to a counselor, and I'm transferring to Champaign when the new semester starts."

Chaos broke loose inside me, Dana. I wanted to throw my arms around Matt so tightly his ski cap fell off. I wanted to scream my happiness so loudly the neighbors rushed to their windows. Only one teeny tiny part of me thought this was a bad idea, too big of a sacrifice, a gift I couldn't—shouldn't—accept.

I told that teeny tiny part to shut up.

"That was really stupid," I said. "What if I don't want you back?"

I could see that possibility hadn't occurred to him.

"You don't want me back?"

"Of course I want you back. But what if I didn't? Then you'd have gone and screwed up your—"

"But you do, right?"

"Yes. But what if I didn't—"

"But you do." He grabbed my face and kissed me. Not a romantic kiss, but one big fat smack, like I'd just saved his life or something.

"One confession," Matt said, holding up a finger. I don't think I took a breath until he spoke again, waiting for the revelation. A girlfriend he still had to break things off with, or a one-night stand with one (or two) of those jungle-juice-guzzling sorority girls.

"I didn't make it official yet," he said. "The transfer. I just talked to a guidance counselor about what would be involved. But that doesn't have the same ring to it, and I really wanted to make a grand gesture."

I punched his arm, and then I kissed him.

Matt worked with Northwestern and U of I over the rest of break to finalize the details of his transfer, and in January he moved his things to Champaign.

The beginning days of our relationship had been good, but this was better. A restart. We had a new appreciation for what we had. *All in since 2010* became our motto, our little inside joke.

Sometimes a quiet voice inside me would whisper that it was wrong to accept Matt's grand gesture. He was sacrificing so much. He'd chosen Northwestern, and now he was choosing me, because I wouldn't let him have both.

But that's what love is, right?

Choosing the same person over and over and over until one of you dies.

38

We had toast and coffee and silence for breakfast the next morning. It was a gut punch to instinctively pause for Champ's greeting and not have him limp over to say good morning. Another punch for the perfect sunny day streaming in through the window, warming his big, empty bed pillow.

"Morning" was the only thing Matt said when I entered the kitchen. I tossed the single word back, though there were at least a dozen other things I wanted to say: *I'm sorry. He'll turn up. I hate myself, too.*

Matt had not stayed out late the night before, just long enough for a drink or two, like he'd claimed. I listened carefully when he got home, assessing the tone of his movements. Keys dropped into the bowl on the credenza. Doors locked, the soft pad of fingers on buttons and the short beep as the security system enabled. A glass of water from the tap. A heavy exhale. A couple handfuls of something crunchy from the pantry.

I waited for the sound of pillows and blankets rustling as he made up a bed on the couch, but instead, there was the soft thud of his socked feet on the stairs, the tiniest squeak from a loose riser halfway up.

I kept my eyes closed while he brushed his teeth and peed in the master bathroom. He undressed at the side of the bed, crawled in beside me, and lay on his back, arms sticking out over the top of the covers, like it was any other evening.

Finally, I heard his one small sigh. It was a funny thing he did every night, Dana. After having heard thousands of its predecessors, I could usually tell whether it had been a good day or not. This one was obvious.

Before Matt could fall asleep, I reached my hand out in the dark and rubbed his arm. It was a statement and a question, that gesture, one we'd done scores of times before when the words were too hard.

He put his hand over mine for several seconds, then let it slip away. It could have meant a hundred different things:

Love you, too.

It'll be okay.

I'm not mad.

Please stop.

Don't touch me.

We'll talk about it later.

In the kitchen that next morning, I was still trying to decipher his behavior. But it was hard to tell from the silence, too easy to read too much into the way he sipped his coffee or flipped the newspaper to the next page.

"I'll call the neighbors again," I said.

I got back a nod.

"And maybe the microchip place . . ."

This time, a sigh. "I already called. They said they'll let us know if he's brought in anywhere. It won't do any good—"

"It's worth a shot, though, isn't it?" I asked. "It won't hurt, and you never know—"

"Where were you?" Matt put down the paper. "Yesterday, I mean. When I got home from work."

"Coffee," I said slowly. I wasn't sure where he was going with this, but I was quite sure I wouldn't like it. "With Morgan."

"You promise?"

A physical slap may have stung less, Dana. I pressed my lips together and took a big stream of air in through my nose. I could feel the ugly flare of my nostrils.

"Yes. I was at coffee with Morgan. My friend. From group."

Matt's smile was cold. Nasty. "Yeah, I know who Morgan is."

Something dropped in my stomach. "What's that supposed to mean?"

"Nothing," he said, shoving his chair back. He picked up his mug and headed for the sink. "Just saying you don't have to tell me yet again who she is."

"What is your problem with Mor—"

"*Is* there a Morgan, Cady?" He'd spun around to fling that at me.

I must have heard him wrong, Dana.

"I mean," he said, "first there was the man in the cemetery—"

"Oh, *him*?" I laughed. He wanted to go *there*? "The man from the cemetery is real, Matt. Very real—and you want to know something else about him?"

But Matt hadn't heard a word I'd said. "And then," he was saying, "you were supposedly at the office, doing work that—turns out—never existed." He set his mug in the sink and turned around, an ugly sneer still smearing his face. "Now Champ is gone because you were out with this Morgan, who, I don't know, I'm sorry, but is she another one of your excuses to check out, Cady? To not be at work or taking care of Champ or talking to me?"

My breath caught in my throat.

Several horrifying seconds of doubt passed—*did* she exist?

Then my senses returned. And my breath; I let it out in one big, relieved gust.

Yes, yes, of course Morgan existed. She was real, as real as Champ's empty bed, as real as the coffin we'd buried you in.

I hated Matt right then, for making me question myself like that.

39

I wanted so badly to talk to you, Dana. To call you up and tell you about Champ, about Matt. You would have cried over Champ. You would have said, "We'll find him," and maybe, "Matt'll come around, he always does," and then you'd have told me just how to undo it all.

But you were still dead.

I was fifteen minutes early to group that Wednesday. Champ had been missing for two days. I'd exchanged texts with Morgan about it, but it wasn't the same. We needed to talk.

Morgan was always right on time, never early, so it would probably have to wait until after, but I would feel better once she walked in and sat down next to me. I always did.

I waited in my metal folding chair as the clock hands marked the minutes off slowly. 5:58—just another minute to go. 5:59—any second now.

At promptly six o'clock, Moira began recapping the Reality of Death exercise we'd done last time. Still no Morgan as she moved on to this week's theme: Moving Toward the Pain.

I thought, at first, that Morgan was just late. But no one showed up late. It was one of the ground rules Moira had set from the very beginning.

The go-round began. Lips moved, voices traveled, heads tilted and nodded, but I was only tangentially aware of it all.

I watched the clock tick to 6:09, then 6:10. My chest began to tighten, like it had the day you'd gone off to Mackenzie's house. Every tick of the second hand on the wall clock over Moira's head increased the pressure, like a ratchet.

Then all the oxygen was suddenly gone, sucked from the room. I wouldn't breathe again unless I left, so I did. Moira's Reeboks squeaked against the linoleum floor as she ran after me.

172 | MARISA WALZ

"I'm fine," I assured her when she caught up to me outside. "Just a stomach bug or something."

Moira looked unconvinced, but she went back inside when I promised her I'd text as soon as I got home safe.

I made it there in seven minutes. It was still light out, another ninety minutes or so until sunset. It had been, and still was, a perfect June day. Clear and sunny, mid-seventies, a gentle breeze whistling through the grass. I closed my eyes, then opened them as a warm breeze blew in the driver's side window, brushing past me like a casual hello.

That sort of thing—the beautiful weather rubbing its warm, sunny face in mine—made everything worse. You'd think it would be the opposite, Dana. You'd think the overcast days would be worse. But the dreary days were reassuring. Validating. *I feel you,* they said.

No, it was the beautiful days that hurt. Anything beautiful hurt. Like the colors in Morgan's yard. They'd slowly started appearing since my first visit. Reddish-purple blooms bursting from the once naked azaleas, lavender hyacinths and yellow daylilies snuggling up against the blanket of hostas curling around the house—a house that looked welcoming, almost charming, in early summer.

Before you get all *Really, Cady? This again?* let me save you the lecture. I wasn't there to sit in my car and watch the shadows in her windows, Dana. I was past that. Morgan was my friend now. I saw her twice a week, talked to her every day; I'd celebrated my birthday with her—gotten drunk with her. I'd told her a terrible secret, and she'd had my back.

So no, I was not going to stay in my car this time. I was going to ring her doorbell and go inside her house. I was going to find out why she hadn't shown up to group. She would be so relieved—so grateful—I was there. That I'd somehow known she needed me. We would split a bottle of wine and talk about it, whatever it was, in the living room I'd always imagined but never seen.

That's not what happened, though. For starters, the doorbell was broken, so I had to knock, which I never like doing. There's no good way to do it; it always sounds angry and impatient.

I gave a few raps, then stepped back to wait, leaning the tiniest bit right, to get a peek inside. Hard to see much. All I got was a glimpse of half a big, cheap, brown couch and an ugly coffee table that looked like it would fit right in at Grandma Ruby's place. I don't say that to be mean, Dana, just to paint the picture.

A faint noise sounded from the other side, then a louder one—the dead bolt unlocking. Then the knob, loose and jangly. My pulse quickened; I could feel it throbbing in my wrist. I'd thought about this so many times, getting out of the car and going up to the house and ringing the bell and—

"Cady."

Morgan looked surprised. Alarmed. I mean, of course. She wasn't expecting anyone, least of all me. I was supposed to be at group.

I gave her a sheepish smile. "Sorry to drop by unannounced like this."

"It's okay," she said, but slowly, like maybe it wasn't. "I just . . . is everything all right?"

"Actually, that's why I'm—"

"And how did you get my address?"

Shit.

"I . . . I got it from Moira." Great. Just great, Cady. Keep digging that hole. "But please don't say anything to her about it," I said quickly. "She wasn't sure she should; I had to beg her like twenty times. I was really worried when you didn't show up to group tonight. You've never missed. And you didn't text me anything about not coming, so I wasn't sure . . ."

Morgan lifted her eyebrows. "Sure of what?" she asked. She was still wary of the whole address thing. I could tell my answer hadn't satisfied her. She either didn't believe it or didn't like it.

"I just wanted to make sure you were okay." I gave her my sincerest look, hoping she'd see I meant well. "So are you? Okay?"

Morgan sighed. "Yes, I'm okay."

"Then why didn't you come to group tonight?"

She hesitated, then the corner of her mouth twitched the tiniest bit, like she was suppressing a smile. "Because I'm not okay?"

I laughed. The smile she was fighting broke free, and she was laughing, too. Better. This was much better.

"Okay," I said, "so invite me in and let's talk it out. If you're not going to come to group tonight, I'm bringing group to you."

Morgan's smile faded. She didn't move aside to let me in.

She was thinking. But what was there to think about? I was her friend. I wanted to come in and be friends, do friend things.

Then Morgan smiled again, but something was wrong. "How about a walk instead?" she asked. "I was actually just about to go on one."

No you weren't. You had the TV on, and you're in your sweatpants.

But I smiled. I didn't want her to think I was hurt. Or insulted. I got it; she didn't want anyone inside her house. It was a sacred space—probably no one had been inside since her son died.

"Yeah," I said. "Sure. A walk sounds great."

Morgan's obvious relief pinched something deep inside my chest. Did she not trust me yet?

I followed her lead as we set off. She asked about Champ and the whole thing with Matt, but I didn't want to talk about that anymore. I wanted to know what was wrong, what had made her miss group.

Morgan didn't want to go there, though.

"I'm not ready to talk about it yet," she said. "It's very . . . personal. And painful."

We were coming up on a dog walker and his lab. Morgan moved aside, and I fell in step behind her as we passed them.

"More painful than keeping it in?" I asked when we were out of ear-shot.

Morgan shrugged. "Maybe."

We walked in silence for several minutes. Passed a bunch of houses that looked just like Morgan's and a few that didn't. I followed her as she took a right turn down another tree-lined street.

"Is it whatever you were holding back the night you talked about that last morning?"

Morgan stopped. She tilted her head, squinted at me. "How did you know?"

Because, I told you, Morgan, I know you. I watch you. Very carefully.

But I hadn't actually told her that, had I, Dana? I'd only said it in my head. Right?

She took off again; I walked quickly to catch up.

"All right," I said, "I'm going to give you the countdown."

Morgan shook her head. "Cady—"

I started counting down.

"Three . . ."

She gave me a look, like *Don't even.*

"Twoooo . . ."

Still giving the look.

"*One.*"

Morgan held up her hands. "Please don't, Cady. It hurts to even think about. I can't imagine saying it out loud. I . . . this thing, my secret, it's bad."

"It can't be worse than mine."

I don't know what possessed me to say that, Dana. Actually, I do know. It was the truth; it was rotting inside me.

"Cady," Morgan chided gently, "you can't keep beating yourself up about that. I mean, yeah, you totally shouldn't have lied to the group about the baby, but you weren't in your right mind—"

"But—"

"—and you meant no harm," Morgan said earnestly. "You just wanted to be part of the group, to be with people who understood. Maybe you'll feel better if you tell—"

"No," I said, shaking my head, "I wasn't talking about . . . that. There's something . . . else."

Morgan blinked. She raised her eyebrows, waiting.

Now what? Tell her? The truth? Where did I even start? *Where did I start?*

Three.

Two.

One.

"I wanted Dana's baby to die."

The look on her face, Dana. Not disgust exactly, not fear exactly, but . . .

"You didn't tell your sister that, did you?" Her voice was real quiet, like the neighbors might hear, like we might get in trouble for talking about this.

"God no."

"So when . . . when did this thought . . . ?"

"That day in my kitchen, when she told me she was pregnant."

Morgan nodded. She chewed the inside of her cheek, thinking.

"I don't believe you," she finally said. She started walking again. "You're not . . . you wouldn't really want that."

She didn't sound half as earnest as she had earlier, when she'd been reassuring me I wasn't a horrible person for making up a dead baby. First that confession, and now this. No wonder she was looking at me like that. So . . . carefully.

"It's true," I said.

Morgan was still peering at me, thinking. "So your sister said, 'Guess what, I'm pregnant,' and your mind just instantly went *there*? To hoping the baby . . . ?"

I shook my head. "No, no, of course not. My first thought was . . . well, the first thing I remember is a feeling, not a thought."

"What feeling?"

"I don't think there's a word for it."

"Try," she said.

I sighed, took a stab. "Devastated?"

"Why were you devastated?" Morgan pointed left; I followed her turn.

"Because it wasn't fair," I said.

There you have it, Dana. I couldn't be happy for you because I wasn't happy for me. I wish I could have been better—more generous—but I didn't have it in me.

I'm sorry. So sorry.

I wasn't mad that you got pregnant, Dana. I wasn't mad about the stupid fucking pact, either. I'd broken the pact before you. I'd been keeping far bigger secrets for far longer. I just didn't think I could handle it if you gave me any of your *Not meant to be* gospel.

Morgan and I came to a crosswalk; a woman in a blue minivan waved us across, and we walked quickly, waving our thanks back.

"So," Morgan said, "how did this sense of injustice turn into wishing . . . that?"

"I don't know." I sighed, exhausted by the confession. "It wasn't any one thing Dana said—it wasn't *anything* she said. It was more . . . the way she was. So happy and hopeful, so sure. Completely, naïvely, blissfully, painfully unaware of what could happen."

"It was just a thought, Cady." Morgan's voice was gentle. "A really awful one, like you said, but still . . . just a thought."

"What kind of person wishes her sister's baby—any baby—dead?"

Morgan thought about that for a minute. "How long did it last?" she asked.

"What?"

"The thought. How long did you wish . . . ?"

A second. Less. A fraction of a second, Dana.

"It doesn't matter," I said. "I thought the thought, and then it came true."

Morgan fixed me with a stern stare. "What happened to Dana isn't your fault, Cady."

"Yeah." I smiled sadly.

"Or her baby."

I nodded.

"This doesn't make you a bad person."

She grabbed my hand. I squeezed hers back.

"What about losing my dog?" I asked. "And blowing up my business? And my marriage?"

The fighting and lying and hiding? And this thing with Morgan? And our fight, Dana? And that walk with the boy?

And the other . . .

"Here," Morgan said, pointing ahead at a park. "There's an empty bench. Let's sit."

She led the way. We didn't talk, just sat, watching the children on the playground run and climb and jump. I thought about the boy, William's boy, taking me to that park to look for my lost dog. I was pretty sure Morgan was thinking of her son.

"I'm sorry for taking us here," I said after some time.

Her eyes stayed fastened on a trio of boys that had to be around her son's age.

"The park was my idea," she said.

"I didn't mean the park. I meant *here,* to this sad place. I swear, I came over to help, not . . . unload all this on you. I shouldn't have told you that. It's too . . . I'm sorry."

Morgan shook her head. "No apologies, remember? Besides, if you knew some of the things that've passed through my head since Christopher died . . ."

"Like what?"

"Oh, I don't know." She was looking away from the boys, but still not at me. "Like . . . like . . ." She glanced around the park, like the answer might be under the monkey bars or at the top of the slide, and gave a little snort. "Okay, like last week—don't judge—but I thought . . ." She started laughing; she couldn't finish.

I punched her arm lightly. "*What?* Tell me!"

She took a good ten seconds to compose herself.

"I thought," she said, "about trying to date again."

Interesting.

She was still laughing. "I know, I know. It's ridiculous—"

"It's not."

Interesting. Very interesting. I could use thi—

"It is," Morgan said. "It's so bad. It's not something I should be entertaining right now. But I think about it a lot, actually. Every couple I see . . . it feels like getting hit with a brick, Cady. Like the way I feel when I see a boy Christopher's age." Her eyes flicked back to the three boys, now huddled around a bike rack. "I'm even jealous of the couples who look unhappy—at least they have someone to be miserable with, you know?"

"Morgan . . ."

"The truth is, I'd started thinking about getting back out there before . . . before Christopher died. I don't need a fairy tale, but it would be nice to have *someone*—anyone."

I gave her a look. "Stop. You're too good for just anyone."

I would not *let her end up with just anyone, Dana.*

Morgan shrugged.

"So, like, what?" I asked, smiling. "You're jumping back into the dating pool?"

Morgan's flush was as red as the faded bricks on her bungalow. "Not exactly jumping. More like thinking. Thinking about dipping a pinky toe into the shallow end of the dating pool."

"Wow, a whole pinky toe?"

Morgan pretended to be offended. Then she laughed. "This is going to sound pathetic, but the other day, I even thought it would be nice to have my ex back."

I frowned. "Your ex? I thought that was off the table."

"It is, it totally is. I do *not* want Reid back. We weren't good together—horrible, really—and he wouldn't have me back, anyway. I know I've told you all about his many shortcomings, but . . . well, I wasn't perfect either. I . . ."

Morgan stopped; her whole face changed. I'd seen her like this one other time, when she'd talked about her son's last morning, when she'd almost but not quite told the group the rest of it. This was it, the thing eating her up inside.

I reached for her hand. "You can tell me, Morgan."

She cast her eyes back toward the playground. I thought that was it—conversation over, she wasn't going to talk tonight.

But then she started to tell me.

"My ex . . ." she said. "He kissed a coworker at a work happy hour one night, back when we were still married. Or, rather, he let her kiss him—there's a distinction, according to Reid. When he told me, I lost it. I just couldn't . . . I hated him so much, Cady. How could he do that to me? To Christopher? To our family?"

I shook my head.

"I wanted to balance the scales," Morgan said. "I wanted to hurt Reid so badly. So I did. I slept with his best friend. I didn't even like the guy—I'd always just kind of tolerated him—but something came over me one night. And I hate myself for that. I mean, part of me still thinks the bastard deserved it, but . . ."

Her eyes filled up. "That's what I couldn't get out at group that night. What if I hadn't been so determined to have my revenge, Cady? What if I'd forgiven Reid instead? Or at least tried to work things out? Would Christopher still be alive?" She choked on his name, the tears crashing down her cheeks. "Maybe Reid and I would still be together, and if we were still together, we'd still be in our old house, not the new one, and Christopher would have never—"

"Stop," I said. "Stop right there. No what-ifs, remember? Moira's rules."

"I know, I know." Morgan swiped at her tears. "You're right. I just . . . I'm . . ."

"I know," I said gently. "Trust me, I know."

Something crept into Morgan's eyes. I recognized it instantly.

"No," I said, pointing my finger at her. "*No*, Morgan. You are not a bad person. What did you tell me five, ten minutes ago? When I told you about Dana's baby?"

Morgan tried to smile, but that sadness still shot through her, and now her chin was trembling, rendering the whole façade fragile, like it might fall apart if she had to hold it in place for one more second.

I dropped my finger, put my hands on the tops of her arms, made her face me.

"You told me I did a bad thing," I said, "but it didn't make me a bad person."

She wasn't nodding anymore.

"You are not a bad person, Morgan."

She didn't even blink, Dana.

"Good people . . . sometimes they do bad things."

Nothing. Had she heard anything I said?

I pulled her against me tightly. I could feel something leave her; her whole body sagged into mine and her shoulders began to shake under my arms. Then a little gasp, a whimper.

A woman pushing a small boy on the swings stared. I didn't care. I kissed the top of Morgan's head; a few strands of her hair stuck to my lips. I pulled them off and smoothed them down, then I brushed the pieces hanging over her ears back behind them, the way I'd wanted to do that first Wednesday night, sitting across from her in the circle. I pressed my temple against the top of her head.

Don't worry, Morgan. I'm going to fix everything.

40

What do you think is most important in a relationship?

I selected *Making life easier for one another.*

If it were the old me, I would have picked *Pushing each other to new heights* or *Diehard devotion.*

But this wasn't for the old me.

It wasn't even for the new me.

Next question. *What do you want more than anything right now?* I went with *To build a safe and secure relationship slowly and steadily.*

What I really wanted—what Morgan really wanted—wasn't one of the prefab options.

What are three nonnegotiable qualities you look for in a partner?

What qualities do you want your partner to like about you?

When are you happiest?

What hobbies do you enjoy?

The questions were endless. The woman I'd thought was my friend began to feel like a stranger. I didn't know how much Morgan liked to cook (I guessed *not very much,* given that she bought a week's supply of microwave dinners every Tuesday night). Nor did I know how many times a week she exercised, if she exercised at all—all I knew was I'd never followed her car to a gym. I didn't know what movies or TV shows she was into, either, just that something was always flickering after dark from the back of her house.

Interests, hobbies, books, food, travel, music . . . by this dating website's standards, I knew nothing about Morgan.

But that wasn't true, Dana. I knew every dark corner of her grief. I could feel her regret and her pain like they were my own.

A banner of support flashed across the top of the screen. *You're almost there, Morgan! Just add a picture or two, and we'll start matching you.*

A knock from the doorway startled me. I spun around to face it. Just Matt, of course. He had a wide smile stretched across his face.

"You at a good stopping point?" he asked.

I looked back at my screen. I was at a horrible stopping point. I was just getting started.

But that smile . . . I hadn't seen *that* smile in a long time. Not since before Champ went missing.

And his voice. It was softer than it had been in weeks.

I should join him. Maybe we would have a nice dinner together. Maybe, if Matt kept smiling like that, I could let the whole thing with that phone call and his leaving the other night go. Maybe he'd forgive me for Champ, and I'd forgive all those missed calls on the day . . . on Valentine's Day.

Maybe I would even smile back, and it would turn into more—a kiss at breakfast tomorrow or a longer goodbye when he left for work. A midday text. All the little things that had once seemed like nothing until they'd disappeared and become everything.

I followed Matt to the kitchen. The table was set with candles and an elaborate meal. Very elaborate, actually—swordfish? Roasted asparagus? Mashed potatoes with rosemary?

Our wedding meal?

Surely . . . surely today wasn't July 11? Surely I hadn't forgotten our anniversary. The asparagus and mashed potatoes blurred together in front of me.

Matt rushed over. "Hey. Hey, hey, hey." He wrapped his arms around me. "Don't feel bad. Please. That's not what . . ."

His words trailed off into a sigh. He probably didn't mean for it to sound like a *Why do I even fucking bother* sigh, but it did.

"I don't feel bad," I insisted into Matt's white shirt. I pulled back, worried, out of habit, that I'd ruined his shirt with foundation and mascara before remembering I hadn't worn any of that in a long time.

Matt rubbed my shoulders. "I'm sorry if it's too much. I knew you wouldn't be up for anything too extravagant, but I wanted to do something—"

"I appreciate it." I reached my hand up to stop his massaging. "I really do. I just . . . I feel bad now. For forgetting."

"I don't care, Cady. Really, I don't. I just had to try to get us back on track—and before you say anything, this has nothing to do with Dana. This is about us, okay? I want *us* back. The same old you and me, transplanted into this strange new world."

That was as close to *getting it* as Matt had gotten.

"I want that, too."

I kissed him then. A real kiss. Probably the realest kiss I'd given him since you'd died. No, not probably. I hadn't kissed my husband—really kissed him, like a wife does—in nearly five months, Dana, let alone doing anything resembling intimacy. Matt had never complained or asked for more, not one time, and I didn't know if that was a good thing or a very horrible thing.

I pulled back and gave him a smile that suggested that maybe, just maybe, there was more where that came from.

"Should I crack open a bottle of something?" I asked as I made my way to the wine fridge. "I'm pretty sure we have some prosecco. A gift from the Mullinses, I think. Ah, here it is."

I pulled out a bottle and twisted it around. It had a pretty orange-and-gold foil label.

"Here, hold this up," I told Matt, holding out the bottle. I reached in my back pocket for my phone. "I want to take a picture of the label."

Matt frowned at the bottle in his hands. "I was actually thinking we'd skip the booze tonight."

"Oh. Okay." I slid my phone back in my pocket. "Are you not feeling well?"

I looked at the table, noticing for the first time there were no wineglasses set out.

"It's not that . . ."

I lifted an eyebrow. "Is this because of my birthda—"

"It's not because of anything you did, Cady. I just wanted tonight to be nice, and alcohol is a downer, so I thought, let's not bring anything into the mix that might bring us down, okay?"

He returned the bottle to the wine fridge and headed back toward our meal. Our wedding meal.

"It's me that's the downer, Matt, not a glass or two of prosecco."

"I didn't say that. I just want a nice night."

"It can't be *nice* if you're going to treat me like I—"

"*Okay!*" Matt said—exploded. "Jesus Christ, open the goddamn prosecco."

He dropped down into his seat and picked up his fork without waiting for me. I yanked out my chair. I took a long, loud swallow of my water.

"Open the prosecco if you want it."

"Forget it."

Matt shook his head. I was tired of everyone shaking their heads, Dana.

"I don't care about the prosecco, okay? I care about being made to feel bad about every goddamn thing I say or do or feel these days."

Matt stabbed the piece of fish he'd just cut. "Nobody's making you feel bad about anything, Cady. You're choosing this. You're *choosing* to interpret everything as some sort of slam against you. The prosecco. Champ. Your parents forgiving William. But not everything's about you. You've always had a hard time getting that, even before Dana died—and I don't mean that as a dig. I'm not saying you're narcissistic or anything, you just don't—"

"*Narcissistic?*"

"There you go again," Matt said, gesturing with his fork, the cube of swordfish still wedged between the tines. "I just told you I *don't* see it that way—"

"Right," I said, "but nobody mentioned the word until you said it."

"I don't think you're narcissistic, Cady. I think you feel guilty about Dana's death for some reason, and I think it's causing you to find fault in everything the rest of us say or do. Because focusing on those things distracts from the real issue."

I had to remind myself to breathe. "And what's the real issue?"

Matt set down his fork. "I don't know, because you don't tell me anything anymore."

"Well, you're wrong," I told him. "I actually am a narcissist."

"No, you're not."

"How would you know?"

"Because I know *everything* about you." He said it like a smart-ass, but I knew he really believed it.

"I used to think the same," I said. "But we don't really know each other all that well, do we, Matt?"

"Cady—"

"Who were you talking to on the phone that night?"

That stopped him.

"What night?"

"The night Champ . . . ran away."

"I don't remember."

"Oh, come on—"

"*I don't remember, Cady.* I can't recall every call or text I get every night. I barely remember what I—"

"I'm not talking about every night. I'm talking about that night. You remember *that* night." I stood up, the napkin I didn't realize I'd put in my lap falling to the ground. "Actually, you know what? Don't tell me. I don't think our marriage could survive it right now."

"Cady, listen to yourself. You—"

"I have secrets far worse than whatever it is you're hiding, Matt."

"I'm not hiding—" Matt stopped. "Like what?"

Like how every time I told him I was at work, I was watching Morgan and her car and her house and her office.

Like how I did just enough every day—some laundry and grocery shopping—to get him to leave me alone, to keep my secret safe.

Like things I couldn't even let my subconscious silently say inside my own goddamn head, like how it was *me* who—

"See?" Matt said, throwing his hands in the air. "You can't even think of one thing. And if you want to know what that phone call—"

"Bet you never knew I gave Ian Doyle a blow job."

Matt's arms, which had been wildly, almost comically, gesticulating seconds earlier, fell to his sides like they'd suddenly stopped working.

I deserved it, all the disgust in his voice and his eyes. I deserved to see my husband look at me like that, Dana. I deserved to see him walk out of the room, to be left standing like a fucking idiot, on our ninth wedding anniversary, in front of a table of candles and untouched swordfish, and to know, with absolute certainty, that this time I'd done it. I'd gone and ruined everything.

41

Funny, or not, how you can trust someone with your life, Dana, but not with your secrets.

Or your phone.

It was August 13. The day before the six-month anniversary of your death. (Sorry, but I may never stop calculating time that way.)

I'd fallen asleep on the couch watching *The Crown*. I know, I know. The Cady you knew never slept during the day. But this wasn't the Cady you knew, Dana. This was the Cady who welcomed sleep whenever it came knocking. It was the only way to turn off the images playing over and over inside my head, like a movie I couldn't turn off.

Anyway, I'd fallen asleep, and when I woke up, the house was quiet, but it felt late. I reached for my phone on the coffee table, but it wasn't there. Strange. I very clearly remembered tossing it down before falling asleep. I shook out the blanket I'd napped with and lifted up all the throw pillows and ran my fingers under the couch anyway, just in case. Nada.

There was no way it was in the kitchen—I *remembered* putting it on that coffee table—but I headed that way, just to prove to myself it wasn't there.

I jumped out of my ever-loving skin, Dana, at the sight of Matt at the kitchen counter.

I had no idea he'd come home. I'd been awake for a good five minutes now and hadn't heard so much as a footstep. Yet, there he was, the back of him anyway, in the white button-up and navy pants he'd left the house in that morning.

I barely got his name out. I don't even think I got to the *T*'s, just "Ma—", but he jumped as if I'd screamed bloody murder in his ear.

"Cady." He said it like my presence was some great surprise.

"What time is it?" I asked.

"A little after five," he said quickly. Scary quickly.

What the hell.

I was about to ask him just that, when I spotted my phone on the counter behind him. I could have sworn . . .

"Excuse me," I said, reaching around Matt to pick it up. "I was looking for this."

Matt stepped out of my way and headed for the fridge. My hand stopped inches short of my phone. The screen was already lit up, though I hadn't yet touched it.

It's no exaggeration to say that my stomach dropped into my ass, Dana.

I'd tucked the dating app into a folder called Shopping, but it wouldn't have taken much effort to find it. And Matt had my password. Up until very recently, I'd had nothing in there to hide from him. *Why* hadn't I changed my password?

I could have called him out on it, but where would that get me? I couldn't prove anything, and Matt didn't seem eager to confess, with his quick answers and shifty glances. Besides, I didn't want another fight. Weeks had passed without us addressing our anniversary dinner, and I suspected we never would. The fifteen-year-old blow job I'd thrown in his face was not the crime; it was the fact that I'd thrown it in his face at all—that I'd *tried* to hurt him. One of those things, like Champ's disappearance, that would never become a funny story in hindsight, no matter how many years we put between it and us.

My marriage was nearly spent, Dana. We didn't have enough capital left to weather another fight. I'd even kept William Fahey's name out of my mouth, though every time Matt snuck a worried glance my way, I itched to blurt out, *I told you so. I told you someone was following me. And guess who it was? That poor, sad, sorry man you all let get away with killing my sister.*

What, if anything, had Matt found on my phone? I didn't know. But I would have to let this go. And also, be more careful. Much. More. Careful.

"Weird," I said, turning my phone side to side, "the screen was on."

I couldn't resist, Dana.

"Huh," Matt said, not turning around from his assessment of the fridge's contents. "You must have forgotten to lock it."

"Huh," I said. "Must have."

Matt quickly changed the subject to dinner. He was going to go upstairs and change, then he had plans to whip something up with the leftover chicken breasts; did that sound good to me?

I told him it sounded great. Then I left, so he could finally close the refrigerator door.

I took my phone up to my office, sat down at my desk, and changed the password before opening up the dating app to check my messages. Nothing good, just the usual catfishers and pervs.

Progress had been slow. For every *maybe* that showed up in my—Morgan's—inbox, there were at least a hundred *hell noes*: the rebounders, the flakes, the guys who had more photos of their abs than their face, the one who asked about my *timeline for intimacy,* the fortysomethings *finally ready to settle down* but *only for the right woman*—which, judging by the requirements stated in their profiles, meant nothing less than Yael Shelbia's head on Barbie's body with Amal Clooney's brain and a 1950s housewife's *traditional values.*

There was the guy who couldn't stop talking about his Tesla, the three who couldn't stop talking about their exes, and the one whose third question was *Not that it matters but . . . bra size?*

It was absurd—*absurd*—to keep sifting through those matches, Dana. But every week there were new possibilities, so I kept looking and clicking and swiping through messages, deleting spam and dick pics, responding to every *Hey* on the off chance it would turn into something real. Something I could give Morgan.

I had two decent prospects—Ben, the kinda-shy-but-warms-up-quickly tech project manager, and Miles, a writer-slash-musician and dog lover. Neither had yet waved a red flag or been snatched up by someone else, nor had they freaked or flaked when I told them I'd lost my son six months ago. Ben said he was sorry to hear that and seemed genuinely interested in how someone even processes something like that. Miles said, *That's rough, sorry.* The point went to Ben. I hoped he might be *the* one, the one that would lead to something offline, in the real world, at a cozy coffee shop or little Italian restaurant.

But no new messages from Ben or Miles, so I actually tried to work. When in Rome.

I opened a few emails, glanced at Jamie's latest list. Nora's name at the top caught my eye. Right. Shit. Her annual black-and-white party. It was her favorite, the crown jewel of all her parties. When she'd finally entrusted it to me after we'd worked together for three years, she told me not to fuck it up or I'd never again plan so much as a birthday party for her dog.

That party was now less than two months away. I should have had the theme nailed down months ago. I should have been knee-deep in details by now.

I pulled up Google, did an image search for *sophisticated amazing creative black and white party,* then a similar search in Pinterest. I could never give Nora the sort of ball that popped up on some *BuzzFeed* top-ten list, but maybe I'd see something that would spark another fresher, more original idea.

It didn't work. I couldn't imagine a world where Nora Donnelly sanctioned a penguin- or soccer ball–themed gala, no matter how bougie I managed to spin it.

I shut my laptop lid and closed my eyes and tried to drum up some inspiration the old-fashioned way.

Black and white, black and white . . . Newspapers. Piano keys. Chess. Dice. Marble. Photography. Old movies. Old movies . . . Old Hollywood?

Yes . . . yes, a bud of an idea began to bloom . . .

And then a chime. My phone. I opened my eyes. A new message awaited me in the dating app; I opened it. Ben. Suddenly I was very aware of my blood, of the fact that it was moving faster.

Hey there.

Hey! I fired back.

Couldn't wait to get off work. Was hoping you'd be on.
I may or may not have been holding my breath . . .
Yeah? Well, I may or may not have waited 15 minutes so you wouldn't think I was too eager.

This was trailed by a crying laughing smiley.

I sent back the blushing cheeks emoji.

Ben replied with the heart eyes one and, having already anticipated this, I immediately sent back the open mouth surprised one.

How long do you think we could talk in just emojis for? he asked.

38 minutes.

Hmm. It might get weird.

Weird could be good . . .

What are we talking about again?

Getting weird.

Oh, right. Did this conversation just take an interesting turn? Ben asked. Or is that wishful thinking on my part?

It's not wishf—

A knock made me jerk in my chair. Matt. I looked up, probably guilt-ily. I'd been smiling—smirking?—at my screen.

Matt didn't seem to notice. "Think you can break for dinner soon?" he asked. "Tacos will be ready in five."

"Sounds great." I sniffed the air, catching faint whiffs of garlic and cumin. "Smells even better."

Matt turned to go downstairs, and I turned back to my conversation with Ben. I hated to leave him hanging. Things were finally progressing. Then again, it would be good to take a break, to keep him wanting more, to show him that Morgan was busy, that she had a life.

I reopened our conversation and wrote back, It's not wishful thinking. I definitely took it there. I added an emoji covering its mouth to suppress a giggle.

Ben sent back whew, with the sweating emoji.

Soooo . . . should we try it? he asked.

I couldn't remember the last time I'd blushed, Dana.

Try what??

Ben's response was a block of emojis.

Oh, that, I sent back with a laughing smiley.

Wait, what did you think I meant??

"It's ready!" Matt's voice called from downstairs.

Shit.

I'm so sorry, I typed, but I have to go. Rain check on the world record emoji convo?

Three thinking dots appeared, blinking over and over, one by one, like fingertips drumming on the screen.

"Cady!"

"Coming!" I pushed my chair out and stood up, then rolled it back under my desk. I knew the sound of the wheels on the wood floor would be heard from downstairs.

I leaned over the desk, waiting for Ben's response. Finally it came.

A frowny face. Then: Right when I was about to ask you out in real life.

My heart pitched. There was my blood again, making ocean sounds in my ears. It was finally happening. I reread Ben's message, soaking up every word. *In real life.*

Real life . . .

"Cady!"

Hold that thought . . . I sent back.

Then: xox.

42

Matt had dinner—chicken tinga tacos—laid out on the kitchen table. There was wine, too, a glass for each of us. An odd choice with tacos, but I got the message. Olive branches and all that.

I sat down and placed my napkin on the tops of my thighs. "Thank you for doing all this."

He handed me two tortillas. "It's no problem at all."

"All the same, dinner's on me tomorrow. I'm going to order you the best takeout of your life." I slid a spoonful of chicken onto a tortilla. "It's a little ways away, but I've got a new place to try. Morgan recommended it."

Matt started to say something, then stopped. He tore a chunk of cotija off a brick and crumbled it over his chicken, then reached for the cilantro. "You talk about her a lot."

"Is that a problem?" I asked.

Matt shrugged as he picked clingy cilantro leaves off his fingers. "No."

"Good, because Morgan—group—they're my . . . they're a big part of my life right now." I'd almost said they were my life, full stop. "The program doesn't work if you don't immerse yourself in it, you know? Besides, you were the one who wanted me to—"

Matt held up his hands, smiled. "It wasn't a criticism. Just an observation."

"Group is helping me," I said quietly.

"I know. My only point is you don't really talk about anyone else at group. It's always just this Morgan."

I shrugged. "She gets what it's like to lose someone who practically defined you . . . and it's not exactly the same, I know, but I *have* lost a child, Matt, in case you've forgotten."

Matt's gaze turned cold. "No, Cady, I haven't forgotten what *we* lost."

He couldn't even say the words. *Baby. Child. Family.*

"You forgot about May 16."

Matt shook his head. "No, I didn't."

"You didn't say anything."

"Neither did you."

I pushed my plate away. "Whatever. We were talking about Morgan."

"No," he said, shoving his own plate away, tit for tat. "You were talking about Morgan. I was sitting here trying to eat my dinner."

I raised my eyebrows. "You were complaining about Morgan."

"I wasn't complaining, Cady; I made a single comment." He sighed. "Let's just drop it, okay? Forget I said anything."

"I can't. You made the comment for a reason. You wanted to make some sort of point, you wanted to rattle my cage, and now you're backing down because you're afraid of what you started. If you've got a problem with Morgan, just—"

"Okay, okay," Matt said, pumping the brakes with his palms. "To be honest, it crossed my mind that maybe you were having an affair with her or something, but—"

"An affair? Oh my God, Matt, really?"

Matt sighed again, as if I were the one being ridiculous. "I was—"

"An *affair*?" I screeched. "First you accuse me of making Morgan up, and now you think I'm screwing her? My imaginary friend?"

Matt shook his head. "I didn't—"

"I mean, do I love Morgan?"

"I *just*—"

"—yes, I think I actually do, Matt." Something on his face twitched, and I rushed to cut it off. "But like a *sister,* not as—"

"*Exactly.* That's what I'm trying to—"

"Besides," I said, feeling a foul little smirk land on my lips, "you know what they say about jealousy. Maybe you're projecting *your* guilt onto *me*. I still don't know who that phone call was from, the night Champ went missing."

"Jesus Christ, Cady, I wasn't done. If you'd just let me—" Matt stopped himself and sighed, twirled his glass by its stem. "It's just odd, okay? How often this woman's name comes out of your mouth. That's all I'm saying.

You've got some of your old fire back, yeah, but it's different. Redirected from Eventually and me and your family to . . . to this woman. So yes, the thought occurred to me, but then . . ."

He looked at me like I might finish the thought for him, but I couldn't, Dana. Not anymore. I had no idea what my husband was thinking.

"Yes?"

Matt looked up to the ceiling, as if it might jump in and help. "But then I thought of another possibility." His eyes traveled back down to me. "Maybe this is some sort of transference thing."

I almost laughed. Almost. "Transference?"

"Maybe? I don't know."

"Transference. You think I've transferred my feelings for you to Morgan?"

"No!" He chopped the table with his hand, making our silverware jump. "I meant Dana, that maybe you're trying to replace Dana somehow."

Replace Dana. Was he fucking kidding me? I reached for my wineglass. "No one can replace Dana."

"I know that. I just think this friendship is moving a little quickly, is all. It seems . . . intense. And you know . . . you know how you can get, Cady."

I set the glass back down. "Yes, you and my mother are both very concerned about *my intensity,* aren't you?"

Matt looked confused, like he truly didn't remember his chat with Mom the night we decided to let William off the hook.

Maybe they had those sorts of chats often, if it wasn't all that memorable.

"I thought you loved that about me," I said, "that I don't do anything halfway. It's what I love most about *you,* you know. That intensity. I mean, who dropped out of Northwestern and transferred schools for who? Talk about intense."

Matt leaned back. He folded his arms across his chest. "I think that worked out pretty well for both of us, don't you?"

I met his smug stare across the table. "Maybe this will, too."

Matt's laugh was mean. "Are you kidding me? Look what it's doing to us. And to Eventually."

"Morgan isn't to blame for this," I said, gesturing between the two of us. "And Eventually is doing just fine."

And it was. Kind of. I mean, Eventually wasn't what it was a year ago, or even four months ago, but the problems—no new jobs coming in, hardly any staff left—balanced out. No events was no problem, because I didn't have the staff to pull them off anyway. So Eventually wasn't doomed or dead. Just . . . paused.

"Is it?" Matt reached into his back pocket and pulled out his phone.

My stomach turned.

"Let's see," he said, flicking his thumbs over the screen. "Q1 was profitable, and so was Q2—just barely—but you're down in Q3, with a few days left in the quarter and only Nora's black-and-white ball on the slate—and you're projected to completely bomb Q4, which is mind-blowing." Matt double tapped something, shaking his head. "With all the holiday and New Year's parties, your projections usually look like a toy company's— most of your annual revenue comes from the last couple months—"

"I know where I make my money, thank you."

"Well, did you know you're not going to make *any* money in December? Or November, or October? How is it possible you don't have a single event booked for the fourth quarter, Cady?"

I frowned. "It's *not* possible. I got deposits for at least two holiday parties way back in January. And the Novaks have a standing contract for New Year's Eve, and—"

"Looks like those events have been canceled." Matt turned his phone around to face me.

On the screen: Eventually's internal revenue forecast.

"Jamie sent you this?" My voice was calm, quiet. I was not angry, not yet. It was more like a falling-down sort of feeling.

"Don't go blaming her, Cady. Someone needs to do something. *Someone* needs to care about Eventually. Jamie said word of mouth has clients dropping like flies, and no one is trained to bring in new ones, and your staff—"

"Okay, fine," I snapped, holding up my hands. "I'll hire someone to step in, a consultant or project manager or someth—"

"A project manager? Are you kidding me, Cady?" Matt laughed in disbelief. "You can't replace *you*. You're the brand, that's what you always say." He shoved a hand through his hair. "You can bring someone in to push paper around and check things off a list, but what about the important stuff? The vision and creativity? Besides, you need to stay busy, Cady. You need something to focus on. Something healthy. And how are you going to pay this person? You've got no—"

"Okay, *okay*," I cried, pushing away the phone he was still holding up like murder evidence.

"No! It's not okay." Matt gestured wildly at his screen. "None of this is okay! You had something great here, Cady, and you just let it go."

"Are we still talking about Eventually?" I asked quietly.

Matt dropped the hand holding the phone. "You always do this."

"What?"

"Turn one thing into something else, so you don't have to face the real problem."

I laughed. The real problem? Matt didn't have a clue.

"Enlighten me," I taunted him. "What's the *real* problem, Matt?"

He shook his head and looked away, behind me. "You already know."

"Tell me."

"I'm not going to say it." He clasped his hands together and pressed them against his mouth, like that might help keep the words in.

"*Say it*," I demanded.

"No fucking way. I'm not stupid. It'll set you off."

I laughed, the sound feral. "Oh, I'm already *off*, Matt, don't worry about that."

He didn't respond. Just kept doing his closed-mouth praying thing with those faraway eyes.

"Fucking say it!" I screamed.

He didn't move, save for his leg, which was bouncing furiously under the table.

I leaned across the table, until I was right in his face. It thrilled and terrified me to test him like that. He'd never once touched me in anger, but that night I felt like I was putting my face right up against a snarling dog's.

"I'm not letting you go until you tell me," I hissed. "Stop starting shit you're too scared to finish, you giant fucking *coward*. What are you scared of? Me? Is it *me*? Are you scared of your little wife, Matt? Is that it? Do you—"

"Yes! *Yes*, goddammit. It's you, Cady. You. You fucking scare me."

Finally.

Finally.

Matt's clasped hands were tightly wound balls now. He'd stopped shaking his leg, like all the pent-up energy had shot up from there and out his mouth.

"The real problem," he said tightly, "the only problem, ever, is your goddamn . . . *obsessions*."

"With Morgan."

"Yes. Today it's Morgan. Sometimes it was Dana, sometimes me. It doesn't matter who, Cady, you just . . . this is why you need to pay attention to Eventually and get back to your old life. You were doing good. When you had Eventually to throw yourself into, you were better. Less . . ."

"Obsessed?" I supplied mockingly.

"Sick," Matt corrected.

I think I'd done a pretty good job of staying calm up until then. Don't you agree, Dana?

I took a real deep breath. "Sick," I said.

"Yes," Matt said. "*Yes*. It's a fucking sickness, Cady, and you need to take it seriously. You need to wake the fuck up."

I jumped up from my chair. Done. *Done*, Dana.

"I would love to wake up from this fucking nightmare, Matt!" I kicked back, hard, sending the chair toppling down behind me. "But I can't. I've tried—I've tried so, so hard—but I *can't*."

I threw my napkin over the tacos I hadn't touched and fled.

Matt didn't try to stop me.

Upstairs in our bedroom, I slammed the door and threw myself onto our bed.

Was this how a marriage ended? Was this what it looked like? Secret phone calls and dead babies and bad financial reports thrown in each other's faces?

And *replace you*, Dana? Did Matt not, after all these years, fully grasp what you were to me? If he didn't get that—if he didn't get *you and me*—he didn't get *me*.

I jolted up, scared that maybe it was true, that Matt had fallen in love with and transferred schools for and proposed to and married a girl he was dead wrong about.

My phone pinged from the dresser, as if asking timidly if it could interrupt.

I got up to get it, then remembered mine was downstairs. This was Matt's phone.

I walked over to where it sat on the dresser, charging in its dock. And I watched helplessly, Dana, as my hands picked up the phone. As my thumbs darted over the screen, tapping out the numbers, our wedding anniversary.

The passcode screen was sucked away, and there, overlaying my and Matt's smiling, tanned faces and the sandy beach behind us, was the new message.

I shouldn't have been doing this. I'd been down this road before, gotten drawn in and eaten up by all the horrible possibilities. It wasn't going to help my marriage. Wasn't going to fix the broken trust or unearth anything good.

Not to mention, it was wrong. I shouldn't have been sneaking into my husband's phone.

Then Matt's guilty jump from earlier flashed in front of me. My lit-up phone screen on the counter behind him.

I could hear Mom in my ear, an echo from our childhood: *Two wrongs don't make a right, girls.*

But you know what, Dana? Neither do one right and one wrong.

I read the text. It was from Nick, head of Matt's on-staff counsel, his most senior advisor. Let's talk in the morning. I'll send a meeting invite.

Just work stuff. I poised my thumb to exit the message and mark it as unread, but a single word caught my eye.

Jail.

My eyes dashed around the screen, reading the whole message, then the one above it, and the one above that. There were only five or six, but the first one seemed to pick up midway through a conversation, as if the ones before it had been deleted.

I reread them again, in the right order this time, starting with Nick's.

> I don't know. Hard to say right now, but it's not looking good, buddy.
>
> **Unreal. I know I fucked up, but I thought this was a sure thing.**
>
> I was sure it would pay off. I knew the guy.
>
> Careful what you text.
>
> **Shit, Nick. Could I really go to jail for this?**
>
> Let's talk in the morning. I'll send a meeting invite.

Oh, Matt.

Matt, Matt, Matt.

What had my husband gotten himself into, Dana?

And jail? Really? Matt? The guy who once drove all the way back to Whole Foods when he discovered he'd only been charged for one of the two avocados he'd brought home? That Matt, going to jail?

It couldn't be.

I couldn't lose Matt.

And what about his business? If he'd gotten involved in some sort of bad investment, what did that mean for MLG? And us? Our house? Could we lose everything?

The walls of our bedroom felt like they were closing in on me as I pictured the losses lined up like dominos, each one tipping the next over with no way of stopping the chain. The baby, you, my marriage, my business, Matt's business, the house . . .

What had Matt done? What had *we* done?

I stared down at the phone, at the little thumbnail icons on his screen. Gmail. Safari. Photos. Maps. Phone.

If Matt wasn't going to play by the rules, Dana, then neither would I.

I opened his call log. Lots of calls with Nick lately. Some other work names I recognized. A whole bunch of numbers with no names attached. I flicked up, up, up, past today's calls, this week's, last week's. I kept going until I was out of August, then past July. June 30, 29, 28, 27, back, back, back, until I was there. That horrible day that hadn't started out too badly. June 17.

There were several calls, mostly from Matt's staff, a couple with a client, one to me, one with the microchip place, another to the vet. Nothing suspicious, nothing off.

But that didn't prove anything, Dana. Just like Matt not replying to my fake Facebook account back in high school didn't prove anything. My husband had been too smart to reply to an obvious catfish then, and he was too smart to keep the evidence of that mysterious late-night call on his phone now.

I checked his photos. Mostly buildings, in various stages of construction or renovation. A handful of pics from our travels, a couple screenshots of some speakers he wanted to buy for the living room.

Email. There were tons. Did he not use folders? Or the trash button? I scanned quickly, but I'd never get through them all; I wasn't even sure what I was looking for, Dana.

Not much in his texts, either. Just dry business logistics, a bunch of those identity verification texts, a long chat history with me, another with his mother, a tasteless meme from his brother, weather alerts, election spam, group chats with friends swapping craft beer recommendations . . .

I closed the texts and opened Safari.

Geez. He had a staggering 106 tabs open. A list of upcoming shows at the Vic, a Home Depot product search for belt sanders, running shoes research, an article from *The Wall Street Journal,* an editorial from *The Trib,* some speaker shopping, a Google search for *dua lipa houdini lyrics,* another for *Cubs game schedule,* another for—

Oh.

Oh, Dana.

A Google search for *morgan keller illinois.*

Next tab: *morgan keller illinois phone number email.*

No. No, no, no.

This was not good.

A search for Morgan? He wanted to *contact* her? For what? *For what?*

I jumped back to his call log, looking for Morgan's number. I didn't have it memorized, but I did remember it had a 708 area code and that it ended with 23, Dad's birthday.

There was nothing with that combination.

I jumped back to his email and searched for *morgan keller,* then just *morgan,* then just *keller.*

Nothing. Thank God. Maybe he'd been unable to find her. Or maybe he'd found her contact info, but decided not to use it. Maybe it was just in case, or he was still thinking about it.

But thinking about what? Calling her and . . . what? Why did Matt want to talk to Morgan? To warn her? Save her? To prove she was real? Jesus. Did he *really* not believe she was real?

I would have to do something about this, Dana.

And I would have to keep closer tabs on Matt.

I didn't want to, but what choice had he left me?

My thumbs moved again, exiting out of the call log, opening the Find My app, tapping People, then Start Sharing Location. Then they were typing C-A-D-Y. They selected my name when the option popped up, and then . . . and then they stopped. One thumb hovered over the confirmation.

Did I really want to start doing this, Dana?

Then again, just because I enabled location sharing didn't mean I'd *actually* track my husband. Maybe I would turn it on and never, ever use it. Maybe I'd turn it on, and one day he'd get in a bike accident or get mugged and left for dead in the woods, and this would be the thing that saved him.

A gentle knock came from the other side of the door. I flinched, turned off the phone, and placed it back on the charger.

But not before I hit that confirmation.

43

I had an idea, Dana: We would have Morgan over for dinner. Matt would see that she existed, and that I was not, in fact, in love with her. That she was, in fact, great. If he just met her, he would understand—and stop worrying. And I could keep going about my fucking plan.

I chose a Friday night. Our Fridays were conspicuously, painfully open now. Having a guest over would be a step back toward the old way— Friday night plans!

Morgan was hesitant.

"I don't want to intrude."

"Please," I begged. "I really want you to meet Matt. I *swear* we won't argue, not in front of you. Or talk about group. Or—"

"It's got nothing to do with your marriage—or Christopher or grief group or anything like that. I just . . . well, I'll feel like a third wheel, Cady."

"Oh." I thought of Ben, how he'd suggested again that "we" get together for "coffee or something" soon. "Do you want me to set you up with someone?"

Morgan burst out laughing. "What? No. God no."

No . . . no, she was right. This wasn't the time.

"I promise you, Morgan, you will not feel like a third wheel. Matt and I are . . . look, give it ten minutes, and I swear you'll feel like you're having a casual night in with old friends."

"Am I getting a taste of that old relentlessness?" she teased. We'd begun sharing more and more of our old lives—what they'd been like, who we'd been before we'd become the twinless twin and the childless mother.

Morgan finally relented, so I told Matt to drop whatever he was doing that Friday. He made out like he was greatly inconvenienced, placing loud, apologetic phone calls to Richard Branson (*Sorry, chap, have to scrap that business meeting*) and Megan Fox (*Terribly sorry about dinner, love . . . some other time maybe*). It was classic Matt, further evidence that this dinner was a brilliant idea. We were playing again, like we used to.

The only thing dirtying my spirits that night was the knowledge of those messages on Matt's phone and my inability to do anything about it. If I confronted him, he'd change his password, start deleting things, maybe even discover that I'd shared his phone's location with my own.

Finding out Matt's secrets would have to wait, but it was good to know he had them too, good to know my instincts had not been off, that I was not delusional . . .

Morgan showed up right on time, just like she did for coffee and group and work. She was wearing her black work pants, but also gold hoops and a little brown eyeliner, neither of which I'd seen her wear before. I went in for a hug just as she bent to slip off her shoes. I waited awkwardly, Matt coming to stand by my side, as she finished.

The vibe was my fault—a product of my great expectations, that this evening was going to solve so many problems. Matt would cease whatever outreach he'd planned on his own; he would end up loving her and she would love us; it would turn into a weekly thing and one day, when she was happily ensconced in a stable, loving relationship with Ben, we'd set *two* extra places at the table on Friday nights.

Morgan finished removing her shoes and stood up again, and Matt stuck out his hand. "Matt. Nice to meet you. I've heard a lot about you."

I had to widen my eyes to stop them from rolling. So formal.

Morgan smiled and let him take her hand. "Morgan, and likewise—on both counts."

In the kitchen, I instructed Alexa to play my *Making Dinner* playlist (or rather, my *Watching Matt Make Dinner* playlist).

As I pulled out wineglasses, Matt picked up the conversation. We got the usual out of the way—*What do you do? Oh really? My cousin's into something like that*—and then we graduated to what good shows we'd seen recently, which got us on the topic of *House of Cards*, which led to a short-lived politics discussion, which somehow evolved into a debate on the regulation of the organic food industry, which reminded Matt of the vegan cosmetics store going in downtown—had we heard about that?—and things finally started to feel right. The ice was melted, the wine was flowing, the Antonio's takeout was warming in the oven, and Matt and I were entertaining—bantering and laughing and topping off drinks—just like we used to.

I dished out lobster tagliatelle and clam risotto, and Morgan complimented the rigatoni arrabbiata, and I admitted it was all from a restaurant.

Then, halfway through seconds, Matt said, gently, "So Morgan, tell me about your son. Cady said he was twelve?"

I fired him A Look. *What* was he doing? Had he been waiting this whole time to say that? To ruin everything? Was that *his* plan, Dana? To hurt Morgan, to save me from her? Or her from me?

But Morgan was not upset. She was relieved. Of course. There was no use pretending I'd met Morgan at a spin class or an event planner's convention, or that her son wasn't dead and that you hadn't been killed and that we hadn't bonded over our struggle to survive these things.

"Thank you." Morgan looked Matt straight in the eyes. "Really, thank you. Everyone thinks I want to pretend it never happened, that Christopher didn't die—it's easier for them that way, or maybe they think it's easier for me, I don't know—but the truth is, I don't want to sweep my son under the rug. Or his death."

"No healing in avoidance," I said with a smile.

Morgan smiled back. "Good old Moira."

"It's good advice," Matt said, nodding. "I'm always telling my team to face the hard things head-on—it's the best way."

Morgan and I exchanged a swift, knowing glance. "There's no wrong way!"

Our perfect jinx, aided by several glasses of wine at that point, sent us into a fit of giggles. Matt was clearly confused, but neither of us elaborated, which deepened that furrow in his brow, which increased the humor Morgan and I found in the whole thing.

I took another sip of my wine to stop laughing or else I'd get hiccups. Morgan's face sobered up a bit.

"Seriously, though. People don't get it. They don't know what to do with themselves around someone like me. Work was the worst. A couple of people said *I'm so sorry* on my first day back and then nothing." She frowned, then shot me a teasing look. "Maybe I should take Cady up on that job offer, after all."

Matt's eyes shot my way, but I kept mine pointed at Morgan.

"Seriously, though," she said, waving her hand. "My job's fine. It could be worse. I just . . . I mean, I don't want to talk about Christopher every waking minute, but it would be nice, now and then, to have someone ask, that's all. That's why I love our coffee dates," she added, smiling in my direction.

Matt finally shifted his gaze away from me. "I can only imagine how hard it's been for you," he told Morgan. "How long ago . . ."

"Christopher died on Valentine's Day."

Oh shit.

"Valentine's Day?" Matt frowned as he searched his memory for the nonexistent time I'd told him about this startling coincidence.

"I know, it's extra tragic, isn't it?" Morgan said drily. "Did you know some people have actually said to me, 'Oh, and on Valentine's Day, too'—as if the real tragedy isn't my twelve-year-old son's death, but the fact that it ruined February fourteenth for me." She rolled her eyes and gave Matt a sardonic smile.

Matt snorted. "Yeah, we know how that goes, don't we?" He shot me a meaningful look.

Morgan's smile fell into a frown. "What do you mean?"

"Just that we've gotten the same sort of comments," Matt explained. "About Dana's accident happening on Valentine's Day—like it might have been more bearable if it'd just happened the next day." He shook his head like *People, am I right?*

"I didn't know your sister died on Valentine's Day," Morgan said, looking at me funny.

"You didn't?"

"You never mentioned it," she said slowly, as if trying to figure out what, if anything, that meant.

Matt looked back and forth between us.

"Hmm," I said. "I thought I did. Maybe it was at the session you missed."

"Maybe," Morgan said.

"Small world," Matt said.

44

I've always loved fall, Dana, but I would have loved it a whole lot more if all the best parts—the cracker-crisp air and the changing colors—didn't foretell all that cold and dark waiting around the corner.

After I closed the door behind Morgan that night, Matt wrapped his arms around me from behind and rested his chin on top of my head.

"That went well," I said.

I did not fully trust yet that the night had gone as I'd intended.

"It did." Matt's arms tightened around me. "Morgan's great. I'm glad you found her."

Found. A more fitting word than he knew, because I had looked for Morgan, Dana. I'd looked for her, and then I'd found her, and then I'd watched and waited, very patiently.

"I don't like that you offered her a job."

I tried to turn around, but Matt tightened his arms around me.

"Why?" I whispered. "Too much? Too *intense* for you?"

"I'm not joking, Cady."

Any other night, I would have bitten back. But I didn't want another fight. There'd been a tiny spark of the old magic alive that night—we'd been *us*—and I was buzzed from the wine and intoxicated by my victory. I wanted more of it; I didn't want it to wash away in our sleep, and I didn't want it ruined because of a fucking job offer Morgan was never going to take anyway.

"You love me this way," I whispered. I pressed my lower body tightly against his. "You love that I scare you."

Matt spun me around and I seared him with an old look I hadn't given him in a long time. I was surprised I remembered how to extend an invitation with my eyes like that.

Matt had no trouble recalling the look or deciphering it. A smirk stretched across his face that he couldn't stifle—it had been ages.

I was nervous—*nervous, Dana*—as my husband led me up the stairs. When you go seven months without, you are acutely aware that it's been that long. But we had no trouble coming together that night. It was—oh relax, Dana, I'm not going to get into the particulars. Suffice it to say, not everything was lost on February 14.

By the next morning, the wine's magic had dissipated into a dull ache. I hardly minded. Our morning kiss over our coffee mugs was reinstated, and there'd been one before that, when Matt had leaned over to put his lips on my forehead before rolling out of bed.

At breakfast, he tossed me interesting tidbits from the paper and shared his opinion (not good) of the day's op-ed. We went to the arboretum after lunch and spent the whole afternoon walking its familiar trails. That night we ordered pizza and ate in front of the TV. We watched a movie. I put my head on his shoulder, he put his arm around me. We were light. We were easy. We were good.

I began taking walks around the neighborhood again. The first time, my fist clenched around the nothing where Champ's leash used to be, but eventually that habit died. I still looked for him, though, when I was out. Nothing—no one—just disappeared. There was always a reason—a gun, a disease, a blocked artery, a car driving too fast, a driver not paying enough attention—always a reason.

I tried not to think like that, though. I tried to focus on the good, on enjoying the rest of September before it was gone.

I started wearing mascara again. I spent longer, more productive days in the office. I posted a job opening on LinkedIn. I figured out our payroll software and caught up on Jamie's paychecks, even gave her a bonus and promised her I'd show up for Nora Donnelly's black-and-white ball.

I put Champ's food bowls and bed in the attic. Fall descended. The summer heat receded. Neighbors began wearing jackets on their walks, flowers disappeared from yards, the leaves on the trees turned the color of flames. There was so much orange. I took a new picture every day. I sent them to Morgan. She loved every one.

I was good—or at least okay. Less edgy, more content. I daresay I was even sneaking up on *hopeful,* Dana.

But I had forgotten.

I had completely forgotten that fall was summer's parting gift, a consolation for what was in store.

45

I had a surprise for Morgan. Two, actually.

I told her over text.

I hate surprises, she texted back almost immediately.

You'll love this one, I sent back.

Doubt it.

Just trust me, I pleaded. Come over tomorrow after work. Matt has a late meeting, so we'll have the house to ourselves.

Why do we have to do whatever this is when Matt's not around?

What are we doing???

Cady???

Fine. I'll be there.

But I really, really, really hate surprises.

"I hate surprises," Morgan said when I opened the door the next night.

I gasped and pressed my hand to my chest. "Why didn't you *say* something?" I said. "I had no idea."

Her smile was dry. "Ha ha."

I hung Morgan's jacket on the coat-tree in the foyer, and she removed her knockoff Rothy's and followed me to the kitchen where I poured us each a glass of champagne.

She arched an eyebrow as she took the flute I offered. "What's the occasion?"

"You." I raised my glass up. "To friends."

She tapped her glass against mine and took a little sip. "So," she said, "are you going to put me out of my misery and tell me what this surprise is?"

I shrugged. "Just a regular old-fashioned girls' night."

Morgan rolled her eyes. "You couldn't have just said that in your message?"

"Nope," I said, smirking over the rim of my glass. "Because you would have kept pressing, wanting to know all the little details, and if I'd told you we were doing a makeover, you would have never agreed to come."

Morgan groaned. "A makeover?"

"Yep," I said, grinning. "It'll be fun."

Morgan looked over my shoulder at her reflection in the big mirror hanging on the wall between the kitchen and the mudroom. She rubbed at a little spot of mascara that had smudged under one eye. "Do I really look that bad?"

"What? No!" I set my glass down on the counter. "You're gorgeous. I just wanted to have a little silly, girly fun. Dana and I used to do this all the time when we were kids. Right up through college even."

Morgan hesitated. She took a big, long swig from her glass. "All right, fine."

I'd take a pity *yes,* even though I hadn't meant to play that card.

I grabbed the neck of the champagne bottle in the same hand as my empty glass, then took Morgan's free hand with mine before she could change her mind. I led her up to the *hers* side of the master bathroom, where I had a big built-in vanity with a giant LED ring light and drawers full of high-end cosmetics.

"This is legit," Morgan said, impressed.

"Sit down," I instructed.

"Yes, ma'am." She pulled out the custom upholstered stool and took a seat.

I set my glass down on the counter and started pulling things out of cabinets. "Hair first," I said, grabbing a bottle of dry shampoo and a blow-dryer.

"Oh," Morgan said. "I don't know if you've noticed"—she flicked her thin, straight strands behind her shoulder—"but the good Lord gave me straw for hair. It doesn't style for shit."

"I'll make it," I said, plugging the dryer in.

Morgan shrugged. She leaned back against the stool and took another sip from her glass. "Do you use all this stuff every day?" she asked, examining everything I'd lined up on the vanity.

"Rarely, these days," I said. "But before . . . back in the day, yeah."

Morgan continued to eye it all as I picked up a round nylon brush and the blow-dryer. "I usually prefer a more natural look," she said.

"Relax. You'll look very natural—an enhanced version of yourself." I maneuvered the brush under a band of her hair. "It takes a lot of makeup to look like you're not wearing any."

I flipped the dryer on before she could raise any more objections, taking my time to add volume at her roots and give those straight, dirty-blonde threads a little shape. When I was finished, she smiled.

"Wow," she said, fingering the delicate waves gently, as if they might pop and deflate. She turned her head from side to side. "It's like you gave me a facelift. I look a decade younger."

Slight exaggeration. But it was a major improvement.

"And I haven't even done your makeup yet," I said, leaning over to grab the primer I'd set out. "Now, I want you to turn around all the way and face me. No peeking until I'm done."

Morgan did as instructed. "I'm a little nervous," she said.

I rolled my eyes. "It washes off, you know."

Quickly, expertly, I applied a light coat of foundation to even out her slightly patchy skin tone. Bronzer on her cheekbones and the tip of her nose, a bit at the top of her forehead. A few swipes of highlighter and contour to enhance her already graceful nose. Some brow filler. A light sweep of coral blush, a tiny black wing of eyeliner, a taupey-mauve swipe of eye shadow, two coats of my favorite Lancôme volumizing mascara in blackest black.

I explained everything as I went along, hoping Morgan would try to keep it up, at least for special occasions. Ben was getting more and more persistent about bringing their relationship offline, and I was feeling less and less inclined to put him off.

"And now for the grand finale," I said, untwisting a lipstick. I applied it in three deft strokes to her already lined lips and stepped back to admire my work.

"You are going to freak," I said smugly.

Morgan's new thicker eyebrows lifted skeptically. "In a bad way, or a good way?"

"You tell me," I said, gesturing at the mirror behind her.

She spun around on her stool, to face the mirror. For a half second, she looked scared, like maybe she didn't recognize herself. Then her jaw dropped, almost theatrically, parting her rose-pink Dior lips. She moved her head slowly in circles, taking in every angle.

"Well?" I asked.

"It's amazing," she said, still checking out the sides. "I can't believe how natural it looks. You kept piling more and more stuff on; I thought for sure I'd look like a clown. But I don't. I look . . . I look *good*."

I grinned. "Told you." I tossed the lipstick onto the vanity and poured us each another glass of bubbles. "Still you, just a spiffier, shinier version of you."

I sipped my champagne as Morgan continued to stare at her reflection.

"Actually," she said, leaning back to get the full effect, "I look like you."

Another sip. "Well," I said, "you are wearing my makeup."

Morgan squinted at herself. "It's not just that . . . the hair, too . . . altogether, it's so . . . wow, dye my hair brown, and I could be your twin, Cady."

We both froze.

Morgan's face bloomed dark red under her foundation and bronzer.

A sick, sinking weight filled my stomach, but something else was soaring in my chest.

"You're right," I said brightly, pretending I hadn't made any sort of connection with her words. "Oh, and that reminds me! I've got one more surprise. Hold on, I'll be right back."

Morgan looked wary as I ran out of the bathroom to my closet, reappearing a half minute later with a bright orange box. I held it out, but she didn't take it.

"Cady." Her mouth hung open again, but not like last time. Not in awe, but something else.

"I can't . . ." she started.

"Yes, you can," I said, rolling my eyes. "Come on, open it. If we're going to be twinsies, we need to go all the way, right?"

Morgan's eyes widened. "It's too much."

"Relax, okay? It's not a Birkin. You can't just walk into the store and get those." I sighed. "This is just a little something, I promise."

I thrust the box toward her, but she backed away, holding her hands up like I was trying to get her to take a handgun or a bag of coke or something.

"I couldn't accept a *handkerchief* from there," Morgan said, pointing at the logo. "Or even a key chain. It's way too much . . . it's too . . ."

I tried to laugh off her protests, but I was starting to get pissed, Dana. And hurt. I get that some people are awkward at accepting gifts, but this was ridiculous.

"Here," I said, setting the box down on the counter between us. "I'll do it, and you'll see it's not such a big deal . . ."

I lifted the lid with both hands, waiting impatiently as it slowly separated from its snug grip on the bottom. I unfolded the layers of white tissue, revealing the orange flannel dust bag.

All the while, Morgan stared, speechless.

I sighed and picked up the bag, tugging at the drawstring. I'd pictured this differently. A different kind of tears shining in her eyes. Less serious protests, all offered while simultaneously tearing through the tissue.

I reached inside and pulled out a medium-sized leather bag. Nothing too extravagant. Just a little something to replace that beat-up Aldo tote. Thoughtful. Practical. Functional.

"And look," I said, pulling the mouth open and pointing inside, "it's lined in orange."

I held it out again, desperately willing Morgan to take it. She pressed a hand to her mouth instead, smothering a cry. I honestly couldn't tell if she was touched or horrified or just stunned by the abrupt reminder of her son, his color.

She began to shake her head and back away, as if I'd said, *Look, it's lined with human skin.*

"I cannot accept that," she repeated.

"Yes, you can," I insisted, still holding it out. "Really, Morgan, it's no—"

"*I don't fucking want it, Cady.*"

I dropped my arm, my heart sinking as low as the bag. *How, how, how* had I misjudged this so badly?

"Okay," I conceded. "I'm sorry. I didn't mean to insult you or anything." I implored her with my eyes, tried to push my feelings up there, so she could see how true every word was. "I honestly thought you would . . . but you didn't . . . and I'm sorry. Really, Morgan, you—"

"It's okay," Morgan said, but it wasn't. I could hear and see something changing, slipping away, and it made the blood in my head hammer faster and harder. I could *feel* the frantic desperation, rising up in me like an actual sickness, like Matt had said. I ached to grab her, to stop her from the exit I knew she was contemplating; I clenched my fists around the stupid bag's straps to stop myself.

Morgan's eyes moved toward the door. Here it came. Just like I'd said, Dana.

She let out a deep breath. "It's getting late. I should get go—"

"No," I begged. "Please don't go. We were having so much fun, before. Look," I said, stuffing the bag back in the duster, "I'll put it away and we'll forget all about it. We can watch a movie or just crack open another—"

"I just don't feel right," Morgan said, putting a hand on her stomach.

"Is it the champagne?" I asked, pretending I didn't goddamn well know it wasn't. "I bet it's the champagne. We should have eaten something, I'm sorry I didn't think of it earlier. Let's order some—"

"No, Cady, please," she said, reaching out her hands. "Please, I just want to go home. Please."

She sounded like a child, Dana. A child, scared at her first sleepover, begging her friend's parents to please just call her mom to pick her up and take her home.

I couldn't make her stay. Not without hurting her, and I didn't want to do that. Ever.

She made as if to help clean up the mess on the vanity, but I told her not to worry about it; I'd do it later, I had nothing else to do tonight. She nodded, not looking the least bit sorry about that last part.

Downstairs, at the door, she slipped her fake Rothy's back on, then shoved her arms into her jacket. When I gave her a hug, she returned it, but she bristled and pulled away too soon.

I forced a smile as she left, willed my voice to sound casual as I said I'd see her Sunday for coffee—"Same time, same place!" I knew from her brief hesitation there would be no Sunday coffee.

She walked stiffly to her car, trying to downplay her urgency.

I stood on the stoop, watching the taillights of her Honda disappear down my street, and when they were gone, I had to swallow down the cry rising up in my throat.

This had not gone as I'd planned.

Obviously.

But that was okay, Dana.

I'd offered Morgan a gift and it was too much—too expensive or whatever—and things had gotten awkward and she'd wanted to leave. So what?

Right?

This was fixable.

It would die down.

She would cool off.

Setbacks were inevitable.

And that's all this was, a little setback.

This wasn't over.

I wasn't a quitter.

I would make it up to Morgan.

And next time, I would get it right.

46

Friday night, end of September, end of dinner. Matt smiled at me from across the table.

"Movie tonight?"

My heart leapt, then sank. I wanted nothing more than the exquisite normalcy of a movie night with Matt, but I'd promised Ben we'd talk. We had to talk. I needed him to help me fix things with Morgan. I'd texted her another apology, and she'd responded, *It's OK,* but that was it, no other reassurances, no smiley or heart emojis.

Plus, it took her half the day to send those two words. So obviously, *it was not OK.*

Matt stood up. "It was just a suggestion." He grabbed my plate and stacked it on top of his as he made his way to the sink.

"No," I said quickly. "I do want to watch a movie. I was just trying to remember the name of this one I saw a trailer for the other day. I thought you might like it."

"Okay, well, why don't you try to find it while I clean up the dishes?"

In the living room, I waited to hear the distant clinks and clanks of forks and plates being loaded into the dishwasher, then I unlocked my phone and fired off a message to Ben.

Last-minute plans with a friend tonight. So sorry—was looking forward to our chat, but she's going through some shit and needs a friend right now . . .

sigh *heart literally cracks open and spills blood onto the couch* Ben wrote.

I know, I'm so sorry. I'm a jerk.

No, you're not. You're a good friend. I'm just giving you a hard
time.

Maybe tomorrow night? I suggested.

I'm supposed to meet up with some friends. I skipped out last
time so . . .

Don't skip it, I wrote back. Sunday then?
"What is this?"
Oh my God, Dana, I jumped halfway off the couch.
Matt didn't notice. He was too busy waiting for an answer to his ques-
tion, which must have had something to do with whatever was on his
phone screen, because he was holding it up like it was a warrant for my
arrest.
Oh God, now what? An updated revenue forecast from Jamie?
"What is what?" I asked, squinting.
His answer was to hand me his phone. I looked down at the screen.
Our American Express transaction history. Shit. Since when—
"Six thousand dollars at Hermès, Cady?" Matt tapped the sides of his
head, miming what was supposed to be a brain explosion, I guess.
"Since when do you monitor the Amex?" I retorted. I was the one who
paid all our bills. As far as I knew, he didn't even know how to log in to
our account. We'd decided long ago that I'd be our household accoun-
tant and he'd be our wealth manager/investor.
Matt grabbed his phone back. "Since we became a single-income
household with a tanking business rocketing down on us," he snapped.
"And when the hell did you go downtown? You don't have the time or energy to make money, but you've got the time and energy to go spend it?"
My mind spun. I didn't want this to come between us. We'd turned
a corner that night Morgan came to dinner. We were back, or coming
back. And this whole thing with Ben, to help Morgan fill that hole she'd
complained about . . . it made me realize I was lonely, too, Dana. Missing something. Something I'd once wanted so badly and now, suddenly,
more so. I didn't want to think about why, about what sick, twisted

meaning might lie behind it, but I wanted us to try again. For our baby. I still wanted us to have that family we'd dreamed about.

"Please," I begged Matt, "let's not fight, okay? You're right. I shouldn't have spent that kind of money . . . I was just trying to fill a void, I guess. Retail therapy or whatever."

Matt's face relaxed slightly. Kind of hard to be mad at someone when they're just trying to get over a tragedy. He still wasn't thrilled about six g's down the drain though.

"Come on," I said, forcing my lips into the shape of a smile, "let's go fire up that movie."

Matt looked down at his phone, thinking way too hard and way too long. I wasn't surprised when he finally shook his head and made some sort of excuse about work calls.

More work calls. Right.

With Nick? I was tempted to ask.

But no, I couldn't give myself away, Dana.

I smiled tightly and said I'd just be upstairs then, reading on my phone or something.

I was already in my pajamas, had been all day, so I climbed into bed and unlocked my phone.

Ben had written back. I blinked my tears away to read his message.

Sunday it is. I'll be counting down the hours.

Awww, I sent back.

The dot-dot-dots began their dance immediately; he must have been waiting for me. Morgan, I mean.

Seriously, he replied. Might make myself one of those paper advent chains and tear a link off every hour until we can talk again.

Ha. An advent chain? What am I, your early Christmas present?

Well . . . I would love to open you up . . .

My face, Dana—my entire body—burned.

That was a pretty bad line, I wrote.

I added the winking emoji to show him I didn't mind.

Sorry, he said. I can do better. How about . . . I can't wait to come down your chimney?

Getting colder . . .

Okay, wait . . . give me one more chance . . .

As I watched the screen and waited, I thought I heard the familiar squeak of the loose riser on the stairs.

I give up, Ben finally sent back. I tried but this isn't me. I'll understand if you want to leave me for someone who has their vulgar-Christmas-euphemisms game locked tight.

I bit back a laugh and started typing back.

I'll have to th—

"What's got you all smiley?"

Gah! Shit.

I gasped at Matt's voice, instinctively snatching my phone to my chest.

"Second time tonight. Maybe I should start wearing a bell or something."

So he had noticed earlier.

He tossed his phone on the dresser and made his way toward the bathroom. Then he stopped. He eyed the phone I was still clutching to my chest.

"What are you doing?" he asked.

"Nothing." I fumbled in my head for something better. *Nothing* was the world's most guilty response. *Nothing* was always something.

"Come on," Matt said, reaching playfully for my phone, "if something's managed to make you smile like that again, I need to know what it is. I could use some help over here."

His fingers closed over my phone.

"Don't," I cried, jerking away.

I swatted his hand without thinking, and he snatched it back like I'd burned him. His eyes flashed with anger.

"I'm sorry," I said quickly.

"What the hell is going on, Cady?"

"Nothing, I just . . . it's work stuff."

He stared me down for an unbearable minute to let me know he knew I was lying.

Then he turned back toward the bathroom without another word. This whole night was unraveling everything, every forward step we'd taken this last month.

I gave him a minute, then I joined him.

"Mind if I brush my teeth, too?" I asked.

He hesitated, then gestured toward my sink—*Be my guest.*

I opened the drawer with my nightly accoutrements—face wash, moisturizing oil, vitamins, toothbrush, toothpaste, floss—as he squeezed a pea-sized blob of Crest onto his toothbrush.

I began, as I did every night, with my vitamins. One fish oil and one vitamin D. There'd been one other, but I'd stopped taking the prescription prenatals after you died.

I glanced at the mirror as I reached for my water glass. Matt's head made a small jerk—he was watching me. I pretended not to notice and made my move, reaching in my drawer for the prenatals. I unscrewed the cap and placed one of the fat green pills next to the others, then filled my water glass, covertly watching Matt as I waited for him to recognize it.

I knew right when he did—his eyes widened slightly, and there was a brief but definite pause in the sawing of his toothbrush. He didn't say anything, but our eyes met in the mirror, and I smiled. A cautious question of a smile that asked, *Well? What do you think?*

He spat out his toothpaste and rinsed with water from his cupped hand—I never understood why he didn't keep a cup by the sink, Dana—then took his time wiping his mouth dry on a towel and hanging it back up over one of the brass hooks we'd spent days vetting.

Then, finally, he leaned one hip against the counter and pointed to the bottle. "You're still taking those."

I nodded.

"What does that mean?"

"It means . . ." What did it mean? Why had I done that? "I guess it means . . . I haven't given up."

That gave him pause.

"Do you want to try again?" he asked. "Is that what you're saying? Because Cady, I don't think now is—"

"I know. Not now, definitely not right now. But maybe one day soon . . ."

Matt looked back toward the pill, still sitting on the counter. "We shouldn't even be talking or thinking about this."

I picked up the pill and rolled it around in my hand. "Why not?"

"Seriously, Cady? Where do I begin?" He started ticking the reasons off on his fingers. "You're waist-deep in your grief over Dana, Eventually is flatlining, Champ's still missing. Then there's this whole thing with Morgan. Not to mention us; we're not exactly in the best place we've ever been. This is literally the *worst* possible time, Cady."

"You're right," I said. "We've lost so much, so quickly." I put the pill down and grabbed his hand, so he would look in my eyes and see how badly I wanted this. "But maybe that means it's the *perfect* time. To bring new life into the world, to help replace what's been lost."

Matt rubbed his forehead, like this was giving him a headache. I didn't blame him. It was a bad choice of words. He thought I wanted to replace *you*.

But we'd already been over how impossible that is.

We decided we'd talk about it another time. Tonight was not the night, we agreed on that much.

Matt left for bed. I washed and moisturized my face and brushed my teeth. And swallowed the green pill.

Matt was already under the covers when I climbed into bed, had already—presumably—done his little sigh, not that I couldn't guess what it sounded like that night.

His eyes were still open, but we didn't speak. I turned off the bedside light and pulled out my phone. There was a little click when I unlocked it.

His voice was quiet. "Who are you talking to, really?"

The air caught in my throat. I could insist it was Jamie. Or I could say it was Mom, but why would I have lied earlier about talking to Mom?

Maybe Sean; that would be unexpected. It might help explain why I'd been so weird about my phone earlier.

"Never mind," he muttered, flipping over so his back was to me. "I think I can guess."

He thought it was Morgan. I didn't correct him.

"Are you about done?" he asked over his shoulder. "You know how the light bothers me."

"I'll wrap it up," I said tightly.

Matt grunted.

I looked down at my phone. Three new messages were waiting.

> Since you're ditching me tonight, the least you could do is say yes to a date next Fri night.
> (That was a question btw.)
> ??????

I changed my answer four times before I finally sent my response.

Yes.

47

Guilt, like grief, has a funny way of making you feel more alone in a crowded room than sitting home alone on the couch or falling asleep in an empty bed. It's the contrast: Them, vibrating with life. You, not.

I went to Nora's annual black-and-white ball. It was the first event I'd been to since you'd died, Dana. The one I'd put off designing until I'd expended all Nora's patience and empathy toward my *situation* and had to deliver something fast.

In 1966, Truman Capote had hosted a "once-in-a-lifetime" black-and-white ball at the Plaza. It was the talk of high society, in part because it was so over-the-top lavish and exclusive—only the cream of the cream of the crop were invited. Perfect for Nora, whose latest voicemail had curtly noted that she was expecting, ASAP, *something for the ages.* I'd texted Jamie a link to an article on the party and, Think you can do something with this?

And she'd done it; she'd really delivered. She'd paid homage to the simple decadence of Capote's ball, then built on it, ensuring Nora Donnelly's event sat a notch above the infamous party of the century.

The ballroom was luxuriously moody. Tall, tapered white candles stuck up like pale fingers from large golden candelabras. Underneath them, red silk tablecloths. In the middle of the ballroom, a four-section jazz orchestra. At every turn, pyramids of Taittinger-filled coupe glasses.

And swimming through it all, a sea of jeweled and feathered masks and black tuxedos and snow-white gowns from another era. The guests had come through, serving as the evening's true décor.

One woman had recreated Candice Bergen's white mink bunny mask and strapless, fur-trimmed ball gown, and over there, that had to be Frank Sinatra and Mia Farrow. There was no mistaking Andy Warhol—that hair!—or Sammy Davis, Jr., singing "The Candy Man" to an unimpressed maharani.

I walked unobtrusively among them in a simple white shift dress and nondescript black mask, listening for any hushed tones of discontent that might signal a problem with the food or the service or the restrooms.

Near the end of my circuit, Nora approached me, leaving her husband—who, short of both sight and stature, required little effort to pull off Capote—to fend for himself against a garrulous and busty interpretation of Harper Lee. The woman was clutching a copy of *To Kill a Mockingbird* to her chest, neither of which—the book nor the chest—was terribly discreet.

Nora, of course, had come as *Washington Post* publisher Katharine Graham, the guest of honor at Capote's 1966 ball. I did not doubt for a second that her long white gown was Balmain, the designer Katharine had worn, nor that it had cost a small fortune to have those jet-black beads custom applied to so closely match the original.

"You're here," Nora murmured in that way she had, leaving you to deduce for yourself whether her words were ones of approval or censure.

"I wouldn't have missed it for the world."

Nora's eyebrows lifted. She sipped her champagne and said nothing, which meant she soon would; she was waiting for the right moment to strike.

I directed my gaze across the room. Harry Belafonte was whispering something in Lady Bird Johnson's ear.

"Jamie did a great job," I said, "didn't she?"

Nora stared ahead, surveying her domain, taking in the bouffant hairstyles and ostrich feathers bobbing over swirls of black wool and white silk.

"Do you have a favorite restaurant, Cady?"

Mmm, yes. Here it came, Dana.

"I suppose I have a few. Kind of hard to pick just one though, isn't it?"

Nora continued to gaze ahead. "Not at all. Au Vin on First Street, half a mile from my house. It has—*it had*—the best cassoulet. Better than I've found in Cannes or Saint-Tropez or even Paris."

"Oh."

"Yes, but then André, the chef, moved back home to Toulouse to set up house with some amateur vintner he met online, and a new chef came in—I don't even know his name, though I suppose I should ask, if for no other reason than to avoid eating at any future restaurants he deigns to ruin. Anyway, the whole place went *en aval.*"

"Oh. That's . . . a shame."

I really hoped Nora wasn't suggesting Jamie had ruined Eventually with this one event, an event that had turned out magnificently. Only in Nora's head could it have been better if I'd had more of my nose in it.

She sighed. "Eventually is just a name, Cady. I didn't hire Eventually. I hired you."

"I'm sorry, Nora. It's been a difficult year."

A hand squeezed mine, and though it was the only one around, the only one it could possibly be, I was still surprised to look down and discover that it was Nora's.

"I know," she said. "And I'm very sorry. But a difficult year can turn into a difficult five or ten years, or an entire life, if you don't give it a deadline."

Suddenly the hand was gone, and Nora was adjusting her sleeves. "I suppose that's enough free advice for the evening," she said. "You have work to do, and for that matter, so do I."

I considered grabbing Nora and hugging her, but before I could embarrass either of us, she was off, talking to a woman in an elaborate headdress with white feathers and a single large diamond dangling between her eyes.

I headed back to the empty conference room we were using as a command center and opened my dating app.

There was already a message waiting: Still on for next Friday, right?

Actually . . . I started to type.

I backspaced over that.

Y-e . . . no, that wasn't right, either.

I sent back the salsa dancing emoji.

Do you like dancing? Ben wrote back.

Does Kanye like Kanye? I started to type, but then I remembered he wasn't asking me. He was asking Morgan, and I had no idea if Morgan liked dancing.

> **Maybe—what about you?**
>
> Let's just say the way you danced around that question smokes my best move.

I laughed and sent back another salsa dancing girl. He sent back a disco dancing guy. In a moment of bold inspiration, I sent the kissing emoji.

My cheeks burned as the typing indicator on Ben's end of the conversation throbbed on the screen. He sent back a shocked face emoji. Then the same kissing one I'd sent, then the blushing one, then finally the one with heart eyes, one right after the other.

Then . . . Did we just have our first kiss?

I laughed out loud in the empty room.

> **Yes, and it was everything.**

I was bracketing the words with two heart eyes emojis when someone walked in. Jamie. She was holding a crystal mask missing a cluster of gems above one eye.

"Got a pair of tweezers?" She held out a fistful of sparkles. "The contessa's mask got trampled on the dance floor."

I shoved my phone shamefully into my purse and started digging around.

"I know I have a pair in here somewhere." I felt their sharp ends poke my fingers just as the venue manager strode into the room holding up a small bottle of superglue.

"You're a lifesaver," Jamie gushed to her.

I held the tweezers out. "You did it," I said, gesturing toward the doors. "Everything is perfect, Jamie. Like the original, but somehow better. And the guests, my God, those costumes . . ." I shook my head. "It's a miracle you didn't end up with a ballroom full of Sinatras and Bacalls, though."

Jamie laughed as she sat down at an empty table. "Ah," she said, "that was solved by the invitations." She used my tweezers to grab one of the tiny twinkling stones. "Each one was addressed to a specific individual or couple who'd appeared at the original ball. Dress code was, *Please come as you did in '66.*"

"That's brilliant," I told her.

She smiled as she applied a dot of glue to the mask, then lowered the tiny gem onto it. I lifted a tick-sized crystal off the table and held it out in my palm.

Jamie smiled. "Thanks, but you don't have to stay back here and help. You should be out there enjoying the spoils."

I snorted as she closed the tweezer's tips around the stone. "I was hardly enjoying myself."

Jamie's face fell.

"I'm sorry, Jamie, I didn't mean . . . the event is great. It's amazing, in fact. You really saved my ass. It's just . . . I have other things on my mind tonight."

Jamie paused, then nodded. "I know. I was surprised you came, actually. I mean, I know you said you would, but . . ."

Her voice trailed off as she concentrated on placing a tiny drop of clear glue onto the stone.

"But I've been messing everything else up, and you thought I'd drop this ball, too?"

She looked up, horrified. "No, Cady, I—"

"Relax," I said, laughing gently. "I *have* dropped the ball lately—a lot— and you've been there to pick it up for me every time."

Jamie's face relaxed. She laid the tiny gem perfectly in place between two others.

"There is something I've been meaning to talk to you about, though, Jamie."

She didn't look up as she reached for another stone. "What's that?"

"Well, I think it should go without saying, but I don't want you to talk to my husband anymore."

Jamie stilled, halting the descent of the next crystal. She turned, still bent over the mask, to meet my eyes.

"I'm sorry, Cady. I didn't want to, but I . . . I didn't know what to do. It was a difficult situation. He—"

"I know I've been MIA and it's caused some problems—serious problems—but Eventually is *my* company, not Matt's." My volume was rising, and I was having trouble keeping my voice steady.

It wasn't even Jamie I was mad at, not really. But she had to stop feeding Matt's fears. She had to know it couldn't happen again.

"If something comes up you can't handle," I said, "you need to call me. Not my husband."

"Cady, I . . ."

"I get that you needed me," I said, holding up my hand to stop her, "but this is not how things are done. You're still very junior, Jamie, and eager to grow; that's why I'm telling you this. I want to help you, but you've got to fine-tune your professional intuition if you want to—wait, Jamie, where are you . . . where are you going?"

She'd set down the tweezers and stood up, and now she was striding toward the small closet at the back of the room.

"Jamie . . . where . . . I didn't mean to—"

"That's the problem," Jamie cut in sharply. I'd never heard such an edge in her voice before. Or any edge, ever. "You never *mean to*, Cady. But you do. You don't mean to no-show events, you don't mean to pass off all the planning to me or forget to pay the bills. But somehow it always happens."

She snatched her purse and coat and made her way back to me.

"Jamie . . ."

She held up her hand, the same way I'd cut her off earlier. "I have been holding your entire crumbling company together for *seven months,* Cady."

I took a deep breath. I would have to backpedal here. I needed Jamie.

"I know. I know, Jamie. And I'm so thankful. I just . . . my only point was that you can't call the boss's husband just because—"

"Cady."

The look on her face. I couldn't name it then, but now I know it was disbelief. Jamie could not believe I was really this stupid.

"I have *never* called your husband," she said.

Everything inside me went cold. "What?"

She rolled her eyes and adjusted the strap of her purse. "I would never call your husband. Not even if Nora Donnelly's bouffant was on fire or Ramona Crawford's orchids rose up and strangled her."

"But . . . you sent him that file with our projections."

"Yeah, because *he* called *me* demanding to see it. He said he was checking in. He checked in a lot, actually. And the truth was, shit was hitting the fan, and I'd been having trouble getting hold of you, and I guess I just assumed you'd asked him to step in and help."

"So you've never called Matt?"

She shook her head.

I closed my eyes. "I'm sorry," I said. "I am so sorry, Jamie. I didn't . . . he said you—"

She cut me off with her hand again. "I'm going home," she said.

"No. Jamie. Please. Let's—"

"I'll email you my resignation tomorrow." She brushed past me. I resisted the instinct to grab her, to try to make her stop and listen.

"Jamie, please don't do this. I'm sorry. I . . ."

But it was too late. She was halfway to the door, striding out of this event and my company without looking back—just the flap of her long black skirt, then gone.

My last employee, the last one keeping my company ticking, breathing, fighting—gone.

I fell into the seat she'd been sitting in, fixing that mask.

Eventually was really, truly dead.

I couldn't do this without Jamie. She was right. She'd been holding it all together. And now she'd dropped the tiny broken pieces back in my lap.

And Matt. How dare he lie to me? How dare he let me—*make me*—think things were so bad that my own staff had to come to him for help?

It was wrong, and it was hypocritical.

But part of me loved it, Dana.

A big part of me had thrilled—shuddered in relief—when Jamie revealed what she did.

Because Matt was a good person, and good people don't break the rules unless they've got something they can't stand to lose.

I hadn't been wrong about Matt after all.

We were very, very much the same.

48

The doers of this world get the glory. The actors. The take-chargers. The bull-horn grabbers.

But there is power in inaction, Dana. In the things we *don't* do, or say.

Matt was checking up on Eventually, on me, on his own. Jamie had never asked him to swoop in and save the day, like he claimed. I wanted—so fucking badly—to hurl the truth in his face.

But there was something else I wanted more.

So I kept the words in my mouth. Put on a smile at breakfast the next morning. Made small talk and laughed and nodded when we went to Mom and Dad's for Sunday dinner. Kissed Matt goodnight. Waited.

Monday morning arrived.

We ate breakfast together. I refilled his coffee when I got up to refill mine. We shared the paper, split the last cranberry scone, kissed at the door, wished each other a good day.

Finally, he was gone. I watched out the window as his taillights disappeared, then waited some more, just to be sure.

It had been awhile—before Valentine's Day, at least—since I'd been in Matt's office. It's the aesthetic antithesis of mine. My bright cream walls are lined with perfectly spaced black-and-white framed photos, every pen and paper clip corralled in its proper matching brass receptacle. Matt's walls are a dark green, his hulking oak desk overrun by shaggy stacks of paper, promotional pens from trade conferences, forgotten Post-its. His diploma and awards and a smattering of unframed four-by-sixes—us on a beach in Tulum, us on a ski lift in St. Moritz—lean perilously at the edges of his crowded bookshelves.

Where to start? What was I even looking for? All I knew was that Matt was hiding something—and I needed evidence to prove it. But what exactly? A legal notice? A financial statement? Love letters? A diary? A *diary*, Dana? *Matt?* I laughed out loud.

I picked up a *Crain's* issue from last year, the one where Matt was named one of Chicago's "40 under 40." I flipped until I found his picture. It was a good interview; I'd read it at least twenty times. I reread my favorite part, toward the end, though I practically had it memorized.

Crain's: They say all the most successful people have a touch of delusion, that there's a kind of requisite audacity in succeeding at your level. What do you say to that?

McKenna: [*Laughs*] I definitely think that's true. You've got to be a little delusional to think, at twenty-five years old, with just a few years under your belt as an entry-level analyst at a single firm, that you're capable of doing on your own what takes most people decades to achieve, if they ever get there at all.

Crain's: So is this perfect dose of delusion something you're born with? Or is it something us regular folks can hope to aspire to?

McKenna: Well, I'm gonna give you the classic politician answer here and say I think it's a little of both. I do suppose some of it's just kind of . . . ingrained. I've always been a bit unrealistic and bullish in assessing my own abilities—in school, on the soccer field . . . and now, of course, in the marketplace. But I do think you need to cultivate those instincts, too, or you'll lose them. The world will knock them out of you, tell you that you can't or shouldn't do a thing, that it's stupid or reckless or that the odds are stacked against you. So you need to surround yourself with things—with people—that have a touch of your brand of delusion. Someone to help you shut out the rest of the world and make you dare to think you can pull it off. And for me, that's always been my wife. Cady.

I smiled as I closed the magazine and returned it to the stack of books from which I'd picked it up.

. . . for me, that's always been my wife. Cady.

I turned my attention to his desk, starting with the drawers. The top ones contained a mess of pens, pencils, paper clips, binder clips, loose business cards. The bottom drawers were packed tightly with files of old projects.

I thumbed through the papers and folders stacked on top of his desk next. They covered the surface, with a small clearing where his laptop had been—I'd seen it poking out of his briefcase that morning. I sighed heavily. That's probably where any real evidence would be.

Even if I found some smoking gun in here, would I realize it, Dana? I picked up a legal pad and squinted at Matt's chicken scratch. Just a bunch of dates. A timeline, apparently, for some deal. And lots of references to AP, whatever that was. Active Property? Asking Price? It all meant nothing to me. A folder labeled Greenview Cap Ex? Another for ISO 14001? And this one, a whole folder for some guy named Alan Prescott?

That was interesting, actually. An entire folder—a thick one—for one person. An employee? An investor? Or potential investor? Did Matt really keep this much intel on his people?

I flicked the folder open and thumbed through the printouts. Whoever Alan Prescott was, his entire life appeared to be documented in these pages. Birth certificate, education records, property deeds, business registrations, a marriage certificate, a divorce filing, another marriage certificate, *another* divorce filing, DMV records, a résumé, screenshots of a LinkedIn profile and a very sparse Facebook page. How did Matt get all this?

I pulled out the résumé, my eye catching on a familiar name. Most recently, Alan G. Prescott was the Prescott half of Elsier & Prescott Development Group, but previously he was a partner at McNally Properties, Inc.

The firm where Matt worked before starting MLG.

What were the exact words in Matt's text to Nick? *I was sure it would pay off. I knew the guy.*

Was Alan Prescott *the guy*? Was he involved in whatever trouble Matt had gotten himself into? I didn't even know Matt still talked to anyone from McNally.

I dropped the folder onto the desk, beside the notepad I'd tried to decipher earlier—the one with the timeline and all the references to AP.

Alan Prescott. Who the hell was this guy and why was Matt so interested in him?

I reexamined the timeline, but it still seemed innocuous. Just the chronology of a deal to purchase a strip mall.

I scanned the other folders one more time, just to be sure. None dedicated to one person.

I pulled out my phone and googled Alan Prescott.

Lots of hits, but a news article from February—oh God, Dana, *February 14*—caught my eye: CHICAGO REAL ESTATE EXECUTIVE MISSING.

I scanned the short piece quickly, absorbing the few facts presented. Prescott, fifty-eight, was a lifelong Chicago resident and a well-known name in the commercial real estate world. Authorities believed he may have been in financial straits; he'd recently liquidated a number of assets, including his primary residence. Police would not speculate on any rumors of foul play at this time. His adult children, ex-wives, and business partner all had no comment. That was it.

I hit the back arrow to return to the Google results, hoping for more— *Missing Real Estate Executive Found Alive and Well!*—but there were only shorter hits in the weeks that followed, noting that Prescott was still missing and police had no new leads to share at this time.

None of the articles said anything about Matt or MLG.

But there had to be a connection, Dana. Matt had once worked with Alan Prescott, and they'd obviously been partnering on a deal together.

That, and Matt had some sort of intense interest in the man.

And now that man was missing.

49

I've always thought intention counted for a lot. Maybe because Mom was always saying things like, *Well, his intentions were good* or *Oh, I'm sure she didn't mean it that way.* People do bad things, Dana—terrible things—but if their reasons are pure, or close enough, that counts for something, right?

These are the things I told myself when I woke up Wednesday, a day that dragged on for what felt like years. Morgan's date with Ben was two days away, and she didn't even know it yet. But tonight she would. I would tell her after group.

I'm not going to lie, Dana. I was a little nervous after the way she'd reacted to the purse.

But this was different. This was something she'd said she wanted. Something she'd practically asked me for.

I just had to find the right way to present it. Morgan would be hesitant. Maybe even defiantly opposed. She'd certainly protest. To reenter the dating scene after however many years away? Scary. Terrifying. Potentially disastrous. And of course, there would be some guilt where her son was concerned. Had she deprived herself long enough to sufficiently grieve him and honor his loss? No, of course not. Never.

I checked the clock all day. Eleven hours to go. Ten hours, forty minutes. Ten hours, thirty-seven minutes.

Finally it was a reasonable hour to leave. I got there a few minutes early, as usual. While I waited for Morgan, I made small talk with Moira, helped maneuver the chairs into a circle, greeted the others.

Morgan walked through the door right on time. I searched her face, but nothing seemed particularly amiss—and why should it? I'd overstepped my bounds a little, and in turn she had overreacted. Now we were both a bit embarrassed, and things would be awkward at first, but we would move past it—we weren't the sort of women who had the luxury of holding on to petty grudges. We had experienced *real* tragedy. We had *perspective*. Thursday night was nothing when you stacked it up against the last seven months.

When she neared, I flashed her the smile I'd practiced in the car. A Thursday-never-happened-I'm-willing-to-let-it-go-if-you-are smile. Morgan gave me a small one back, hesitating briefly before taking the chair beside me. It was the last one left; no one had sat in it because they all knew that spot was reserved, and none of them knew about Thursday. Not yet.

"Hey," she said.

"Hey." I cleared my throat. "Um, listen, I need to talk to you about something after this."

Morgan frowned as she tried to situate her big tote bag on the floor without it falling over. "Sure, okay. Everything all right?"

"Yes. Totally. I just have something—" I wanted to say something about a favor or proposal, to grease the wheels a bit, but Moira was already launching into the session. She held her phone at arm's length, reading from it loudly.

"Impending doom," she said. "Loss of control. Panic. Feeling stressed, overwhelmed, detached, numb, desperate, tired, tense, weak, restless, avoidant. Difficulty controlling worry. Trouble concentrating. Trouble sleeping."

She looked up, dropped the phone to her side. "What am I talking about here?"

Obvious. We answered in a single chorus: "Grief."

"Grief. You all agree?"

We nodded.

"Well, according to the Mayo Clinic and other sources, these are symptoms of fear." Moira sat down. "Does this surprise anyone?"

We shook our heads.

"Why not?"

"Because grief is scary," a man two seats down piped up.

"How so? What is your grief causing you to fear?"

We threw the answers into the circle like cards in a game of rummy.

"Being alone."

"Losing it."

"Never getting better."

"Or being able to move on."

"That it will happen again."

That was Vivian, the mother of the girl killed in a car accident after homecoming.

Moira leaned forward. "What are you afraid will happen again, Vivian? Death?"

Vivian nodded. "I have two other children, both younger than Emily, and that's all I can think about now—what if something happens to them, too?"

The circle of heads around me bobbed.

"I couldn't bear that," Vivian cried. "I really couldn't. I'm barely surviving *this*. Sure, as a mom, as a parent, you worry about something happening to your kid. But deep down, you know it's irrational—statistically speaking, your child should outlive you. And when you consider everything you do to protect them—make sure they wear seat belts, talk to them about drugs, enforce a curfew, get all the vaccines—well, if you do all that and it still fails you, where does that leave you?"

Beside me, Morgan swallowed.

"I think we can all relate to that," Moira said softly—softly for her. "It's that fear of the unknown, isn't it? If it happened once, why the hell couldn't it happen again? And worse—what *else* could happen? What else should I be fearing that I don't even know enough to be afraid of?"

Vivian stretched the sleeve of her sweater over her hand and raised it to swipe at her eyes. "Exactly."

"This is why grief feels like fear sometimes. Because grief is what happens when our worst fears come true." Moira turned back to Vivian. "Tell me, Viv, this feeling . . . is it fear, or is it grief?"

Vivian rubbed at the mascara stains on her sleeve. "Does it matter?"

Moira shrugged. "It's helpful to know what you're dealing with. Grief and fear might feel a whole lot alike, but fear is how we react to a clear and present threat, like a gun in our face or a fatal diagnosis. Grief is how we cope with those threats once they actually happen. It can be helpful to understand the distinction, because fear is more future focused, while grief is more concerned with looking back."

"Oh," Vivian said. "I suppose . . . I suppose it's fear then."

"And what does your fear do to you?"

"It stops me."

"From what?"

"Everything. Living my life. Moving forward. Making decisions. Appreciating what I still have—my husband, my other children . . ."

Moira nodded. "Fear destroys trust. Trust of other people and the world and ourselves—maybe especially ourselves. And if you can't trust anything, it's really hard to move forward. It feels a lot safer to stay right here, right where you are, doesn't it?"

We all nodded, but it was me Moira singled out next.

"Talk to me about that, Cady. Why is it so hard to move forward without trust?"

"Because it doesn't feel safe?"

"Don't *ask* me. Tell me. Is trust—a lack of it—making you feel unsafe?"

"Yes."

"Yes! Damn right it is. Because when we don't have trust, we feel afraid, and when we're afraid, we tend to pull back from life." Moira eyed me, like she was guessing my next answer before she even asked the question. "Who don't you trust, Cady?"

"I don't know."

"Your husband?"

I thought of Matt. His lying—about Jamie and about that phone call. Breaking into my phone, searching for Morgan's contact info. The long hours at work. Those text messages with his lawyer, the possibility of *jail*. How impossible it was to tell him everything—to tell him *anything*—these days.

"Yeah, I suppose."

"And the rest of your family?"

"I don't know, yes. Maybe."

"The universe?"

"Maybe? I don't know."

"What about yourself?"

"Me?"

"Yes," Moira said. "Do you trust yourself?"

Of course I trusted myself. What kind of a question was that? If you can't trust yourself, Dana, who *can* you trust?

"Yes."

Moira raised her eyebrows. "Are you sure?"

"Yes. I think so."

"You think so." Moira squinted at me. "Let me ask you this, Cady. Do you trust yourself to make good decisions? Ones that won't hurt you or the people you love?"

"I . . ."

"I'm not trying to change your mind or pick on you," Moira said, leaning forward. "I just want you to be really honest with yourself here."

"I . . . I guess I don't trust myself."

"Don't let me talk you into anything. You either do or you don't."

"I don't." I took a deep breath, let it all out. "I thought I did, but I . . . I don't."

"That's okay," Moira said. "That's okay. Good job; thank you, Cady."

"Thank you, Cady," the group murmured.

Moira moved on to Freida and Emil—what did they fear, now that the worst had already happened?

Morgan reached over and squeezed my hand.

She didn't say "*I* trust you," but that's what that meant, right? Why else do that, right then, at that moment?

Morgan trusted me.

A cold sweat broke out all over my body. I feared she'd feel it on her hand, but she was already pulling away.

I gave her a quick glance and forced myself to smile my thanks.

It shouldn't have been that way. My heart should have been cartwheeling in my chest, knocking into my ribs. This should have been a major victory, a big step forward. I'd been working so hard to get here, to earn Morgan's trust. I'd opened myself up to her and told her my secrets and gently pulled out hers.

Still, she'd often side-eyed me when I talked about you or Matt or

William, and she hadn't invited me into her home, not even when I was standing there on her doorstep. Sometimes I caught her wary glances, like she sensed what I was really about, the way Mom had always known when we were up to something, no matter how good we—I—got at telling a convincing story or covering our tracks.

But now Morgan finally trusted me, Dana.

I hoped she'd remember that when I told her about Ben.

50

"That was brutal, huh?"

We were packing up our bags with more of Moira's handouts, grabbing our jackets off the backs of our chairs and slipping them on.

I shrugged and slung my purse over my shoulder. "No more so than any other night, I suppose."

Morgan gave a little grunt of agreement as she slid her arms into a faded canvas jacket.

"So, hey," I said, braving it, "do you still have time . . ."

"Oh, right," she said. "Sure, let's talk."

We walked in silence. I tried to pull up the script I'd practiced in my head, the plan for how I was going to lay this all out, but my nerves had wiped my mind clean.

Just chill.

Relax.

I always did this to myself, Dana. Got ten steps ahead of a thing, living and breathing a worst-case scenario that hadn't even happened yet and nine times out of ten never happened at all. Odds were, Morgan would be thrilled. Or amused. Or unsure but curious. Maybe, possibly, a little annoyed.

"You're starting to scare me," she confided as we reached the double doors leading to the parking lot.

"Don't be silly," I said. I pointed toward a cluster of trees several yards away, where we could talk without being overheard by anyone leaving behind us.

She followed me over, and as soon as we stopped, she gave me a nervous smile. "So what's up?" she asked. "Is it Matt?"

Matt? Why would she think I had to talk to her—ask her anything—about Matt?

I shook my head. "Not Matt." I gripped the straps of my purse. "I . . . well, I had something I wanted to tell you. Something I wanted to ask you."

Morgan lifted an eyebrow. "Okay, shoot."

"Well . . ." I said, drawing the single word out as the rest scrambled to organize themselves. "Remember how you said you were thinking about getting back in the dating pool, before your son died, and how sometimes you wished you had someone else around to be miserable with?"

Morgan did a funny little snort-laugh. "Yes . . ."

That she was finding humor in this was a good sign, Dana. She'd put up a fight, sure, but this was what Morgan wanted—she'd said so, hadn't she?

She just needed a push—like the one I'd given her to get her "loss story" out, or the ones Matt and I had given each other to escape our stagnant careers, or the ones I used to give you, when you weren't sure you could ask for the raise you deserved or go for the cute guy sitting alone at the bar.

"Well, I found someone for you to be miserable with." I grinned. "How'd you like to dip that pinky toe into the water?"

Morgan's brown eyes stretched so wide and round, it was like looking down into two full coffee mugs.

"I swear to God, Cady, if you brought someone here . . ."

Her saucer eyes darted around, as if a man with a big red bow on his chest might pop out from behind a car.

"No," I said quickly, reaching for her hand. "No, no, no. I would never . . . ambush you like that. No, I have this friend, his name is Ben. He's a tech guy—a little shy at first, but once you get to know him, you won't be able to get him to stop talking—and he's *so* nice. Funny, but serious, too. And more importantly, he knows what we're—you're—going through, kind of."

Morgan looked skeptical. "Really."

I nodded. "He had a rough go last year—his dad died, and then, shortly after, he and his fiancée split. He's been gun-shy about dating ever since, but now . . . well, anyway, I told him about you, and he's really interested. He wants to meet for coffee, or dinner—whatever you're most comfortable with."

Morgan took her hands back and covered her face with them. "Oh my *God*. I can't believe . . ."

Her words trailed off into a laugh—a nervous but *excited* laugh.

"Remind me never to tell you anything again," she said.

"So . . . ?" I gave her my best beseeching look. "What do you think?"

"I think dinner is more than a toe. It's a whole goddamn foot, Cady."

"Nah, it's just dinner—or coffee, if you want. Whatever."

"*Just* coffee? My plan was to stew over the idea for a few more years, then *maybe* set up an online dating profile or something, then *maybe* talk to some dudes . . ."

"Well, no need to do all that. Ben is a great catch—cute, too. I can show you a picture . . ."

"It's not that. I'm not looking for a lady-killer, just . . ."

"A nice guy to not be lonely with."

Morgan sighed. "Exactly."

"Ben could be that guy, Morgan."

She scrunched her lips. Tilted her head. She was considering it.

"All right."

My heart jumped into my throat—

"I'll think about it."

—and dropped.

"Think? For how long?"

Morgan laughed. "I don't know. A couple weeks, maybe? I'm not prepared to make a decision today."

I frowned.

"What?" Morgan asked. "Is this guy going to turn into a frog or something if he doesn't get a date tonight?"

"I just don't want anyone else snatching him up. He's really great, Morgan."

"I thought he's been single since last year, when his fiancée dumped him."

"She didn't dump him, it was mutual. And he's been single by choice. Now that he's looking again, though . . ."

Morgan made a face. "If he's that hot a commodity, he's going to want more than a boring, grieving old . . . *potato* to grow moldy on the couch with."

"You're not a boring old potato; what does that even mean? Besides, Ben is a staunch homebody himself—and he already knows all about your son. Trust me, he's perfect for you, Morgan. Very down-to-earth, and get this, he claims to be shy in real life, though you totally wouldn't know it from—"

"What do you mean, real life?" Morgan frowned. "I thought he was your friend."

Shit.

"So wait, you've never met this guy?"

"Well . . ."

"Is he some sort of online friend or something?" Her brows were so tightly pinched they were almost touching.

"Yes," I said slowly. "Or something."

Morgan waited, her amusement gone.

"I met him on a dating app."

Her eyes narrowed. "You're on a dating app?"

"Yes. I mean, well, kind of. Not *me* . . ."

"*I'm* on a dating app?"

"Yes."

"*You* went on a dating app, pretending to be me."

When she put it like that . . .

"Yes." I gave her an apologetic, please-don't-be-mad-at-me smile.

Morgan shook her head. "I don't understand. How . . . how did you think this was going to work? Were you thinking I'd actually go on this date and keep up your sick game? Pretend like it really had been me talking to this guy all along? Was that your plan?"

"I . . . yes."

Morgan scoffed at that. "So what, do I have like a whole profile out there or something?"

I drew a deep breath. "Yes."

Morgan stared out at the parking lot forever. At nothing. For one wild minute, I was sure she would just up and leave, and I'd never see her again.

Finally, she looked back at me. "Let me see."

I tried to mask my relief as I fumbled to pull my phone from my bag. The motion lit up the lock screen—the wallpaper was a candid shot of me and Matt on our wedding day, laughing about something I couldn't remember anymore. I held us up to my face to unlock the phone.

My home screen appeared. I opened the app and navigated to Ben's profile.

"Here." I handed my phone over. "That's his profile photo, but he's got a few others in there. He's a project manager for a start-up, and he loves to cook and hike—and here, look at this," I said, taking back the phone to scroll through the photos. "He has a dog—a four-year-old lab mix that he absol—"

I stopped. Morgan was staring, not at Ben's picture but at me.

"Not this." She spat the words out at me, gesturing at the screen. "*My* profile."

"Oh." I felt myself sinking into the pavement. "Right."

I tapped the profile icon and handed it over. I had little choice.

Morgan read her headline out loud, her brows arching higher with each word: "Caring and Down-to-Earth Homebody Looking for Same."

I couldn't read her reaction. She didn't look pleased, or amused, but she didn't look *more* angry than she'd been a minute earlier. Maybe she was relieved that it wasn't as bad as she'd feared. I mean, if I was going to put her out there, at least I'd been honest.

Then something caught Morgan's eye. She pressed her index finger and thumb together over it, then pushed them apart to zoom in.

"This photo . . ." She looked up, and her coffee eyes had somehow turned blacker. "You cut Christopher out."

Yes. I had, Dana. She only had a handful of photos out there, and they all had her son in them. I'd felt bad—really bad—about that, but having no pictures is a big red flag in the online dating world.

"Morgan, I'm sorry. I didn't have any other photos, and no one's going to talk to a woman who doesn't have a—"

"Shut up."

"Morgan, I'm really sorry about the photograph. But—"

"I don't give a *shit* about the photo!"

A small flash off to the side briefly stole my attention. We had an audience. Vivian and Ruth had emerged from the school and were on their way to their cars. They'd stopped their chatting to glance back at us. I didn't care.

"It's not the photo," Morgan hissed, quieter. "It's *everything*, Cady. The photo and the profile and the chatting and the . . . the *gall*. You didn't want

Matt to rescue you or your business. You didn't want your parents to tell you to forgive the guy driving the car that killed your sister. *But you think*"—she thrust her finger to within an inch of my nose—"you can put me out there and . . . and *impersonate* me and talk to people about Christopher like he was your son? Your loss? *Your tragedy?* Fuck what Moira said about there being no right or wrong way, Cady. This is not right. *You* are not right."

Her parting look chilled me in spite of my jacket and the scalding shame.

This was wrong, very wrong. I could not go back home, leaving this hanging between us. I could not bear it. I had to fix this. I had to try.

But before I could decide how to stop her, she stopped on her own.

Right in front of my car, staring at the LTS PRTY vanity plates for far too long. I held my breath for several long terrible seconds until, finally, she turned and strode back toward me, her arms stiff rods at her sides, her fingers wrapped into fists, all her tightly curled fury directed straight my way.

I should have known right then that I would regret ever coming here tonight.

"You've been to my house," she said. "You sat outside, in your car."

"No. I mean, yes, I . . ."

"How many times?"

"How many . . . ?"

Morgan crossed her arms and stepped forward until she was only a foot from my face, which sounds like a lot but isn't, not when you're staring into eyes that look capable of spitting bullets.

"You know what, Cady? You *have* helped me."

Despite her tone, and her eyes, and the way her jaw stretched so tightly against her skin that it looked like one of them—the jaw or the skin—might break, I dared hope, for one foolish second, that she meant it.

"I have?"

Morgan nodded. From the corner of my eye, I could tell our audience had grown. Several more group members had stopped, or slowed their walks to their cars, to watch.

"Yes," she said. "Hating you is taking the edge off my pain. So thank you, Cady, yes. You've helped me. Mission complete. *Now stay the fuck away.*"

I pulled my head back as if the words had slapped me in the face. I'd always pictured her as the quiet, *I'm-so-disappointed* type. Not this.

I closed my eyes, so I wouldn't have to see her anger. Her hatred. I'd tried to *help* this woman. I cared about her—I *cared*, Dana—and I'd tried so fucking hard. I'd turned my back on my career and messed up my marriage for her.

"That includes group."

I opened my eyes. "Morgan . . ."

But she was gone. Getting away from me as fast as she could.

51

Matt was still at work when I got home. I waited for him on the couch.

Something about the quiet thud of his wallet on the credenza and the careful clink of his keys in the bowl let me know something was wrong. Something *new* was wrong.

Maybe he'd had a rough day—maybe something to do with those texts from his lawyer. Or maybe he'd had to fire someone or a building had burned down.

But no, it was probably much worse than any of that, Dana. I'd had this same feeling before, when I'd seen Sean's five missed calls last Valentine's Day in that parking lot downtown.

He walked into the living room and sat beside me on the couch, his outer thigh only inches from mine.

I angled my head his way and rubbed his back. "Hi."

He didn't say it back. He was looking at his hands. At the ring on his left one.

"I'm going to ask you a question," is how he prefaced it. "And I don't want your explanations or justifications, I just want a yes or no."

I nodded.

"Have you been . . . watching Morgan? Following her?"

My hand slipped off his back.

After everything I'd done for her, Dana. After all my efforts and energy and sacrifices, she wasn't satisfied with scratching me out of her life and cutting me out of group. No, she had to mess with my marriage. With Matt. Matt, who didn't even like her, who'd once doubted she even existed.

"Yes."

Matt nodded, like my answer was a foregone conclusion he'd only been verifying as a courtesy. He didn't even look surprised. In his eyes, I'd become a person capable of such things.

"How did she get your number, Matt?"

He hesitated, then nodded, like the point was mine. But it wasn't.

"Who's Ben?" he countered.

That bitch.

"Is that who you were talking to the other night?"

"I—"

"Are there others? Or just this Ben?" Matt shook his head and laughed, scaring me. "What am I saying? It doesn't matter. One is . . . this is . . . it's . . ." He looked around the room wildly, as if asking the TV, the candles, the framed wedding photograph on the bookshelf for help. "What the *fuck* were you thinking, Cady?"

I flinched at his brutal tone. "I . . . I don't know. She was so lonely, Matt, and I wanted to help her, so I started . . . I started looking for someone. For her."

Matt stared at me, incredulous.

"I just wanted to help her," I said quietly.

"Help *her*? Morgan? How has she helped *you*, Cady? Huh? How? Because I don't see things getting any better around here. In fact, as far as Morgan's concerned—"

"That's not true—you said things were getting better; you said you could see the old bits!"

Matt flopped back against the couch cushions. "That was before I realized you were lying again."

"Lying? About what?"

"About Eventually. About Morgan. About where you are when you aren't here."

"So you're the only one allowed to lie?"

Matt's eyes narrowed.

"What's going on with McKenna Land Group, Matt?"

He laughed. Laughed, Dana. I didn't see what was so funny.

"Wow, Cady," he said, shaking his head. "Wow. I mean, I should have known you'd find out—you always do somehow—but . . . yes. Shit's hitting the fan. I fucked up, okay? I went in on a big deal with a guy—"

"Alan Prescott?"

Matt hesitated. Something twitched in his jaw. "Yes." He proceeded again, slowly. "I bought this huge lot in Lakeview from him. The location was amazing. The possibilities for developing it were limitless. But turns out, Alan didn't have the right to sell it. Not without his partner. I knew Elsier was a cosigner, but Alan said he was on board, and there were two signatures on all the paperwork. I would have never wired the money if it wasn't all in place. But everything was fake. Forged."

I could feel my face screwing up with disbelief. "How is that possible? You have a whole team of people who check—"

"I didn't go through my usual process." The twitch again in his jaw.

I blinked. "Why not?"

Matt sighed. "I couldn't find any investors in time. Alan led me to believe he had two other serious buyers lined up and he was in a hurry to off-load it to fund another project. I tried raising the funds with my usual go-tos, but they all said it was too good to be true. I'm not stupid, I knew that sort of property, in that location, doesn't come on the market every day. But I also knew the potential upside was huge, and when these sorts of opportunities come up, you have to act. Fast." Matt rubbed his face with his hands. "And I knew the guy, Cady. He wasn't some schmuck off the street. He—"

"You worked at McNally together."

Matt's eyes narrowed. "Yes."

"So how did you get the money, if you couldn't find an investor?"

Matt flinched.

"Oh God." I gasped. "You used your own."

His flinch deepened. "Kind of. I reallocated some funds from other projects."

"You reallocated investor money," I said slowly. "Without their permission." I closed my eyes. I never would have guessed Matt capable. "That's misappropriation, Matt. You could—"

"I only reallocated my own stake in those projects. I got the rest from a loan and the sale of a few assets. And I stopped taking a salary."

"So you're off the hook? Legally? Criminally?"

Matt sighed. "It's a gray area," he muttered. "We're trying to figure it out."

"You and Nick."

The mention of Nick, the obvious implication that I'd read his text messages, sent the guilt flying out of Matt's eyes. The anger was back.

Before he could turn it around on me, I said, "Well, that explains a lot, doesn't it?" Matt's forehead furrowed, like he couldn't fathom where I was going with this.

"Without the safety net of Eventually," I explained, "we might be headed for bankruptcy." I smirked. "You weren't trying to save my ass, Matt. You were trying to save yours."

His head shot up, eyes flaring. "I was trying to save *us*," he bit out, "because I thought that's how this worked: I get your back, you get mine."

"Why didn't you tell me?"

"Why the fuck do you think?" he bellowed. "It was horrible timing. I couldn't add one more thing to your plate. You were barely hanging on as it was."

"So this all happened after Dana died."

He didn't answer.

"Before? It happened before, when things were good, and you didn't tell me?"

Matt hung his head, shook it.

I remembered the date of that article, CHICAGO REAL ESTATE EXECUTIVE MISSING.

"That day," I whispered. February 14.

He nodded. "Like I said, bad timing."

"That's why you didn't pick up."

Matt grimaced. "There was an article in the paper that day, about Prescott going missing, about his financial troubles. The same Prescott I'd just wired a shit ton of money to not even a week earlier." He took a deep breath, let it out, closed his eyes like it hurt, like he'd done that day in the hospital. "When you called, I was in the war room with Nick, confessing my sins and trying to figure out what the hell was happening and how bad it was."

Matt opened his eyes. I think he expected me to apologize, Dana. To say I was so sorry, if only I'd known, I understood now, it was okay.

But I couldn't. I couldn't forgive him. I know how that sounds, but if you knew—

"So now you know," Matt said.

Yes.

Now I knew.

But if I hadn't gone through his phone, Dana—if I hadn't confronted him—how long would he have kept this to himself?

"Kind of hypocritical," I said tightly, "giving me shit about Eventually when all along—"

"Not even close," Matt snapped, jamming his fist into the couch cushion. "I'm busting my ass trying to fix a mistake, while you're sitting on yours, letting it all slip away without so much as lifting a hand to try to stop it."

My will to fight was nearly spent. First Morgan, now this. I was going to lose this battle too, but I took my last shots anyway.

"Jamie never called you," I said calmly. "*You* called *her*. You were checking up on me."

Matt looked like he wanted to laugh, or throw something, or both.

"And that's how Morgan got your number, too, isn't it? You called her. *My friend.* You tried googling her, but that didn't work, so you broke into my phone and got her—"

"No, Cady. Don't. Just don't, okay? This—" he said, gesturing to me, sitting up straight again, "is not the same. Yes, I reached out to your assistant, and yes, I protected you from everything going on at MLG. But this thing with Morgan . . . it's . . . it's just *not right.*"

Those had been her words, too.

"And you told her—told everyone in that group—that we had a *baby*?"

No.

No, she wouldn't have, Dana.

She'd said she understood.

I shook my head, so confused. Hurt. "No. I mean, yes, I did, but then I—"

"You said we had a baby," he said again, more slowly, letting it sink in deep, permanently staining his vision of me. "And then you told them it died? A baby named *Dana*?"

"*I did have a baby!*" I jumped up from the couch. The pillow tumbled off my lap and fell onto Matt's feet. He kicked it angrily.

I stood there, looming over him, radiating heat. "I did have a baby, Matt. Maybe the baby wasn't real to you, but it was to me. *I grieved that life.*"

Matt jumped up, too. What had seemed like a normal distance between us on the couch felt too close standing. I wanted to take a step back, but I didn't.

"You think I wasn't sad?" he demanded. "You think I wasn't devastated? Really, Cady?"

"You said it could have been worse," I cried. "You said at least it happened now, and not later." *Imagine if we'd lost her after she was born, Cady. At four months, or four years, or fourteen years.* "You said at least we didn't have to go through that. Like our child wasn't real. Or didn't matter. Like the pain wasn't valid . . ."

Matt's eyes went wide. He was trying to find something to do with his hands, running them through his hair, then making fists. Finally he hung them around the back of his neck.

"I was trying to be positive," he said. "It *could* have been worse. And I know it hurt, Cady, I hurt too, but you were so . . . down. I couldn't . . ."

"Of course I was *down*, Matt!" I was much too loud for how close we were standing, but I didn't care. "I lost a child. Our baby was real, and Morgan got that. She was the only one who got it. Or so I thought."

Matt pulled his head back to look at me. I could see his pain; deep down, I knew this was hard for him, too. But it hadn't hurt him the way it had hurt me, and I hated him for that sometimes.

Especially this time.

But that wasn't fair. And it was stupid—pointless—to fight about who had it worse, especially now. Things had been looking up; I'd thought we still had a chance. I was going to bring it up again. Our plan. Trying for our family again. I was waiting for the right moment . . .

"I'm sorry," I whispered.

He shook his head. "I know. But I don't care anymore, how sorry you are. What does that mean anyway, Cady? *What* are you sorry about?"

"Everything. It just . . . it all got out of hand . . ."

Matt snorted. "I'll say. Following a woman in your car? Impersonating her? I mean, my God, Cady. That's not even . . . it's not . . . right. Not normal. It's not *legal*."

I swiped at the tears clouding my view of him. Matt didn't understand. If he only knew—

"I can't do this anymore, Cady."

There it was. Finally.

I dropped back onto the couch.

"You're leaving me."

The words barely came out. My throat had become too thick to breathe, let alone speak.

Seconds that felt like lifetimes passed before Matt said, "I don't know what else to do."

He wasn't looking at me anymore, but at something—the nothing—behind me. The big empty house we'd tried so hard to fill.

52

Why in God's name I showed up to that date with Ben, I will never know, Dana. Because I owed it to him? Because he deserved to hear it face-to-face? Because I was curious? Lonely? Losing it? *Losing my goddamn mind?*

We met at a cozy restaurant in Little Italy. It was everything I'd imagined. Snug romantic nook. Candles. White tablecloths and red wine. Soft music and hushed murmurs and the light clatter of forks against plates, the faint clinking of glass kissing glass.

Every detail, just as I'd pictured it. Except one.

It should have been Morgan walking through the front door with a racing heart and shaking hands. It should have been her, looking hesitantly at each strange face at each table, wondering if she'd recognize him from the six photos posted on his profile. Morgan, exhaling her relief when she did. Morgan, pretending to be confident as she reached the table and was just feet, inches, centimeters away . . .

"Morgan?"

I blinked. Of course he thought I was Morgan. That's who he was sitting there waiting for, so of course that was his first guess when I stopped just inches from the table, sweating through my silk blouse, gripping my purse with white knuckles and clammy palms. No matter that I was more than ten years younger than Morgan, no matter that my hair was the wrong color and my lips were fuller and my nose—

Oh God. It was happening, Dana. He was standing up, getting out of his chair. He was going to hug me.

"No," I said. "No, I'm sorry. I'm Morgan's friend. Cady."

"Oh." Ben stopped three-quarters of the way to standing, thoroughly confused.

He sat—plopped—back down.

"She's not coming, is she?" he asked.

I shook my head.

Ben hung his head, then glanced up at me with one raised, bemused eyebrow. "She could have just messaged me. Didn't have to send a personal messenger."

"It was a last-minute decision," I said. "She was going to come. She really wanted to, but it's just . . . it's hard. Her son . . . she's not ready . . ."

Ben nodded. "Yeah. I half expected this, to be honest. There was always something a little . . . off about Morgan."

Off. What the fuck. Why did everyone say that?

I sat down across from him.

"Don't tell her I said that," he said quickly. "I don't mean it in a bad way. It was just a . . . a feeling that something wasn't quite right. I could never put my finger on it, but . . ."

"But you knew," I said.

Ben sighed. "Yeah, I guess I did."

"It's not you, Ben . . ."

He snorted. "Right. Famous last words."

"No, really. She cared about you. It's just . . . it's the timing. What happened . . . her child . . . that's not something you just forget, or move past . . ."

"I get it. But why . . . why'd she even bother . . ."

"She thought she was ready," I said softly. "She wanted this. *She wants you.* But there's something else she wants more."

"Her son."

"Yes."

Ben shook his head. "I should have known better. I *did* know better. When Morgan talked about her son, I could tell . . . she was consumed with it still, his death . . . six months isn't enough time."

"Eight."

"What?"

"Eight months," I said. "Not six."

Ben closed his eyes. "Right. Sorry."

"Ben . . ."

He opened his eyes, and I could see his disappointment, could hear him beating himself up in his head—he'd known better, shouldn't have gotten his hopes up like this; he'd had a hunch and ignored it.

Looking in his eyes—he had the most imploring green-brown eyes, Dana—I was furious with her. Yes, I'd started this. Yes, it had been me talking to Ben. But it was Morgan who'd said no, Morgan who was throwing him away.

"Here," I said, reaching into my bag. I rummaged around blindly until my fingers closed on one of the pens rolling around the bottom and then a crumpled gas receipt. "Don't give up on her, Ben." I unlocked my phone and pulled up her number, copied it down on the receipt. "One day . . ."

I didn't finish, just handed the number over. This was literally out of my hands now, up to him. And her.

Ben looked dubiously at the paper. "You sure she wants me to have this?"

"Yes." I didn't have to fake the certainty in my voice. "She does. She just doesn't know it yet."

He shook his head, but he carefully folded the receipt, took out his wallet, slid the paper behind a credit card.

"You never know . . ." I said.

Ben smiled sadly.

I stood, blinking back tears. I'd been so close on this one. I'd really hoped . . .

"I hope you find what you're looking for, Ben. I mean, Morgan does. Her words, not mine. She wanted me to tell you that."

He gave me a *Yeah thanks, whatever* smile. "For what it's worth, I hope she does, too."

I fumbled around in my head, looking for some words or sentiment that would make this better, less bleak and wasteful. But there was nothing. I left him with a sad smile and a "Take care."

As I walked away, my resentment was soaring. Why couldn't she have just—

"Cady."

I turned.

Ben had gotten up from the table and was closing the gap between us.

I don't know why—guilt, probably; it makes you paranoid—but my first thought was that he'd somehow figured out it was me this whole time, not Morgan. And for one wild, terrifying, thrilling second, I waited to see if he would grab my shoulders and kiss me, or grab my neck and not let go.

Neither, of course.

"Thank you," he said. "For coming today. You're a good friend."

I choked back a bitter laugh and tried to smile, for him. "I don't know about that, but thanks, Ben."

"No, really." His hand shot out and touched the top of mine. My skin tingled, even after he dropped his hand, which was almost immediately, as if he thought maybe he shouldn't have done that, after all. His face was so earnest, so boyish.

"Morgan talked about you a lot," he said. "All good things," he reassured me, misreading the look on my face. "She's really lucky to have you." He smiled. "Her words, not mine."

53

The sky was persistently gray now. The air was sharp. The streets were quieter. The sidewalks were coated with wet leaves and decimated worms.

I sank into my grief like it was a warm bath. I mourned the latest deaths—of my friendship with Morgan, of her relationship with Ben, of Eventually and my marriage—even more deeply than I'd let myself grieve you, Dana. I lived in the same clothes for days. I ordered takeout for dinner, ate the leftovers for lunch, made do with coffee for breakfast. I watched entire seasons of shows, unable to recall one single character or plotline afterward. I cried for an hour straight at the sight of Champ's blue chew ring under an armchair.

I watched the balance in our checking account sink to just a month or two's worth of bills. Soon, I'd have to dip into our savings, which we couldn't afford. Eventually and MLG may have been raking in the dough those last couple years, but we'd been living large, Dana. Treating ourselves to a big house and luxury cars and nightly takeout, enjoying our newfound prosperity for a bit before we got serious about saving for retirement and contingencies.

I noticed Matt wasn't making any withdrawals from our checking account or charging anything to our Amex. I wondered if he'd opened his own checking account and credit card. I worried about what that meant.

I needed you more than ever, Dana. You would have known just what to say to make it all a little more bearable, a little less tragic and irreparable. You always did. In college, we used to call you The Counselor, remember? It made you sound like a mob boss or something, especially when we said it in horrible Jersey accents. So I don't know, maybe Mom was right. Maybe you were destined for your chosen path.

My one bright spot was when Matt called on Sundays—four of them had passed now—to check in, like I was his ailing grandmother or something.

This was how the rest of October passed. I might never have noticed it was gone, or nearly gone, if it hadn't been for an unexpected visitor.

I was in three-day-old sweats, half watching *The Crown,* starting to crave my nightly takeout, when the doorbell rang at four o'clock on the dot. It was the first time it had rung since Matt left. Maybe that's why I let myself hope it was him, though he still had his keys and he'd never hinted at coming home during the few texts we'd exchanged.

But it wasn't Matt standing on the porch. It was another man, a stranger, dressed in all black. Dried blood crusted around a gaping wound above his left eye. Standing beside him were a small ninja and a towheaded Princess Jasmine.

"Trick or treat!"

The children waited expectantly while I processed their demand: *Trick or treat.* Halloween. Candy. They wanted candy. I didn't have so much as a stick of gum, Dana. I was only peripherally aware it was October, let alone the thirty-first day of it.

I mumbled something about being right back and fled to the kitchen, where I found a couple granola bars in the bowels of the pantry. I returned and deposited them in the kids' pillowcases just as two Harry Potters and a Pikachu appeared in the driveway, pumpkin-shaped treat buckets thumping against their knees as they advanced.

I shut the door and turned off all the lights and the TV. I pulled a cashmere throw up to my nose and got a hair stuck to my lips, and cried when I realized it was Champ's.

Despite the closed door and our new double-glazed windows, I could hear the "Trick or treat" chants ricocheting off the neighbors' houses. Old memories pushed their way up, Dana. You and me trick-or-treating on a sunny day, Mom following behind with her new digital camera, Dad with his half-heartedly concealed Coors. A different year, in the snow, shivering in our thin polyester costumes and down jackets. Afterward, sorting our candy into piles, making trades—five Jolly Ranchers for a peanut butter cup, two peanut butter cups for a Fun Dip. You, third grade, pouting in your half of our peanut butter and jelly sandwich costume, so pissed about being the brown peanut butter while I got to be the purple jelly.

I could see the images like they were photographs I was holding in my hands. They made me smile. I might have fallen asleep, warm from old memories and the blanket, if it hadn't been for the doorbell, again.

I checked the time on my phone. 8:19. Trick-or-treating was supposed to be over—village rules. Yet the long brass bells of the door chime were starting up again, setting off another round of Beethoven's Fifth.

I sighed and stood, letting the blanket fall away. In the pantry, I found a single-serving bag of pretzels and made my way to the front door, hoping it was just one persistent kid out there and not a whole stoopful.

"Where the hell have you been?"

Only one person, Dana—an oak tree of a woman with brassy split ends, a Radiohead T-shirt, and white Reeboks—could have shown up on my doorstep, unannounced, and not promptly received a closed door to the face.

"Moira. What . . . what are you doing here?"

I poked my head through the doorway, steeling myself for what I might find: The rest of the group? Morgan? Was that why Moira was here?

"Look," I said, "I don't know what Morgan told you, but—"

"She didn't tell me anything." Moira craned her neck to get a look behind me. "You going to let me in or what?"

I sighed.

Moira sighed back. "I've seen a messy house before."

"It's not that."

"Well, okay then. As long as you don't have a hot date or a dead body in there, I'd like to come in and chat." She rocked forward on the toes of her Reeboks, then back down again.

A chat. I did not feel up for a chat. Especially one with Moira. I loved Moira, but conversations with her left me tapped out, and I wasn't starting with much to begin with.

But Moira was Moira, and she was looking awfully comfortable and permanent standing there on my stoop. I gave her a resigned *You win* smile and stepped aside.

In the living room, my blanket lay abandoned in a cashmere puddle on the floor. The TV was frozen on Princess Di as she emerged from a livery car in her legendary black revenge dress.

"Pretzels?" I asked, holding up the little bag.

Moira shook her head. "I'm good."

I tossed them on the table and picked up my blanket. "Make yourself comfortable," I said, gesturing around at the seating options.

Moira chose the couch. I sat at the other end, pulling the blanket into a ball on my lap.

"I had you pegged as fancy," Moira said, "but this is something else. Nice house."

"Thank you. About the house, I mean. I don't know how I feel about being pegged as fancy."

"It's the purse," Moira said. "Looks like one of those five-hundred-dollar kinds."

I smiled—really smiled—at that. "Dare I ask what you came here to talk about, Moira?"

Moira laughed. She had a soft, pleasant laugh. The first time I'd heard it, I'd done a double take. I'd expected something loud and barky.

"Sorry," she said. "I didn't prepare an agenda. Just checking in to make sure you're okay."

I opened my mouth to reassure her, then stopped. "I started to say I'm fine, out of habit, but I think it's obvious I'm not."

"Of course not. Your child—your baby—died. And your sister. *Your twin sister,*" she added, as if I could forget. "And you've got a ketchup stain on your sweatpants, and your hair hasn't seen a comb in days."

It was sriracha, not ketchup, but I wasn't sure what correcting her would prove.

"Wow, Moira. Don't hold back." I smiled to show her I was teasing. But the reminder that I'd lied about a dead baby to this very real mother—to an entire room of real mothers and fathers—stung. I narrowed my eyes. "Are you sure Morgan didn't tell you anything?"

"Swear to God and George Clooney," Moira said, holding up her hand. "I mean, sure, I asked if she knew why you'd stopped coming, but she just got real quiet, and I thought, *You know what? That's between them.* No,

I came here of my own accord. Believe it or not, I care about you guys. I don't get paid for this, you know. Well, I do, but trust me, it ain't much."

I shook my head. "I miss you, Moira."

"You know where to find me."

"I know, but . . . it's complicated."

"Yeah, so's rocket science. But someone figured it out, right?" Moira adjusted herself on the couch so she could face me head-on. "Seriously, though. Tell me. What's going on? Not whatever happened with you and Morgan, but with you."

"I don't know, Moira."

"Sure you do. Come on."

"I really don't."

Moira folded her arms. "All right then, why aren't you coming to group anymore? Let's start there."

"I . . . Morgan and I had a disagreement. I betrayed her trust, and now she doesn't want to see me."

Moira stared at me blankly, waiting for me to continue. I sighed. "I didn't mean to hurt her. I wanted to *help* her. But it all got so screwed up. And then—it's kind of complicated—but my husband left me. And my business is destroyed. And my dog . . . my dog ran away. I think. Kind of." My eyes were filling up, but I didn't even try to hold the tears back. I let them fall, fast and furious. "I've fucked everything up, Moira. Like *everything.*"

Moira nodded. "Yeah, well, that's why they call it shit hitting the fan and not shit being delivered in a neat little box with a bow."

"I didn't *set out* to mess it all up. Obviously. It just . . . it's like one thing, and then another . . . and each time it gets that much easier to cross that next line—isn't there a word for that? The law of motion or something? Inertia?"

Moira didn't answer. She was watching me. Intently.

"What?" I asked.

She raised her eyebrows. "Aren't you forgetting something?"

I squinted back at her, confused.

"You just gave me a whole laundry list of the things that are going wrong," she explained, "but what about your *grief*, Cady? You never talk about Dana."

My brows furrowed. "Yes, I do. Or did, anyway. I talked about my sister at every session."

"Exactly," she said. "*Your sister*, but not the child."

The child. My eyes stung, filling up with tears that made Moira and my living room blur together like a Monet.

"Why don't you talk about the child, Cady?" Moira's voice was a soft, non-Moira-like hush. Her face, not so soft. Very Moira-like. Set. Determined. Waiting, just like in group. She wasn't going to let it go until she got something out of me.

I didn't have the strength to fight her. I let it all out. The truth about the baby that was really a miscarriage that hurt so bad that I'd wished something would happen to your baby, too.

I waited for Moira to hate me, to tell me Morgan was right all along and to forget what she said earlier about coming back to group, that she'd better never catch me around that school or those honest, honorable, *real* parents ever again.

"Do you remember," she finally said, so softly and quietly that I was sure it was some kind of trap, "what I told you about grief?"

I raised my eyebrows. "You've said a lot of—"

"The first day," Moira said impatiently. "What did I say?"

I smiled. "That our grief is a peanut butter cup." I smiled wider. "And there's no wrong way to eat it."

Moira nodded, her face serious. "Well, that's not entirely true."

My smile slipped away.

"There are, of course, exceptions." She leaned forward, her Radio-head T-shirt stretching across her boxy chest, making Thom Yorke's eyes widen. "I wouldn't, for example, condone violence as an acceptable means of managing your grief. Or robbery or adultery or drug abuse."

"Or lying about your dead child to crash a parent bereavement group," I said quietly.

Moira wobbled her hand. "That's more of a gray area."

I gave her a skeptical look.

"In my book," she explained, "intention counts for a whole heck of a lot. And I don't think you intended to hurt anybody, Cady."

Yes, *yes*. Hadn't I been saying that all along, Dana? That good people can do bad things? That it's our *intentions*—

"So back to this inertia crap," Moira said, the softness gone from her voice. "It doesn't work with the good stuff?"

I shook my head, confused. "What?"

"The inertia or whatever," Moira said impatiently. "If you were to, I don't know, send your husband flowers or put up a missing poster for your dog, it couldn't possibly, just maybe, lead to a *good* thing? And then another and another?"

I scrunched up my face. "Smart-ass."

She laughed. I gave her a tired smile. "Can we be done with the therapy session?"

Moira hesitated, then looked around a bit awkwardly. I realized she thought I was kicking her out. "Fine by me," she said, and before I could stop her, she slapped her hands on top of her thighs, like she always did before she stood up, like any good Midwesterner did.

I reached my hand out. "Wait," I pleaded. "You came all this way. Do you want to stay? We could watch *The Crown*. And order Chinese."

Moira hesitated again.

"Please? It'll be a good step—eating dinner in front of the TV *with* a friend, instead of alone."

"Can we order pizza instead?"

"Sure."

So I ordered pizza and we resumed *The Crown*. Diana finished emerging from that car and got on with her dinner in Kensington Gardens. The Queen tutted over Charles with PM Major. Moira watched silently, and I watched her, turning her words over in my head, the ones about one thing leading to another. How maybe it doesn't only apply to the bad stuff.

"You're right."

"I know," Moira said, not taking her eyes off the screen. "What about?"

"Fixing things. Or trying to, anyway. I'm going to get Matt back. And fix things with Morgan. And save Eventually."

Moira finally turned away from the TV to look at me. "I'd start with the dog, personally."

I laughed at that, even though I was pretty sure she was serious.

Then I settled deeper into the couch and pulled out my phone and—I couldn't help myself, Dana—it's like it wasn't even me, like I was just a spectator watching my thumbs dart across the screen of their own volition, watching as they opened the Find My app, selected People, then Matt. It wasn't me doing any of that.

But it was me who let out a little sigh when the circle with his face popped up on the map, right over one of MLG's condo buildings, right where he'd told me he was staying. I let my screen fade to black and relaxed into the couch cushions.

I pulled up Morgan's Facebook next, then Morgan's Instagram, Morgan's ex-husband's second wife's Instagram (no, Dana, Morgan *hadn't* mentioned wife number two; that took some digging), and Morgan's mom's Facebook (that one was easy; I'd just had to yank a photo off the internet and pretend to be a fellow quilter looking for like-minded buddies).

Yes, I was still doing it, Dana. Still up to my old tricks. And some new ones. I know I said I wouldn't follow Matt. That I'd only *enable* the tracking feature; I wouldn't use it, not unless I had to.

But that's the thing about inertia that Moira didn't get. It takes a lot more to keep a good thing going than it does to let a bad thing run its course.

54

I found Champ. Sort of.

Matt had said the microchip place would contact us if Champ's chip was scanned, but I thought it was worth the thirty-second call to double-check.

A cheerful woman named Arlene listened as I explained the situation, how it had been months since Champ went missing, but we were still holding out hope.

"Of *course*," she said. "Let me check the notes." There were a couple clicks and a *Hmm*, then, "It says here that we called the number on file the evening of June 17, after we received a call from Countryside Animal Hospital."

"Yes," I said eagerly, "that's our local animal hospital."

But June 17? That was the day Champ had gone missing. Maybe they'd called the wrong number—but surely they'd have tried again by now?

"Right, well," Arlene said, "someone brought your dog in, and the clinic scanned the chip and alerted us, and we alerted the primary contact on file—Matthew McKenna. Is that your husband?"

"Yes. That's my husband, but . . . he didn't . . . didn't answer? You didn't get ahold of him?"

Arlene made a little humming noise as she read through the file.

"I'm sorry," she finally said. "I don't see that detail in the notes. It just says the primary contact was notified, then I see the ticket was closed out, which usually indicates we made contact."

That phone call, the one I'd thrown in Matt's face over and over again . . .

"Right. Okay, well . . . thank you, Arlene."

"You're most welcome. Is there anything else I can help you with to-day?"

"No, thank you."

I called the animal hospital and spoke to a sympathetic woman named Charla, who confirmed that Champ had been brought in the night he went missing, suffering from the lacerations and internal bleeding he'd sustained after being hit by a car on Elm, just one street over from ours. He died of his injuries within an hour of arriving—they'd administered morphine to make his last moments peaceful—then his scruff was scanned for a chip. Matt was called; he arrived to settle the bill and say goodbye to Champ's body. Then he came home to me, where he sighed under the covers and let me put my hand on his arm, and God, how fucking fitting was that, Dana?

The first thing I did after hanging up was grab a trash bag from under the kitchen sink. As I made my way to the attic, I snapped it open. The angry pop was satisfying, so I gave it another good crack.

The attic door had always stuck a little, but not this time; I opened it with the same force I'd used to crack that bag open. At the top of the stairs was a small pile: one large dog pillow, two depressingly clean stainless-steel bowls, and the handful of toys I'd kept finding around the house. I'd stashed it all up here, out of sight but not gone, waiting, just in case.

"No more just in case now," I said out loud as I wrestled the pillow into the bag.

I spoke to Matt as I threw the bowls in, then the toys.

"How dare you."

"Thank you."

"You lied to me."

"You protected me."

"I can't believe you kept this from me."

"I can't believe you shouldered this on your own."

"You should have told me."

"You should hate me."

I lugged the bag downstairs. As tears—fat, angry drops—rained down my face, I tied a tight knot at the top and threw it in the trash bin in the garage. One of Champ's toys gave a short squeak of protest as it hit the bottom.

Or maybe it was a goodbye squeak. I hadn't gotten the chance to say goodbye, Dana. Matt had—he'd gone in and said goodbye that night; the woman at the clinic had said so. Maybe there was a little box of ashes somewhere in the house. Maybe not. All I had for sure was that bag of garbage, so I went back and lifted the lid, and I said goodbye.

There are no perfect goodbyes, Dana—I'd already learned that much—so I did not pity myself too much as I stood there, alone and crying in our cold garage, talking to a dead dog's last earthly possessions at the bottom of a garbage bin that smelled like chicken teriyaki and old bananas.

Then I went back inside, and I sat on the couch, but I did not turn on the TV. I started making lists.

This was good, Dana. The old Cady was never without a list. Ideas for parties and home improvement projects and Matt's birthday gift and baby names and nursery themes.

My new lists were in my head. Among them:

Things I've Irreparably Fucked Up

Reasons I Don't Deserve Matt/Dana/Morgan/Mom & Dad/Champ

Ways to Save Eventually

Things I Should Have Told Dana

Things I Shouldn't Have Told Dana

Ways to Make Things Right with Morgan

Ways to Fix Things with Matt

Ways to Fix Everything

But how to fix everything? How to fix *anything*?

I couldn't. I'd tried, but I'd made everything worse.

I needed to try something different.

I needed help.

Help.

Yes, that's what I needed, Dana.

I needed to get some fucking help.

Therapy.

Matt would laugh—or maybe not—if he were there, witnessing me come to that conclusion, the same one he'd come to way back in February. I pulled up Yelp on my phone and typed in *grief therapist* and our zip code. The first name that popped up was Gene Callahan, CAGCS, of Callahan & Associates. I tapped the phone number below his name.

As the call rang in my ear, it occurred to me that I hadn't read his reviews or checked his star rating. No matter; this wouldn't work anyway. An entire grief group didn't fix me, so how could one CAGCS, whatever that was?

"Callahan & Associates, this is Lauren speaking."

"Yes." I realized I wasn't sure what, exactly, to ask for. "My name is Cady McKenna. I'm looking to start therapy? My twin sister died earlier this year, and I . . . I understand you offer grief counseling."

"I'm so sorry about your sister, Ms. McKenna. But yes, we do. We have several counselors and therapists that specialize in grief. Did you have a particular one in mind?"

"Callahan is fine." Must be, right, if the company was named after him?

Lauren took my name and insurance information. Less than five minutes after pulling up Yelp, I had my first session scheduled for the following week. I could have done this ages ago.

It was too late to go back, though, Dana.

Or was it?

I picked up my phone again and made one more appointment. I'd wanted this for so long, Dana . . . and what did I have to lose now?

55

Grateful. *Grateful*. I'm not kidding, Dana. *Grateful* was the word that greeted me when I showed up—twinless, jobless, Matt-less, Morgan-less, hopeless—to Mom and Dad's front door on Thanksgiving. GRATEFUL, spelled out in swoopy cursive letters on cheap orange chipboard, perched next to a dopey-looking scarecrow inside a wreath of polypropylene leaves. I took a picture with my phone, then let myself in.

Turkey, garlic, rosemary. It brought me right back to last Thanksgiving, stepping through that same door, greeted by those same smells. Except last time, Matt was by my side, and you and Sean were waiting in the kitchen, helping Mom mash sweet potatoes and debating whether the stuffing needed more salt.

This year, Mom hastened from the kitchen, calling to Dad that Cady and Matt were here. She had on her apron, the one with orange flowers and the cranberry sauce stain. Dad followed, in a Bears sweatshirt and blue jeans older than me.

We exchanged hugs and Mom looked me over, settling my hair around my shoulders the way she always did, like she was fixing something. It used to drive me up the wall when we were teenagers, but now I welcomed it.

Dad tilted his head to peer behind me. "Where's Matt?"

I hadn't told them yet. When Matt first left, I hadn't believed it. *He'll be back tomorrow,* I'd thought. One night apart, and he'd realize how wrong it was, this separation, how much he missed me.

That was stupid, of course. We hadn't argued over unfolded laundry or who left the kitchen lights on. And it had been months since I'd been me. He'd had plenty of time to get used to my absence.

"Work emergency," I said.

Dad's eyebrows twitched. Mom frowned and said he'd be missed, that it was a shame he wouldn't get to enjoy the pie, that she'd just have to send extra home.

Dinner was exactly how you would imagine, Dana. The same as the year before, just divide the joy by a thousand and subtract three people and nix the part where we go around the table saying what we're grateful for. There was no talk of *gratitude*, despite that wreath on the door.

After dinner, I settled onto the sofa, hugging one of Mom's festive fall pillows to my stomach. It had embroidered maple leaves and claimed OUR NEST IS BLESSED. I picked at the $14.99 HomeGoods sticker while Dad turned on the TV. Mom followed behind with the old-fashioneds—we were maintaining all the traditions, apparently, except for one.

Mom handed me a glass first. "I'm sorry Matt had to miss, but I'm happy you're here."

Happy? We couldn't really be happy, could we? Ever again? Without you?

When we all had our glasses, Mom made a simple toast: "Happy Thanksgiving."

"Happy Thanksgiving," Dad echoed.

"Yes," I said, tapping my glass against theirs.

I took a sip. It was good. Strong. I took a picture with my phone, zooming in on the orange peel curlicued over the rim.

We drank in silence, excepting the occasional "Oh, come on!" or "Somebody get this ref some glasses" from Dad.

After one particularly loud outburst, Mom turned to me with a *Men!* smile. "Think Dana's up there rolling her eyes with us?" She looked up, toward where you supposedly were.

When our old-fashioneds became just orange peels and ice, Mom clapped her hands together. "Well, should we cut the pies?"

Right, the pies. I didn't know why all this was so surprising, Dana. It was Thanksgiving, and this is what we did on Thanksgiving, apparently come hell or high water or your death.

In the kitchen, Mom lifted the tinfoil lids off the pumpkin and pecan pies she'd baked that morning. It had been too much food when it was six of us; it was ludicrous for just three. I watched as she rummaged through her utensil drawer, looking for the pie servers. Another holiday tradition, the search for that elusive second server.

"Here." I reached around her to pull the utensil from its embrace with a metal whisk.

"Ah, thank you, sweet girl. What would I do without you?"

We both stiffened at the question. Or maybe that was just me. Maybe it was only me who was thinking, what *would* Mom do if something happened to me, too?

I pulled the pecan pie toward me and cut three thin slices—the thinnest I could manage, though I knew, no matter how small they were, we would moan when we were finished, clutching our bellies and exclaiming over how good it was, but also how *rich,* as if it were a surprise that the pecan pie was, for thirty-some years running, every bit as filling as the year before.

When I was done, I looked at Mom. She hadn't sliced into the pumpkin pie yet. She was still holding the server in her hand, watching me.

"How are things, Cady, really?"

She knew, Dana. She knew something wasn't right, something more than the pain of missing you on this special day, a day we'd never spent apart. I wondered if Matt had called her. If they'd had one of their little chats about me.

"No worse or better than things are with you or Dad or Sean, I suppose."

She looked unconvinced.

"I'll be fine. I have Matt." The lies slid right out.

"That's true." Mom smiled sadly. "I'm glad. Something like this . . . some couples find it hard to weather." She turned back to the counter and finally sliced into the middle of the pumpkin pie. "Your father and I . . . we put on a good face, but it hasn't been as easy as we might make it look."

I frowned. "Have you been fighting?"

She shook her head. "No. It's just . . . different. Your children become part of your identity as a couple. With Dana gone, something is gone from us, too." She smiled. "We'll be okay, though."

Ugh, my heart, Dana. I'd been so wrapped up in myself, I hadn't noticed. I'd assumed that unlike me and Matt, Mom and Dad had found some solace in each other.

"Come here." I wrapped my arms around Mom and squeezed. I thought she might be crying, so I didn't let go.

She was still in my arms when she said, "Cady?"

I pulled back.

"I wanted to ask you something. A favor."

"Of course, anything."

"I want to have a memorial for Dana and the baby. In February."

"Okay." I didn't think you would care about a memorial, and I selfishly didn't want a reenactment of your funeral. But if Mom wanted to mark the anniversary with some sort of ceremony, if it would help bring her closure or peace, I would go, of course I would.

"And," she said, watching me carefully, "I want you to put it together."

I almost said yes, Dana.

Yes, of course I would do this for Mom, for you. If commemorating the last three hundred and sixty-five days with catered sandwiches and all your best photos taped onto trifold poster boards would make Mom happy, of course I would do it.

But it wouldn't make Mom happy. And I didn't do memorials. I did parties. Big, elaborate, joyous affairs to memorialize life's happiest moments, not its saddest ones. And I hardly even did those anymore.

"I'll think about it."

Mom smiled sadly, like she knew I wouldn't really.

I followed her back to the living room with our three plates of pie and settled beside her on the couch. We feigned interest in the game, though it wasn't even on; it was just an insurance commercial.

I was already too full, but I took a couple small bites to please Mom, then set my plate aside and checked my text messages. Nothing new. The last exchange was between me and Matt, hours earlier. Sterile *Happy Thanksgiving* messages to pass on to his folks from me, and from him to Mom and Dad.

I sighed and exited the messages, pulling up Pinterest instead. I scrolled through my feed, sifting through the recommended posts, clicking on one that caught my eye: a DIY tutorial for painting your own "sunshine and sunbeams" mural.

I smiled in spite of myself. So cute, and it would be perfect for a boy or a girl.

I pressed save and added it to my private *Nursery Inspiration* board.

56

We should have spent that next day shopping, keeping the tradition alive. Braving packed parking lots and long lines in the pursuit of deals that, deep down, we knew were not really deals. Breaking for lunch, swapping in-law and mutual-friend gossip, game-planning the rest of our shopping trip, lamenting the cute jeans we'd talked ourselves out of. That's what we should have been doing, Dana. Instead, I was planning your memorial.

Trying to, anyway.

I couldn't do it, though. I didn't know the first thing about such events. All my experience lay in letting the good times roll.

That doesn't mean I didn't try. I went into the empty office that Black Friday, hoping it would trigger some old event planning muscle memory, but as I sat in the skeleton of my once vital, thriving company, googling *beautiful memorials,* I found no inspiration. Eventually was dead, and I had slowly killed it, and all Google's suggestions sounded like an encore of your funeral. I tried coming up with my own ideas, but nothing felt appropriate. A photo booth? Dana-themed, with cardboard cutouts of your face on little sticks? A backdrop of white roses, like the ones we'd placed on your casket?

Clearly, I was not the right person for this. I called Mom and tried to tell her.

"But you *are,*" she argued. "I don't want to do it if you're not going to plan it."

I sighed. I didn't like the idea of the party at all, whether I was planning it or just showing up.

"I'm not, Mom. I do celebrations. This . . ."

"But that's just it! I *want* to celebrate Dana's life. I *want* it to be a party. Only you can do this justice, Cady. Who knew Dana better than you?"

I sighed and promised to give it another go.

Back to Google.

Fun memorials, I typed.

Oh.

Well, Dana.

Apparently some people actually *do* have photo booths at memorials—with cutouts of the honoree to boot. Guess I was onto something. Somehow, I didn't think Mom would love that.

Potlucks were a big thing, too.

And balloon releases (though I didn't think a bunch of birds and turtles choking on latex was how you'd have chosen to be honored).

I slammed my laptop closed. I couldn't do it. This wasn't my *thing*. I'd never done anything like this.

Well. That wasn't entirely true.

In fact, wasn't this how I'd started out? Kind of? Small personal events as favors for friends and family? I'd even done that cancer remission party.

God, Dana. How had I started there and landed here?

I frowned, looking around my sleek office with the high-end furniture and original artwork, remembering how it started, all the papers and ideas scattered around that tiny secondhand dining table in that cramped little apartment in the city. It had been a long time since I'd thought of Eventually's early days. I'd never really stopped to look back, not until recently, when I'd told Jamie my company's origin story. What came next—my success story—had happened so fast.

But it didn't "just happen." Nora Donnelly happened. Without her . . . I don't know if I'd have made it.

I'm sure I must have told you the whole story before, right?

I'd been in the business for a little over a year, remember? I was profitable, but not by much, and only because there was so little overhead. I was charging nominal fees, just to get experience and generate word of mouth.

Then Nora left me a voicemail, inquiring about *procuring my services* for her *next fête*. I'd debated calling back. The woman sounded difficult.

But I was building a business; I didn't have the luxury of turning anyone away.

So I called. Turned out she was the sister-in-law of my friend Gwen, and she'd loved what I'd done for Gwen's wedding. It was a small event, but special. I'd hand-strung this beautiful hydrangea canopy over the aisle with a florist friend. And we did couches instead of chairs at the ceremony. There was one long table for dinner. It was different . . . intimate.

Anyway, Nora loved it and asked Gwen for my card.

A week after her first call, we met at her house in *the best part of Hinsdale,* which is an absurd five words to string together, because it implies there's a part of Hinsdale that isn't to die for. Nora ushered me through her massive house quickly, no time to gape at or even process its size and opulence. I was there to be shown one thing, and that was the very large, very exquisite outdoor space—I hesitate to call it a *yard,* Dana.

I hesitate to try to describe it at all. There were these flowers, so many flowers, all so striking and exotic, that surely they weren't really growing in the Midwest. And the trees. Giant century-old elms and oaks and willows hugging the borders of the property. A large, amorphous pool tucked behind a row of flawlessly manicured hedges, like a hidden natural pond. And the lawn—I'd never paid attention to lawns before, Dana, but this one was greener and lusher and more tightly clipped than Medinah Country Club's golf course.

"What do you think?" Nora asked. "Could you do something with this?"

"Absolutely." I could have put card tables and citronella lanterns in that yard, and it would have been spectacular. "But . . . the occasion?"

Nora swooped her arm out. "To show off the new landscaping, of course."

"Oh," I said. "Right. And, um, your budget?"

Nora smiled. "Let's see your ideas and your estimate first, and then we'll talk—and remember, I called you because I want *different.*"

I returned the following week, armed with my ideas. I walked Nora through each one: First, the grand entrance, a dramatic arch of white roses leading guests to the immaculate gardens. Then the mismatched crystal chandeliers hanging from the massive oaks. The plush couches, like the ones Nora had admired at Gwen's wedding, arranged into intimate conversation nooks around the lawn. Then the smaller details: the giant stalks of calla lilies and the three-foot ivory candles that would surround the pool, the long oak dining tables and their supersized centerpieces—generous bouquets representing flower varieties found throughout the grounds.

And over there, atop a simple wood platform, against a backdrop of lavish ferns and strings of white fairy lights, the band would play—a local, folksy quartet Matt and I were fond of, not the expected jazz band or stuffy string quartet.

"You wanted to celebrate your landscaping, right?" I asked Nora. "So that was my inspiration—take the existing beauty of the yard and just . . . exaggerate everything."

Nora said she loved it—*adored* it.

But then she asked me what it would cost. I handed over my estimate, and she immediately made a face. My heart sank. The price I'd quoted her was a steal, Dana.

"This can't be right," Nora said, handing the sheet back.

"I'm sorry, but—"

"You'll barely cover your materials for that amount, let alone your cut."

"Oh," I said. "Well, I'm waiving some of my usual fees."

Nora gave an impatient shake of her head, her bleached blonde bob swinging over the tops of her bony shoulders. "Why would you do that?"

"Because you're Gwen's sister-in—"

"Oh, pssh," she said, waving me off. "Look around you, Cady. I don't need a discount. In fact, let me give you a piece of advice that will serve you well in attracting . . . a higher caliber of clientele. *Do not undervalue yourself.* To anyone with real money, that word alone—*discount*—is gauche. Anything worth having is worth paying through the ass for—that's how people of a certain tax bracket think, understand?"

I nodded.

"Now, here's what we're going to do. I'm going to give you what you asked for, plus another ten percent, because I don't want you skimping on anything. And then I'm going to give you another ten grand on top of that for your time and your eye. You can use it to get some nicer clothes and a decent logo," she said, making a face at the branding on my estimate sheet.

The emblem in question was a simple circle with a big E inside. I'd designed it myself with a free online logo generator.

"And in exchange," she continued, "you'll give me a party that doesn't look like Pinterest and Etsy vomited all over my yard."

I nodded slowly, still stinging from the logo comment—and the dig at my wardrobe. I was tempted to say, *Thanks but no thanks, lady. I don't need your charity.* But the truth was, I did. I needed every job I could get.

And if I was going to succeed, I could do it a whole lot faster in a world like this, where people like Nora Donnelly paid *that* kind of money for a single night. A ten-grand profit from one event?

I've never worked harder on an event, Dana. I earned every single one of those ten thousand dollars, and at Nora's party, I handed out my card (with a chic new logo) to several of her friends, Nora watching out of the corner of her eye like a proud patron.

That was it. I was off and running, no time to stop and ask if this was what I wanted. Which was fine, because I did want this, once. It was fun. I loved what I did—at least, I had. The creativity and the stakes and the challenge and the freedom and yes, the glamour and the glory, Dana. I'd lived for the rush of event day, and I'd savored the satisfaction when it was all over, another smashing success in the books, twenty more potential clients heading home with my card in their designer purses.

But then I remembered how hard it was to come back to work after . . . after February 14. How vacant the idea of another six-figure, five-hundred-guest, black-tie, gold-plated event had left me feeling.

I looked at the empty chair across my desk, the one in which Jamie had always sat. I pictured her there now, blue pen poised, her Moleskine balanced on her knee.

"Get out," she would have said. "Nora Donnelly? I can't believe you've never told me any of this before!"

She would have seen that it made me a little sad—wistful, nostalgic—for the old days, when things were simple, and I was planning the sort of events that meant more than just another feather in some rich lady's Dior cap.

"Do you ever miss it?" she might have asked. "The feel-good events?"

"Sometimes," I would have admitted. "But I'm fine," I'd reassure her. "Better than fine. I'm really proud of Eventually. Besides, it's a moot point now."

Jamie would have shrugged at that, or challenged me with one of her perfectly manicured eyebrows. I could hear her voice, chirping her infinite optimism in my ear: "It's never too late to go back."

And I would have smiled. Sweet, naïve, hypothetical Jamie. She didn't know how wrong she was.

57

Why? Why was I there? That was the first thing the therapist, Gene Callahan, wanted to know at my first appointment.

Wasn't he supposed to coax that out of me, one thirty-dollar co-payment at a time? If it were as simple as saying it out loud, I wouldn't be sitting there on his couch.

Gene Callahan. Imagine, Dana, flipping to the men's section of a late-nineties JCPenney catalog. The first man who pops into your head is my therapist. He waited patiently for me to answer his question, one chino-clad leg folded over the other. He had on a plaid button-up, tucked neatly into the waist of his pants, the cuffs of which were tugged up, revealing thick brown socks that matched his bargain-box loafers.

As for his face, it was unremarkable, except for his eyelids and brows. The former were thick with folds—heavy looking—and the latter were always raised, probably to keep the former open. It must be wearing, taking in other people's problems in addition to your own.

"It's hard to say," I finally answered.

Callahan nodded. He thought I meant that it was complicated or that I didn't know why I was there or what my problem was. What I meant, though, was: *It's* hard *to say. It would* hurt *to say it. Maybe it would even—*

"Why don't you start," Callahan suggested, "with telling me what feelings brought you here?"

"I feel . . ."—I searched the blank walls in my head for the right label—". . . bad."

"By *bad*, do you mean guilty bad? Sad bad? Bad bad?"

"Yes."

A patient smile. "What do you think is making you feel bad?"

I inhaled deeply, to get more air for all the words. "Well, my husband left me. That was . . . God, two months ago now. And before that, my identical twin sister—and her unborn child—were killed in a car crash. That was 292 days ago. And in between there, I managed to run my business into the ground, get my dog killed, and make and then lose the only friend who could possibly come close to understanding what it was like to lose Dana."

A pause. "Dana was my sister."

"Is that all?" Callahan's smile thawed me a degree. I liked that he didn't take my trauma too seriously. It was all sobering enough without making a point of it.

"No. There's more."

"I know."

I must have visibly tensed, because Callahan smiled, making his eyes disappear. "There's always more. You wouldn't be here if there wasn't."

He asked more questions. What was my relationship with you like, Dana? What was our childhood like? What about Matt? Our marriage? It had been over nine months since you'd died; why therapy now?

"Let's talk about this friend," he said. "Morgan."

I took a deep breath, Dana, and I told him everything. Well, everything after that first night I went to grief group. Not before, not the hospital. But I told him about her house. The bricks and the rust and the azaleas. Her hair. The way her ears poked through, and how it didn't bother me, not at all. The tilt of her head when she listened. Sunday mornings. How she was never late, never early, always right on time. Orange. The color orange. It was everywhere. My birthday, the lemon drop shots that made me whisper in her ear. Her loneliness. Ben—his emojis and his bad jokes. The date he wanted so badly. Her disgust. Her anger. Her space.

Morgan. I'd walked in hesitant to say anything about her at all, but I ended up saying a whole lot. Why? I don't know, Dana. Maybe because I was holding so much back, and if I was going to leave the house and pay thirty bucks for this, I might as well try, at least a little.

Maybe because a very small, very terrified piece of me wanted to see if he could pull that splinter out of me, too.

58

After nine weeks—*nine weeks, Dana*—I worked up the nerve to ask Matt for a date.

He suggested coffee. On a Tuesday morning.

Coffee. Hardly a romantic date, hardly a date at all.

Remember how you helped me get ready for my real first date with Matt, sixteen years earlier? I don't remember what I ended up wearing, just that you and I spent an entire afternoon selecting The Perfect Outfit. I tried on everything in my closet and yours, and you modeled the finalists so I could get the three-dimensional view. I'd forgotten about that particular perk.

Anyway, what to wear? It was just coffee at Wheelys. I wanted to show some effort, though—some progress—so I chose black jeans and a fitted cream sweater and a layered gold necklace. I blew my hair out and curled it into soft waves.

My old *Getting Ready* playlist kept me company while I applied my makeup—blush, mascara, a thin stripe of dark brown eyeliner, a coat of lipstick that almost perfectly matched my natural color.

I was twenty-four minutes early, because I knew Matt would be at least fifteen minutes early and that was part of the plan: Look nice. Show up early. Be relaxed. Mention the therapy. Tell him how much it's helping. Keep it light. Smile. Bring up a few good memories. Don't bring up *her*.

I requested a booth by the window. It would be more comfortable and intimate, more conducive to a long chat that would lead to easy smiles and old feelings and talk of moving back in.

When Matt arrived, I would order a coffee and something to eat—*Look at me and my healthy appetite!* Maybe I'd get the avocado and egg sandwich, his favorite, so he would remember the time I'd tried to reproduce it at home for his birthday. (He'd gotten tears in his eyes. I'd assumed it was due to my thoughtfulness, but it turned out it was the amount of salt I'd used.)

But maybe old memories, even happy ones, weren't the way to go. Maybe I'd order something unexpected, like a pink vanilla mocha or a sakura smoothie, some sort of symbol—*New and different, but better!* Or maybe I'd order whatever took the longest to make, to give us the extra time. All good possibilities, though I thought my first idea, the avocado and egg sandwich, was best, since it most aligned with my plan to remind him of the good—

"Hey."

He looked different, Dana. I couldn't explain it, couldn't pinpoint what it was. He hadn't grown out or cut his hair, hadn't started a beard or missed a shave. He didn't look more tired or heavier or thinner or happier. He just looked different.

Suddenly I was nervous. Or excited. I don't know. Something similar had happened when he'd gone to LA for a big industry conference the year before. When I'd picked him up at O'Hare and seen his face for the first time in a week, I'd had the weirdest, giddiest feeling, like we were back to being complete strangers. I'd *giggled,* Dana. I was junior-year Cady Wilson again, and he was Matt McKenna, senior varsity soccer player, telling me I better give him my phone number.

Now I echoed Matt's "Hey" back, wishing I'd gone in for a hug. But it was too late. He was already sitting down.

"You look nice," he said.

"Thanks." *Nice?* I looked the absolute best I had in months.

"It's really good to see you."

God, Dana. What next? *Good to see you, too? How are your folks? Pretty pleasant day out there if it weren't for this wind?*

Fortunately, our server came. I ordered a coffee and the avocado and egg sandwich. Matt didn't seem to notice. He ordered just an espresso, which I tried not to overanalyze.

"How are things at the house?" he asked when we were alone again.

"Fine." Actually, the water was draining slowly in the master shower and the pilot light was out in the fireplace and our checking account balance had dropped to four digits, but I didn't want us to get trapped in the matter of domestic issues.

"You missed some especially delicious stuffing at Thanksgiving," I told him. "And a scandalously rich pecan pie."

Matt smiled sadly. "I know. I went to my parents', but it felt wrong, not being together."

I nodded. We hadn't spent a holiday apart since we'd been teenagers.

"I still have some stuffing in the freezer. My mom made the same amount she always does, even though . . ." I trailed off. No need to say it. "Anyway, there's at least a full serving left, and some slices of pie, if you want to stop by and grab them. You don't even have to say hello. Just come in, take the Tupperware, and go. I won't judge."

Matt laughed. "That's okay. It's all yours. I'll eat double next year to make up for it."

Next year. Did he believe things would be back to normal this time next year?

We fell silent again. I racked my brain for a better topic.

"I'm seeing a therapist."

Matt's eyebrows shot up. "Really? That's great, Cady. I'm . . . proud of you. Is it helping?"

I shrugged. "I've only had one session so far. But I'm going to keep going. I'm hopeful."

"Good, I'm really glad. I . . ."

God, why was this so hard, Dana? Sixteen years together, nine of them married, a thousand perfect moments and easy conversations in between, and it all got flushed away after ten bad months and a handful of weeks apart?

Our server returned with our drinks and my sandwich. I stirred some cream into my coffee but didn't touch my food.

"I really miss you," I said.

Matt put down his little espresso cup and sighed. "I know, I miss you, too."

My stupid eyes filled with tears, not part of the plan. "I know about Champ." Also not part of the plan. I was supposed to keep this light. Happy.

But a wall of tears rose up in Matt's eyes, too. "I didn't want you to feel bad," he said. "Worse."

"I know."

I pressed a napkin under my eyes. Matt smiled sadly. This wasn't what I'd planned. I was messing this all up.

"I want to launch a new business." I didn't know why I'd said that—I hadn't made any such decision—but as soon as the words were out, I knew they were true. "A new Eventually," I explained, "but focused on more charitable events."

"Like fundraisers?"

"Fundraisers, benefits, memorials, subsidized events for nonprofits and community organizations . . ."

Matt watched me closely, like he was trying to figure something out. "This is . . . wow. A whole new venture, huh? It's a bold move. Very brave. So . . . you."

I flushed from the praise. "I don't have it all figured out yet," I admitted. "Far from it, actually. I have to tie up loose ends with Eventually first— I've taken down the website, but I still have to dissolve the LLC and who knows what else. And I'll have to figure out how to run a nonprofit— maybe I can get grants or something? I don't know. It's completely outside my wheelhouse, and I've only just started to really wrap my head around the idea—*What?*"

Matt hadn't said anything, but he had a funny little smile on his face.

"Do you remember," he said, "what you told me when I was starting McKenna Land Group?"

"I probably told you a lot of things."

"You said, *Keep it simple, stupid.*"

I rolled my eyes. "I didn't call you stupid."

"Whatever." Matt smiled. "Point is, I'd been overcomplicating every-thing. You gave me great advice then, so I'm giving it back to you now: Don't overcomplicate the thing. Leverage everything you already have. Don't bulldoze Eventually and start over; expand it. Parlay it into something more."

"Like a separate arm or something?"

Matt shrugged. "Whatever. I'm just suggesting you consider pumping oxygen back into Eventually and see what happens—maybe it's not too late to resuscitate it."

"I can't. I've burned all my bridges. Not even Nora—"

"Bridges can be rebuilt."

"But what if I don't want that anymore? The lavish balls and posh garden parties? That's the whole point of the new venture."

"I know," Matt said gently. "But if you can get Eventually alive and kicking again, you could use the profits to *fund* the new venture. You could use what you've already created to launch this next chapter. Maybe even win Jamie back and properly train her to keep the luxury side going, so you can focus on—Cady, what are you . . . what's wrong?"

I was crying. I couldn't help it, Dana. My husband, across the table from me, both of us talking fast and dreaming big again. It felt so familiar, and yet . . . not. It had been so long. It was sad, but it was good, too. There was something left, something to go back to and keep fighting for, if we could just find our way there again.

And if the next couple months went as planned, there would be even more reason.

I smiled through my tears. "This feels like the old days, kind of."

Matt smiled back. "Yeah, kind of." He glanced at his watch and frowned. "I should get going," he said. "I've got a lunch meeting in Oak Brook."

A lunch meeting. That's why just the espresso.

"Work stuff?" I asked.

"Yes."

"How is . . ." I started to ask about the bad deal, then thought better of it.

But Matt had already seen where I was going. His face fell, and I wished I hadn't brought it up.

"They found Prescott," he said. "In Costa Rica. He's being extradited this week."

I nodded. I already knew that. I had Google Alerts for his name set up on my phone.

"What about the legal stuff?" I asked. "And your investors?"

Matt's eyes darted around us before he answered. "Nick thinks we have a decent case if any charges are brought," he said, lowering his voice. "A lot hinges on what the investors do, or don't do, about it, honestly. When I first told them, they . . . well, they were pissed, of course. They still are, I imagine. But if MLG or any of its ventures tank, we all lose." He leaned forward. "We're going to sue Prescott and his company for damages, and there's a better chance of success if we band together. Turns out, given the right incentive, people are willing to overlook this sort of thing. If you can believe that."

I could.

Matt exhaled heavily. "Whatever happens, I'll never so much as roll through a stop sign again, Cady. I might end up really lucking out . . . but it scared the shit out of me."

I shook my head. "Not luck," I said. "Reputation. Respect. Credibility. That's why you're going to be okay. You're a good person—everyone knows that. You made a bad mistake, but you owned up to it. That . . . that counts for a lot."

My eyes began to water. Matt gave me a funny look. "You're going to be okay," he whispered. "You know that, right? I mean, if this does end up going bad . . ."

"It won't."

"But if it does," Matt pressed, "you'll be okay. I made sure of that. No matter what happens with MLG, they can't take the house. Or go after our assets or Eventually. The way the company's structured, we're not—"

"I know," I said. "I'm not worried about any of that."

I really wasn't, Dana. Besides, I could get it all back if they did. I could claw my way back up. I could do anything, if I wanted it bad enough.

Matt checked his watch again.

"Sorry," I said. "I know you have to get going." I smiled and reached my hand out, put it on top of one of his. "This was good."

"It was."

Matt moved his other hand so it was on top of mine, so mine was sandwiched between his, warm from his warmth. He was always so warm, even though he kept the thermostat so low—or had, when he'd still been living at the house. I started to make a joke about that, about keeping the house at seventy-four to my heart's content, running up that gas bill, but Matt opened his mouth at the same time and a funny little buzzing came out.

No, it wasn't coming from Matt's mouth—that was just timing—but from his pocket, from his phone. He reached for it, and I caught his half-second flinch when he saw the caller ID. It was as fleeting as a blink, but I had been paying very, very close attention to Matt this whole time, and I know what I saw.

I can already hear you defending him, Dana—*Come on, Cady, a flinch?*—but it was his next move—that guilty glance my way, to see if I'd seen—that cemented my certainty.

My husband was still hiding something.

59

The best time of year to buy a new car is at the end of it. Black Friday through New Year's Eve. That's what Matt had told me anyway, two years earlier, when he'd driven me to the local Land Rover dealership to buy the car I'd had my eyes on for months.

I didn't care about any of that now, though—the financing offers and rebates and special leases. I just wanted to get rid of that beast.

New year, new car, new me.

I went to the same dealership I'd bought the car from and told the first person I saw in khakis that I wanted to trade it in. I didn't try to downplay my urgency, though I knew the smell of my desperation would cost me several thousand dollars on both the sale of my old car and the purchase of my new one.

A potbellied man with thick black hair and a mustache with a lunch crumb stuck in one corner walked around the car, appraising it like it was a show horse or a Rothko. His metal name tag said *Don*.

"This ever been in an accident?"

"Nope."

"Anything wrong with it?"

"Nope."

Don finally paused his circling and stuck his hands in his pockets. "Well, I think I could get you a fair trade-in value for her."

Fair. Right. For whom? Whatever, it didn't matter.

"What're you looking for?" he asked. "An upgrade in the same class? We've got a brand-new—"

"Not another Range Rover," I said, shaking my head. "Something smaller."

Don looked around the showroom. "We've got some Jags if you want—"

"Something less . . . conspicuous," I said.

"Less conspicuous." He looked around again, stroking his mustache. "This is a Land Rover / Jaguar dealership, ma'am. I'm afraid all I've got is something big and conspicuous, or something just . . . conspicuous. Maybe you should try Toyota."

"Will they buy a Range Rover?"

Don shrugged.

So it was that I found myself at Leroy's Fine Used Cars, two towns over. I accepted a trade-in offer on my car that would have made Matt pass out on the showroom floor, then doubled down by buying a three-year-old black Camry for an equally scandalous price.

As I drove off the dealership lot, I could feel the loss of those extra four thousand pounds like a fresh haircut swinging over my shoulders.

60

It was still December, early to mid—who knows. It drags when you're sludging through it, then it's just a blink-sized memory, like how your entire childhood feels about as long as a chapter in a James Patterson novel by the time you're thirty.

Sean and Mom came over to the house to discuss your memorial. That's right. *Sean and Mom*. I invited your husband, Dana. It felt wrong to exclude him. And in the words of every single person in our family every time we talked about you, Dana, *This is what you would have wanted*.

Anyway, I made sure to invite them on a weekday, so when they asked, "Matt at work?" and I nodded, that would be that.

I knew this event wasn't really for you, that you'd never know or care about any prayers or slideshows or vigils or released doves. This was for us, because there was nothing else to be done about your death. This memorial was something, and that was better than nothing.

I had a slideshow prepared, as if Mom and Sean were any other clients and this were any other event.

"Wow," I muttered as I pushed play on my laptop. "I haven't done one of these in ages."

Mom grabbed my hand and squeezed as the music started. I'd stitched together short clips of some of your favorite songs, the ones I planned to play at the event.

The first images were of the venue: a big empty former gallery that was sometimes used for pop-up art shows, but mostly for weddings or other large events. It was a beautiful blank canvas. Elegant, like you—but also unfussy, like you.

I'd swiped photos of the space from the venue's online gallery and tweaked them to give a visual of what I had in mind, starting with the timeline. In lieu of poster boards or a table laden with frames, I envisioned hanging photographs and mementos of your life on the gallery walls, creating a massive timeline that would weave up and down hallways and through rooms, taking guests on a poignant tour through your thirty-two years.

I'd rendered some examples for them, stop number one being your first few days of life. Inside a large gilt-framed shadow box was a big black-and-white photo of baby you (it was hard to find a good shot of just you, Dana; we'd spent our earliest days snuggled up like two cats). Alongside it, your tiny socks and a handful of smaller photographs—Mom kissing your cheek, Dad holding one of us in each arm like a pair of machine guns.

Sean's smile shook as more of the timeline passed by, as we got closer to what we knew was the end, and Mom made a small horrible sound when it finally came: an eight-week sonogram in a tiny gold frame.

I'd meant that to be a somewhat happy thing (in your last days, you'd known such ultimate love; you'd had such hope) and as a symbol (the great circle of life, the timeline ending so similarly to how it had begun), but I don't think either of those things occurred to them in that moment.

Mercifully, less turbulent images followed: The candles and the wildflower bouquets. A sushi bar and two signature cocktails (French 75 and Aperol spritz, of course) and the string quartet that would play instrumental versions of the songs I'd selected.

When it was over, I took my time exiting out of the program, giving them a minute to take it in. Despite the lighter tone of the last few slides, the timeline shots had been difficult to watch—even for me, and I'd known what was coming.

But when my laptop screen turned black and I caught Mom's reflection in it, she didn't look wrecked. She looked—I turned to double-check—yes, she was disappointed, Dana. And Sean looked confused.

What the fuck. I'd *delivered* on this. I'd reached deep down inside to make this beautiful and meaningful, to represent you in every way, from the colors and music to the lighting and the venue and the food. It was *you.*

"It's kind of . . . sad, isn't it?" Mom asked.

"It's a memorial, Mom. It's supposed to be—"

She shook her head, cutting me off. "I know. It's just . . . well, your parties are usually more . . ."

"You didn't ask for a party. You asked for a memorial."

"Yes, but with your special touch." She looked up, a plea in her eyes. "I want us to celebrate the years we had with Dana, not . . ."

"Not mourn all the ones we don't?"

"Exactly."

I closed my laptop and ran my fingers around the edges. A party. For you. For us.

A celebration.

"I'm sorry," Mom said, gesturing to my closed laptop. "It's not that I don't love all this, Cady. The timeline was beautiful and the venue looks lovely. It's just . . . maybe it's the tone. If we could just make it more . . ."

"Lively?"

"Yes," Mom said, relieved. "More like your usual stuff, but with the heart you put behind all this," she said, waving at the computer again.

I didn't know if I could do that, but I'd promise Mom anything if it would chase away those shadows in her eyes.

I got up to make coffee, throwing ideas over my shoulder about how we could *liven up* your death.

We could start with the music. I'd chosen all your favorite slow jams, the moody ones we'd blasted in our dorm after you'd had a bad breakup or when we'd just felt in the mood to indulge ourselves. But I could take those out, replace Adele and Paramore with the Lumineers and Chairlift. I queued up a quick playlist of ideas and let them run in the background while we continued our brainstorming.

"I love the timeline," Sean was saying, "but maybe it could be a little . . . happier?"

I nodded. "I like the more poignant moments, so I don't want to take those out—but maybe I can lighten things up by mixing in more fun shots, like the one of Dana pouting in the PB&J costume."

Mom laughed. "And that one of the two of you with Tupperware bowls stuck on your heads? I think you were four. That's one of my favorites."

"Definitely that one, then."

"Maybe the food could be more laid-back, too?" Sean suggested.

Mom scrunched up her nose. "Did Dana really like sushi?"

"Loved it." Mom would never fully come to terms with the fact that we were no longer the seven-year-old girls who would only eat buttered rice and plain spaghetti. "But I agree," I said. "We can make the food more playful, but still sophisticated."

A small smirk touched my lips. "Dana never outgrew corn dogs . . ."

"Or Fruity Pebbles," Sean added. "We always had a box in the pantry. Whenever I'd tease her about it," he said, looking away so we wouldn't see his misty eyes, "she'd sing that old commercial, with Fred Flintstone? It was so bad. I loved it . . ."

Yes, Dana. That sounded just like you.

I cleared my throat and blinked away my own tears. "Well, there you go," I said. "We'll serve little corn dog hors d'oeuvres, and I know this great bakery in Wheaton; I bet they can whip up some sort of Fruity Pebbles–inspired pastry. Okay!" I clapped my hands together. "I think we're getting somewhere."

It was the first time in ten months I'd felt any sort of spark working on an event.

Later, I snuck glances at Mom and Sean as I walked them to the door. Mom was excited, and even Sean had gotten into it, and I think we all had mixed feelings about our mixed feelings.

Mom pulled on her coat. "Okay, so you're going to call the bakery and the caterer, and Sean and I are going to go through the photo albums."

I nodded. "And I'll email you the guest list—I could use a double check to make sure I'm not missing anyone."

The light dimmed in her eyes, and I wondered what I'd said wrong now.

"I forgot," she said, drawing the words out carefully, like peeling a sticker off bit by bit so it didn't tear. "I wanted to ask you about inviting William."

"William . . ."

Mom looked down at the purse strap she was now fidgeting with. Sean cleared his throat.

Oh. *William.*

"The driver," I said.

"Yes."

No.

Anything but that.

Anyone but him.

I couldn't say that, though. Not without Mom asking why. Even though she thought she knew the answer, she'd turn it into a discussion, another opportunity to move the needle, to make me forgive him, or at least start to—for my sake, for my closure—and I didn't want to have to lie to her, or anyone else, any more than I already had, Dana. I was tired of it, so damn tired, but I couldn't tell her the real reason I hated him, the real reason I could not forgive William Fahey.

"Okay," I said.

61

Christmas was not Christmas. It was just a Wednesday at Mom and Dad's. No you, no Sean, no Matt. The three extra stockings dangling from the mantel mocked me.

I'd finally told Mom and Dad about Matt—our troubles, his leaving. I had to—first Thanksgiving, now Christmas? I gave them the executive summary, no details—especially no fifteen-year-old-blow-job-confession or fake-dating-website-profile or secret-phone-call details—and to their credit, they didn't shower me with questions or too many pitying glances. But I knew their restraint was a show, that deep down, it was one more thing for them to worry about.

A couple days after Christmas. A Friday. I should have been working on your memorial, finalizing the menu with the caterer or sifting through the pictures and other mementos Mom had gathered for the timeline. But it was the holidays, and you were gone, and Matt was gone, and Morgan, too, and I guess in many ways, so was I.

I was restless, caught in some kind of limbo between the old me and whoever I was becoming. I tried to watch a new show, some friend drama thing, but I couldn't get into it. I flipped through my Pinterest feed and social media—nothing added since I'd looked five minutes earlier. I opened my email, though I'd just checked that, too, but—oh!—something new. And not just the usual spam or utility bill, but something I'd been waiting for.

The next step.

I . . . I'd set something in motion, Dana, and I'd been waiting for further instructions, for whatever they said was next.

Now it was here. I opened the email and clicked on the link and digitally signed and initialed all the right spots on the informed consent document. The nurse had explained at my last appointment that, even though we'd done this before, we had to do it again each new cycle.

Thank you. Your form has been submitted.

One step closer. I closed my email and opened Safari. If I got my form, they must have sent Matt's, too. I logged into the fake email account I'd set up for him. It was scary easy to update his email address; I'd just told the receptionist that his old one had been hacked, and she'd plugged the new information I'd given her into her computer, no questions asked.

Funny how everybody trusts a woman who wants a baby, Dana. I would have done anything to get mine.

After I signed Matt's form, I checked the time on my phone. 5:18 P.M. He was probably still at work. I navigated to the Find My app and, yes—still there.

I went to the kitchen and ate a spoonful of peanut butter from the jar. I took a glass of water to the living room. Restarted episode one of a series I had zero interest in. Checked my phone. 5:31. I checked on Matt. Still at work.

The show rolled on. I kept my thumb on the phone screen, watching Matt's face hover over McKenna Land Group's offices, waiting for it to move, waiting for him to go home—no, *no*. Not home. That condo wasn't his—*Oh, there we go.*

The circle with Matt's face was moving now. East on Forty-seventh, west on Wolf. In a few minutes he'd be home, and for the rest of the night, I would check in every so often, ensuring he was right where I'd left him. I'd picture him in his bachelor pad, cooking up elaborate little meals, doing things his way—putting as many capers as he wanted in his marinara sauce, leaving towels on the floor and facial hair in the sink. Watching war documentaries and college football, playing *Animals* on full blast, to his heart's content.

I watched on the map as Matt neared his condo building. His little circle was moving awfully fast. He'd have to slow down or he'd—yes, he'd gone and missed the turn, Dana. Now he'd have to swing back around . . .

No . . . No, he wasn't doing that. He was going right past the next street. Where was my husband headed?

All I'd wanted was the reassurance that Matt was in that condo, eating dinner alone, watching TV until it was time to turn in. I wished for very little these days, Dana. Just the steady lull of our newly separated lives. I'd lowered my expectations to pathetic levels and now, apparently, even the simplicity of a routine evening was too much to ask for.

I grabbed my keys.

***

He must have had an appointment. A client dinner. Drinks with a buddy? Or a date—a date, Dana?—with some gorgeous, bubbly, levelheaded woman from work or the grocery store.

Oh God, I remember naïvely thinking as I drove. *That would be the worst.*

When I'd left the house, Matt was still moving on the map on my phone, so I'd driven in that general direction. Now his face hovered somewhere in Riverside's downtown area. Probably a restaurant or a bar.

He'd stopped moving at 6:14. No doubt his plans were for 6:30. Typical Matt. We'd never shown up at an airport gate less than ninety minutes before departure time, and we often got to the movie theater before they even started rolling the ads. At parties, you'd find us ringing the bell at the appointed hour on the invitation, no matter how many times I assured Matt that the hosts didn't actually want you there on time.

I drove up slowly to the place my map was telling me I would find my husband, and sure enough, there was his Audi, parked in the lot of a little Italian diner.

He'd be inside by now, so I let the car roll past the front. The red gingham curtains on the windows and doors reached high, allowing only about a foot of visibility to the inside. All I could make out was the flicker of candlelight against brick walls and the soft twinkle of white Christmas lights. I had to use my imagination to see the small, intimate tables with red checkered tablecloths and cozy booths, to hear the hushed voices and the soft clinks of wineglasses toasting good news and new beginnings. The restaurant didn't look fancy, but at the same time, it was just the sort of place you went to be romantic—to impress a first date or celebrate an anniversary or rekindle an old flame.

I turned my attention back to the parking lot as I passed the front door. I could not imagine Matt here for a client dinner or to grab a beer with one of the guys or to meet up with his parents. It was just too—

Too . . .

Well, Dana.

This was interesting.

Parked in front of the restaurant, between a Corolla and a Prius, was a little red Honda Civic. And on this Civic's bumper was a bright blue magnet that read PROUD PARENT OF AN HONOR ROLL STUDENT AT BROOKS MIDDLE SCHOOL.

62

I could have waited for them there, in my new inconspicuous Camry. I could have waited for my husband and my *friend* to emerge together, hand in hand, or maybe with his arm slung around her shoulders, pulling her and her frumpy down jacket against him until her fake Rothy's arched off the pavement, until her face was just inches, then half an inch, a quarter inch, an eighth away from Matt's, until there was nothing separating her lips from his or her hands from his chest, resting on the lapels of his coat, getting Champ's fur stuck to her gloves . . .

Or I could go inside. I could go in there right then and confront them, demand their answers and their apologies and their shame.

But what if I was wrong, Dana? What if it was all just a giant coincidence? Maybe Morgan was there on a date—maybe I'd inspired her—and maybe Matt really was with a client. Maybe Morgan would stop by Matt's table on her way out to laugh about what a small world it was.

But no, Dana. That wasn't it. There's no such thing as a coincidence.

I got out of the car and marched toward those gingham-cloaked doors. Tears fell down my face, burning my skin as they traced their way along the same tracks over and over again.

I blamed myself as I strode across that parking lot. I hated myself.

But *no*. It wasn't me. *This* wasn't my fault. *This* was Morgan. I blamed her. Then Matt. Then you—why did you have to die, Dana? Everything would be okay *if you hadn't died*. Then William, because it wasn't your fault you were dead; it was his. Then Morgan again—no, Matt. Morgan. You. It was all of us. We'd all . . . no.

I had started this. Me. *Me.* I was the one who'd gotten us here, to this parking lot. I was the one who'd lost Matt. The only person you and I had ever failed to pull a switch on—remember that? He'd known right away.

I'd asked him how; we hadn't been able to fool Mom and Dad in years, but even our aunts and uncles and our closest cousins and friends fell for our act nine times out of ten. He'd just shrugged and said it wasn't that hard, that you and I were nothing alike. I hadn't believed him.

"Come on," I'd begged. *"How did you know?"*

And so he'd laid out all the differences, Dana. Stuff I'd never noticed. I rubbed my lips together a lot, apparently. And I kept touching my hair—you were less fidgety. I made eye contact longer, Matt said, and I tried to stop my sneezes, which made them come out sounding funny. And I always said *anyway,* especially when I was getting a little long-winded with one of my stories.

"And your crooked smile," he'd added. "Dana doesn't do that."

"I don't have a crooked smile."

"Yeah, you do. You only pull it out for my really bad jokes, the ones you don't want to laugh at. Your mouth does this sort of thing." Then he'd done a very unflattering demonstration.

Why had I let myself lose a man like that, Dana?

I hesitated when I got to the entrance of the diner. I didn't have a game plan, just anger and fear and adrenaline. That was never good. I couldn't just walk in there . . .

No, no, those were excuses, Dana. To delay what had to be done, to protect myself from what I would find.

Three, two, one.

I opened the door—yanked it—startling a woman on the other side. I mumbled an apology and moved aside, letting her pass. She gave me a side-glance as she went by, so I must have looked some kind of way, but I didn't care, because I was right, Dana.

I was fucking right.

There they were.

Together.

No small world.

No coincidences.

Morgan and Matt, across from each other at a cozy table, just like I'd imagined, with two wineglasses and a little candle, their knees practically touching—maybe *touching touching*—underneath.

I didn't need to give myself a countdown this time. My legs carried me over there without any hesitation. It took until I was a table away for her to spot me. Her hand—the one that had touched mine in that waiting room and started all this—flew to her chest. She was shocked.

Then, just as quickly, scared. Horrified.

Good. She should be. I'd been a good fucking friend, Dana. Maybe not perfect, but good, or at least good-intentioned. There was a time I'd have done anything for this woman. *I'd offered her one of our embryos.* I didn't even have a child of my own, Dana, yet I had been willing to do *that*.

And she turned around and did this . . . this . . . whatever this was?

I'm even jealous of the couples who look unhappy, she'd said. *At least they have someone to be miserable with.*

She was punishing me. Morgan was punishing me, just like she'd done to her ex.

So I don't know, maybe this *was* right. Maybe this was how it was supposed to be. My punishment for what I'd done to Morgan, good intentions be damned.

But I couldn't let her have Matt, Dana.

Anything else. A job, a lung, an embryo, Ben, my last dollar, my undying loyalty . . .

But not Matt.

I don't know how long I stood there, but eventually I realized they were both staring at me. If it was possible, Matt looked more scared than Morgan did. He was the first to speak.

"Let's talk outside," he said.

I wanted to shake the panicked look Morgan shot him right off her pale face—how dare she think she had any right to his concern, his protection?

I waited outside for what felt like a lifetime while they did whatever they were doing in there. Settling the bill. Getting their stories straight.

Finally, they emerged, not hand in hand, as I'd imagined earlier, but with Morgan cowering just behind Matt. Then she made a break for it— she was *running*, Dana. Like I was going to . . . what? Hurt her? Did they really think . . .

"Morgan!" I shouted.

"No, Cady." Matt shot out his arm and stepped in front of me. I hadn't made the slightest move to go after her. She was in no danger. This must have been the plan they'd been making in the restaurant. She makes a run for it while he protects her. From me.

I didn't say anything until her car was gone.

"Dinner," I said. "With Morgan."

Matt sighed. He started to open his mouth, but I cut him off. "And the phone call? When we got coffee? Was that her?"

"Yes."

"Okay. Wow."

"She was upset, Cady. I had to—"

"So you're talking. You and Morgan."

Matt held up his hands. "I wanted to make sure she wasn't going to cause any trouble. She needed someone to talk to, so yes, I took her calls. The stalking, the whole dating profile thing . . . and she said you gave that guy her number? Really, Cady?"

He took her calls. I couldn't—

"Morgan could have had you arrested or something! Sued you, I don't know. I wouldn't blame her if she did. But," he said, catching the flash in my eyes, "all I wanted was to protect you, Cady."

"By snuggling up to her in some cozy little restaurant?" I spat.

A couple, our age, holding hands, did a shoddy job of pretending not to be interested as they walked by.

Matt shook his head. "It wasn't like that. Morgan was angry and scared. I tried to reassure her, but let's be real, Cady. Imagine if someone were following *you* around . . ."

"I wasn't *someone*, Matt. I was her friend. And it wasn't what she's making it out to be. I—"

I stopped myself. Matt was getting that closed-off look again, the one he'd permanently worn around the house in the weeks before he'd left. It would do no good to try to explain. He would never understand. No one would.

"I know you didn't mean Morgan any harm, Cady. You could never hurt anyone—"

Oh, never say never, Matt. Everyone knew that. I definitely did, now.

"—but you did. You hurt her."

"You didn't have to go to dinner with her."

Matt grabbed the sides of his head. "You're right, I didn't. But you know what? I wanted to, Cady. I've been holding in a lot. I couldn't talk to anyone else—my parents, our friends—because I hoped one day we'd be better, and when that time came, I didn't want it tainted."

"I see. So Morgan became your confidante," I said. "You confided in each other about how miserable I was making you, and you—"

"I wasn't—"

"And you bonded over that, and one thing led to another—because that's how these things always work, don't they? First you become friends, and then before you know it, you realize you're falling in love with her."

"No," Matt said, jerking backward. "*No*. What?"

"Look around, Matt. This isn't the sort of place two friends go to shoot the platonic breeze. That's what coffee shops are for."

Matt hung his head. "We usually do get coffee."

"Usually? *Usually*, Matt? How long has this been going on?"

"Nothing's *going on*, Cady." His voice was a hiss now. "It was a few phone calls, a couple coffees . . . then Morgan texted saying she was having a rough week—that Ben guy called her—and she needed to talk. I never thought . . ."

Matt's voice trailed off as something, some sort of recognition, dawned across his face.

"What?" I snapped.

His eyes were circles now. Big horrified circles.

"What did you do?" he whispered.

"Me?" I meant it to come out in a hiss to match his, but it sounded more like a squeak.

"You only ever doubt me when you feel guilty about something *you've* done."

"Come on, Matt. You're—"

"No," he interrupted, waving me off. "No, it's true. You gave me so much shit when we got back together in college. You were so sure I must've had a fling while we were broken up. You grilled me all the fucking time, for months. And come to find out, all these years later, your paranoia was just your own goddamned guilt, because *you'd* hooked up with someone else."

I swallowed.

Matt shook his head. "I haven't done a damn thing wrong, which means . . . God, Cady, what the fuck have you done?"

63

"I'm going to stop."

"Oh?"

"Yes. Morgan, the watching . . . I have to stop. I know that now."

Callahan leaned back in his chair. "Is this a New Year's resolution?"

I shook my head. "No. Just a resolution. One I happen to be making at the end of the year."

"When are you going to stop?"

"Soon. Very soon. I've given myself one last watch."

"And then what?" Callahan wanted to know. "Then what will you do, Cady?"

Wrong question. He always asked the wrong questions, Dana.

"It isn't what I'm going to do that we should be talking about," I said. "It's what's already been done."

Now I had his attention.

"And are you ready to talk to me about that?" he asked. "Ready to start at the beginning and tell me what it is you think you've done?"

What I *think* I've done. As if I'd imagined it all. If only.

"I don't know," I said. "I want to, but . . ."

"Would it help if you told Dana?"

"Dana?"

"Yes. If you could talk to Dana, would you tell her?"

We weren't supposed to play the what-if game. Moira had said so.

"I can't talk to Dana. Dana is *dead*."

"So?"

So? *So?* God, he was an unusual therapist, Dana. Not that I had anything to compare him to, but I couldn't imagine he'd been taught in therapy school to give his patients the old *So what?* He was either brilliant or completely inept, and I wasn't sure which I preferred.

"Why can't you talk to Dana?" he pressed. "I talk to my father all the time, and he's been dead for eight years. Haven't you ever talked to yourself? Cursed an empty house when you stubbed your toe or broke a glass? Yelled at the universe for being unfair or at some jerk on the highway who would never hear you?"

"You don't think," I said slowly, "that talking to my dead sister like she's here is a bit of a step back?"

I tried to imagine what Matt would have to say about this. But it had been days since we'd fought in that parking lot, and he hadn't so much as texted.

"I think you can find a healthy way to talk to Dana. You don't have to include her in conversations at the dinner table. But you could, say, write her letters. Or start a journal, to fill her in on what she's missed. Or, if you don't like to write, you could record a video or audio diary on your phone. You could even talk to her in your head, if you like."

"Talk to her in my head."

"Yes."

Hello, Dana.

Hey, Dana.

Hey, little sis.

"I could try."

We wrapped things up shortly after that. I gave Callahan my co-pay and my word that I'd be back next week.

In the car, I thought about his suggestion.

"Hello, Dana," I said aloud. "Hey, Dana. Hey."

Stupid. I couldn't talk to you. You were dead. So much for this guy—now I would have to find a new therapist.

In the meantime, at least, I had my new plan. I'd given myself one last watch, and tonight I was going to use it.

I drove to Morgan's house and parked my Camry along the curb, a house and a half away. Different car, same view, same regrets, same winter chill biting into my bones. I found myself cataloguing all the sames: the pulsing blue light, the neatly shoveled driveway, the naked azaleas, and the dirty snow, and then . . .

And then I found myself talking to you, Dana.

The sun is leaving for the day, I told you, *and I probably should, too.*
I shouldn't be here at all, I confessed.
This has to stop, everyone says so. It's not healthy, Cady. It's not right. Not normal, not legal.
But I'm only watching.
Watching never hurt anyone . . .

64

"Okay, Cady, are you ready?"

I nod.

I am very ready.

It's February 5—no May 16, but it'll do. Especially if it works this time.

The doctor tells me I'm going to start feeling very relaxed. She pushes a syringe into the IV bag hanging by my head. There's an orange label on the bag. It has my name on it.

These are the only thoughts I have time for before the drugs hit, making me feel open and loose, like all my secrets might slip out.

The doctor's voice narrates every step.

I'm inserting the speculum now, just like we do for Pap smears.

Putting the catheter in . . . passing through the cervix . . .

Okay, Cady, I'm going to begin placing the embryos . . .

I watch everything happen on a monitor hanging on the wall. The fuzzy little orbs are pushed through the tube and released into my womb with a dramatic thrust. It feels like I am watching history being made.

I feel none of it.

The whole thing lasts fifteen, maybe twenty minutes. I don't recall being taken out of the cold surgical room and back into one of the curtained stalls down the hall.

The nurse who is attending me has long purple fingernails and a name tag that says *Jade*. She asks how I'm feeling.

"I wish my husband were here," I tell her. The last two words sound slurred in my ears.

Jade smiles kindly. "I know, sweetie," she says, patting my shoulder. "But he's got that work thing, right? He's got to take care of business and make sure y'all are ready for this baby. Or babies," she adds with a wink.

I nod. It feels like I'm still nodding, even though I'm pretty sure I've stopped.

"All right," Jade says as she fusses with her clipboard and a monitor. "You keep resting. I'm going to update your friend in the waiting room, let her know you've probably got another forty-five minutes or so until the anesthesia wears off enough to go home."

I start to nod again, or keep nodding, whatever, but then I remember what I told Moira this was for. A test, a biopsy. I couldn't ask her to pick me up from an actual embryo transfer. The doctor may have bought the *My husband wanted so badly to be here but had this last-minute work emergency* story, but Moira would be suspicious.

"Wait," I call, reaching for Jade's retreating back.

She stops and turns.

"Just tell her the procedure went well, okay?" I say, struggling to get all three syllables of *procedure* out in the right order. "Don't mention the details, please. She's squeamish about stuff like this."

Jade grins. "Got it. No gory details."

"And plus, HIPAA," I add, but my words come out long and listless, and it sounds more like *And plush, hippo.*

Jade laughs and disappears, pulling the curtain shut behind her. I doze off. When I wake up, I still feel tired, but my head's clearer and my words don't stick to my tongue anymore.

The doctor stops by to fork over a small stack of printed instructions—avoid strenuous activity, schedule a pregnancy test for fourteen days out—and to let me know that the procedure went well. Textbook, she says.

She squeezes my shoulder before she leaves and says, "I've got a good feeling about this one."

A good feeling.

Can she say that?

Can she say that, Dana?

She didn't say anything like that last time.

314 | MARISA WALZ

She must be very confident this go-round, to say someth—
No, Cady, stop.

It was just a throwaway comment. I'm reading way too much into it.

I cannot get my hopes up, Dana.

Cautious optimism—good. But this unfettered expectation welling up inside . . .

Jade finally decides I'm ready to go home. I'm handed off to Moira, who walks ahead of the wheelchair they've pushed me out of the clinic in. There's a lot of fussing by Moira and an attendant as I'm situated in the passenger seat of her Buick.

Moira follows her GPS instructions to my house. I am so grateful she agreed to this. There's no one else I could have asked. And she was so happy—so eager—to help. Who doesn't want to help a woman so heartbroken, so utterly destroyed by grief, that she'd gone and lied about a dead baby, just so she could talk for one hour once a week with people who understood, who got what it was like?

But as grateful as I am for Moira, I don't want to talk. I close my eyes so she thinks I'm sleeping.

A good feeling, Dana.

The doctor has a good feeling about this one.

I shouldn't make too much of it, but I can't help myself.

The odds are better this time around. Last time, we only implanted one embryo. This time, we opted for two. And since it was a frozen transfer, there was time for genetic testing, to identify the strongest two embryos, to give us the best chances.

Listen to me, Dana. *We. Us.* As if Matt were a part of this.

A moan escapes my lips.

Moira glances at me. "That much pain from just a test? Dang, woman. You must really want a baby."

I look out the window at the local breweries and boutiques drifting by at exactly the speed limit.

"I do," I whisper. "I really, really do."

I just wish it were Matt driving me home right now. I wish we'd done this together, the way we planned, and dreamed.

Not this way.

But as Dad always says, Dana, *It doesn't have to go as planned, it just has to go.*

And anyway, there's one thing that will go *just* as we'd originally hoped.

Matt is going to be very, very surprised.

65

It's Memorial Day—yours, Dana, not America's. I'm at the venue, answering last-minute caterer questions and solving A/V hiccups as adeptly as if I'd never stopped, when Matt walks in, sixteen minutes early. We've only seen each other a couple times these last two months, since our argument in the parking lot of that little Italian place.

He holds me extra tight now—because he's missed me, or because he knows today is going to be hard? When he talks, his chin knocks softly on the top of my head.

"I know it's bad form to come early . . ."

"It's okay. I'm glad you're here." I pull back to see his face. "I was actually counting on you being obscenely early."

Matt glances at his watch. "Sixteen minutes is hardly obscene."

"I want you to come home."

He's clearly not expecting these words—not in this moment, without any sort of preamble. He frowns, searching for the right answer. "What about . . ."

"I know, but . . . hold on." I tell him to wait right here as I run out of the room.

My purse is stowed in a desk drawer in the venue manager's office. I pull it out and remove the folded white paper I slipped inside this morning. Then I run back down the hall to the front room and thrust it into Matt's hands.

His eyes scan the words—fearfully at first, until he realizes what it is. "Is this for real? It's official?"

I nod, tears filling my eyes. "I even have my first client booked."

"Let me guess," he says. "The OG? Nora Donnelly?"

I nod again, my throat still tight, waiting for him to notice it.

A grin unfurls across his face as he looks down at the license for the new, nonprofit arm of Eventually. "Wow, Cady. Congratulations. This is . . . this is huge." He keeps reading, and his smile stretches wider and crinkles the skin around his eyes. "You named it Grand Gestures."

"Do you remember? In college, when I came home from winter break, and you were waiting outside my parents' door with your grand gesture?"

His eyes are shining when he looks back at me. "Of course I remember, but . . . you named your new business after me?"

"It's not just a new business, it's a new start. And yes, I did. If it weren't for you . . ."

Matt doesn't seem to be listening. He's looking at the certificate again, inspecting it more closely, and now he frowns. "Are you sure this is real, Cady? The seal looks funky. And this signature—"

I snatch the paper back. "Okay, okay—it's not set in stone yet. I just applied for it a couple days ago, and it takes a few weeks for the real deal to come in the mail, but that doesn't have the same ring to it, and I really, really wanted to make a grand gesture."

Matt laughs, and for a whole second—maybe two—the toll of the last year vanishes from his face.

But then he stops. He's remembered something—everything, maybe—and it's taken him out of the moment.

He folds the paper back up. "This is nice . . ."

I know that tone. "But?"

"I don't know if it's enough to . . ."

I nod. "I know."

"I just don't—"

"You don't have to say anything, Matt. It's okay. I get it. I don't deserve or expect your forgiveness. This is my punishment. What I get."

"It's not about forgiveness, Cady. Or punishment. I just don't know if I can . . ."

"I know. Me either."

He doesn't know if he can forget. If he can move forward. If it could work.

But he might not have a choice. I touch my belly.

The test is scheduled for Wednesday.

Three more days, and then we'll know.

66

I don't know what to say about the memorial, Dana. It's a success? That feels wrong, somehow. I wish I never had to plan this sort of event for you. I'd much rather be throwing you a baby shower or helping Sean pull off a surprise birthday bash for your thirty-fourth.

Everyone you've ever smiled at seems to be here. Mom and Dad and Sean and Matt, of course. Aunt Sharon and Uncle Jerry, Uncle Paul and Aunt Erica, Uncle Bill. All our first cousins, except Cody, who's at police academy training. The teachers from your school, the principal and all the office staff, the custodians and the students—so many students. Our college roommates and childhood friends and neighbors. Your last two hairdressers and the woman with those ridiculous microbladed brows who always did your nails. At least two dozen people I've never laid eyes on before. Moira is here, in an honest-to-God dress and black Crocs, and Nora stopped by and touched my hand again. Even Mackenzie fucking Arlington turned out, accompanied by a shellac-haired douchebag with a Gucci belt buckle and a *pocket square*.

They all love what Mom and Sean and I have done. The timeline brings almost as many smiles as it does tears, and the upbeat playlist lifts some of the weight. The corn dogs are a hit. I managed to glam them up with gold sticks and a gourmet condiment bar. There's a glass bowl of buffalo sauce, bright orange. I take out my phone and snap a photo.

"You did it."

The voice comes from behind me. I recognize it instantly; there is nothing threatening about your husband or his voice, Dana—even when he's angry, he's as dangerous as a puppy—but his words . . .

"What do you mean?" I try to sound nonchalant, but the words tremble on their way out.

"What do you mean, *what do I mean*?" Sean asks loudly.

I want to shush him and suggest we do this somewhere else, away from prying eyes and perked ears.

But then he says, "*This*," and waves his hand. "The memorial. It's perfect. It's Dana."

The memorial. He's talking about the memorial.

I want to laugh or cry or hug him. I do all three, and I'm not sure which takes him aback the most, but he recovers quickly, his surprise replaced with a kind of wistful, rueful look.

"Dana's up there, you know, smiling down on all this," he says.

Are you, Dana?

"She'd be touched, Cady. Every detail . . ." He looks around us.

"It wasn't just me," I remind him. "If it weren't for you and my mom, it would have been a total sobfest instead of . . . this."

"Me and you and your mom," Sean says. "The dream team. Who'd have thought?"

I laugh. "Definitely not Dana. If she really is watching, she's not smiling. She's laughing."

Sean grins. "Come on now. We weren't that bad, were we?"

I don't return his smile. "I'm sorry," I say.

I wait for him to ask, *For what?* just so I have to spell it out, so he can revel in my apology a bit longer. But he doesn't.

"You loved Dana," Sean says, "and she knew that, Cady. Dana never doubted you loved her. Not even . . . not even those last few weeks."

It's better than an apology, not that I was looking for one.

Sean gets whisked away into a hug by someone I don't recognize. I turn my attention back to the party, to the guests. I field their condolences and their praise for the event, mostly the latter.

Dana would have loved this, Cady . . . captures her brilliantly . . . such a touching detail . . .

"Excuse me. Cady?"

This time, the voice is not familiar.

I whirl around, and face him.

I knew he would be here. He RSVPed, so I expected this moment, and I've been steeling my insides for it like I'm bracing for a crash, but—just as I knew *one day* you'd die, Dana—when it actually happens, it sneaks up on me and I am wholly unprepared.

"Sorry," he says, reading my face. "I didn't mean to scare you."

I swallow. I collect myself. "And at the funeral? Or when you showed up outside my work? I suppose you didn't mean to scare me then, either."

William hangs his head. Today he's in a suit. No green jacket. When he looks up again, he meets my eyes. "I'm sorry. I wasn't in my right mind. The accident . . . I didn't know how else . . . I know I upset you, showing up like that, but that wasn't my intention. I never wanted to make things worse. I just . . . I had to see you."

"Why?"

William shrugs, but his answer is quick—he's contemplated this before. "To reassure myself you'd be okay? To punish myself with proof that you weren't? To fix it, somehow? I'm sorry, I don't know."

An unsatisfying answer, Dana, but I understand better than I care to admit.

"I'm sorry," he says. He looks me square in the face, and he does look wretched. "Sorrier than you'll ever know. I will never stop regretting those three, four seconds I looked down. I wish I had a better excuse—I wish I could say a dog jumped in front of my car or my kid was getting sick in the back seat or my brakes went out, but I can't. It was just my phone . . . a text . . . a stupid, unimportant, goddamn text . . ."

Some socially conditioned, well-mannered piece of me itches to give this pitiful man false reassurances. *It's okay. Don't worry about it. You didn't mean to. It was an accident.*

I don't. It's not okay, and he should regret it, every day for the rest of his life. I can tell from just these three minutes we've spent together that he will.

But—I can't believe I'm saying this, Dana—it doesn't bring me any peace. His very real remorse, his obvious suffering, doesn't make me feel better, and I realize it wouldn't make much difference to me if the inverse were true, if he were completely remorseless. It changes nothing. There's nothing he can say or do to make it any better or worse.

William's arms are hanging awkwardly at his sides. I have never not thought of this man without thinking of his arms. How you died in them.

Now I find myself drawn to them, the way I was drawn to Sean's that day in the little waiting room, when he held me, and I sought out any last traces of you.

What would it be like, Dana, to be held in *these* arms, to close my eyes and search for you? If I reach for this man, if he takes me in, could you and I be connected, however faintly, one last time? Would I feel you there? Would I get a glimpse of your last minutes?

What was it like, Dana, dying in a stranger's arms?

67

The snow in her yard is still slashed with dirt, the azaleas still naked and gnarled. The paint in the bottom corner of the living room window still festers with rust, curling back from the house in distaste. The television flickers like a heart rate monitor, letting me know she's still there, still kicking.

I came here right after the memorial. I know, I know. The last time was supposed to be the last time. I can hear your disapproval—*supposed* to be, Cady?

Look, I meant it when I told Callahan I wasn't going to watch anymore. I intended to stop this. I had good intentions—I always have good intentions. You know that, Dana. I had them when I snuck Morgan's last name out of the hospital, when I tracked her down online, the first time I drove to her house. When I joined group and befriended her . . . I always *meant* well.

But I knew the last time I came here it wasn't going to be the last time, and I know today won't be the last time, either, the same way we knew Mom wasn't going to stick to that Atkins diet and you wouldn't really swear off tequila forever after Cinco de Mayo 2011. One day—maybe in a year or two, a week, or even tomorrow—I'll be back. Because Morgan still needs me, and what kind of person—what kind of animal—would I be if I abandoned her *now*?

Sometimes, you have to help people, no matter what.

I haven't always . . .

I mean, if I could go back and do it all over . . .

But I can't. I can't go back, it's too late.

I think I'm ready to tell you about that now, Dana.

68

I was thinking of happier times. Of you, full of life and light. You, the way your nose scrunched up when you laughed really hard at something. You, two years ago, tipsy from champagne, dancing in big circles in a sparkly green dress at a New Year's Eve party in Manhattan—

Party. Fuck.

I remembered the client meeting I was supposed to be heading to and called Jamie to have her reschedule it. I told her there was a family emergency, and she just said, "I'm on it. I hope everything's okay?" Jamie was great, a lifesaver.

Now if only Matt would pick up. I tried him again and again. Nothing, nothing.

Another stop sign approached, and I picked up my phone. Maybe the GPS or the bad memories had drowned out the sound of Matt's return call. But no, there was nothing on my screen. Unbelievable. He could respond to my stupid Valentine's Day meme that morning but now, *now*, he was unreachable?

The GPS was in my ear again: *Make a left-hand turn in three hundred feet.*

A simple left turn.

But everything was so loud.

The GPS.

Your disappointment.

My angry words.

Two hundred feet.

A voice in my head: *Let her be okay. Don't let Dana die. Don't let the baby die.*

Matt's voicemail: "You've reached Matthew McKenna . . ."

"Matt, call me. As soon as you get this. It's bad—"

And then the bang. A car. Someone, another car, had slammed into the side of my Range Rover.

Fuck.

I looked in my mirrors. My side mirror, the passenger mirror, the rearview. Nothing. There was no one there. I'd imagined it. I'd conjured up another crash. Just my imagination. Thank God.

But it had been so loud. So real . . .

The farther away I got, the more I could make out as I looked back. Funny how that happens, Dana. I wasn't sure, at first, what I was seeing in my rearview mirror. A pile of some sort that hadn't been on the ground just moments before. I struggled to make sense of the objects. Wheels. Spokes. Handlebars. A coat. A coat lying on top of a bike. But that didn't make sense. Why would someone put a coat on a bike?

And how did it all get there? It wasn't there before, when I'd made that left turn.

And *why* would someone put a coat on a bike?

I kept asking myself that as I drove away. Maybe I could have put the pieces together sooner if I hadn't been so consumed with other things—thoughts of you, of getting to the hospital, of Matt not picking up his goddamn phone.

It took me until the end of the next block to figure it out, and when I did, I turned around. Immediately. I really did, Dana. I made a right, then another and another. I circled back. Of course I did.

I approached slowly, like a wild animal inspecting a deserted campsite. The scene had changed. From this new angle, head-on, I could see that the coat was not just a coat, that a body lay crumpled inside it. A head of sandy hair stuck out the top and lay unnaturally still across the pavement. The small limbs hanging out of the bottom of the coat were tangled with the bike, impossibly contorted, as unmoving as its top pieces.

Then movement—there was movement now—one of the arms moved. And the head, it was lifting—wasn't it? Yes. Not by much, and now it was settling back down, resting on the sidewalk, but it had tried; I'd seen it move.

More movement. A woman. An older woman was bent over the boy now—I was pretty sure it was a boy—and she was doing her best to juggle the cell phone pressed between her shoulder and her ear, but she had to manage the leash of a small white dog, all while she ran her hands over the boy's coat and head, searching for something—a wound, a pulse, a breath, whatever the voice in the phone pressed to her ear was instructing her to do.

The next minutes still replay in my mind like a movie I might have watched years and years ago, everything I retained living as blurry snippets inside my head . . . the intersection, the bike, its orange handlebars, the unmoving coat, the old woman, the frantic white dog vibrating at the end of its leash, all of them getting bigger and bigger as my car approached.

Then a voice, Dana. A voice telling me to turn around. It was the woman from the navigation. She wanted me to turn around, she wanted me to *Proceed to the route*.

To my shock—to my absolute horror, Dana—the car obeyed. It stopped its approach toward the boy. It pulled into a driveway. It reversed.

As it drove away, I looked back in the rearview mirror. The bike and the coat and the old lady and the little dog grew smaller—less real—the farther the car drove, the closer it took me to you.

I should make it turn around, I thought.

But I hadn't hit him, Dana. He'd hit me. I hadn't done anything wrong.

But that didn't mean I could *leave*.

If someone had a front door camera and the cops got their hands on the recording, they'd see me fleeing in my big black Range Rover and I'd be in a world of trouble.

Or would I?

Any video would show what the boy would surely tell the doctors and his parents at the hospital: that he'd run his bike into my car.

And my car hadn't so much as flinched from the impact. It was too big, the boy too small. It was totally plausible I'd had no idea.

And if the boy didn't remember anything, or . . . or if he couldn't, for whatever reason, speak, the cops might not even realize a vehicle was involved. How would they know?

A doctor—or, oh God, a coroner—wouldn't be able to say what, exactly, caused a broken bone or a concussion. Could be a car, could be the pavement.

Still. It was wrong. I should go back.

I should *definitely* turn around.

But also: There was already someone helping.

And: What more could be done?

And: I had to get to you, Dana.

You.

You, every time.

Over anybody or anything, under any circumstances.

Make a left turn in three hundred feet.

You needed me, Dana, and the child already had someone.

Besides, what good would it do to stay?

Make a left turn in one hundred feet.

I didn't even know CPR.

And someone was there helping. She'd probably already dialed 911.

Your destination is on the right in two hundred feet.

Besides, I didn't hit him; he hit me. *He* ran his bike into the side of *my* car. I hadn't seen a helmet—he should have been wearing a helmet.

Where was his helmet? His mother should have made sure he had a helmet.

Where was his mother?

Acknowledgments

Writing a book can be lonely, but publishing it is certainly not. I will never be able to adequately express my thanks for my editor, Sarah Cantin, who made my oldest, wildest dreams come true when she offered for this book. Thank you for getting, at the bird's-eye view and the worm's too, this story. Endless awe and gratitude to my agent, Hannah Mann, who was so confident about me and this book that, in hindsight, I don't see how we could have ended up anywhere else but here. The entire Writers House team has been amazing: thank you to Sydnee Harlan, for pulling me out of the slush pile; to Genevieve Gagne-Hawes, for so deftly wielding the red pen that made this story really shine; to Tom Ishizuka for your fascinating insights and guidance into the world of film and TV options.

Thank you to my brilliant publicist, Katie Bassel, and to my marketing maven, Erica Martirano, both of whom made sure Cady's voice could be heard far beyond my own reach. Thank you to Olga Grlic, for designing That Cover; it's everything I dreamed but also more than I could have ever imagined. Drue VanDuker, thank you for all the things I can't see you doing over there—and for reassuring me that my last-minute commas and trifling word changes are not obnoxious. Thank you to Hilary Zaitz Michael and Sanjana Seelam at WME, for thinking this book might look good on the big screen and for all your hard work to give it a shot.

Thank you to all those who I cannot see working behind the scenes to bring this book into the world. And thank you to the many people I have yet to meet on this journey to publication; there are many months between now, as I sit here writing these acknowledgments, and publication day, but please know I am grateful for you.

The writing (and reading) community is unparalleled. Thank you,

Julie Mosow, for your brilliant and incisive wisdom on what this book needed (and what it didn't) but more importantly, for listening and caring. Andra Miller, thank you for reading. Your praise came at a critical time—and showed me that I was not crazy to think this book was maybe, sort of, kind of good. April Gooding, beta reader extraordinaire, thank you for your keen insights into what was making the early drafts of this manuscript sing (and what was horribly out of tune). Jeneva Rose, thank you for your honest, unfiltered, and often hilarious advice—but especially for that one piece of advice (it was life-changing). Jessica Payne, thank you for being generous with your time, advice, and support; you are a true friend to the entire writing community.

Thank you to all my many friends and family who supported me on this long road and for your faith in my ability to actually pull this off (or at least the grace to fake it). Special thanks to: my outlaws, Susan and Dennis Walz (signed copies for everyone in Sue's book club!); Pam Drews (who introduced me as an author to everyone long before I was even a twinkle in any publisher's eye); and Ami Grandy (for reading some very rough drafts).

To my parents, Jim and Tammy Knudsen, thank you for all the love, support, and billions of other things you've given me over the years but especially for passing down your bottomless energy, unmatched work ethic, debilitating perfectionism, and slightly delusional confidence in my skills and abilities—basically, everything I needed to defy the odds and see my name on the cover of this book.

And finally, most importantly, to my Dans and Isla: I love you guys so much. I am so thankful for my husband, Dan. You never, not once, complained or made me feel guilty or silly for continuing to plug away, often very late into the night, at these one-in-a-million (or something like that) odds. And Dan Jr. and Isla . . . it may seem strange to dedicate such a dark and twisted tale to your children, but it's not the story inside this book that I dedicated to you. It's the other story: the one of a little girl who had an impossible dream that came true, because she decided it should be so. Do something cool with your lives, have fun, be happy, be you—*I love you.*

About the Author

Anna Cillan

Marisa Walz is a Federal Reserve executive who also writes novels about people behaving badly. She lives in the Chicago suburbs with her husband and two young children.